CHROME MOUNTAIN

A NOVEL BY

BEN SCHNEIDER

CREATOR OF AIRMAN ARTLESS

outskirts press

Chrome Mountain

v2.0

This is a work of fiction. The events and characters described herein are imaginary and are not intended to refer to specific places or living persons. The opinions expressed in this manuscript are solely the opinions of the author and do not represent the opinions or thoughts of the publisher. The author has represented and warranted full ownership and/or legal right to publish all the materials in this book.

Outskirts Press, Inc.
http://www.outskirtspress.com

ISBN: 978-1-4787-9925-2

Library of Congress Control Number: 2018904463

PRINTED IN THE UNITED STATES OF AMERICA

To my parents, Rick and Bonita,
the best friends I ever had.

CALIFORNIA: PRESENT DAY

Astride her rumbling Harley-Davidson, Sonya McCall waited impatiently for the green light. She'd traveled northeast along I-80, turned south on River Road and, for a few miles, followed another road edging the north side of Lake Tahoe. She gazed over emerald treetops to feast her eyes on the expanse of azure water that sparkled beneath the high noon sun. While enjoying the vista, she hoped to reach her destination before dark. To her, it would be bliss to see Becky Lugo again. They could talk and laugh about the lawless life in Sacramento she was leaving behind. So far, Sonya's favorite moment of the year had been when she'd phoned her distant friend, explained her plight, and was sincerely invited to come live with her.

Out of utter boredom, Sonya studied the eighteen-wheeler in front of her. The forty-foot trailer had a faded paint job with vertical red and yellow stripes backgrounding the words FUN ZONE CIRCUS on both sides. She guessed the circus had been officially shut down and the trailer was sold to some company prepared to repaint it once it arrived. To the right of the bold rococo text was a laughing clown's disembodied head, large enough to swallow her two-wheeler. It seemed as if the cartoon clown found hilarity at her misfortune—being stuck at a red light that seemed to have no intention of turning green.

She glared at the portable, trailer-style traffic light, barely visible with the semi in front of her. Boulders had fallen from the pine-cloaked mountainside, limiting the road to one lane. She counted five cars going the other way and hoped the light would not stay red much longer.

Songs from jays in the nearest trees competed with the distant growl of another motorcycle. Beneath her German half-helmet with a maroon paisley pattern, Sonya's raven-black curls flew in the wind as her head spun to see behind her. Beyond two SUVs, the road curved behind a cliff. Then the second Harley appeared.

Even from two hundred yards away, she recognized the rider, Brock Laxdal—third-in-command of the malicious biker gang she'd once been a part of. With pearl-white hair flying from his chin and helmetless balding pate, Brock quickly closed the gap between them, passing the innocent motorists. Sonya realized that even if Brock had never seen her before, he could still confirm her identity by reading LVISCHK on her license plate. Brock parked his Fat Bob left of her Low Rider. Sonya remembered the skewered skull tattooed on his muscular arm bared by his denim vest. While struggling to hide her tension from being caught in the act of desertion, she lowered her sunglasses. Frown lines, wrought from years of stress, were flanked by almond-shaped eyes of deep blue—one ringed by purpled skin that had recently met her ex-boyfriend's fist.

"What do you want, Brock?" she asked in her typically forceful but weary voice.

"Levi has every last one of the Screamon Demons looking for you, Sonya!" he bristled, keeping his shades on. "You have some explaining to do, girl! You left our leader confused and heartbroken last night. He also said that thousands of our hard-stolen cash went missing from his safe. I'll bet my left eye that bread is in your backpack. And you won't answer your phone!"

Sonya remembered the hell she'd gone through during a lunch stop in Colfax. After reading a few of Levi's threatening texts and hearing one of his nasty voicemails, she'd made herself unreachable via phone. It had been a hassle, blocking some of the gang-related numbers in her list of contacts while dealing with interruptions from other numbers before she could get to them. She'd almost been incited enough to let the costly smartphone follow her burrito wrapper and empty soda cup in the waste bin.

"*And*...I see you're not wearing your vest with our gang's emblem," Brock added. He would have mentioned one more thing had he known about it—she'd stolen Levi's license plate and put it in her saddlebag as a keepsake while giving the cops an excuse to pull over the revolting ringleader sometime in the near future.

As he chewed on a wad of smokeless tobacco, his eyes examined her shapely figure. Over a tie-dye T-shirt with six shades of blue, she wore a multi-pocketed jacket of washed black leather. Her faded blue jeans were mildly tattered and tucked down black biker boots adorned with studded straps. Fingerless gloves of goatskin leather protected her palms from blistering as a camouflage bag with four tones of gray was slung across her back.

"Do you have something to tell me?" he asked scornfully.

"Yeah. You might get run over if you don't move," she sneered. The next westbound motorist honked his horn and swerved to avoid Brock; his wheels were a foot left of the road's centerlines.

"You always did have a smart mouth and too much spirit. I guess that's why Levi liked you so much. So, tell me something, girl. Why'd you leave town...and where you headed?"

"Sydney."

Her true destination in the Silver State was the last thing she wanted anyone in the gang to know; if they found out, it would put Becky in jeopardy.

"Sydney...what? Is that some town in Utah? Idaho?"

"Australia, you geographically challenged halfwit! I'm going to Sydney, Australia."

"Very funny! *I'll* tell you where you're going."

"Where?" *He can't know where...can he?* she thought nervously, certain she'd never left any clues behind.

"Back to Sacramento."

He doesn't *know. Thank God.* "No, I don't think so."

"Yes! You! Are!" He spat dark brown gunk on the blacktop, stressing his demand. "Don't tell *me* 'no,' stupid girl! Turn that bike around. I'll follow you. Levi wants you back. He may even forgive you for what you did."

"What *I* did? What about what *he* did to my eye?"

"I'm sure you said something to deserve it."

"No, I didn't!" She wasn't about to explain how Levi had come home drunk after a very bad day and started the altercation by pestering her for sex, even though he'd forgotten to buy more rubbers. Then he'd ended the fight by assaulting her for not making an exception. After punching out her will to resist and having his way with her, he'd added insult to injury by boastfully admitting she wasn't his first victim and probably wouldn't be his last. With his massive limbs, mixed martial arts training, and years of street-fighting experience—three things she didn't have—the "gentle" giant had shown her what a monster he truly was.

Weeks ago, the odious gang had unknowingly revealed to Sonya that robbery was no longer the most severe of their felons. She'd been planning to leave the Screamon Demons after observing the murdering and torturing. Her last night with Levi had expedited that plan. There was no doubt in her mind if she stayed with these sordid lawbreakers much longer, she'd end up rotting in a ditch somewhere.

"Where's the cash, Sonya?" Brock scowled. "I need to know before we go back."

"What cash?" she shot back.

"Don't play games with me. The dough is in that backpack, isn't it?"

"See for yourself!"

While pushing her wraparound shades back up her aquiline nose to hide the direction of her eyes, she could feel her heart thumping; it knew exactly what she was steeling herself to do. She set her kickstand and dismounted her ride, reminding Brock of her seventy-one-inch stature. The straps of her backpack were shrugged off her leather-clad shoulders as her veiled eyes noted the lower tip of his gun's holster exposed by the hem of his vest.

"Here, Brock, have a look." Her right hand dangled the bag over his bike's handlebars.

Brock reached for it, not seeing her left hand filch his Smith & Wesson.

With an adrenaline-fueled shove, she put the crook and his ride on their left side—a move she'd never thought herself bold enough to do.

Knowing the attack would fan the flames of his temper so hot that he might rashly pull another gun and start shooting, Sonya acted quickly. Her right hand shot under a flap of her open jacket and came out gripping a shimmering Beretta; she didn't know if Brock's revolver was loaded. With a leg pinned under his motorcycle, he stared down the barrels of her gun and his. Then she moved her pistol to his front tire, thumbed down the safety, and turned her face away while squeezing the trigger.

BOOM!

With a shrill hiss, the wheel deflated, tossing her black mane with foul air. An empty shell plinked across the asphalt as acrid smoke escaped the muzzle, now trained between Brock's eyes again. His brawny arms raised in surrender as onlookers in the SUVs froze. His soot-black vest hung open, and she briefly scanned the front and other side of his waist. No weapons.

Sonya casually tossed Brock's revolver behind her. Dismayed, he watched the gun—a gift from his mistress—vanish over a cliff. Straps securing a Mossberg shotgun to the Fat Bob's rear fender captured Sonya's attention. Velcro ripped as she undid the straps and chucked the twelve-gauge firearm off the same ledge.

"Lose the rest of your weapons!" she ordered her superior, glaring down at him while re-donning the knapsack—a bag filled with cash adding up to seventy thousand dollars.

"What weapons?" he bit back.

"Last chance!" She held the firearm closer to his face.

"I don't have any, crazy broad!"

I think he's telling the truth, she thought as he continued ranting. *I really don't feel like frisking this pathetic pig; he'd like it too much.*

"I hope you know what you just volunteered for: weeks of more pain than you can imagine…times *ten*!" he carried on. "Levi will—"

"Levi will do *nothing* to me again! Now, do yourself a favor, lowlife! Go tell that sad pile of excrement that you couldn't find me. I'm done with him, I'm done with Sactown, and I'm done with the Screamon Demons. He can lead all you unholy scum to the bottom of the Pacific for all I care!"

The Beretta was returned to the holster harness under her jacket as she mounted her ride.

✞

Brock wriggled out from under his fallen Harley. The woman's long hair flew as her Low Rider roared away, passing the semi and the now-green light. The trucker had been too mesmerized by the scene to notice the light change.

"Stupid whore!" Brock snarled, glancing at the punctured front tire of his beloved Fat Bob. *Now, I need a different ride. Oh, I forgot, I* do *have one more weapon.* He got to his feet, pulled a snub-nose revolver concealed at his right ankle, and sprinted for the Kenworth tractor. Seeing the criminal hold the small firearm high, the scared driver raised both hands out his window. "Get out!"

The trucker didn't hesitate to open his door and vacate the driver's seat. Once he was standing on pavement, the revolver's short barrel was pressed under his chin and the trigger squeezed, producing a resonating *POW!* Taking no time to watch the driver crumple, Brock climbed in, recalling experience he'd had in such vehicles. While growing up with his truck-driving mother, she'd trained him to operate semis to put in more hours while sleeping.

He disengaged the air brakes, put the Kenworth in gear, and stepped on the gas, spewing a noxious cloud from the exhaust stack. The rearview mirror showed him the adults coming out of their now-distant SUVs. They raced over to see if the dead trucker could be saved. Brock decided once he'd made his leader's double-crossing lover just as lifeless as the tractor's previous driver, he'd be done killing for today.

"I told you, boss!" he grumbled to himself, imagining Levi sitting next to him. "I told you last year that spirited whore looked like too much trouble! Why wouldn't you listen to me? What were you thinking, letting her become one of us?"

Brock remembered he'd not yet texted the leader of the pack, letting him know he'd found Sonya. *It can wait,* he decided.

Sonya sped down the right lane of the serpentine mountain road, flashing by yellow tractors and construction workers in hardhats, all busy removing landslide rubble from the other lane. Half a mile later, the other temporary traffic light came into view, facing the same way she was heading with seven cars waiting in front of it.

After moving in another S, she slowed her Harley to a stop, scarce believing what was downhill a quarter mile ahead of her. Minutes ago, a transit bus had overturned when the driver tried to avoid a deer he would have been better off running over. The bus was on its side, blocking both lanes with its front against a cliff face and the rear hanging over steep downhill terrain. Getting around the passenger vehicle would not be possible.

"You've got to be kidding," Sonya huffed, noting the descending road beyond the bus curved right into a mile-long C. To her immediate right, she spied a narrow stairway for hikers. The trail bore multiple steps and landings while leading down the forested slope and eventually meeting the same road. It was not just a shortcut; it was the only way to bypass the obstacle ahead.

Her attention returned to the distant bus. As tempting as it was to take the shortcut with no delay, she felt her conscience beckon her to go straight first; there might be injured passengers in need of her help. Near the overturned vehicle, a few people stood around as some sat and nestled their injuries. From the distance, it was difficult to tell if her assistance could be used.

A distant grinding sound persuaded her to look over a shoulder for the source. Beyond the treetops, the same tractor-trailer with loud colors and laughing clown head came into view. The semi rounded a cliff and bashed the light and first motorist into the ditch. Instead of stopping, the Kenworth shifted up through the gears. She could hear the diesel engine roar as smoke trailed from the exhaust pipe. Albeit the accelerating rig was too far for Sonya to see the driver, she was certain the reckless driving meant Brock was behind the wheel.

Various questions filled her head. *Why did I let that scum live? How did he commandeer that semi? Did he threaten the driver? Or did he kill him? With what weapon? Maybe a weapon concealed... at his* ankle. *Man, I'm so stupid! Why did I not check his feet? Since I showed that sadistic creep mercy, that trucker is probably dead. I need to man up before Brock's rampage costs more lives! I've never killed anyone in my life, but I must kill now!*

She maneuvered the Low Rider so the front wheel was inches from the first step of the hiker stairway—a surefire way to put herself well out of Brock's reach. The risks of riding down the steps were not what made her hesitate, but the likelihood of the gang member driving the massive semi through the bus and killing more people in an effort to catch up with her. She would not let that happen and felt somewhat responsible for the outlaw getting his hands on the eighteen-wheeler.

Rearming herself, she watched the tractor approach with a grumble that conveyed Brock's homicidal resolve. When it was fifteen seconds from T-boning her two-wheeler, she aimed the Beretta, verifying the wild driver in her sights was who she thought.

Kill or be killed, Sonya! No more hesitation!

The trigger was pulled and, with an ear-piercing flash, her second bullet left the barrel. The slide kicked back, letting an empty shell fly free. She swiftly re-holstered her gun, feeling no need to see what happened next. Revving the Harley's engine, she began the daunting descent of the long stairway.

✞

Gyrating through the air, the nine-millimeter slug closed the distance between itself and the tractor's windshield. Without slowing, the shot made a spiderweb of cracks in the glass, bored into Brock's left eyeball, and exited the back of his skull. His head bounced lifelessly off the seat's leather headrest, slimed with his dark red blood.

Gravity tipped his body forward, causing his arm to pull the steering wheel right. Before he plopped across the floorboard, his head knocked the shifter into neutral. As the engine's volume dropped, the eighteen-wheeler drifted off the road, taking down a speed limit sign and a cluster of mailboxes. Then the right wheels found steeper terrain. The circus-colored big rig tilted into a deafening roll down the mountain—when it was lined up with the stairway.

✞

Spruce trees, mostly dwarfed dead ones, flashed by as Sonya's ride carried her further down the steps. Booming sounds from the tractor-trailer provoked her to glance back. The eighteen-wheeler was not far behind, rolling sideways again and again. Each time the clown face flashed into view, it seemed resolved to devour her.

Hundreds of panicked chickadees filled the air as trees and the stairway's rails were demolished by the revolving rig. Losing its wind deflector, rearview mirrors, and exhaust stack, the giant vehicle produced an immense dust cloud in its wake.

It was catching up.

The biker's heart raced as she eyed her deficient progress down the stairs. Another backward glance showed the mammoth wreckage of the semi was about six car-lengths behind her. A third glimpse showed less than two. She could not outrun the rolling steel hulk. It would squash her like a house-sized boulder.

The trees flanking the stairway thickened.

Nature spared Sonya's life, slowing down the tractor-trailer's thunderous progress. A sigh of relief escaped her lungs.

The delay was only temporary.

With the roof caved in, the Kenworth uncoupled itself from the floppy trailer as it pivoted around a large fir tree while upright. Then it began bouncing down the steps with the aid of its wheels.

More timber railing exploded out of the steel behemoth's path. Chunks of wood caught in the radiator grille as the Kenworth neared Sonya's bike with earsplitting ferocity. She wanted to go faster, but couldn't without losing control and falling, inevitably going under the tires of the unstoppable wheeled beast.

A frightened black-tailed deer, going almost the same way, grazed her handlebar with its shoulder, nearly taking her down. One of the tractor's rear tires came loose and bounced ahead of it, missing Sonya's head by inches.

The stairway led her through a narrow gap between two ancient homes supported by stilts on their downhill sides. Behind the Low Rider, the tractor still did not slow; it broadened the gap, producing piles of wooden debris.

The Kenworth's dented bumper came within six feet of Sonya's rear fender.

Six feet became four feet.

Two feet.

Then it did the unexpected—drifted left, leaving the stairway. Instead of rear-ending her, it *passed* her.

Winded from dread, Sonya slowed her bike to let the colossal truck move further away. It took down more trees and collapsed three more stilt houses. She neared the bottom of the stairway, watching the runaway vehicle roll across the road. An old RV screeched to avoid hitting it. The disintegrating tractor headed down another forested grade that would likely carry it all the way down to the lake. Once Sonya reached the street, she stopped her Harley and looked both ways.

"What's going on?" the driver of the halted RV exclaimed.

The biker gave an "I don't know" gesture with one hand and gazed left—the way that led back to the overturned bus.

Should I go help them? she questioned herself.

She faced right, finding two ambulances and a firetruck coming in an exaggerated response to the bus accident. With sirens howling and red lights flickering, they flew by, dodging the RV.

I don't think so. What could I do that the ambulance crews can't?

Believing the emergency vehicles were going the wrong way, the RV's driver shouted after them. Not knowing about the bus, he thought they were responding to the tractor he'd almost collided with. Sonya ignored him, revving her Harley's throttle. She steered right and continued down the road as if nothing had happened.

Pacing down a picnic table's smorgasbord of cookout food, Trey Radisson put a cheeseburger together as he listened to the lively conversations around him, mainly his sisters, Sherri and Denise, rambling on about their unfair supervisors. He had come to Colorado for a family reunion his father, Rody, had put together. Nearly fifty relatives had shown up and were all having dinner at Winter Park Resort. If it wasn't the middle of summer, they would be surrounded by skiers gliding by.

Trey reached for the mustard bottle and paused as the rhythmic thudding of a helicopter caught his attention. Conversations dwindled as everyone searched for the rotorcraft that sounded too close to be hiding behind anything. Like everyone around him, he scanned the entire arch of the cerulean sky, finding no hint of an aircraft. The unseen rotor blades thundered closer, tossing potato chips, paper plates, and napkins off the table. Still, the uninvited chopper's exact location remained a mystery. Most of the puzzled faces turned west—where their ears told them the rotor's loud thrum was coming from. Doubts of the direction faded when people noticed the lawn mostly littered on the east side of the table.

RAT-TAT-TAT-TAT-TAT-TAT-TAT-TAT-TAT!

The only visible sign of the machinegun racket was in the west sky. Like a strobe light, gun flashes with no gun flickered in the same place.

Trey turned left to see Sherri collapse with a bloodspot on her T-shirt. Denise went down next, losing some of her head to another bullet. With steaming holes in their bodies, more relatives were cut down by the fusillade. Trey stood petrified with out-and-out horror, not knowing why the resort's innocent guests were under attack by an invisible gunship. Comfort food, soda bottles, and spots of the emerald lawn burst from shots that missed their mark. The screams became fewer as the body count rose.

The hail of bullets stopped when only Trey and Rody were standing. With utter disbelief, they goggled their loved ones scattered about the yard, no longer breathing. *Why-why-why is this happening?* Trey's mind demanded to know. *Why, God, why? Why!*

The *WHUMP-WHUMP-WHUMP!* of the invisible rotorcraft grew quieter with increasing distance. Soon, there were no sounds at all. Trey faced his red-bearded father as if to ask him if everything they'd seen had really occurred.

Rody turned to his son, his gray eyes peering over oval sunglasses. "Now, see what happened?" he said far too casually. "All this because of your stupid invention."

Trey turned where he guessed the helicopter had gone. He wanted to die as well, knowing *he* was the reason no one had seen the airborne attacker coming. Trey had invented a cloaking device that could render anything it was attached to entirely undetectable to every living eyeball on the planet.

Tossing his covers, he sat up in bed.

Sweat filmed his terrified face as he fought for breath. When his pulse slowed and vision cleared, he scanned the familiar features of the room—*his* room. He was euphoric from knowing he'd been in his home in San Antonio the entire time, not where the horrible incident had transpired. But it *didn't* transpire. This was reality—where he'd not yet introduced his secret to anyone.

He turned to his digital alarm clock, showing 4:08 A.M. Wanting to return to standby mode for four more hours, he sprawled back down on the bed. Then he thought of the nightmare, which was not the first one.

Why do these bad dreams keep coming? he thought. *This has been going on nearly every week since I started the invention. This last one was by far the worst of them all. Funny how it happened the same week my revolutionary device became operational. I could introduce it to the company and become one of the richest citizens of San Antonio. Plus, I've always wanted to make scientific history, like the ones who have inspired me—Darwin, Einstein, Hawking, even my dad. And now I* could.

However, could something like the dreams become reality? Could my contraption fall into the wrong hands and cost more lives than I can count? Of course, it could. Why have I wasted so much time on this scientific path? What was I thinking? I was thinking only about my *future? What about the* world's *future? Why have I never thought of* that? *The world's future affects* my *future. If not mine, my kids', if I ever have any. And what about my niece and nephews?*

Why did it never occur to me that anyone who would travel with a cloaking device, such as a chopper pilot, would never do so, unless...their intentions were evil? This can't happen. It just can't! I will not be responsible for any dark realities that are even remotely similar to those ghastly events haunting my dreams. As sad as it makes me, my goals of early retirement, making scientific history, and impressing my father will have to be forgotten. I'll have to give those weaker projects at Envisiocom a shot instead.

He got out of bed and went straight to his garage. When he flipped the light switch, fluorescent bulbs buzzed as they lit up the room, with his tan Toyota Corolla on one side, worktable on the other. Scattered about the table were science-related notes and tools that had aided his creation of the apparatus. Fastened to the old car's hood was the cloaking device, an odd-looking stack of circuitry the size of a shoebox. The name of Trey's creation was the VV1—Veiler, Version 1.

I have to end it now. I can't take any more of those nightmares.

A mallet was taken from a toolbox atop the table. He approached the Toyota with it, wanting to see the miracle gadget perform one last time. His hand felt its way through the multicolored wires for the correct switch and flipped it. A few scarcely audible bleeps could be heard as lights twinkled through the circuitry. After forty seconds, the red READY light came on.

He flipped the second switch.

Yellow radiance hummed, coating the entire Toyota. Then—

—all signs of the vehicle were gone.

Trey set his hammer down on the hood that wasn't visibly there. The tool seemed to defy gravity. He grinned, gliding a hand across the cold, solid contours of the invisible Toyota.

"Truly remarkable," he sighed. "I'll miss this thing."

He felt for the switch and flipped it back off, making the car reappear. Then he unfastened the VV1 from the hood and set it on the worktable. The hand gripping the hammer came up.

But it would not come down. He imagined the device morphing into bundles of banknotes that totaled to millions. Atop every packet, Franklin shook his head no.

Should I really do this? Or should I heed Ben's advice?

Thoughts of prosperity that the device promised ran through his head. It's what he'd worked nearly a year to achieve. Now, it was ready. He could bring the VV1 to Envisiocom and watch it deliver a thriving future to him and his fiancée.

Memories of recent nightmares returned to the conflict within his brain.

It could have only been God who'd troubled my sleep with those terrible previews of a possible future. I've never had such reflections on my own; I only focused on making the invention operational.

Enough! Less thinking, more hammering!

Trey inhaled deeply and closed his eyes. The steel-headed mallet came down in a shrill crash. He repeated the action five times until the VV1 was reduced to unrepairable wreckage.

What have you done? a scolding voice echoed in his head.

He ignored the unforgiving words and dumped the VV1's remains in the trash. Research notes followed. He took the metal trash can outside and set it on his back porch. Then he turned to find matches and lighter fluid. An hour later, the can contained only smoldering ashes.

CARSON CITY, NEVADA

With cold sodas in one hand, Sonya McCall and Becky Lugo were in the latter's backyard, sitting in lawn chairs and watching hot air balloons drift over the town. They'd counted eleven so far in the evening sky filled with clouds the color of wine and yams. Unsure if there was some kind of event going on, Becky petted her white Chihuahua on her chubby thighs and faced Sonya, thinking of all the stories of lawlessness she'd just shared with her old high school friend.

"Did you *really* do all that wild stuff?" she asked in a teasing, unconvinced tone.

"Indeed, I did," Sonya replied. "But if you think I'm proud of it, I guarantee you I'm not. I was stupid to join that gang. I used to lie to myself by thinking I was too cool for the law. Later, I learned I was too fool for cool."

Becky chuckled. "So far, you've lived a far more interesting life than I have. I'm so low on courage and high on weight, I wouldn't last one day with people like that."

"Weight is not really an issue in that gang. Lots of its members are more fat than muscle, so don't think less of yourself for that."

"I try not to. Still, I wish I didn't lack the motivation to go to the gym."

"Well, if it's any consolation, some of the nicest people I've ever met *never* exercise. But, at the gym, I had no trouble at all finding a rude jackass. That's why I stopped going…that and the outrageous membership fees."

"I believe you. I guess my courage is the main issue. Since I'm so low on *that*, I'll never get on a motorcycle. They scare me."

"There's nothing wrong with that. By the way, you have no idea how much this means to me, letting me crash here and stuff."

"Well, Rosco here is good company." Becky cradled the sleepy dog on her legs. "But, unlike you, when I talk to him, he won't say much back." She kissed the Chihuahua atop the head. "So, what *was* the straw that broke the camel's back?"

"Sorry?"

"What made you leave them?"

The tormenting memory of the rape revisited her mind. "Well, there was *this*." She raised her shades for two seconds, showing Becky her bruised eye that made her wince. "Compliments of my vile ex." She decided to keep the terrible events after the punch to herself.

"Good for you for having the courage to leave him. Too many women think verbal abuse and black eyes are what true love is all about."

Sonya nodded, recalling other crimes. The felonies were not less severe than the assault she'd endured, but at least they were not committed against *her*. Still, they were too harsh for Becky's ears and needed to be sugared in a lack of details.

"Also, the gang grew a lot more evil this year and started murdering and torturing people." Her friend still covered her mouth in shock. "I couldn't be a part of that. Some of those depraved bikers did things every week that would have probably earned them the death penalty…which doesn't get used often enough in California."

"It's not used much in *any* state," the blonde woman added, raising her drink to her lips. "But, even when the penalty is death, people *still* break the law, you know."

"Not repeatedly." The raven-haired beauty casually sipped her orange soda the second after her witty response left her tongue.

Becky spit her beverage on her lawn and shivered from a fit of laughter. "Touché, girl, touché. I forgot how much fun you are to talk to. Sorry I didn't try too hard to stay in touch."

"Hey, I don't blame you; I wasn't much of a friend." *Why did I say that?*

"You weren't? Why do you think that?"

"If you don't remember, I'd prefer to keep it that way." She ignored Becky's puzzled face, recalling the cruel remarks she'd heard from other students about her friend's weight. Instead of rising to her defense, she'd made a few quips of her own: *"Every time she swims, she has to refill the pool." "When I threw a paper wad at her, she didn't feel it." "Last time she rode in the back of the bus, I heard the rear bumper scrape the pavement."*

The next thing she recalled was that she'd never said such things when Becky was in the room. But that didn't make it okay. She'd been too worried about what others would think of her if they'd known she occasionally hung out with the overweight blonde after school. If she could relive those years, a few blabber-mouthed students would have lost teeth to her fists.

"Is there something you would like to tell me?"

Sonya considered her next words. "Only that I don't recall doing anything nice for anyone in those days." *Good cover.*

"You were pretty much the only one who talked to me our senior year." Being reminded of this made Sonya feel worse about the fat jokes she'd made. "Are you in touch with anyone from our graduating class?"

"Nope."

"You're kidding."

"I'm *not* kidding."

"Didn't a lot of guys hit on you?"

"None who were worth my time. I've been like you most of my life—a loner. And I'm not sorry. Remember what happened to most of the dumb gals from our class who were social butterflies?"

"I *do* remember. They were all suckered into the same trap—the life of a single parent."

"Exactly. They were nothing but followers. Miserable clones of each other."

"I may be no parent, but I will always be *single*." Becky sighed and looked despondently at her lawn.

Sonya wanted to cheer her friend up. Failing to recall any worthwhile relationships brought her to her next point. "*I* intend to stay single for *years*. Despite what society would have you believe, having no boyfriend or husband is no sign of failure."

With a smile, Becky thanked her friend for the thought-provoking words. "Yeah, you're right. I can't deny that my lack of physical appeal has probably improved my character. With Rosco, my TV, and a few books to read, I'm doing all right. That's certainly better than living with some deadbeat guy who could ruin my life."

"True, true. Every deadbe—"

Sonya was interrupted by the *Peanuts* theme song ringing from a pocket of her jacket she'd draped over her chair. She got up to answer the smartphone, barely audible over Becky's profusion of wind chimes.

Please don't be Levi or one of his cronies, Sonya thought, certain there were no numbers she'd forgotten to block. *And please don't be Levi with a borrowed or stolen phone.*

When she took the phone from the pocket, the touchscreen displayed GRANDMA.

"You're kidding," she gasped in disbelief, letting the ringtone continue for ten seconds. Her finger reluctantly glided across the screen to answer the call. "Hello?"

"Sonya, it's Iza...your grandmother," an elderly voice said weakly.

"I'll be right back," the biker told her friend and walked away, dodging so many yard ornaments that people likely wondered if Becky sold them. Sonya entered the squeaky back door of the shabby house and sat in a broken-down easy chair. "Grandma?"

"Yes, dear."

"It's been a long time. Why are you calling me? I thought you said you didn't want to talk to me again."

"Sonya, I want your forgiveness. I should have never disowned you just because you were dating that Levi guy and hanging out with that motorcycle gang. I know I've been a terrible grandma and—"

"I left Levi, Grandma. And I've left Cali." She thought of the time she'd taken a selfie of herself with Levi nearly a year ago. Then she'd spitefully sent it to Iza's smartphone with a proud text about how she was dating the leader of the most dangerous biker gang in Sacramento. After one look at the text and the outlaw's picture, Iza had told Sonya she no longer considered her family.

"You've left California?" the old woman asked in disbelief. "You're kidding. I thought you'd never leave."

"It's true. I'm living with a friend in Nevada. I'm ready to change my ways. You were right to disown me. I've been very stupid the last five years. And, yes, you have my forgiveness. Maybe someday, I can earn yours."

The breath Sonya heard in the phone spoke of the elderly woman's relief. "You already have my forgiveness. You have no idea how happy I am to hear these words from you, babe. I prayed every day for a moment like this. You've just now given me more joy than I've felt for a very long time." Seconds of silence crawled by. "I wish that was all I wanted…but it's not."

"Go on."

"I've had a stroke, Sonya."

Her granddaughter felt a lump in her throat. "What?" she wheezed.

"A stroke. I had one last week. I can't get around the house very well. I need help. And I can't afford a caretaker. I don't know how much time I have left."

Sonya's azure eyes welled as thoughts of how her life could have been the last five years filled her head. She wished she'd stayed where she'd grown up—Artesia, New Mexico, where Iza lived. She wished she'd found work there and never disrespected the poor old lady's wishes.

The year after Sonya's high school graduation, Cody Wiggins, her third boyfriend, had promised her a better life in California. Much to her grandmother's dismay, Sonya had moved there with Cody, only to discover he could move mountains easier than he could keep promises. After losing his job and making a lengthy chain of thoughtless choices, Cody ended up in jail, leaving Sonya to fend for herself.

With too much pride to return to Iza's home, Sonya had spent years struggling to keep her head above water in the Golden State. Her attitude and short fuse had made it far more taxing than it had to be. She'd gained and lost numerous jobs, apartments, and boyfriends—a circle of folly she couldn't seem to avoid repeating. The more the cycle echoed, the more her depression swelled. She wanted excitement in her life, not drama. But the world never seemed capable of fulfilling her wants.

One night, she'd gone to a biker bar to toss back a few tequila shots while mulling over a plan to end her life. The plan was forgotten minutes after she'd met Levi for the first time. The gang leader had begun searching for a new girlfriend only a week after the death of his last girl, Candy. A rival biker gang had murdered her with nine-millimeter shots that were intended for Levi for his failure to pay his debts. Since Levi was not home, they settled for Candy and burned the house down, not knowing Levi had plenty of other places to live.

After meeting Sonya, paying her tab, and conversing with her for two hours, he'd decided she would make a perfect replacement for Candy. He was smitten by Sonya's looks, bravado, and clever remarks, while she was drawn to his power and willingness to take her under his wing. Against the advice of his followers, Levi had welcomed her into the Screamon Demons, albeit he'd not known her long. Months later, through no fault of Sonya's, the gang had turned too barbaric for her taste as Levi's drinking spiraled out of control.

So many places I've been when the only place that ever mattered was near my poor grandmother, who'd helped raise me, she thought.

Sonya was Iza's only grandchild, while Sonya's father, Derrick, was her only child. Though Derrick was never responsible enough to stay employed or afford his own place, he'd loved his daughter dearly and taught her everything he knew about his passion in life—motorcycles. If not for him, she would have never acquired her own keen interest in Harley-Davidsons. While repairing or upgrading other people's bikes, working part time as a locksmith and training his daughter to be his little helper at both jobs, Derrick barely made enough income to get the family by.

Then, a month after Sonya turned fifteen, Derrick got killed from riding his bike while intoxicated. He might have been saved by the love of a good woman, which he'd never had. Kali Rojas, the selfish vixen he'd married once they'd learned she was pregnant, had deserted the family for another man when their daughter was three. When Sonya was seven, the McCalls swallowed their pride and attended Kali's funeral after learning lung cancer had claimed her life.

Sonya was almost four when her mother had left the house for good, but not before Iza had futilely begged Kali to stay. Seventeen years later, Iza went through the same experience again—this time with her granddaughter, the last of her family. The memory now pained Sonya deeply.

Why did I abandon Grandma, like my despicable mother? I did even worse by leaving her when I was the only family she had left in her life. I forced her to live alone for five years. What was wrong with me? Hasn't Grandma been through enough already? I was so stupid to get aggravated by her harmless rules and ditch her! And where did I go? I went to Cali with that pathetic lowlife, Cody—a decision that led to me wasting five of the best years of my life! What was I thinking?

She sniffed and wiped her eyes with her tie-dye shirt. "Okay, Grandma, I'll start heading that way tomorrow."

"Oh, God bless you. Thank you." Further words of gratitude flowed from Sonya's smartphone, making her smile ear to ear.

SAN ANTONIO, TEXAS

Polishing off the last of his bologna sandwich, Trey sat at one of the breakroom tables at Envisiocom—his place of employment. "So, Vyron, what's *your* team working on?" he asked the black coworker seated across from him.

"A lawnmower that runs itself," Vyron replied. "We're still having trouble getting the darn thing to tell the difference between cut grass and *un*cut grass."

Trey nodded. "I would buy one. I never liked cutting grass, but my neighbor *really* doesn't like it. He hates mowing his lawn so much that he put flower pots over all the sprinklers." Vyron almost gagged on a bite of his egg-and-salmon sandwich. "His sprinkler system is possessed or haunted or something. He can't shut it off."

A manager across the breakroom switched off the TV mounted to the wall. The silence made both inventors and other brilliant minds turn their heads. Everyone watched as the bespectacled woman taped a note to the darkened flat-screen.

"Why, Abbey?" the nearest man said, annoyed he was missing the news.

"Because the CEO said that too many of you abuse this privilege," the manager replied to the whole room. "You get so engrossed with the TV that you don't realize when your lunchbreak is over."

She left the room with deaf ears to the objections that followed her out the door.

Every complaint Trey heard sounded just like he felt. Knowing he was partly to blame for Abbey's actions made him feel worse.

"Let me see. 'This will not be turned on for…thirty days,'" Vyron read the screen's note aloud. "Huh. I ought to post that note on my *wife*." As everyone within earshot chuckled at his quip, he thought of how much he despised the medication his other half was on; her multiple prescriptions for numerous health issues constantly snuffed out her libido. *You can endure anything if you find the funny side of it*, he reminded himself, smiling at his misfortune.

"Find a chick on the side to have flings with," someone proposed.

Vyron met eyes with the idea's source—a coworker who was well-known across the corporation for his lack of principles outside of work. "No, thanks, Brice. No one ever had a mistress without distress. How about keeping your debased ideas to yourself?"

Brice raised his arms out to his sides. "Why you gotta be so negative?"

"What's wrong with negativity?" Trey chimed in. "We have it for a reason."

"What reason is that? Negative feelings are a waste of life."

"I prefer to think of them like a check engine light on my car. When *I'm* down, it lets me know something is wrong with my life. That way, I'm reminded to fix it."

"Last time I checked, Brice, there's a *lot* going on with *you* that needs to be fixed," Vyron put in. "Maybe your life wouldn't be such a hot mess if you weren't smiling all the time, pretending everything's fine."

Knowing how right Vyron was erased Brice's smile and left him speechless. He returned his attention to the conversation at his own table.

"*That* shut him up," Trey scoffed as he stood. "I'll see you around."

"Later," Vyron said with a wave.

Trey returned to his tidy cubicle decked with action figures of various sci-fi film characters. His framed graduation certificate from the California Institute of Technology hung over his flat-screen monitor. Sighing, he logged back on to his computer and began typing up his latest diagnosis on improved video conferencing equipment he and his team had been working on. He'd always hated doing this. Upper management never seemed to understand that by demanding progress updates three times a week, they were only *slowing* their subordinates' progress. There were even rumors going around that the reports were usually not even read by the managers.

After typing three lines, a four-inch window popped up on the monitor, showing a smiling Filipino woman. "Hi, Trey," she said gleefully in perfect English. "Busy?"

"Hang on, Zuri," the inventor replied to his fiancée. He donned a headset and plugged it into his speakers, muting the woman's voice to everyone but him. "Can you hear me?"

"Yes. I got us reservations for this evening at Bella on the River. Trust me, you'll love this restaurant. I've heard it's one of the best in San Antonio. When you're done at work for the day, I say we have ourselves a little celebration dinner."

"What are we celebrating?"

"Your invention, silly—you know, the one that could probably afford us half a dozen yachts someday?"

Zuri was the only one he'd told about the VV1. The day after he'd made the invention operational, it had excited him so much that he couldn't wait to show his girlfriend what it could do. She would not be happy once she heard about his change of plans.

Trey met her doting gaze, thinking of how much he wanted the next two months to pass; after that would be their wedding day. She would be Zuri Radisson instead of Zuri Navarro. Until then, he would try to learn more about her. Reason told him he knew her well enough, yet something he couldn't fathom was missing.

They'd met at Envisiocom ten months ago when she'd worked as an assistant for the company's Hazmat and Safety Monitor. After six months, she was terminated for borrowing an access card she wasn't authorized to carry. When Trey had asked her about it, she'd told him she'd left her card home by mistake and her supervisor needed inspections completed in the restricted area before lunch hour. Two weeks later, she'd told Trey she'd found a new job with the airlines.

The inventor was not certain why she'd taken an interest in him. She said it was his character, but he felt there had to be more. Until they'd met, experience had taught him his nerdy, introvert persona gave him no appeal to the other gender. Plus, with a flaxen Jewfro, beaklike nose, deep smile lines, protuberant eyes, scrawny frame, and unstylish wardrobe—mostly faded plaid shirts, never-ironed khakis, and white sneakers—no other woman had ever given him a second look. Zuri, on the other hand, could have possibly become a supermodel, at least in the Philippines.

Trey would not be engaged to her now if it wasn't for all her talk about cherishing his company and wanting many more years of it. Then there was all the physical affection she'd shown him. Thirty-one years old, he'd never been in love before and couldn't resist the idea of proposing to her. She was the first person outside his immediate family to make him feel so important. To him, it was a truly blissful day when she'd gladly accepted the engagement ring he'd bought her.

However, he was still unsure of why she seemed a tad mysterious. He guessed it had something to do with all the out-of-town trips she took every other week. She'd told him her occupation required her to fly to various parts of the country for training purposes, and security policies forbid her to voice details to a single soul. Since Trey loathed airports anyhow, his curiosity stayed too low to press her for details.

With large gray orbs, he studied her features on the screen: lank black hair, monolid eyes, flawless teeth, fair skin with a gold undertone.

"How did I ever become this fortunate, Trey?" she said with sheer admiration. "Your outstanding brains are going to buy us nearly anything we want."

His heart sank as he thought of the painful news he had for her. Hearing her speak of the dreams he would deny them made it worse. However, it would only get harder if he waited. It was time he got it off his chest.

"I had another bad dream last night, Zuri," he began.

"Yes?" she urged him on.

"Well," he resumed after a long pause, "it was like all the other bad ones, only worse. There was an invisible helicopter shooting up a picnic I was having with my family. I think—"

"No!" she cut him off, waving a finger. "Don't even go there, Trey. I don't want to hear silliness like that."

"Like what?"

"Don't 'like what' me! I know where you're going with this. You think that VV1 of yours will end up in the wrong hands."

"Well, yeah, it could. Imagine how disastrous—"

"Na-a-a-a-a! You need to bring that thing to work, sell it, and make us rich." Her face turned hopeful as she clasped her hands at her chin. "Right, sweetie?"

Why allow this to drag on? Just give her the bad news. he told himself.

"I destroyed it," he said flatly.

Her slanted eyes became impossibly large. "You. Did. *What*?"

"You heard me. The VV1 is gone. It was a stupid invention. I never should have made it. And I've made up my mind to not make another one. I'm sorry if—"

"I can't believe this! What, I mean, *what* were you thinking, Trey? Are you an idiot?"

"I don't think so, Zuri. Are you a gold-digger? You're certainly talking li—"

"Trey!" someone to his right huffed.

The inventor's head spun to find Gus, his grossly overweight boss. He stood in the entrance of Trey's cubicle, glaring at him through a pair of trifocals.

"Yes, sir?" he said timidly.

"Chitchat with your lady during lunch hour, understand?"

"Yes, sir. I'm sorry. It won't happen again." He removed the headset.

Shaking his balding head, Gus moved on. When Trey turned back to his computer screen, the window that had showed his fiancée was black with DISCONNECTED in the center.

What just happened? She's never hung up on me before. What's going on? I thought we were in love. With no success, he tried to reconnect with her.

NEW MEXICO: THREE YEARS LATER

Despite its rusted roof of corrugated iron and clapboard walls, bleached to a dull gray by decades of hot summers, the ancient house was still inhabitable. The only lit window of the two-story shack bore a cockeyed sash framing six panes of grimy glass, two of which were cracked. Sonya McCall was inside, sprawled on her late grandmother's worn-out sofa, where she'd dozed off to a weather report on the TV.

A distant metallic *thump!* from outside startled her. She sat up to see out the window, finding nothing in the darkness.

Have the Screamon Demons found me? she thought worriedly. Nightmares of being found by the vile gang had often troubled her sleep. If the lawless bikers were on her property, they wouldn't find the same woman they'd known three years ago who was nearly helpless without a handgun. Back then, she'd been like a goldfish swimming with sharks. But, after leaving the sharks and moving to New Mexico, she'd done a few more things out of fear for her life. She'd given up smoking, become savvier with firearms, jogged twenty miles a week, and attended self-defense classes. She'd also done so much weightlifting, her supervisor at her waitressing job called her Brawny Barbie since her pale face had not lost its doll-like quality.

She ran in the kitchen and reached in a narrow gap formed by a vintage yellow refrigerator and a wall covered with peeling, floral-patterned wallpaper. Her hand came out gripping a fully loaded Remington shotgun. She switched off dim, candle-style lights and peeked through the dining room window's threadbare drapes. The distant laughter of a teenage boy reached her ears.

This smells more like the activity of vandals than outlaw bikers. Whoever's out there, they picked the wrong day to mess with my property. They won't get a head start from me getting dressed to go outside.

Sonya already had on jeans, shoes, and T-shirt—the same clothes she'd worn to work that day. It had been such a long shift, all she'd wanted to do after returning home was collapse on the couch.

The screen door flew open from her fierce exit and bounced off the timber wall, causing a warped clapboard to fall loose at one end. Gripping her Remington in one hand, flashlight in the other, she sprinted through the darkness, following the gravel driveway to the road thirty yards south. She spied a pickup's taillights going west as she neared Hermosa Drive. The flashlight was shined on Iza's mailbox.

As she'd suspected, someone had struck the mailbox again with a bat—someone who needed a good beating in her opinion. This time, it was caved in at the center, rendering the three-digit address number a slight challenge to read. Over the number, the box read GIBBS—Iza's maiden name. Forty-one years ago, Iza divorced Sonya's alcoholic grandfather, Hector McCall, and had her last name legally changed back. She would have also changed her *son's* last name, but knew Hector's volatile reaction to such a move would be more than she could handle, albeit Hector had rarely come to visit Derrick.

Ever since Iza had passed away from another stroke four months ago, her granddaughter had never felt the need to update the mailbox. Furthermore, allowing the box to display any last name that was not hers made her feel safer. Sonya was unsure of the need for such paranoia. Levi had never seen her ID and, as far as she knew, he still thought her last name was Meadows. She would have told him her *real* name, but had become exceptionally fearful of identity theft a year prior to meeting him. When she'd lived in Stockton, her naive roommate had her life unimaginably ruined by a con artist "boyfriend."

Sonya stood in the quiet road, hearing only the crickets chirping. She recalled how little she cared about the mail—credit card offers, coupons for products she never bought, bills already covered on autopay, nothing more. Taking one more glance at the distant taillights, she guessed the delinquents had switched off their truck's lights while near the mailbox so they wouldn't be seen committing their misdemeanor.

The next vandals who see my *mailbox will lose interest fast.*

She pumped the shotgun and fired. The box was blown off its oak post, twirling in the air with a week's worth of mail escaping.

K-CHAK! BOOM! K-CHAK! BOOM!

Splinters flew as two more twelve-gauge rounds sundered the post. The mailbox thudded on the side of the paved road. Admiring her handiwork behind a cloud of tart smoke, she recalled how clumsy she'd been with weapons this size back in her lawless days.

The hysterical screaming of two teens shocked her.

She spun, shining the light across the street. *There* were the vandals, running from their hiding place behind the shell of an old pickup truck a stone's throw from the road. It had been left there by last week's tornado—a close call she'd never forget.

Terribly horrified by the gunshots, the roguish boys raced toward nothing but darkness in the flat, treeless field.

Such easy targets they're making themselves, Sonya thought. *They are so fortunate I don't put vandals out of their misery.*

One kid spun to glance at Sonya's light, hoping she wasn't pursuing him and his pal. The pause of his flight was brief, but long enough to show her the wet spot on his tattered jeans.

"If you're gonna destroy my stuff, do it right!" she thundered after the fleeing duo.

What is wrong with kids now days? Haven't the people of Artesia, like the owner of that wrecked truck, already been through enough during and after the twister?

She headed back to her decrepit abode, unconcerned with who else might have been alarmed by the gunshots. The neighbors lived more than a hundred yards away, much further than the Woodbine Cemetery, where Sonya's grandmother had been buried. She'd not inherited much in addition to the secluded home.

The *Peanuts* theme played from her smartphone in her back pocket as she neared the rickety porch. When she took the phone and eyed the screen, it blinked BECKY CALLING. She immediately thought of asking her blonde friend if she would mind her returning to Nevada and moving back in with her; it was getting lonely with her grandmother gone.

"What's up, Becky?" she answered chirpily.

"They're coming for you," her friend whispered.

"What?"

"They're coming for you, Sonya." Her breaking voice was filled with dread.

The black-haired woman's pulse quickened. "What do you mean?"

"The Screamon Demons found me. They know I know you."

Feeling entirely defeated, Sonya let her eyes fall closed. "How is that possible?"

"I don't know, but they broke in and told me to tell them where you went. I told them I didn't know. Then they beat me until I agreed to unlock my smartphone for them. They went through my contact list and found your name and New Mexico address. Now, they're coming for you. I'm so sorry." The blonde woman sobbed hysterically.

"Becky, calm down. How did they find you and how did they know you know me?"

"I don't have any idea."

"Why did they let you live?"

"One of them—some guy called Po—has been watching me until the others verify you're really there in Artesia."

"Po?" *Must be a newbie*, she thought, not recalling the name. Then she wondered why Becky's contact list was not enough proof of her New Mexico address. *Her phone would have said either "Sonya McCall" or "Sonya," not "Sonya Meadows." Maybe* that's *why the gang is unsure the address is accurate.*

"Yeah, Po. He said he might torture me later if his boss tells him to."

To coerce me to give myself up. "How are you talking to me right now?"

"Po is supposed to be watching me, but he drank too much and passed out minutes ago. So, I took my phone back and now I'm hiding in the bathroom with Rosco."

No wonder she's whispering. "Geez, Becky, the bathroom? Seriously? You need to get out of that house...*now!*"

"I can't. Po nailed the doors shut, and the nails are too high for me to reach. Just get out of Artesia. I need to hang up now and call the cops bef—"

"What are you doing in there?" the cruel voice of Po shouted from the background. Then there was fierce rapping on a door, which roused excited barking from Becky's Chihuahua.

"Oh, no!" Becky wailed. "He's awake! That creep is awake! Oh, my—"

The next thing Sonya heard from her smartphone was the door being kicked in.

"What the hell? You just called the cops, didn't you? Big mistake, you fat slut! Well, I can't stick around *here* anymore, can I? One last thing to do before I leave!"

Garbled sounds of Becky's fear and the biker's rage followed.

A gun went *POW!*

"Becky!" Her friend had gone silent as Rosco continued barking. After another *POW!* Sonya heard nothing.

7

SAN ANTONIO

Red and blue lights flashed in front of a five-story structure labeled ALMIGHTY IT. Squad cars, news vans, and vehicles belonging to hostages cluttered the corporation's parking lot. The last of the late workers from the first four floors, mostly software engineers and information-technology architects, had exited the building only minutes ago. After they'd heard about the police activity, curiosity persuaded them to clock out early, go outside, and pry. Then they were informed of the trouble occurring on level five.

No one outside had any way to hear the bickering within the walls of the establishment. To everyone still on the top floor, the quarreling was loud and clear.

"Pele, get real. You know this never works. How do y—"

"I told you not to talk to me, Justin!" the livid Samoan threatened, training his snub-nosed revolver on the hostage's head.

"All right, all right. Don't shoot. Forget I said anything," Justin pleaded with hands raised.

With his back against a copy machine, Trey Radisson sat on the carpeted floor near Justin and the rest of Pele's hostages, all anxious to get out of this fix and go home. A wall clock showed it was 7:55 P.M. Every worker on the top floor was supposed to go home almost an hour ago.

Pele neared the floor-to-ceiling windows and beheld the numerous blinking lights that meant trouble for him. "I swear, I'll kill whoever called these pigs!" he groused. Sweat glazed his tan face as he turned toward his shortest hostage. "You should not have fired me, Dan, you stumpy lowlife. All I wanted was the promotion I worked years to earn, and you give it to some jerk who hasn't even been here half a year. Then you terminate me just for saying something about it?"

"Not just that—you were rude and late to work almost every day." Dan spoke boldly.

"If I have to off any of you idiots, you're going first!"

Grating sobs from the female employees were giving Trey a headache. Deciding he couldn't take any more, he tapped on Justin's shoulder, recalling how his colleague frequently took pills for migraines.

"What?" Justin whispered.

"Do you have any aspirin?" Trey asked quietly.

"Something like that."

"Can I have one?"

"No."

"Why not?"

"They're prescription pills. What if you have an allergic reaction or something? If you die, I don't want you suing me."

"Okay, never mind." Trey shook his head, visualizing a ghostly version of himself in a courtroom. Then he recalled how life had been when Pele was still employed at Almighty IT. Even though Trey never agreed with some of what the disgruntled Samoan had said about the company, it felt good to be the first person Pele had talked to. He was the closest thing the bitter ex-employee had to a friend. They'd worked together as software engineers for almost a year.

Trey was ready to forget all about his past with the armed man. For months, he'd suspected Pele was psychotic. Now there was no doubt. The former coworker's short fuse seemed to make him one of a kind. All the other Samoans Trey recalled working with were always civil and quite brilliant.

My bladder is killing me! Trey thought, noticing the soaked spot of carpet surrounding the seated backside of Jody—the first victim of Pele's rule against bathroom breaks. *I want to go home and watch TV. I'm sick of all this!*

Then he fathomed a probable escape. However, his idea didn't benefit the others.

Why should I care? Justin, married with three kids, is sleeping with Regina. Cindy and Jody are self-centered and lazy. I've heard of people fainting from overworking. Jody proved at her desk one time that underworking *can have a similar effect. Maybe instead of drinking all that Cran-Apple juice every day, she should have coffee instead.*

As for the others, LeRoy and Meredith are extremely rude to everyone while often flirting with each other, not caring how their spouses might feel about it. Every week, Derrick and Jason compete with each other to see who filled their weekend with the most debased events, as if it's something to be proud of. Dan, who has clearly never missed a meal, uses company money to buy himself fast food. Plus, he talks to me and the rest of his subordinates like we're stupid and worth less than the dirt beneath his feet. Most of us tune Dan out for the same reason he *tunes out his bratty kids at home—important words never leave his mouth.*

Everyone I respect made it out of the building before Pele came in and waved his gun around. Well, I want out too! I'm sick of heeding my ethics. Every time I do that, I get screwed! Look what happened to me three years ago—I got rid of my problematic invention, possibly saving the world, and everything still *goes bad for me. My fiancée disappeared from my life without a trace. Envisiocom went out of business, forcing me to take* this *stupid job. Now, I'm surrounded by jerks with no concern for anyone but themselves.*

Well, maybe it's time for Trey *to think only about Trey. Maybe it's time I show these dishonest morons how they make* me *feel every day. Yep, that settles it! I'm getting out of here and going home! My TV is waiting on me.*

"Pele?" Trey called out, his tone oddly blasé.

"What?" Pele retorted.

"I have a plan that will make those pigs take you seriously."

Pele's free hand beckoned him over. Trey stood and slowly approached him, trying not to show any hints of pain from his full bladder. As the overweight Samoan goggled the window, Trey winked at the other nine hostages who looked concerned for him while remaining uncomfortably seated on the carpet. Everyone knew he was up to something and wanted to insist he not try it.

"Pele, listen to me," Trey began, keeping his voice only audible to the tan-faced man. "What we need to do first is lure the cops into the basement. I will go out the front door and claim that I escaped. Then I will tell the pigs that the activity up here is just a diversion and that you and the hostages are actually in the basement. They will send every trooper down there if I tell them you have eight other accomplices."

"What good would that do? Why the basement?" Pele asked.

"Haven't you ever wondered why no one goes down there?"

"I heard they were remodeling it."

"Not true. The fire suppression system down there is the obsolete kind—the *dangerous* kind that sucks all the oxygen out of the air. They haven't taken it out yet…*and* the damn thing still works. I will lead the cops down there, run the other way, lock them in, and pull the switch."

Pele chewed this over. "Forget it. I'm not ready to be a cop killer. Besides, I can't release anyone. Not even you."

"Pele, I'm your friend," Trey cajoled him. "Don't talk to me like I'm one of the other losers in this room. I'm like you—a disenfranchised American who is ready to get even with all the injustice surrounding him. At least give me some credit for *that*. This company has screwed *both* of us over. We need to show them *we* are in charge, right? We're going to win here. You just have to let it happen."

Trey's bulging gray eyes were filled with assurance as they bore into the dark monolid orbs of the armed man. Instead of denying him his release, Pele continued to sweat and shiver with uncertainty, just as Trey thought he might.

"I'm with you to the end," he continued. "Besides, if you don't want to kill the pigs, let me lead them on a wild goose chase. The basement also has an access door to the sewer. While they waste time down there, I will lock them in and you can pistol-whip your promotion out of our selfish boss and get out of here, or whatever you want to do next. Okay, friend? Now, let's show everyone that no one, *no* one messes with Pele Lameko."

"Fine, but hurry back."

"No problem."

Trey exited the room and took the elevator to the ground floor. Then he entered the men's room. If not for the irate Samoan forbidding everyone on level five from leaving his sight, Trey would have used *that* floor's restroom half an hour ago.

"What an idiot," he snorted, thinking of the disgruntled employee as he stood in front of the urinal. Then he thought of all he'd told Pele to dupe him into releasing him. *I can't believe he fell for that. I must be a better liar than I thought. I hope I never feel compelled to do anything like that again. I never liked liars much.*

A minute later, Trey washed and dried his hands. Like every time he used a public restroom, he reached over the door for the self-closing mechanism and pulled the closer arm to one side, cracking the door open a few inches. He gripped the edge of the door and pulled it open the rest of the way, not knowing how many unwashed hands had been on the door's handle.

Trey nonchalantly entered an elegant lobby trimmed in shiny mahogany and accented with brass columns that flanked paintings of the CEO's predecessors. The only sounds were his footfalls on the polished marble floor and the trickling of an oval fountain. When he exited the spacious lobby through automatic glass doors, the media massed around him with mics, lights, and cameras. Then the questions came.

"Can you tell us about the situation?" one well-dressed woman asked.

"Did he let you go?" asked another.

"Has he harmed any hostages?"

"Did you escape?"

"Do you have—"

"What are you TV people going on about?" Trey grumbled, silencing everyone. "All I did was go to the bathroom! Leave me alone!"

Two San Antonio police officers who'd neared the entrance with the news crew returned to where their comrades waited. "Forget him; he doesn't know jack," one of them affirmed. "He must be from one of the lower floors."

As Trey expected, the media ceased the questions and cleared a path for him. With no further interference, he strode over to his tan Toyota.

Against his wishes, he thought of what the cop had said. *They think I don't work on the fifth floor. That will all change if they watch the recordings from the surveillance cameras on level five. Then what will happen to me?*

Forget about it, a voice in his head told him as he got in the Corolla and drove away. *What kind of theories will help you sleep better tonight? How about this: Maybe the cameras were not even on. Even if they were, the cops at Almighty IT won't be worried about you; they have bigger fish to fry.*

During the last three years, the cash Sonya had stolen from Levi's safe had gone from $70,000 to $15,300. She was sure the last of it would have been spent by now had she not taken her part-time job nearly two years ago—after Iza had recovered enough from her first stroke to be left home alone for a few hours. Sonya put seven paper-clipped packets of twenty Franklins each in her backpack as the remaining $1,300 joined the few Jacksons already in her wallet. Atop the cash, other items were added to the knapsack: toiletries, undergarments, lighter, water bottle, her grandmother's photo.

She chucked off the mildly soiled T-shirt that advertised her place of employment, changed her sports bra, and entered the feebly lit bathroom to brush her hair. The sink's elliptical mirror had endured eight decades of excessive moisture from the shower and bore unsightly black spots that were far too large for the rococo-style frame to hide. Sonya utilized her brush, sick of looking at the ancient mirror and thankful this would be the last time. The reflective wall antique never failed to remind her of what a fleapit she was living in.

When Levi and his chums find this eyesore that I call home, they'll probably burn it down, she thought. *That might be a favor to the entire street.*

Once the tangles were gone and the center part was straight, Sonya's raven ringlets hung in twin curtains that framed her ivory face. She didn't look often at her reflection in *any* bathroom; it reminded her of high school when a few callous students had stereotyped her as a creepy Goth girl.

This is no time to reflect on my teenage years. I never got a chance to ask poor Becky how long ago the Screamon Demons got my address. They could be just hours away...if not minutes. Time to go!

She put on a clean T-shirt with FAITH: (F) FORWARD (A) ALL (I) ISSUES (T) TO (H) HEAVEN printed across the front in white Castellar text. The blue jeans and underpants she'd worn to work that day were swapped with fresh ones. After tucking in her dark gray shirt, she changed her socks and put on her biker boots. Once her favorite belt was buckled on, she shrugged into her nylon shoulder harness and secured it. Her fully loaded Beretta was returned home to the holster fixed to the left strap.

After switching off every light, she carried two items out the back door—her camouflage backpack and her late grandmother's floral-patterned suitcase, which she'd filled earlier with her own stuff. Both bags were taken to a barn that Derrick had converted into a garage before Sonya was born. After flipping on the warehouse-style lights, she donned her fingerless gloves and leather riding jacket she'd left hanging on her Low Rider's left handlebar. Her smartphone and wallet were shoved down interior pockets before the jacket was zipped closed. For her firearm, she opened the bottom drawer of a rusted filing cabinet, took out four extra magazines and a box of nine-millimeter cartridges. The fifteen-round clips were filled to the max and shoved down exterior pockets.

She opened the top case over her Harley's taillight and the leather saddlebags flanking the passenger seat. All three compartments were filled with various items from Iza's old suitcase: clothes, snacks, Bible, smartphone charger, flashlight, pillow, street atlas, and water bottles. From cluttered shelves, she took three items and added them to a saddlebag: an unopened box of cartridges, components for a dome tent, and her father's lock pick kit.

Derrick had trained her how to use the twenty-four plastic-handled hooks that were tucked down pockets inside a monogrammed leather case the size of a paperback novel. He'd provided her with another skill to possibly use someday to make an honest living. Instead, she'd used the skill—and the same kit—to aid the Screamon Demons on their robberies. She still wasn't ready to forgive herself for that. However, it was a good thing she'd brought the kit to California eight years ago; she'd also used it to crack Levi's safe full of stolen cash—an enormous help for her and Iza's financial needs the past three years.

Eyeing the D.H.M. engraved on the kit's brown cover, she apologized to her father's spirit for the time she'd misused it. As she packed the kit in her two-wheeler, her feelings of self-reproach led her to think once more about Becky. She'd desperately wanted to go save her from being murdered in cold blood, but Nevada was not even in her time zone. Two years after high school, since Becky had grown sick of living near her overbearing mother, she'd moved to Carson City after her father offered her a job as a scheduler in his vet clinic. Sonya felt like cursing both divorced parents—one for driving Becky away, the other for *keeping* her away.

How did the gang know to go to Becky's address? she asked herself again, knowing she'd not been at her place for very long. She figured Levi must have bribed some cop for aid. The cop could have helped Levi discover her real last name and traced her phone's location. She'd heard every smartphone had a tracking device with a location history being recorded somewhere. Levi could have noted Sonya's phone was at Becky's address for two days. But Sonya could fathom no explanation as to why he failed to note the next address.

For two more days, Sonya had traveled to Artesia. Three days after her arrival, she drove Iza to Albuquerque to see a friend. While there, Sonya went to the phone store and, as a precaution, swapped phones and got a new number, thinking it safer to make the switch while in a city far from Artesia. The only thing she'd not changed was her area code and address; the phone company still showed her living in California.

Since she'd changed phones three years ago, she could not understand why the Screamon Demons just recently found out about Becky. Or *how* they found out. Sonya had not been back to Carson City for the entire three years. It made no sense.

I'm glad I never told Levi my real *last name; I'm sure if I did that, he would have found me a lot faster.*

She thought of the time she'd answered Levi's query of her last name. After almost saying "McCall," two things had occurred in less than a second. First, she recalled her hapless roommate from her past in Stockton before pronouncing any letter after the M. Then she thought of the dull, flat views she'd seen for years around Iza's home and said "Meadows" before she could stop herself. Despite thinking the false name was silly, she'd felt compelled to accept it—in any successful relationship, you only had one chance to get your own name right. After falling for Levi and moving into his costly domicile, she'd wanted to tell him her *real* name, but feared his temper too much. When the biker gang turned too barbaric for her taste, she knew she'd never let the cat out of the bag.

Before opening the garage-style door, Sonya studied the outbuilding's interior, remembering how it had looked during her childhood and teen years. It was once a private motorcycle workshop, cluttered with half-assembled Harleys, spare parts, and toolkits. *I learned so many valuable things from Daddy inside this barn. I miss our visits. I miss his jokes.*

The timber structure was now occupied with other things she would miss: her late grandmother's old Subaru Forester, a treadmill, dumbbells on a three-tier rack, the padded bench Sonya used with the weights. Over a year ago, a coworker had sold her the fitness equipment for dirt-cheap since her husband had injured his back and couldn't use it anymore. She would miss the other servers she'd worked with. For tomorrow, she made a mental note to call the manager of the Mexican restaurant and let her know she was quitting.

Sonya noticed Levi's old California license plate hanging right where she'd left it—over the four-drawer filing cabinet. Displayed across the white vehicle sign in blue letter was MESWME—the ideal set of characters for any wrongdoer searching for trouble. Of course, one look at Levi's size made most trouble dealers look the other way, knowing they would get much more than they could give. Sonya saw the tag as a trophy since it had belonged to one of the most—if not *the* most—feared outlaw in Sacramento. Smiling, she wondered what sort of complications she'd caused the repugnant ruffian by taking the plate.

The license tag was unhung from rusty nails in the ribbed, cobwebbed wall. As she added it to a saddlebag, she eyed her own tag for a moment. Forgettable alphanumerics were embossed in red across the yellow plate. To her, it was still a great improvement over her old California plate that had read LVISCHK. She could scarce believe she'd spent actual money to have her last tag personalized to honor the atrocious leader of the Screamon Demons. Once she'd obtained her New Mexico plate and attached it to the Low Rider, she'd wasted no time digging a hole in the backyard and burying the old tag.

In one move, she turned off the lights and pushed the button to raise the motorized garage door. After scanning the flat, moon-glazed landscape, she straddled the motorcycle. When she turned the key, the engine screamed to life. She turned on the sole headlight, donned her maroon helmet, and pulled out.

Halfway down the driveway, she stopped to take one last look at her grandmother's darkened house. Derelict or not, she would miss the place—her home for most of her life. It was now nothing but a diversion for Levi and his gang at some time in the near future.

"Good-bye, Grandma. Good-bye, Daddy," she whispered, imagining Iza and Derrick were still alive and waving to her on the front porch. "I'll always love you."

She neared Hermosa Drive and turned right, accidentally rolling over the remains of the mailbox. At the first opportunity, she headed north.

Trey's last hour at Almighty IT would have been a thrill to any normal person. But he was not normal; he was far too drained by how society was crumbling to be fazed by much of anything. As he sat quietly behind the wheel of his Toyota, driving to his house near Lackland Air Force Base, his negative reflections on life flowed freely.

I hate my job! It never brings me any excitement. I thought a disgruntled employee waving a gun around would be an exception, but I was still *bored. What else do I hate? I hate struggling to pay bills. I hate how I didn't trust my VV1 enough to introduce it to the world and end my financial concerns. Since I* still *don't trust it, I'm never going to rebuild it.*

I hate living alone and having no one to come home to when I get off work. I hate how interesting women are hardly ever single. When they are, they always have an excuse when I ask them to go out with me. If I want some extra income, maybe I should try writing a book about how to repel women. It might be worth a shot since I'm the complete opposite of a chick magnet. Wait a minute! Who would buy a book like that?

I hate Zuri for disappearing from my life with no explanation or warning. All the signs tell me she was only interested in my ability to make her rich. What a freeloader! And I was too stupidly in love to realize it. Then she stopped answering my calls and texts. But I just can't believe she moved out of her apartment without telling me! Where in the world did she go?

Next, Trey recalled the first eighteen years of his life. He'd been raised by good parents who'd brought him to church every Sunday. The church had constantly emphasized how important it is to love people. *It's so hard to love when there is so much to hate.*

Then he realized he was parked right outside his dull two-bedroom house. *How long have I been sitting out here? Why am I not inside yet?*

After locking his car and entering his nondescript residence, he parked himself in his favorite place on Earth—a well-cushioned recliner. After leaning the chair as far back as it would go, he took the remote off an end table and turned on his widescreen television. Backgrounded by police lights, a news reporter spoke into her mic.

"I'm standing in front of the Almighty IT corporation, where police—"

Trey changed the channel, not interested in hearing about things at work. Another well-dressed news woman on the screen gave her own report.

"More bad news in Phoenix, where Civic Gains Bank was robbed today by the Chrome Falcon terrorist group. Every employee and customer was brutally murdered and not a single dollar was left behind. This is the fifth reported robbery and ninth reported sighting of the extremists. Police and FBI are still working towards tracking down anyone associated with Chrome Falcon, but, as far as we know, they have yet to find any leads."

Trey studied the image next to the reporter's head. A black rectangle was the background of Chrome Falcon's symbol—a silver avian figure with crowbar-like wings spread and hooked beak turned right.

"Ironically, the locations where the four other reported robberies took place are nowhere near Phoenix. Never occurring in the same state, they include Sacramento, Birmingham, Bangor, and Frankfort. Police are speculating Chrome Falcon may be behind many small-town robberies that have occurred all across the U.S. in the past two years. But how they cover their tracks so well and move so quickly from state to state remains a mystery."

A scene of a Phoenix police officer replaced the reporter. He stood beside a highway, giving his story.

"We were tailing a black semi with the Chrome Falcon emblem on the side of the trailer. After they blew out our tires and took down our chopper with an RPG, all backup units that were inbound to their whereabouts couldn't find them anywhere." The cop stared despondently off into space, uncertain what to think. "I don't know how they do it. That's quite a trick too, hiding an eighteen-wheeler that fast. In all my years on the force, I've never seen such evasive suspects."

Videogame music from Trey's smartphone jarred his attention from the TV.

"Hello?" he answered.

"Hi, Trey. It's your mother," an enthused, squeaky voice said. "How are you?"

"Good. Nice to hear from you. How is Dad?"

"He's fine. Did you know your sister, Sherri, is engaged now?"

"No, I sure didn't." *It's about time*, he thought, recalling all the stories he'd heard about her sneaking around with boyfriends.

"Her boyfriend, Jeff, proposed to her last week. You haven't met him, have you?"

"Nope."

"They have their wedding date planned for February of next year."

"Uh-huh." *Of course they're in no hurry; the way Sherri lives, life after her wedding will have few surprises.*

"Are you currently seeing anyone?"

Trey rolled his eyes. "No, Mom."

"No one? No one at all?"

"Nope." *If only I could be one of those rare people who can go their entire life relationship-free and still be happy.*

"Still haven't heard from Zuri, I guess."

"No." A reminder of the Filipino woman was the last thing he wanted. They'd not spoken since the day he'd given her the news about him destroying the VV1. Then his boss chewed him out, causing him to miss the moment Zuri disconnected. "Like I said, she just vanished three years ago. No offense, but I would rather not talk about her."

"No problem. Well, your father and I were wondering when you could come up to Winter Park again. We would love to see you and show you our new house."

Trey thought of his boss and coworkers he'd left behind. When he'd winked at them, they'd likely had high hopes he would save them from their predicament. Once they learned he'd feigned ignorance of the hostage situation and claimed to be in the restroom, albeit the latter was true, they would be livid at him, assuming they survived Pele's wrath. Trey could not think of a better time than now to quit the job and leave town for a while. With his experience, he could always find another job once he returned to San Antonio.

"How would you feel if I started heading up there tomorrow?" he proposed.

"Oh, that would be wonderful!" she cheered. "Absolutely marvelous! You have the new address, right?"

"I don't think so. Can you text it to me?"

"Sure. It's 47 White Gales Drive, Wint—"

"No, no, no. *Text* it to— You know what? Never mind. Let me find a pen." Remembering how far behind the times his mother was, he got up to head for his kitchen, where a notepad and mug full of pens were sitting on the counter. "Okay, you were saying?"

"It's 47 White Gales Drive, Winter Park."

He scrawled down the address. "Got it." *I should stay out of this city for at least a few weeks.* "By the way, may I stay with you and Dad for…a month?"

"As long as you want. Wow! They must really like you at work."

"I'm sure they do."

NORTH OF LUBBOCK, TEXAS

The following day, Trey had been driving his tan Toyota Corolla for hours with the cruise control usually set to seventy-five miles an hour. For a half hour, the passing scenery along I-27 had been relentlessly flat and devoid of trees. He looked forward to seeing different surroundings sometime after he had lunch somewhere in Amarillo. To reduce the tedium of the drive, he listened intently to his MP3 player connected to the car's radio. The current track was a comic's story about his first job at an adult novelty store.

"So, there I was, trying to keep up with the register. The idiot working next to me says, 'Holy crap, man, you work too slow!' I said, 'It's my first day working with a cash register. Cut me some slack.' Then the manager walks up and says, 'You know, if this kind of work is too much for you, maybe you should try a simple, low-class job first. Then, you can gradually work your way up to one of these *higher*-class jobs.' And I said, 'Well, from the looks of this merchandise, this is not a higher-class job.'"

Like the comedian's audience, Trey broke into a mild fit of hilarity. He glanced in the rearview mirror at an old maroon Camaro, the only vehicle tailing him. He wondered what the obese couple behind the grimy windshield was talking about.

✞

"What happened to the windshield?" the driver's wife griped after waking up from a nap.

"We passed some pickup with a Rottweiler hanging his head out the window," her husband explained. "That dumb dog drooled in the wind and it got all over our car."

"How disgusting!" She swigged a large soda she'd bought two hours ago at a drive-thru.

"People who let their dogs slobber out the window like that shouldn't even be on the highway."

Deciding her drink was too watered down from the melted ice, the chubby woman spat the mouthful of Coke out her window, not seeing the hapless hitchhiker their Camaro flew past. "You got that right," she agreed and regarded the filth on the windshield. The dog had only been responsible for half of it; the rest was from bugs colliding with the glass. "Use the washer fluid."

"I ran out. I'll get more in Amarillo."

✞

A mile further north on I-27 was the first vehicle ahead of Trey's Toyota—an eighteen-wheeler of an arts and crafts store chain. A jackrabbit watched the semi roar by, then warily hopped up to the blacktop, intending to cross. The furry critter's nose twitched as its long ears aimed skyward, listening for any sign of danger.

Sudden electronic whining sent the hare scurrying back the way it came. A pair of four-inch-thick poles sprouted from the ground through concealed apertures near both shoulders of the two northbound lanes. In eight seconds, the black hexagonal bars reached fifteen feet and stopped with a *CLACK!* Red lights blinked once atop the twin shafts. With a sequence of clicks, the posts pointed at each other with two dozen three-inch-long emitters that studded the columns from top to bottom. The emitters produced a fifteen-feet-high energy field that hummed like a swarm of robotic bees. For two seconds, the thin web of green light blurred the view behind it before turning almost entirely invisible.

✞

Trey watched as the Camaro swerved into the fast lane and passed him. When it was a few car-lengths ahead of him, he noticed the two black poles much further ahead and barely saw distortion between them. His first guess was a mirage.

What are those things for? he thought when he eyed the distant columns. *To make sure I'm not speeding?* Since the highway kept going beyond the posts, he saw no reason to not drive between them. *Probably the sunlight playing tricks*, he theorized about the "mirage," recalling a drive he'd taken years ago through the Mojave Desert. He couldn't recall the reason behind the trip, but vividly remembered one thing he'd passed on the way—Nevada's Ivanpah Solar Power Facility. *Uncanny things occur when thousands of mirrors direct the sun's energy to a trio of solar boilers.*

He observed the sports car ahead of him approaching the gap between the poles at eighty-two miles an hour. The driver didn't seem aware of it since he wasn't slowing. Then Trey remembered how grimy the fat man's windshield was.

The Camaro's nose met the flat rectangle of barely visible energy—

—and burst into a hundred tendrils of light that scattered across the power field.

The rest of the car followed at half speed, fragmenting into more white vines of condensed matter. The twin bars absorbed every trace of it, leaving behind no clues the Camaro or its occupants ever existed.

After goggling the two-second process with utter shock and disbelief, Trey decided he didn't want the same thing to happen to him.

He stomped down the brake pedal. Tires locked up and screamed across the asphalt as the speedometer dropped. While skidding to a halt, his northbound car spun forty degrees. Facing northeast, it stopped and rocked faintly with the bumper two feet from the energy field.

Trey stared at the bizarre marvel before him. *This is nothing at all like a solar power facility; this is something* far *more advanced. What is this high-tech...thing that can dissolve cars?* He gazed through the transparent power field at the greenish scene of road, land and sky—a view that quivered as if he were looking over a fire.

His shock of curly, flaxen hair fluttered in the wind as he opened his squeaky car door and stepped out to look closer, listening to the odd metallic drone from the energy web. Then he beheld the web's maker—the two hexagonal bars flanking the divided highway's northbound lanes. His focus went to the emitters that lined the inner sides of the poles, keeping the power field active.

He picked a rock off the side of the road and tossed it between the columns. With a hissing static sound, the rock blasted into tiny coils of bright light that flew into the bars and vanished, just like the Camaro had done. Then he recalled a few key scenes from a sci-fi film he'd seen a year ago.

He didn't notice the miniature camera focused on him from under a nearby bush.

Startling its sole observer, the energy field winked out with a loud *ZAP!* as if a dragonfly had collided with a high-voltage bug killer. The emitters retracted and the posts made an electrical whir as they shrank back into the earth. Once the peaks of the bars were below ground level, sod-covered hatches made a startling thump as they closed over them.

Trey's bug-eyed gaze had repeatedly shifted right and left, trying to capture the activity on both sides of the pavement. Seconds after the hatches closed, he forgot where they were located; the grass growing on them provided impeccable concealment.

This thing is incredible! What's it for? Who built it and why? What did it do to the maroon car? Did it kill the people inside? Should I call the police? What wo—

BEEEEEEP!

His heart skipped as he spun, finding a six-wheeled Ram truck halted one car-length behind his Corolla.

"Hey, bud, you want to get out of the road?" the young driver griped through his lowered window. "What's wrong with you?"

Still in shock, Trey regarded the hillbilly for an instant before giving his surroundings a brief once-over. Then he realized his car was blocking both lanes.

"S—sorry," he stammered and clumsily got back in the Toyota. After shutting the driver-side door, he glimpsed the pickup's owner again. The man's cowboy hat made it obvious he was shaking his head, clearly thinking he'd encountered a moron. Trey further convinced the hick of his theory by trying to bypass the hidden piece of hazardous technology.

I don't know what that contraption did to that Camaro, but I'm not letting it perform its "sorcery" on me or my car.

In the off chance the "traffic vaporizer" resurfaced, Trey drove across grass for a few yards before returning his Corolla's tires to the blacktop. As he stayed in the slow lane, the annoyed redneck revved his black truck past him, giving Trey the one-finger wave. A black-and-brown dog hung his head out the right rear window and eyed the tan Toyota falling behind. Wind tossed saliva from the Rottweiler's dangling tongue.

How come every time I meet a jackass with road rage, he's driving a big pickup? Is the size of their vehicles meant to make up for the size of something else? I hope I don't see that irate hick again when I reach Amarillo. If he'd been a few car-lengths behind me for the past five minutes, he would have seen that dangerous machine too and understood why I stopped my car.

Trey recalled his last idea—calling the police to show them the peculiar device.

What's the use? As well hidden as that thing is, I'll never find it again. This lonely highway has had no landmarks for the past five miles. Encountering that pickup didn't help my memory either. But where did that Camaro go? Are the people who were inside it dead?

Should I tell the police what I saw? Will they believe me?

He thought about last night when he'd talked his way out of a hostage situation—with help from a silver tongue he didn't know he had. Then, he didn't bother to help the cops.

How seriously will the police take what I did in San Antonio? Or, what I failed *to do? That was a terrible idea. What was I thinking? On second thought, I don't want to talk to cops. I need to keep going. That stop didn't help my travel time.*

McCALL RESIDENCE

With a smoldering Churchill cigar in his yellowed teeth, a menacing, bearlike man stood where Sonya's gravel driveway met Hermosa Drive. Like two onyx marbles, his inherently livid eyes scanned all directions for any sign of the disloyal woman. His bulging muscles, seventy-nine-inch stature and third-degree black belt made him the toughest hooligan in his posse—a reason he was elected the leader. His tattooed scalp was shaved from the ears forward as waist-long hair hung from the back in a gray braid. From his ruddy, weathered mug, salt-and-pepper whiskers hung in a thick trucker-style mustache and plaited goatee.

An excess of erotic and macabre tattoos covered most the skin of his burly arms and shirtless torso. He wore silver-tipped biker boots, zipper-slashed trousers, and fingerless riding gloves with zinc spikes. A nickel-studded belt supported the monogrammed holster of his Taurus revolver, barely visible beneath the hem of his upper garment—a denim vest with the team's crest embroidered on the back.

The image stitched to the soot-black vest was a half-melted pewter skull, bearing multiple horns and broken teeth. A tangerine glow escaped its spectral eyes and yawning jaws. Over the diabolical cranium, LEVI studded a cherry banderole with gothic caps as

SCREAMON DEMONS lined a teal streamer at the emblem's base.

Behind the biker boss, five Harleys were parked in the driveway. Sporadic sounds of glass breaking could be heard from the ancient house as three of Levi's henchmen ransacked the place. Like the trio inside, the fourth biker's appearance below the neck mostly imitated Levi's.

"Yeah, boss, this is the place," he assured. In his massive hands was Sonya's mailbox, not only crushed but also Swiss-cheesed by her shotgun. He scrutinized the ruined metal from every angle. "The numbers are torn, but I can still tell what they are. I guess Sonya ran over it with her motorcycle."

"You know, Melvin, I never thought that stupid broad belonged on a Harley," Levi grumbled around his cigar. "She belongs in my house, bearing me sons and cooking me steaks."

His minion nodded, but wanted to laugh. *That would be a neat trick. How could any man turn a fearless hellcat like Sonya into a docile homemaker?* "Is that what you'll make her do if you find her, boss?" he queried, dropping the smashed mailbox where he'd found it.

"You mean *when* I find her. No, what's the use? Sonya is not obedient and probably not fertile either. Therefore, she doesn't deserve the privilege of being my girl. She deserves to be shot in every place that will *not* kill her. And that's what I'll do to that slut when I find her. Then I'll find other ways to make her beg for death."

Melvin eyed his superior, uncertain how to reply to the rancorous words. He decided no reply at all would be best. *Remind me to never make* you *mad,* he thought and then brought to mind the stolen money. "Do you think she'll still have the seventy thousand, boss?"

"After this long? Not likely. But her stealing from us is actually the least of what I'm peeved about."

"Right. I think you're mad enough to punch newborn babies."

"You're damn right, I am!" Thrice, he caught his right fist in his left palm, pretending the latter was Sonya's face. "Let's not forget what *else* that whore did. She took my license plate, which led to me getting pulled over when I was alone with an empty gun and a nearly empty tank of gas. Then the cop discovered the warrants against me, called for backup, and I had to serve twenty-eight months. Once I got out of the slammer, it took me a month and thousands in cash to buy Officer Hudson to find out where in Nevada Sonya was last seen."

"How did you know to have him check Nevada?"

"Remember three years ago when I sent riders in ten different directions to find Sonya?"

"Yes."

"Brock Laxdal was the only one who never returned to Sacramento. Remember him?"

"I do."

"He's the one I tasked to see if Sonya took the most direct route to Nevada. Brock's Fat Bob was found near Lake Tahoe, but there was no sign of *him*. I know Sonya had something to do with his disappearance. What I *don't* know is why Brock didn't have enough brains to text me as soon as he saw her."

Melvin nodded. "Didn't you once say that Hudson found surveillance footage of her?"

"That's right. After that excruciating month of online haggling with Hudson, I had to wait five *more* months for him to find a recording of Sonya in Carson City with that friend of hers, Becky Lugo. Then he needed another two months to ID Becky and get her address for us."

Melvin did the math, thinking aloud while counting his sausage-like fingers. "One, five, and two equals…eight? *Eight* months? With all those assets the cops have that we don't, it took him that long?"

"Of course. Hudson is extremely busy…and a hard negotiator. Eight months, plus the twenty-eight I was in lockup make three years. Sonya has wasted *three* damn years of my life! No one does that to me and gets away with it! When we find her pretty face, it won't be pretty for long! I can't believe she never even told me her real last name!"

"Becky's phone said 'Sonya *McCall*,' not 'Sonya Meadows,' right?"

"Yeah. Hudson had already searched his computer for a Sonya Meadows and had no luck. So, I had him look up every Sonya *McCall* in the country just before we left Carson City to come here. One of the driver's license photos he found matched the picture I sent him. He also said that Sonya's address history includes *this* address—the same one we found on Becky's phone."

Melvin noticed the name on the flattened mailbox. "If this is the right address, why does the mailbox say 'Gibbs,' boss?"

"According to Hudson, Gibbs was the maiden name of Sonya's grandma who croaked four months ago."

"Oh." Melvin faced the tumbledown house a stone's throw away. He could barely read the trio of black Celtic-style numbers fixed to the clapboard wall near the front door. He verified the dwelling's three-digit address matched the one on the wasted mailbox. "That's one sorry-looking abode, isn't it?" he thought aloud, stroking his thick black beard.

"Indeed." Levi's chapped lips spat out the finished cigar. "Let's go help the others."

When they neared the ramshackle porch, the other bearded outlaws came outside. The chubbiest of the three—barely supported by the rotting floorboards—handed the boss a photo album.

"What is this, Jed?" he asked, flipping pages. "Oh, I see." The light binder included dozens of pictures—mostly of Sonya from almost every year of her childhood and teen years. A few photos included her late father and grandmother. "This is definitely the right house."

"I also found this, boss. Look at page twelve," the pudgy man said, handing Levi a street atlas. "The highlighter markings say she went to Mexico."

He dropped the beat-up scrapbook on the overgrown lawn and scrutinized the right page of the atlas. "Manzanillo?"

"That's right." Jed noticed the lack of incisors bared by his superior's pleased grin. "But maybe that's a diversion."

"Diversion? Don't make me laugh. Chicks are too stupid to think of *that* concept."

"Uh…whatever you say, boss."

Levi rolled up the atlas, stuffed it down a thigh pocket, and looked up at his waiting followers. "Okay, boys, we have our new destination. As I said in Sactown, Sonya took thousands of dollars three years ago—cash I meant to go to all of you for being my five best Screamon Demons. When we find that turncoat-slut, we will show her no mercy. Agreed?"

The half circle of Viking-like faces nodded.

"Good. Now, let's torch this pathetic hovel of hers and ride south!"

Minutes later, the dilapidated house and barn were ablaze as five manned motorcycles roared to life and departed. The last two of the gang rolled over the mailbox's remains.

NEAR COLORADO SPRINGS

With her leather-clad back against her Harley's steel frame, Sonya sat and watched the scarlet disc of the sun inch down beyond the horizon. A stone's throw from I-25, she'd found an elevated spot inside a cedar grove where she planned to spend the night. The next city was five miles north, but since she didn't know when she'd be employed again, she wanted the $4,000 in her checking account and the remainder of Levi's dough to last as long as possible. What she'd spent last night for a motel room in Roswell pretty much equaled the total cost of her other expenses that day—pancakes in Roswell, fuel and a snack in Wagon Mound, and a steak dinner in Pueblo. By settling for the tent a few days, her money would last twice as long.

Stoking her campfire, she wondered if her ruse in her late grandmother's house had worked. *Have the Screamon Demons found the other street atlas? Are they now on a wild goose chase in Mexico?* The thought made her beam and chuckle.

Her next thought was like a bucket of cold water on her mirth—her driver's license would expire in three months. In order to get another license—and a job—she needed an address.

I can't believe I'm homeless now. I can't go back to Artesia, and I only knew one person outside of my hometown who would have allowed me stay with her. And, now, she's gone! I don't know how, but someday, I will make Levi regret the day he invaded Becky's home.

As for me, where will my *home be? I guess it will be this stupid tent, but only for a few days...I hope. I need to set it up now, but I detest hassling with those stubborn rods. I'll do that later. Right now, I think it's time to decide where I'm going. What city and state am I going to call home?*

Since her smartphone's battery was dead, she took out her street atlas and flipped through it, quickly scanning webs of red and blue lines that meant roads. The thought of going as far as Montana quickly lost its appeal. *Too cold*, she thought. *Not enough to do.* She didn't realize her narrow view of the Big Sky Country and several other states had come from ignorant students from her high school years—teens who wanted their classmates to think they knew more than they actually did.

She flipped to North Dakota. *Same problems, only worse. Too windy.* South Dakota. *Almost as bad.* Nebraska. *Same.* Wyoming. *Ditto.* She rashly rejected Kansas and Oklahoma as well since tornados terrified her.

Colorado's page was given more scrutiny. By the time the sky turned black, her frustration drove her to put the entire atlas in the fire. She didn't need it to find Denver—her original and most sensible idea. She could find a place to live and work in Colorado's largest city. Being a country woman who despised traffic and other stressors of big-city life no longer mattered; it was not easy to stay invisible in a small town. Besides, Levi would not be expecting her—or any other Harley owner—to move to an often-cold state.

From her backpack, she took out the photograph of Iza. She studied her grandmother's careworn face in the firelight. Twenty-eight years ago, when the picture was taken, Iza was beautiful for a fifty-year-old woman. Her kind blue eyes had often welled during the most defiant acts of Sonya's teenage years.

Flooding her mind were treasured memories—ones she'd locked away out of hatred back when her grandmother relentlessly tried to protect her from herself. Figuratively speaking, Iza frequently saw Sonya walking toward cliffs and warned her every time. All Sonya saw was a nagging old hag. She began to question herself.

Why was I so stupid? Why did I waste years of my life, hanging out with the wrong crowds? Then, I moved from bad crowds to the worst of them all—the Screamon Demons. For nearly a year, I dated the atrocious bully who leads them. Why? Was it mainly out of spite for Grandma, knowing she'd never approve?

The more she chewed this over, the more convinced she was that "yes" was the answer to the final question.

What a defiant idiot I've been. I saw my only true friend—the same one who'd brought my beloved father into the world—as nothing but a pest!

"I miss you, Grandma," she whispered, seeing a tear from her watering eyes land on the snapshot. "I miss taking care of you." She recalled the last two and a half years of Iza's life—the best years of *her* life. She'd left her lawless life in Sacramento behind and come home to live again with the poor old woman who'd loved her more than life.

The three months following her return to Artesia were a disturbing but thought-provoking time. As she got reacquainted with a few of the locals, she'd learned most of her high school class, not including the dozen dropouts, had gone down roads as bad as or worse than hers. Half the young ladies her age had children with no father willing to stay in their lives. As reckless as she'd sometimes been with boys, Sonya was a tad surprised *she'd* never gotten pregnant. Other graduates had chosen suicide, some had gone missing and some were in jail or drug rehab. It seemed everyone was either dead or dying.

Most of the ones who were still alive and doing well had only their close relationship with God to thank for their contentment. At Iza's request, Sonya regularly attended church with her. The pastor, Frank Giles, still remembered Sonya from the days she'd been learning to walk to when she'd become a rebellious—and fatherless—teen and stopped attending. Even during the first fifteen years of her life, Sonya and her father had only come an average of ten times a year, much to the displeasure of Iza, who'd never missed a single Sunday.

Sonya would never forget words she'd heard from one of Frank's sermons three years ago: *"Despite popular belief, you can't entirely blame chance, situations, or hardship for molding you into the person you are today. You're mostly defined by only two things.* Two... *things—what you* will *do and what you* won't *do."*

The words made her want to hear more. For eight Sundays in a row, Frank's poignant messages gave her harsh reminders of her own mortality while also stressing what she *could* have to look forward to—mainly Heaven. The more she heard, the more appalled she'd grown by her poor judgment in California.

She'd asked herself the same question at least a hundred times: *What was I thinking, getting mixed up with that atrocious biker gang?* Then, while hearing a ninth sermon that year, Sonya made a choice—one that led to her righting the rest of the wrongs in her life.

She'd given her life to Christ.

She would always remember the joy in Iza's wrinkled face when she'd returned to their pew from the altar. Then there was the long embrace that followed. If not for her walking difficulties, the frail old woman would have gleefully joined her granddaughter as she went to the front of the crowded room to pray with Frank and pour her heart out to God.

I'm really going to miss Frank too.

After replaying the cherished memory in her head a dozen times, her attention went skyward to the profusion of stars.

"Grandma, I know you're up there." She spoke softly. "I know you're in a better place. But now that you've left this life behind, I don't know what to do with *my* life." She blinked away another tear and took a deep, shaky breath. "What should I do? Should I become a vigilante? That could be fun, certainly more exhilarating than dating another loser guy. I would really like to help someone less fortunate than me...but I don't know how. And I wish I wasn't sick of being alone...but I am. How pitiful."

For minutes that felt like hours, she wistfully eyed the print again. "Is Denver really the best answer? If God's listening to you, please ask Him to give me a sign. I don't know where to go." Then she put the photograph to her slim lips.

A deafening roar pounded her eardrums.

Her scream was lost in a ferocious gust that blew out her campfire and fluttered her long black mane. Then the wind and sound died down nearly as fast as it came. In the cobalt sky was the source—a massive helicopter that had flown past her.

It was too dark for her to discern details of the aircraft's odd black shape. With its tail aimed toward her, it looked like a flying saucer with rotor blades, which glowed red at the tips. It was flying north, following I-25.

In the midst of the smoldering black-and-orange remains of her fire, she stood and dusted herself off, winded from shock. "Is that my sign?" she asked herself, eyeballing the copter as it thrummed away.

At 10:35 P.M., Trey was more than ready to find lodging in the next town. He'd been driving for hours and wanted nothing more than to stretch his weary bones across a motel bed. The inviting lights of Colorado Springs blanketed the skyline ahead. As his tired gray eyes drank in the pleasant view, he grinned and thought of a hot shower.

Blue-and-red police lights flashed on the shoulder of the southbound lane. Trey slowed down his Toyota and glimpsed the activity he was passing by—a Ford Mustang that got pulled over for speeding. Then his attention went to his MP3 player. The current tune was a techno trance song that had been playing for over ten minutes through the Corolla's speakers. Once it finally ended, the next was a pop tune—a love song mostly targeted toward female teens.

"How did *that* crap get on here?" Trey griped, hitting the skip button. What came on next was the work of a comical-satire artist he couldn't recall the name of. Marching band music played in harmony to a children's choir. They were singing a parody of a song he'd not heard since his last visit to Disneyland.

It's a world of bastards who grind my gears.
It's a world of hoes who have got no fears.
There is no end to crime. We get screwed all the time.
It's a flawed world after all.

It's a flawed world after all.
It's a flawed world after all.
It's a flawed world after all.
It's a flawed, flawed world.

It's a world of cancer. A world of hate.
And there's shysters, thugs, and inebriates.
Deadly fumes from our cars. Can we please move to Mars?
It's a flawed world after all.

Annoyed by the whirling of an approaching helicopter, Trey turned up the volume. But the loudness of the chopper's engine also increased. He sighed, wishing the bothersome racket-maker would hurry up and move on, but it didn't.

"Get out of here, stupid eggbeater," he muttered. "I can't hear my tunes."

The *WHUMP-WHUMP-WHUMP!* of the copter's rotor grew louder. Suddenly, he was driving in a pool of radiance from the whirlybird's searchlight trained on his car. His pulse swelled as he wondered what anyone in an aircraft could possibly find so interesting about him.

"Stop your vehicle, immediately!" a loudspeaker boomed. The rotorcraft moved ahead of the Toyota, flying backward to face him. Trey squinted from the xenon searchlight glaring through the windshield. "I repeat, stop your vehicle immediately! You will be fired on if you do not comply!"

He applied the brake and brought his car to a halt. Then he put the shifter into park, thinking this might be the FBI or Army out searching for some significant criminal and thinking they'd found the right man. Then he shuddered with apprehension as he recalled what he'd done at the Almighty IT company.

Is that what this is about?

Switching off its searchlight, the massive copter slowly descended to the highway twenty yards ahead of him. It landed almost entirely sideways, blocking passage to the city. With the aid of his headlights, Trey studied the fantailed gunship. With all the black surfaces and angles, it greatly resembled a stealth helicopter he'd once seen at an airshow years ago. But this one was at least double in size.

A red neon light trimmed the canopy sheltering a pilot and gunner. Just below the cockpit was the fuselage's oddest feature—a three-feet-thick weapons pod, octagonal in shape when seen from below. The pod was three times the width of the cockpit, making the base of the aircraft too wide and flat to require wheels or landing skids. As the six blades of the main rotor formed a red halo with their lighted tips, the base of the large rudder encased the tail rotor.

On the tail boom, Trey noticed a silver symbol—a falcon with hook-like wings spread and head turned right. He immediately recalled when he'd seen this symbol on the news the night before he'd left San Antonio.

The Chrome Falcon terrorists want me?

"Stay where you are," the gunship's pilot ordered. "We have people on the way to come get you."

Winded from fright, Trey heard the chopper's engine slow. His bulging eyes glanced nervously in all directions, finding no safe haven.

I'm sick of considering my next idea. Thinking about it is making me very edgy. How about less thinking and more doing...before I have a serious panic attack?

He yanked the shifter from *P* to *D* and floored the gas. The Corolla's tires screamed as they spun on the blacktop. He drove the car off the road, skirting the landed aircraft. Once he returned to the asphalt, he took fleeting glimpses of the highway ahead, mostly keeping eyes on the rearview mirror. The red ring of light from the copter's rotor blades grew smaller with distance.

Then it began ascending to pursue him.

Trey turned off all the Toyota's lights, hoping the darkness would keep him invisible. His speedometer read eighty-five miles an hour. Every time he heard the grinding of gravel on the highway's shoulder, he corrected his steering. Light from the city ahead reflected off the clouds above, nearly providing enough illumination to see without headlights.

In the rearview mirror, he could still see the chopper's red light ring. Then the blinding searchlight came on again, shining on the highway in sheer determination to find him again. The rotorcraft was some distance away—a rapidly shrinking distance.

Ahead was an underpass, pitch black against the horizon's glow. As he went under it, Trey allowed the car to coast down to thirty. Then he left the northbound lane, doing a U-turn across the grassy divide to the southbound lane, willing himself to not touch the brake and reveal his location. He coasted back to the underpass, finding the aircraft thrumming north with its light on the wrong lane. When it passed him, he stomped on the accelerator.

He exceeded seventy, adjusting his steering when he heard the tires meet the highway's ridged shoulder. A backward glance showed the daunting copter still heading north. Seconds later, it was no longer in sight.

The headlights were turned back on. Trey panted and perspired as he continued speeding south. Hundreds of yards flew by, and his heart slowed as his elation rose. He laughed triumphantly, scarce believing he'd successfully evaded the gunship. The only thing that distressed him was knowing he might have to sleep in his car instead of Colorado Springs.

Police lights came on behind him.

The flickering blues and reds tossed water on the flames of his euphoria. He immediately recalled the busted speeder he'd passed before the gunship's arrival.

His speedometer was at ninety.

How will I explain this?

The tan Toyota slowed and pulled over. The patrol car parked behind him, keeping the bothersome lights flashing. Yellow curls of Trey's Jewfro swayed as he rapped his head thrice against the steering wheel.

Of all the times a cop could show up.

He shut off the engine and flipped the switch to lower his

window. Then he waited for what felt like hours for the cop to review his nearly flawless record. Every three to four years, he was pulled over once—mainly to receive a warning for passing a stop sign at two miles an hour instead of stopping.

What will I tell the lawman when he asks about my embarrassing speed? The truth? Will he believe me?

The policeman finally got out of his black-and-white Dodge Charger and approached the Corolla. Trey kept his hands visible on the steering wheel, knowing it would make the cop less edgy. His apologetic gray eyes met the sergeant's distrustful gaze when he was near his door.

"I clocked you at ninety!" the pudgy cop snapped. "Are you stupid or what?"

"Well…I was being followed, sir," Trey replied, a bit stunned by the man's rudeness. "Someone was threatening me."

"What kind of vehicle were they driving?"

"They were driving a helicopter."

"Right! That's the dumbest thing I've heard all week. How much have you had to drink today, jackass?"

"None, I swear."

"The sweat on your funny-looking mug tells me you're a liar. I'm giving you a sobriety test. Get out of the car!"

This just isn't my night!

Droning from a helicopter took the lawman's focus north. Trey hung his head out the window, turning fretfully the same way to see the pilot had overcome his ploy.

Definitely not my night!

Beyond a miles-long row of transmission towers that soared nine stories high, the rotorcraft came with its searchlight still on. Then the chopper rose to avoid the high-voltage power lines supported by the steel lattice towers.

If Chrome Falcon wants me, I guess I'm done running; it doesn't seem to be helping much. I'm unarmed and driving this pitiful Toyota. They have some kind of war chopper. I just can't win. I might as well let the answers to my questions come to me.

The searchlight shined on the patrol car and then moved to the Toyota, where it stopped. Trey eyeballed the gunship behind him and then turned to the cop, who stood motionless, gawking at the light.

"Still think I'm a liar?" he flared. The tense sergeant glanced at him.

Despite the rotor's thunder, they heard the chopper arm itself. *K-CHAK-CHAK!* Near the searchlight was the abrupt flickering of a machinegun.

RAT-TAT-TAT-TAT-TAT-TAT!

Twenty-millimeter rounds holed the cop's chest and back, dropping him to the pavement. Trey jumped in his seat, gawping in horror at the corpse as chills ran down his spine. The size of the wounds and the rate of blood loss made it abundantly clear the lawman couldn't be saved. He was dead before he even hit the ground.

The rotorcraft launched a rocket. Hissing its way downward, the smoking projectile went directly for the black-and-white.

Trey squinted as a bright, earsplitting blast tossed the patrol car skyward. Hood, trunk, and doors flew open from the explosion. Doing a half twirl, the flaming Charger soared ten feet high and came down, top first. In a heap of wreckage, it landed noisily where it had been three seconds ago, now with tires in the air.

Trey's shocked eyes had taken in every second of the extreme moment. Through his window, he goggled the burning patrol car a moment. Then his attention turned to the hovering gunship, still slanting the light down on him.

"Do not attempt another escape!" the pilot ordered through his loudspeaker. "We will not hesitate to fire! Get out of your vehicle, now! Hands in the air!"

Trey complied, not wanting what happened to the rude cop to befall him. His khakis, plaid shirt, and mop-like hair fluttered in the aircraft's wind as he faced it, standing in absolute surrender.

These psychos are awfully desperate to take me alive. I doubt I can escape them twice. Time to find out what they want.

He heard three pistol shots.

Looking over a shoulder at his four o'clock position, he saw something in the darkness a stone's throw away—a gun booming and flashing twelve more times in less than eight seconds. Most of the bullets sparked off the gunship's rotor and fuselage.

The pilot cursed from two rounds glancing off the canopy, leaving white, golf-ball-size blemishes. "Who's firing?" he asked edgily, pulling back on the cyclic stick.

"Relax," the gunner told him. "The canopy is bulletpr—"

Electric light exploded and zapped around the aircraft as it backed into the power lines. For a moment, night became day, forcing Trey to momentarily turn away, lest he go blind. The rotor blades sliced most of the cables, producing a gyrating ring of sparks. The fuselage wobbled and spun, its searchlight shining everywhere but on the Toyota's owner. Flying out of control, the rotorcraft drifted west with its fuselage twisting counterclockwise. Trey watched in awe as the chopper came down.

In the background, the lights of Colorado Springs blinked out, darkening the horizon.

Steel clanged as the tail boom caromed off the nearest transmission tower, spinning the fuselage clockwise—and faster. The helicopter drifted east, coming down on the northbound lane. As it crashed, the main rotor tangled with sagging power lines.

More spark eruptions preceded a shrill orange blast that filled nearly half the night sky from Trey's viewpoint. A hundred lumps of flaming wreckage flew in all directions. Feeling the explosion's intense heat, Trey covered his ears and turned away. He flinched as one piece of debris barely missed his Corolla.

All turned quiet except the crackling fires on the scattered ruins.

Trey's bulging eyes drank in his surroundings—the totaled police car, the dead cop, and the flaming wreckage of the culprit. As his mind replayed the unforgettable crash, he could scarce believe any of it had transpired.

A single headlight seized his attention. It shined from the same place he recalled seeing the gun flash before the copter lost control. Atop her growling Low Rider, Sonya emerged from the darkness.

Trey had not expected the one responsible for the gunship's crash to be female.

What other surprises does this night have in store for me?

She stopped five feet from where he stood. Beneath her maroon half-helmet, wind tossed long curls around her oval face, bathed gorgeously in firelight—from fires she'd started. Despite the Goth-like contrast between her hair and skin, to him, she wasn't a bad-looking woman.

"Thank you for saving me from those…psychos, ma'am," Trey told her.

"No problem," she replied, smiling and deciding she felt more heroic than she'd ever felt in her life. "Oh, I forgot." Without looking at her Beretta, she pulled it from under her jacket, swapped its empty clip for a full one, returned it to her holster.

"I doubt the nearest city is thankful, but *I* truly am."

Showing more flawless teeth, she tittered. "You're funny."

She brought down a chopper and killed the power of Colorado Springs less than five minutes ago, and she's already telling me something like that? Nothing fazes her, he thought.

"Very good shooting," he praised her, not sure what else to say. "Well done!"

"Well, I couldn't help myself. I despise cop killers."

A robbery in Sacramento returned to her memory. She, Levi, and three others entered a jewelry store with masks on and guns drawn. Barrett Knox, one of Levi's least liked minions, had shot and killed an off-duty lawman in front of his family, albeit he'd surrendered his firearm. The horrified faces of the cop's wife and two small children had deeply etched themselves into her memory. While Levi had put a knife through Barrett's hand just for being a loose cannon and raising police interest in the gang, she'd wanted to make amends for the cop's family.

"Who were they, anyhow? What did they want with you?" she asked, giving their surroundings a couple of once-overs for further threats.

"I wish I knew."

The way she checked their environs reminded Trey of the first time he'd seen the gunship. Fretfully glancing north and south, he thought of the pilot's words: *"Stay where you are. We have people on the way to come get you."* He was pleased to see no signs yet of the "people on the way."

He extended a hand to Sonya. As she reluctantly shook it, he explained himself with the verbal rapidity of an auctioneer. "Sorry, I've got to go. It was nice to meet you, ma'am. Thanks again for your help. I need to disappear before the chopper's friends show up. Bye."

Puzzled, she watched the anxious man jump back in his car. He did a U-turn around her bike and went north in the southbound lane to avoid the fallen power lines. He swerved here and there to dodge flaming ruins of the rotorcraft. She thoughtfully eyed the departing taillights as the Corolla crossed the highway's grassy divide and followed the correct lane to the dark city.

Interesting fellow, she thought. *Nerdy, but cute. Very polite. I like his hair too. Funny-looking, but stylish. I could tell how humble he is without even talking to him. His outdated clothes, dull car, and frank gray eyes gave that away. I like him already. He makes me laugh.*

She scanned the fiery remains of the gunship. *Who are these cop-killing crazies? How did they afford this once-fancy helicopter? Why are they after that nice man? Should I try to find out? That poor guy might need my help again.*

14

The only lights in the powerless town were the headlights of other motorists. To Trey, it almost felt as if he were still miles from any city. He'd driven long enough for his heartrate to return halfway to normal. He wanted to put his need for rest ahead of all other concerns, even the thought of Chrome Falcon finding him again. After driving ten minutes without further problems, he grew more confident the "people on the way" would not find him without the gunship's aid. The rude cop who'd been murdered by the copter had his sympathy, but he would have done him no favors by staying with his body.

Okay, now that all the excitement is over, how will I find a motel in all this darkness? he asked himself. He kept driving north on I-25 at forty miles an hour, hoping someone would reroute the power before he lost his patience. *How long will this take? Surely the sliced power lines were not the* only *way to keep this town on.*

"What am I doing?" He scowled and took the exit to Bijou Street, not wanting the other radicals—if there even were any—to spot him on the highway. When his tan Corolla was seven car-lengths from the dark traffic light, he pulled over onto the right shoulder. The Toyota was put in park and the hazard lights were switched on. Then he reclined his seat all the way, hearing only the nonstop click of the car's orange lights. He doubted he'd fall asleep soon; his pulse was still rather high.

The moment he pillowed his head in his hands and closed his eyes, power to the city was reactivated. Darkness vanished in all directions as Colorado Springs came back to life. Still used to the blackness, Trey squinted his eyes. Out his left window, he saw the sign of a twenty-four-hour restaurant illuminate on the opposite side of the highway. South of the restaurant, a motel lit up.

Now, I know where I'm sleeping...or at least lying abed.

✞

At 5:30 A.M., Trey had finally managed to fall asleep in the stale-smelling motel room, but not before hours of channel surfing and compulsively drinking water. After turning the TV off, he'd wasted almost as much time not sleeping; instead, he'd tossed and turned in the bed and made trips to the toilet every half hour. Stopping the flow of disturbing theories of what could later befall him had been a challenge. Blocking out the unsettling memory had been no different. He wished he could un-see the entire thing, especially the lawman's gruesome demise. He'd wondered most of the night if the rude cop had a family. Unbearable thoughts of kids sobbing, knowing they would grow up without their father, had wrenched his heart like a wet towel.

Then he'd flipped the pillow over after leaving tears on the warm side. Thinking about the tough, attractive woman on the Harley—his final thought before drifting off—had helped him put all other thoughts in check.

Who was she? Where did she come from? Why did she interfere with Chrome Falcon's business and save me? She put herself in extreme danger—for me. Me! *No woman has ever done anything like that for me. She's one hot, gun-toting biker. Why do I find those last two traits appealing? Maybe it's because I'm a weirdo. Does that beauty dig weirdos? Will I ever see her pretty face again? Is there any hope at all that I could make her fall for me? She* did *tell me that I was funny.*

At 1:37 P.M., he rolled under the blankets to face the other way and check the time that glowed bright red on the bedside table clock. After last night's bedlam, he'd not expected to get any rest at all, much less eight hours of it.

He remained abed without sleeping for ten more minutes and said a silent prayer for the patrolman's loved ones. Then he took the TV remote off the mahogany nightstand, aimed it at the flat-screen beyond his feet, and pushed power. When a cooking show came on, he didn't hesitate to change the channel. Seeing a cartoon, he flipped it again, thinking a few minutes of a sitcom before a meal next door would be nice. Breaking news was on the third channel.

Chrome Falcon's logo was over the reporter's shoulder.

Trey sat up, bulging eyes glued to the TV as he heeded the anchorman's words.

"Police have investigated the blackout that occurred last night."

The next thing on the screen was the gunship wreckage and downed power lines, filmed from a hovering news chopper. Trey decided the damage was far more obvious in the daylight. As the camera panned across the scene, the reporter carried on.

"A helicopter had crashed through power lines near Colorado Springs. According to the symbol on the aircraft, it is the property of the Chrome Falcon radicals. Neither of the two men in the chopper survived."

Again, the screen showed the reporter behind the counter. Next to him was a photograph of a familiar face—the cop Trey had seen murdered fifteen hours ago.

"Sergeant Lloyd Derrickson, father of three, was brutally murdered and his patrol car destroyed at the same time and place of the crash. The shots that killed Derrickson match those the aircraft was armed with. Police have concluded the pilot of the aircraft unintentionally flew into the power lines just after opening fire on Sergeant Derrickson. Just before he was shot, he had reported the Texas tag number of a tan Toyota Corolla he'd pulled over for speeding."

The photograph from Trey's driver's license replaced the deceased cop's picture.

"The number was matched to the owner, Trey Radisson, who'd driven off just after the tragedy. Authorities believe the chopper pilot was protecting Radisson from the police, raising the likelihood that he is in league with Chrome Falcon."

Trey's picture filled the entire screen.

"If you see Mr. Radisson, do not approach him and alert authorities immediately."

As Trey's heart raced, he stared in disbelief at the TV. *This is not happening! The cops' speculation on last night has branded me a fugitive! None of this would have happened if Chrome Falcon didn't want me so badly! What do they want from me? Why is all this happening to me?*

He wanted to put his foot through the flat-screen as thoughts of wrath and despair darted through his mind.

I hate presumptuous cops who have loose tongues around the press! I hate Chrome Falcon! And damn the media! And damn every person who watched this bogus story and now hates my guts! The entire world has turned against me! Life has been kicking me while I'm down an awful lot lately. Now, it is over! Definitely over!

He looked out his window, thankful he'd parked the back of his car a foot from the wall of the hotel; his license plate couldn't be read.

Are the cops scouring the city for tan Toyota Corollas? Or are they searching south of town? It was obvious the cop had stopped me as I was driving away *from the city. While they waste their time south, maybe I can escape from the north side—where I planned to go anyway.*

He thought about last night when he'd checked into the motel. The only local who'd seen him in town was the man who'd handed him the keycard to his room.

Was he watching the news just now? Doesn't matter. I need to get out of this town. I need to get out now! Only four words make sense: Winter-Park-or-bust! I will go see my family one last time... or die trying!

DENVER

Continuing north on I-25, the tan Toyota stayed five miles below the speed limit as it approached Colorado's capital city. Trey hoped he'd drawn no suspicious eyes when he'd passed through a fast-food drive-thru in Castle Rock. Hunted or not, he was starving. As he shoved the last of his chicken sandwich in his mouth, his nervous glimpses at the rearview mirror never ceased. He was rather surprised he'd been driving for over an hour and still not been pulled over.

Then he thought of his destination.

If I make it to Winter Park, what then? Will there be police cars waiting for me on White Gales Drive, where my parents live? Has the media or FBI made any harassing visits to their house yet? If not, have Mom and Dad seen the news about me yet? Will they tell me to leave once I get there... if *I get there?*

He didn't want to think about it anymore. It calmed his nerves more to keep believing the authorities were concentrating their search south of Colorado Springs. But he still couldn't resist glancing at every white car and black car that passed him on the interstate. It would do a cop's career a lot of good to catch someone "in league with Chrome Falcon." He doubted he could ever forgive the media for this. He also wondered who the cop was who jumped to conclusions too fast about his encounter with the radicals.

That bigmouth lawman ruined my life! Whoever that jerk was, he should never be allowed to talk to the press again! Will his chief make him pay for this? I truly hope so!

Feeling his smartphone buzz, he took it from his pocket and eyed the screen that read MOM CALLING. *Tell me she doesn't know. Please, tell me she doesn't know.*

He swiped the screen to answer. "Hi, Mom. How are you?"

"Trey, why are you on the news? What are you mixed up in?" she asked fretfully.

Damn it! She knows. "Calm down, Mom; that's misinformation. That Chrome Falcon group was trying to capture me and a cop got in their way. But I got away from them."

"I'm worried sick. What do those people want?"

"I don't know and I don't care. All I care about is coming to see you and Dad."

A wailing police siren reached his ears and fired up his pulse.

"And I'm on my way there," he continued. "For right now, I've gotta lose a tailing panda car. Wish me luck."

"You've gotta *what*?"

The phone went in his pocket after he disconnected the call. As he passed a medical center, he spied one patrol car with flashing lights in the rearview mirror. The driver was clearly not showing any interest in the other motorists. Trey could feel his heart hammering in his chest. He wondered why he'd not stolen someone's Colorado license plate to replace the one from Texas that had just incriminated him.

Reason told him he should pull over, let the arrest happen, and give the police all the time they needed to discover there was nothing to link him with the terrorist group.

But what could happen while I'm in custody? he asked himself. Then he grasped the answer. *Once the Chromes discover my location, they will murder every cop they have to just to acquire me. They clearly have the means and cruelty to do that. One dead lawman in Colorado Springs is already too much for me. I will not let others in*

Denver die because of me. God, if You're reading my thoughts and You see things my way, please help me lose this tail.

Without a second thought, he swerved over into the fastest of the four lanes and applied more gas. The orange speedometer needle climbed…seventy…eighty…ninety…

Trey kept shifting between the two fastest lanes, dodging other vehicles. The patrol car was still on him.

"What the hell am I doing?" he asked himself, uncertain he was making the right choice. He searched for anything outside to take his mind off his predicament. His Corolla passed a red Ford Explorer. The young woman behind the wheel was only going five over the speed limit. On the rear window of her SUV was a small yellow sign that read BABY ON BOARD. "So, you're a new mom, huh? Whoopi-doo." Next, he spied a lawyer's billboard and wondered if he should write down the phone number.

Traffic thickened during the next three miles, forcing Trey to keep his Toyota in the thirties. Road construction transpired ahead after a sign on the shoulder that blinked PREPARE TO STOP. The next sign read PREPARE TO BE IRRITATED. Trey managed to keep at least two motorists at a time between his car and the tailing patrol car. Searching for things to read along the highway didn't help his anxiety. However, the black Corvette he was tailgating gave him a chuckle. The driver had also attached a BABY ON BOARD sign to the rear window, but he'd written NO on the top and YAY! on the bottom.

Trey noticed a cop on a motorcycle had come to participate in the chase.

Then, all four lanes came to a complete halt.

I'll miss this car.

Without a second thought, Trey opened his door and ditched the Toyota. His shock of curly hair flew over his sweat-glazed face as he dashed between the two leftmost lanes, following the broken white line on the asphalt. Fumes from the stopped vehicles were already making him nauseous.

This day is showing me new depths of my stupidity. Am I really protecting the Denver police? Or am I just delusional? Why can't I make myself stop running?

The cop on the motorcycle entered the same gap between the halted lanes of traffic, sighting his fleeing suspect fifty yards ahead of him. The police bike roared louder as its rider grew determined to reach Trey before he got far.

Between two quick breaths, Trey peeked over a shoulder, seeing the lawman swiftly closing the distance between them. Another glance showed less than ten yards remaining. He slowed down just enough to grab the unlocked lever of a Porsche's passenger door. Then he continued sprinting, leaving the door of the yellow sports car standing wide open.

As the driver bellowed protests after the runner, the cop cringed and applied his brakes, fishtailing his motorcycle. There was no way around the Porsche's door and he was going too fast to stop in time. The car lost its door and the patrol bike lost its rider.

The white blanks painted on the blacktop continued flying under Trey's sneakers. He wished he'd spent more time at the gym; he couldn't continue like this for long. Another means of transportation was essential. While sprinting, he began a desperate search of the bright blue sky for any sign of a helicopter. If the police sighted him from the air, his full-out run was futile. As far as he could tell, no choppers had shown up yet.

A stone's throw ahead of him, the traffic was moving again. He had mere seconds to become someone's stowaway. His first choice was a black limousine to his right three strides away. He faced the way he'd come, finding the cop back on his motorcycle. Trey estimated fifteen seconds before the lawman reached him.

He ran between the limo's rear bumper and the front of a semi to disappear from the cop's view. As he'd suspected, the right rear door of the stretched sedan was locked when he pulled on the lever. Then he noticed another way inside. He climbed atop the trunk, the roof, then allowed himself to drop through the open sunroof. Two seconds later, the lawman's bike passed the eighteen-wheeler, finding no sign of the suspect. He rode on past the black limo, looking in all directions.

Though the cop had not seen where Trey went, someone in the rightmost lane *had* seen.

Inside the limousine, he faced a rich, young couple who were dressed as if they were going to prom. Trey sat in the center of the vacant rear seat, facing the dazed pair who had their backs to the chauffer.

"Who are you?" the blond man in a tux asked.

"The highway warrior," Trey jested, still winded from the dash through traffic, though he liked the new car smell. He shoved a hand down the pocket of his khakis and extended his index finger, as if he were concealing a gun. "Want to see my revolver?"

"No, no, that's okay," he replied docilely with hands raised. While the man was close to tears, his wife, wearing a formal red dress, seemed not the least bit alarmed.

"I know who he is, Brad!" she cheered in utter interest as the limo started moving again. Trey guessed the woman was too witless for serious matters. "I saw this guy on the TV. Trey Radical is his name…I think." Trey didn't bother to correct her. "He's one of those…Crow Falcon terrorists. We have a celebrity in our car! Isn't this exciting?"

Brad stared in disbelief at his wife, now giggling. "Wanda, you're hopeless."

"Ma'am, please don't call me a terrorist," Trey said. "I'm not with those people. In fact, I despise them with a passion. The media has got it all wrong."

The blackened window behind the chauffeur came down three inches. Everyone heard the elderly driver's questions. "Do I even want to know what's going on back there? Or why the car shook a minute ago?"

Brad faced Trey, who shook his head. "No, Lyle. Everything's fine." As Wanda cackled from randy ideas of what could have made the limo shake, the window whined back up.

When traffic stopped again, someone tapped on the right rear window.

Trey turned, expecting to see another cop. Instead, he saw the woman from last night who'd saved him from the gunship. Her unexpected appearance left him frozen on the limo seat.

Hi, gorgeous. Didn't think I'd see you *again*, he thought.

When she rapped on the tinted glass again, he flicked the window lever just enough to reveal his big gray eyes and hooked nose.

"Trey, you'd better come out of there," she warned. "The cops are gaining on you. If you want to escape this traffic, it will only happen with *my* help."

"Please move on, ma'am. You'll give away my location," he implored, albeit he didn't entirely want her to leave his presence. He liked looking at her and wanted to know more about her, but knew his wants and likes were irrelevant right now.

"That's already happened. Look at the trucker behind you."

When he looked out the back window, he could see the semi's pudgy driver eyeing the limo fretfully while pointing at the license plate. As he talked on his smartphone, he looked close to having a panic attack. Trey guessed the driver had recognized him earlier when he'd jumped through the sunroof.

"Come on, Trey," Sonya prodded. She coasted forward on her Harley far enough for him to open the back door. He slowly exited the limo, loathing the idea of leaving its seclusion.

"Bye, Trey! Nice to meet you!" Wanda called after him as he

shut the door.

"Are you getting on or what?" Sonya said over her shoulder and put her shades back on. Trey reluctantly mounted the passenger seat behind her, setting his feet atop the second set of footpegs. He took one last glimpse at the tractor's unnerved driver, still on his smartphone with his fat finger directed at him.

"Stop watching the news, jackass!" Trey hollered at the trucker.

"Hang onto me!" the biker cautioned.

He complied, finding himself a tad infatuated; she was a very pleasant armful. *Focus*, he chided himself. His heart skipped as the Harley growled forth.

"Don't worry, Trey," Sonya shouted over the wind and engine. "The police on their best day are not as good as me on my *worst* day. It's nothing for me to lose tailing cops."

Twenty minutes later, nine wailing cruisers from the Denver Police Department were in the wake of the Low Rider. Trey and Sonya headed east on I-70 with Strasburg several miles ahead of them and the edge of Denver two miles behind them. With the aid of black steampunk goggles Sonya had loaned him, Trey's bulging eyes stopped watering from the wind in his face. Much to his shame, he looked behind them and counted sets of flashing blue-and-red lights.

"Now there are *nine* panda cars on our tail," he reported, noting the Harley's speedometer read only seventy. "When is the part where you *lose* the police supposed to happen?"

"Shut up!" she returned. "Something's up with my transmission. I can't go any faster."

"We were supposed to go *west* of Denver. Why are you going east?"

"Wake up, Trey! When there are cops after you, you take detours."

"How do you know my name, lady? Did you watch the news too?"

"Yes. By the way, my name is Sonya, not Lady."

"Nice to meet you…again. May I ask why you're helping me?"

"Because you deserve it and I have the time. And it's…kind of fun." She decided firing the "lucky" shots at the enemy rotorcraft was a tad more exciting than now.

"Kind of fun," Trey repeated. *Is this woman crazy?*

"Oh, and I think God wants me to do this. Long story."

Yeah, she must be utterly mad. "I hope I get to hear it sometime. But, by now, the cops probably know exactly who you are. They've had plenty of time to look up your license plate."

"It's fake. Well, not *completely* fake. It used to be on my ex-boyfriend's bike. I have my *real* plate packed in the left saddlebag."

"Oh." *Maybe there's still hope in helping her out of this mess.* "Listen, Sonya, if you drop me off and leave me to the mercy of the Denver P.D., I'll forgive you immediately. I'm already in huge trouble. I didn't want to bring other people down with me." He hoped his words were enough to persuade her to stop the Harley and save himself from further embarrassment…before more cameras were on them. Then, she could continue struggling to escape the law.

"I can't do that. I'm very sure God would not like that." The night before, the chopper could have flown over her at any time. But it happened right when she asked God for a sign.

"I see." *I guess my shame will drag on.* "Well, how will we lose these cops?"

"Have faith!"

"Right…faith," he scoffed, noticing the helicopter from Fox News staying at their eight o'clock position. "Speaking of faith, can you see that whirlybird over there?"

"Whirlybird?" She peeked over a leather-clad shoulder at the following rotorcraft. "Oh, *that*. What about it?" Her attention returned to the miles of highway ahead. She didn't really want to think about anything behind her two-wheeler.

"My faith will really soar as long as Fox News is airborne. Soon, th—"

RAT-TAT-TAT-TAT-TAT-TAT-TAT!

Near the aircraft's tail boom, thirty-millimeter rounds perforated the hull. Smoke trailed from the sputtering engine as the news copter nose-dived to the yellow field. The slowing rotors snapped off when they met the flat terrain. A roaring blast scattered flaming pieces of engine, fuselage, tail boom, skids, and the chopper's occupants across the dead grass and westbound lanes. A trio of motorists screeched to avoid the debris.

"Did someone just shoot down Fox News?" Sonya asked.

"I think so," Trey replied, twisting to look behind them for the source of the bullets.

A gloss black airplane the size of a Boeing 747 was seconds from flying over the speeding black-and-whites. Sonya's passenger watched the eastbound jet lower its landing gear and retract a thirty-millimeter cannon on its left side.

"Who shot them down?"

Blocking out much of the sapphire sky and sun-crested clouds, the plane flew past the cops and their target with the earsplitting shriek of turbine engines. Then it touched down on the highway, casting extensive shadows with its sixty-four-meter wingspan. Fifteen car-lengths ahead of the Harley, rear landing gear met asphalt with a steamy, rubbery squeal. The massive tires spun on both shoulders of the divided highway's two eastbound lanes.

"*They* did," Trey answered casually as he pointed ahead of Sonya's shocked face.

"What the...? Why is this jumbo jet in front of us?"

Trey couldn't hear her over the cry of the four engines mounted beneath the wings. On the tail's vertical stabilizer was the Chrome Falcon emblem.

"The Chromes are back," he groaned, wondering if anyone else had thought of that nickname for the terrorists.

The howl of the engines lowered, slowing the jumbo jet down so the Harley could catch up. With a hydraulic whine, a broad hatch opened beneath the tail. A loading ramp with small wheels on the edge slowly lowered to the highway, revealing the dark interior of the cargo plane. As Sonya maintained her speed, the gap between the ramp and her Low Rider was ten car-lengths and dropping. It was clear the aircraft's crew meant for her to ride up the incline and enter their plane. Then she and Trey would be rescued from the tailing police.

Why are the Chromes willing to do this? Trey pondered. *What do these odd, well-funded extremists want with me? Will being in their custody be worse than police custody? Probably. Once the Chromes find no further use for me, they will most likely slay me as indifferently as they did Sergeant Derrickson.*

"What should I do, Trey?" Sonya asked over a shoulder. "We're between a rock and a hard place."

"Back off. Don't accept their rescue offer. This is our chance to prove to the authorities I'm not with these psychos," he replied.

"Good point."

"We might as well let the cops catch us now."

She chewed this over. Albeit she wasn't thrilled by the slim chance of her past offenses in Sacramento being discovered, she nodded in agreement; the alternative was being in the custody of cop killers.

"I'm slowing down."

The plane's pilot was losing patience. Albeit the motorcycle that carried his target was under five car-lengths from the ramp, it kept backing up, as if seeking police protection. By flipping a switch on his complex control board, he activated the engines' revolutionary thrust reversers to help slow the aircraft. The copilot triggered a cutting-edge brake system on all three landing gears, showing astounding control of the momentum. The wheels, of a weight and durability unmatched by other jets of this size, produced a brief screech.

Not anticipating the sudden stop of the seventy-meter-long jet, Sonya found herself without time to avoid the ramp. Against her will, she drove onto the steel incline and entered the plane, applying her brakes the entire time. The first police car's driver had the same problem.

The motorcycle fishtailed across a smooth section in the floor of the cargo hold. As the tires skidded, the duo cringed, certain they would collide with something in the darkness ahead.

A black safety net shot up in front of them. With the bike, they fell over in a heap, entangled in the crossing nylon strips.

When the black-and-white screeched to a halt, its bumper was over the Low Rider's rear wheel. Sonya killed the bike's engine. The cruiser's driver shifted the lever to park, unsure of what else to do. Regardless of his unprecedented situation, he didn't want to back out of the plane and increase the distance between him and the suspects.

Behind the halted aircraft, eight patrol cars had managed to stop before colliding with any part of the plane. The drivers and their partners got out to aim pistols and rifles down the insides of the cargo jet, searching for any hostile beyond the first black-and-white.

The ramp began to whine back up as all the mechanisms that had stopped the aircraft were switched off with a chain of clicks. The shriek of the turbine engines increased, propelling the heavy craft further down the highway as the ramp completed its closure.

Without bothering to pursue, the disheartened lawmen watched the jet carry off more than their suspect; it had also captured two of their own men—the main reason none of them had fired their guns. The mammoth airplane approached takeoff speed. Both men in the cockpit gritted their teeth anxiously at what was ahead. Sweat beaded their foreheads as the aircraft's landing gear left the pavement and cleared the rail of an overpass by ten feet.

As the airplane climbed higher, two cops exited their captured cruiser, pistols drawn. They fought to stay balanced with the tilt of the aircraft as it turned west to fly back the way it had come. Scanning the dimly lit surroundings of the cargo jet's interior, they neared the netted heap.

"Freeze!" Officer Balfour warned, aiming his Glock at the pair of suspects. His shorter partner, who'd been driving, did the same. Trey and Sonya raised their hands in capitulation, staring fretfully through the net at the duo in uniform. "Okay, Mr. Radisson, I hope you're happy!" Balfour thought of the other lawmen who had been left behind on the ground. Without them to back him up, he spoke with more confidence than he felt. "You and your girlfriend, whoever she is, just added kidnapping police officers to your long list of charges!"

A bright green dot appeared on the chests of both cops.

"Now," Balfour continued, "go tell the pilot to land this thing bef—"

RAT-TAT-TAT-TAT-TAT-TAT-TAT-TAT-TAT!

Both officers collapsed with smoking holes in their uniforms.

The netted duo turned to the source of the stuttering gunfire and removed their eye protection for a better view. From the shadowed front of the cargo hold, two green lasers shined through a rolling cloud of gun smoke—lasers mounted on scoped assault rifles. The duo bearing the firearms made a menacing entrance as they stepped beneath the room's only light with the tart smoke drifting away. The loose black jumpsuits the cop killers wore were multi-pocketed and silver-trimmed with the gleaming Chrome Falcon symbol pinned to their left breast pockets. Their utility belts and field boots looked befitting of a SWAT team. Silver helmets with tinted goggles and vented face masks hid their features well. Pinned to their upper right arms were horizontal bars, as shiny as their falcon symbols. The first man wore three bars, indicating his rank of sergeant, as the second, a corporal, wore two bars.

The corporal faced the airplane's starboard side and stepped toward it. He took a lever jutting from a wall groove and flipped it up with a *CLACK!* LED lights with protective DVD-size covers of Plexiglas lined the floor and ceiling. Flush with the steel surfaces, the lights came on sequentially from front to back, revealing every detail of the empty cargo hold.

The sergeant neared the two captives under the net and shined his weapon's laser on them. "Give me your phones!" he ordered in an unnatural, low voice through his face mask, designed to disguise his real voice. It reminded Trey of a bass singer speaking through a fan.

Can you say, "Luke, I am your father?" he thought, almost laughing.

This is no time for stupid sci-fi references, another voice in his head scolded. He slowly pulled his smartphone from a pocket and held it through a gap in the mesh.

Sonya did the same.

The sergeant's left hand warily came off the firearm long enough to take the phones. "Keep your hands up!" he demanded, unsure if they were armed. Sonya discarded the idea of reaching beneath her jacket for her Beretta.

A third man in the same kind of uniform came through a door leading to the rest of the plane and shut it behind him. Shorter than his two comrades, he had one bar on his right arm.

The corporal strode over to the floored cops, both gasping for air with no blood escaping the holes in their chests. Their dropped guns had slid too far away for them to reach from their supine positions. The corporal looked down into Balfour's blue eyes that pleaded for mercy. Ignoring the suppliant look, he set the selective fire switch on his rifle to *3* for the three-round-burst mode and aimed where the officer's bulletproof vest wouldn't save him.

RAT-TAT-TAT!

Then Balfour's sniveling partner.

RAT-TAT-TAT!

The pair under the net cringed at the brutal homicides.

As dark red blood escaped from the cops' heads, their murderer safed his weapon and slung it over a shoulder. He tucked the dead men's pistols down his large thigh pockets, then struggled to move Balfour's corpse.

"Get rid of these, Private," the sergeant commanded, offering the short man the two phones. "The cops will trace them." The private took them. "And go help him." He obeyed, helping the corporal toss the uniformed bodies into the patrol car's trunk. Then he closed the lid and took up a ratchet as the corporal strode up to a small control panel on the left wall with a column of three buttons.

The bottom one was pushed, causing the ramp behind the cruiser to open again. Wind howled as a view of Denver four thousand feet below was revealed.

The private hit the driver-side window with the ratchet, failing to break it. He ineffectively tried three more times.

"Give me that!" the corporal said crossly in the same choppy voice as the sergeant, taking the heavy tool from the private. "Now, go get that broom." The private made an apologetic gesture and went to fetch a push broom from the front of the cargo hold. The corporal reduced the window to glass pebbles with one blow so he could access the shifter. "Hold down the brake," he told the private, who returned and stuck the broom handle through the window to keep the pedal down. His accomplice pulled the lever from park to neutral.

Five pairs of eyes watched in mild awe as the police car rolled backward out of the ascending plane and plummeted. Then the corporal pushed the high button on the panel to close the ramp. Seconds before it shut entirely, the private remembered to toss out the two smartphones.

"Come get this netting off of them," the sergeant ordered, still holding his gun ready. His two subordinates drew titanium flick knives from their utility belts and approached the heap their captives were entangled in. As the nylon bands were sliced, Trey squinted from being so near the razor-sharp blades that extricated him and Sonya from the netting.

✝

Thousands of roaring NFL fans filled the stands at Sports Authority Field at Mile High—the home stadium of the Denver Broncos. Little regard was paid to the advertisements and words of team spirit flashing relentlessly on the surrounding jumbotrons. The Broncos were ahead of the Seahawks by three points. The scoreboard showed HOME: 28, VISITORS: 25. It was the fourth quarter with a minute and fifteen seconds remaining. All Seattle fans were zealously awaiting the field goal kick from the forty-yard line that would tie them with Denver.

Ryan McKee, the Seahawks' primary kicker for the past two seasons, stepped onto the emerald AstroTurf. Both teams prepared for the next play as Bronco fans booed McKee, who took his position on the field. Seahawks fans bellowed their confidence in McKee, but their voices were overwhelmed by the Bronco fans who brought sweat to the kicker's forehead. As they bellowed their wish for his failure, he was sure he'd have no appetite after the game if he satisfied them.

His kicking foot flexed this way and that as he called upon its strength. He took deep breaths as his dark squinted eyes rested on the spot where the ball would be. Then his gaze settled on the neon orange goalpost. *Piece of cake!*

The ball was hiked to Carl Rose, the holder.

Bronco players tried to push through the Seahawks in an effort to thwart the field goal. With a violent exhale that tossed a drop of sweat over his partial face mask, McKee began his advance. Rose instantly readied the ball beneath his finger. McKee counted every step that brought him closer to the ball. Once he was near enough, he brought back his kicking leg, praying it would not disappoint him and the entire team. Then his cleated shoe met the ball. All eyes were on it as it left the ground. McKee beamed as he watched the ball flip and fly on a direct course that would carry it between the two neon posts.

The patrol car that had fallen from the cargo plane crashed down noisily on the goal post, bending it out of the ball's path.

The struggle on the field stopped as players and refs turned to what had fallen from the sky. The entire crowd was silenced by the unprecedented event. A pyramid of dazed cheerleaders collapsed, forming a head-turning heap. A morbidly obese fan of the Broncos stood, dropping the nachos he'd bought from the concession stand. They landed on the couple seated in front of him, staining their hats and shirts with cheese sauce. Nothing moved in the stadium but the football and the digital imagery on the jumbotrons.

All eyes were on the ball as it flew into the net without passing between the posts. Refs exchanged glances and shrugged shoulders…then two of them made the "no good" gesture. The most witless Bronco fans cheered as everyone else exchanged questions about what would happen from this point forward. After getting over the shock of what interfered with the game, a broadcasting official made quips of how Denver's finest felt about the Seahawks.

OVER THE ROCKIES

Once Trey and Sonya were freed from the netting, the corporal produced two sets of handcuffs and secured the prisoners' hands in front of them. Then he cut the straps of Sonya's backpack, took it off her person, unzipped it, and turned it upside down. Her melancholy eyes were on her stuff piling up at the corporal's feet: undergarments, toiletries, lighter, a water bottle and, most especially, the paper-clipped packets of cash. Everyone but her regarded the money with mild shock, wondering where she'd obtained it.

"Well, look at that!" the sergeant said in an eerie disguised voice. "Corporal, bag the dough and we will divide it three ways later. Private, search them."

Downcast from watching the money being taken from her, the biker let her head sag forward. She was further distressed by the actions of the short man: removing her helmet, frisking her entire body, and taking the extra magazines and firearm she'd owned for years. With his helmet still on, no one could tell if the private got much delight in searching Sonya's shapely figure. His only noble deed was letting her keep her wallet. Then he moved over to check Trey's person and found nothing.

With the sergeant leading and the corporal bringing up the rear, all five people filed through the door that led to the rest of the plane.

In the next room, they were flanked by two rows of plastic seats facing each other. The right row lined a window-studded wall as the left was against a partition in the center of the jet.

"Sit!" the sergeant ordered, pointing to the sleek chairs on the left. The pair complied, uncomfortable with the lack of upholstery on the built-in seats. Their knees nearly touched those of the armed trio who installed themselves by the windows and faced their captives.

During a minute of silence, Sonya swallowed to pop her ears from the increasing elevation, hearing the muffled drone of the engines more clearly. She and Trey did what little they could to comfort their cuffed wrists in the tight, cold metal. Then they noticed the nametags just above the Chromes' goggles. The private on the right was Skewer, the corporal on the left was Tricks, and Frosty was the sergeant sitting between them.

Trey decided it was time to break the awkward silence. He saw no harm in it since the Chromes clearly wanted him alive. "Interesting names you guys have," he said coolly, not noticing Sonya's concerned look. The masked trio faced him. "So, what are your *real* names?"

"My name is Not Your Business," Frosty said. He pointed to his comrade on his left, then the one on his right as he introduced them. "He's *Never* Your Business, and *his* name is *Mind* Your Business."

"Fair enough."

These three aren't much fun. Why would they be? They're cold-blooded killers.

Trey recalled the moment he'd first seen the plane. "May I ask you guys a different question—one that's harmless to your identity?" Frosty nodded. "Did you really have to shoot down that chopper? I mean, I don't like Fox News either, but that seemed a bit extreme."

"We don't need our business televised," Tricks explained.

"Where were you headed?" Frosty asked.

Trey thought fast; he didn't want to reveal where his parents lived. "To see her," he lied, pointing to Sonya, who tried not to glare at him for it. "She lives in Denver." *How about turning this discourse to more relevant matters*, he admonished himself. "So, what do you guys want with me, anyway?"

"We need you to work for us," Frosty replied. "Our commander heard you know things that could be useful to our science team."

"Who told him that?"

"You'll find out."

After more quiet, Tricks spoke again. "Let's get rid of her, Sergeant," he proposed, pointing to Sonya as he faced Frosty. "You said that we only came for Mr. Radisson. *She's* of no use to us. We can dump her and the bike as we did the coppers."

Sonya's heart raced as the fearless light in her eyes faded.

Trey thought quickly for some dissuading words. "Wait, please!" he implored, showing his palms to the three terrorists. "She's all I have in this world. Besides, she's a…a scientist…like me. There's more to her than meets the eye. If it's my knowledge you want, you should know that her ideas have a way of…refining mine."

Frosty faced Sonya, then Trey, then Sonya again. Then he faced Tricks. "The girl stays. At least until we talk to the colonel." The corporal's head hung.

Sonya's hand gripped Trey's. His protruding gray orbs met her almond-shaped eyes of azure. "Thank you," she mouthed without voice.

"Besides, during tomorrow's mission, we'll be meeting with someone I know who will give us at least three K for the bike," the sergeant added.

The Harley's owner looked daggers at him.

"When you were…" Everyone heard the scarcely audible words from Private Skewer. The heads of Frosty and Tricks swiveled to face him as he tapped on the speaker of his face mask. "When you w—" He thumped it harder, not sure why it wouldn't mask his real voice.

Frosty reached over and flipped a concealed switch on Skewer's mask. "You gotta be smarter than your helmet, Private," he said disdainfully.

Without interruption, Skewer repeated his words in the voice of his superiors. "When you were south of Colorado Springs last night, you must have seen one of our CF Gunships crash. Can you tell us why?"

Sonya looked nervously at Trey, recalling the time she'd spent an entire clip on the rotorcraft and miraculously brought it down.

"What's a CF Gunship?" Trey queried.

"Chrome. Falcon. Gunship," the annoyed private retorted. "You know, the armed helicopter that ordered you to stop driving so that other members of our organization could come pick you up?"

"Oh, *that*. I have no idea." He thought fast for words to protect Sonya. "I guess the pilot was a clumsy idiot who didn't see the power lines."

The guilty one let her breath out. *Good cover, Trey*, she wanted to tell him.

From around a corner near the front of the plane came a tall, lanky man. He wore a charcoal dress uniform and appeared to be in his fifties. Beneath his ironed slacks, shiny black shoes *clunked* across the steel, diamond-tread floor. The Chrome Falcon emblem shined on his scarlet beret and on the buckle of a wide belt encircling his dress coat at the waist. A single falcon's eye, embroidered on both upper arms of his coat, bore a pupil as red as his felt cap.

As the man strode up to the seats, the sergeant and his subordinates stood as one to salute him. When he returned the respectful gesture, they sat back down. The two prisoners regarded his oblong weathered face. A full gray beard and sideburns were kept neat and short like a chinstrap. His cobalt eyes, contrasting vividly with his ruddy skin, turned to Trey.

"Hello, Mr. Radisson," he said with a British accent, stopping two feet from Trey's knees. "I am Colonel Epperson, one of the leaders of our organization." He held out a bony hand. Trey raised his snug restraints and tentatively shook hands with the colonel, noticing the falcon cufflink inside his coat's sleeve.

"Colonel Epperson." Trey said the name as if tasting it. "Is that your *real* name?"

"Mind your manners!" Tricks snapped, pointing at him. "You're speaking to a Chrome Falcon officer!"

"Calm yourself, trooper," Epperson advised flippantly. "This chap is no soldier; he's our guest...sort of." He faced Trey. "Yes, Mr. Radisson, that is my real name. We only give our *troopers* fake names."

"I see."

"I must apologize for our frightfully sloppy efforts at bringing you into our custody. I know they've costed you your reputation with the authorities. Unfortunately, we've been having technical difficulties with the drones we've had following you."

Trey considered the man's words, understanding how the rotorcraft had found him. "I see," he repeated. "So, where are we going?"

"To your new home at CFCC."

"Where?"

"Chrome Falcon Command Center. I'm quite sure you'll come to fancy it there. You will be entirely untouchable to the police now." Epperson followed his words with a smile that was meant to be reassuring.

"Why is that?" Sonya queried.

Epperson gave her an annoyed look, then turned to Frosty. "What's the story on *her*, Sergeant? Is there a reason we're keeping her alive?"

"Yes, sir," Frosty replied. "Mr. Radisson said that she's also a scientist and he needs her. She's sort of his right hand, I guess."

"We'll see."

"Attention, all personnel. Prepare for landing," the pilot's tired voice boomed from the overhead speaker. Epperson took the empty seat next to Trey and, like his henchmen, buckled his seat belt. The two captives glanced at each other, shrugged, and secured their own belts. They noticed through the windows behind the helmeted trio that the Rockies were unusually close. As the plane slowed to landing speed, the hydraulic groan of the landing gear lowering could be heard through the floor.

"You two might want to close your eyes," the colonel warned his captives.

✞

Stars multiplied over the Rockies as the sapphire sky turned navy blue. A trio of mountain goats nearly lost their footing when the jumbo jet screamed past their peak. They watched the aircraft drop lower than the skyline and head directly for a mountainside. No hikers or climbers, if there were any here, would have been able to fathom why the heavy craft was on a collision course for the peak. But they would not have taken their eyes from the plane since they would expect to see a dumbfounding crash. Then they'd see something entirely different.

Secured to the steep mountainside were two hexagonal columns, like the pair Trey had encountered between Lubbock and Amarillo. Instead of fifteen feet, the twin shafts stood over a hundred feet high and were seven times thicker. They also generated a barely visible energy field, offering more than enough width and height for the mammoth cargo plane to pass through.

Fixed to the wall of rock three yards behind the field's center was a flashing white beacon. This allowed the pilot to know where the nose of the plane must hit. Without the aid of the beacon, the pilot could fly too high, too low, or too far to one side and crash into the mountain.

With landing gear fully lowered, the aircraft made contact with the greenish energy field, bathing the jagged terrain with unnatural light as the plane's matter rapidly condensed. With the brilliance of lightning, the wings passed through, producing the most deafening static sound of the process. Two seconds after the nose had hit, the tail completed its own "evaporation" into the columns. Then darkness returned to the land.

A wall of bright light moved swiftly from the front to the back of the plane, leaving everyone aboard feeling tingly. When Trey and Sonya opened their eyes, they noted the view behind the masked trio. Studding a wall of granite were steel columns flashing past the windows. The aircraft had instantly gone from flying over the Rockies to rolling on its landing gear through an immense tunnel. Since the plane's interior had darkened, overhead lights came on.

"What just happened?" Trey asked, clearly astonished.

"We just passed through a TF—a teleportation field," Epperson replied. "We usually call them Green Gates. Ever heard of them, chap?" Trey shook his head. "Of course, you haven't; no one on the planet has them…except us. Only *our* science team knows how to create them. They are truly remarkable pieces of technology. This entire plane and all the matter inside it has been instantly condensed, transported from Colorado to…CFCC and restored to its original form." The colonel had obviously almost voiced the command center's location. "That's what Green Gates do. You would have saved us all a lot—a *whole* lot—of hassle and hell if you'd just driven your bloody car through the gate we set up between Lubbock and Amarillo."

"So, *that's* what that thing was." Trey mulled over the new info, still astonished by the advanced machinery. "Now I know why you Chromes are so untouchable." His mind replayed his first encounter with a Green Gate. "It didn't seem like the gate stayed on for very long."

“I had a team monitoring you from here at CFCC. They could see you on a hidden camera near the gate. They switched the gate off because they could tell you were not going to drive through it anyway—not after you saw what it did to that maroon Camaro. Plus, they didn’t want the man in the pickup behind you to see the gate. In fact, we don’t want *anyone* who isn’t one of us to know about our Green Gates.”

“I see. But what happened to the Camaro?”

“Against our wishes, it ended up at this place. So, unfortunately, we had to dispose of the people inside.”

“You monsters,” Sonya muttered, scowling and shaking her head as she eyed the floor. Her words mirrored Trey’s thoughts.

“Well, we didn’t *mean* for them to drive through the gate. When we activated the gate, we only expected *Trey* to pass through it,” Epperson explained.

“And it wasn’t like we could turn the Camaro’s occupants loose and risk them showing someone the gate’s location,” Frosty added.

“And they would probably tell people what they saw *here*,” Skewer put in.

“Enough of this stupid woman!” Tricks flared, slapping the armrest of his seat. “We don’t have to explain ourselves to her!” Pointing at Sonya, he faced Epperson. “Colonel, with all due respect, I think she should die! Trey’s a liar! I seriously doubt she’s a scientist!”

“Calm yourself, Corporal,” Epperson ordered with a placating hand raised. “I will allow her until the end of tomorrow to prove her worth to us. If she fails, you may execute her yourself if you’d like.”

Sonya felt her heart quicken again, but managed to hide her anxiety.

✞

The black airplane slowed to a halt in a more spacious part of the tunnel—the other end of the underground runway. Over a hundred warehouse lights with LED bulbs hung from the jagged stone ceiling. Nearby was an immense door of reinforced steel with a yellow

02 centered on it. If door two was open, even the jumbo jet would have no trouble exiting.

Minutes later, the cargo ramp opened. As the colonel strode down the steel platform, Trey and Sonya followed him. Behind them, Frosty and his two subordinates walked abreast, holding their assault rifles ready.

Trey's curious gray eyes followed the way the cargo plane had come. A white center line painted on the tarmac was for aiding the pilot's efforts to steer the plane and keep the wingtips away from the granite walls. Lining both sides of the runway were flashing green lights. They ran down the two-mile-long tunnel and terminated at an enormous steel door labeled *01*, identical to door two, but too far for him to see well. Flanking door one were the Green Gate's columns that were switched off seconds after the jet had landed. If the gate ever failed to function, door one would open if the plane had a dire need to leave the base. Trey guessed the purpose of door two was for ventilation during takeoff.

Half a mile down the subterranean runway was an enormous display board hanging high enough for the plane to clear it. From this distance, Trey could scarcely read the green lettering on the board—TF14: DENVER. He guessed there were probably more than fourteen Green Gates scattered across the country and maybe more in the base.

By pushing a few buttons from somewhere around here, perhaps I could reset the runway's gate to take me to another gate near Las Vegas, New York, possibly even Paris, he thought, eager to know many things the Chromes were unlikely to tell him. *How many gates are there? Where are they located? Are any outside the country? Where on the planet is* this *place?*

Near the nose of the aircraft, four men and one woman, all in uniform, entered through a personnel door and scurried around the plane to inspect and service it. Trey and Sonya noticed the five maintainers wore what Frosty and his followers wore, minus the belt and helmet.

The colonel's party of six left the runway's great cavern through a different personnel door that led to another cave, not as long, but still gargantuan. There were no windows or skylights to reveal the command center's presence. Instead, the place was limned by more warehouse lights that dangled from a ceiling of pipes and rafters eight stories high.

Hundreds more personnel wore jumpsuits, mostly male, 30 percent female. Nearly half were American; some were European or Russian and many were Arabic or North Korean. Paying no heed to the captives, they all stayed busy, carrying boxes, operating electric forklifts, maintaining high-tech equipment. As most of the bustle transpired on the cable-strewn concrete floor, more took place on a maze of catwalks and office boxes overhead. Twelve armed troopers, dressed like Frosty and his two followers, marched in formation to a training seminar, saluting the colonel as they passed by.

Monitors the size of theater screens hung high at every corner. Most of them showed constantly changing numbers that not even Trey, a proficient mathematician, could fathom the meaning of. Two other screens showed a Chrome Falcon official speaking as the largest monitor showed a neon red outline of the United States. All across the map were dots, each labeled TF with a different number after it. According to a legend in the corner, the red dots indicated inoperable teleportation fields, the blue dots indicated the inactive ones, and the green dots were active ones. Trey counted thirty-eight blue dots, twenty-three red, and one green.

Two to three times a minute, a computerized woman's voice echoed through the colossal chasm making announcements over a PA system. The voice told some names they had a phone call while other names were summoned to various places within the subterranean base.

Trey and Sonya continued to drink in the imposing environs as they were led through an aisle in the activity. Then they followed a causeway lined on both sides with yellow-and-black safety tape instead of railing. Ten feet below the walkway's left side, maintainers crawled all over eight dormant gunships. On the right were clusters of cubicles where techies were up to no good on headsets and computers.

"What do you think *those* geeks are doing?" Sonya whispered in Trey's ear as she looked downward at the workspaces.

"I don't know. Maybe trying to hack government systems," he guessed, pensively eyeing the sixty-plus computer screens. "Some might be spreading malware. Some could be recruiting or keeping up relations with other extremist groups and...maybe trying to annex them."

"I hope you're wrong."

"So do I. Maybe I *am* wrong and they are just doing some harmless data entry. Whatever it is, I'm sure their preferred browser is Google *Chrome*." The quip drew a grin from Sonya.

"You two stop talking!" one of the troopers behind them warned.

"And keep moving!" ordered another.

Trey kept gawking at everything they passed. He no longer thought of Chrome Falcon as a terrorist faction; it seemed more like the beginning of a terrorist *empire*. Revolutionaries from all over the planet were united here, convinced they were part of something greater than the rest of the world—even America.

It's like the Nazis have been reincarnated, he thought fretfully. *If their ultimate goal is to dominate the U.S., they are undoubtedly starting off well.*

A heavy pair of automatic steel doors whined opened when the six drew near. They headed down a lengthy hallway, passing propped-open double doors on the right. Inside a large room, twenty uniformed men and women stood at attention as a captain reprimanded the group about performance lapses. On the left was a more spacious, high-ceilinged room filled with rows of people wearing black shorts and matching T-shirts bearing the Chrome Falcon symbol. Over a hundred voices counted aloud as jumping jacks were performed in unison.

After being led through three more corridors and down two stairways, the two captives could not hold back questions any longer. Trey was the first to speak.

"Where are we going?" he asked the colonel.

"To your holding cell," Epperson replied. "Don't worry, chap; it's almost as nice as a room at a fifty-dollar-a-night motel. If your behavior impresses me the rest of the year, I'll move you to something akin to a Hilton suite." He glanced at his gold Tiffany watch, reading 10:45 P.M. "We have much to discuss, but it can wait till tomorrow. After we talk, I'll introduce you to our science team. As for tonight, we'll bring you food and water. I would suggest you two get a shower and some rest."

SACRAMENTO, CALIFORNIA

Wade Grimes was snoring peacefully in his king-size bed when a sudden yelp made him wide awake. If he'd heard it one more time, he might have been able to identify the voice's source or gender. But the only thing he heard next was his wife's question.

"What was that?" she asked nervously with a Hispanic accent.

"A dead man!" the gang member replied, certain there was an intruder in his abode with a sick sense of humor. The couple had no kids or dogs, and it was far too late for visitors. He tossed the covers aside and pulled a heavy Smith & Wesson from the drawer of his nightstand.

"Wade?"

"Stay here, Jackie."

The Latino woman sat up in bed, watching her husband tiptoe out of the dark room and into the darker hallway. Creeping around his spacious house, Wade was on high alert with a tense trigger finger. He searched his memory for unpleasant encounters with rival gang members. Nothing recent came to mind. There was no one he could think of with a strong motive to invade his Mediterranean-style home—one of the town's most difficult domiciles to find. He even kept his residence a mystery to most of *his* posse.

He checked the four empty bedrooms where kids would be

sleeping after Jackie's fertility treatments started working. After verifying the closets and bathrooms had no signs of life, he sidled downstairs, hearing absolutely nothing.

The corner of his eye caught movement at the living room window.

He spun, blasting a round through a pane. It was only the shadow of his favorite oak tree shaking in the wind.

He turned again, firing the revolver twice more at a clattering noise. It was the icemaker in his fridge dispensing more cubes in the tray. The bullets had put two leaks in the freezer door.

"Who's there?" Wade roared. After fifteen heartbeats of silence, he flipped on lights in every room, finding nothing that could have produced the sound. Utterly confused, he checked windows and outer doors, verifying they were all secure. Then he headed back to the master bedroom. *A stray dog. Just a stray dog passing through my property,* he speculated.

With her stained-glass lamp on, Jackie was still sitting up in bed, now eyeballing Wade with disbelief as he entered the room.

"Don't know what it was," he told her, putting away the firearm.

"It was *me!* I had a bad dream!" she flared.

His dreadlocks and ten-inch beard flew when he spun his head to return her incredulous look. "What? A bad dream? What do you mean?"

"Have you lost your mind?"

"*My* mind? What about *yours*? How can you shriek at something in your sleep and then say, 'What was that?' Silly woman! I thought there was someone in our house! Now, we have a window to fix and a fridge to replace!"

"I can't believe you did that." Muttering something in Spanish, she took the remote off her nightstand and turned on the TV atop a dresser across the room. "You need to get rid of your stupid guns."

He got back in the bed. "But, honey, *everyone* in the gang carries."

If anyone else on the planet had objected to any facet of his lawless lifestyle, he would have blackened both their eyes. Only around his other half was he this vulnerable.

"I'm the gang's second-in-command and I have to set an example," he added.

"I don't care." Jackie was sure she would have left Wade a long time ago if he wasn't so well off and constantly spoiling her with gifts. She neither knew nor cared what the source of his income was. When he'd told her he managed a factory, it was a sufficient answer for her. She never felt compelled to go see the plant or find out what products it yielded.

"Why is the TV on? Don't you want to go back to sleep?"

"How can I sleep *now* after you acted like a trigger-happy lunatic?"

Wade chewed this over as he eyed the revolving ceiling fan. "Good point. I'm also wide awake."

On the screen, he saw a blonde anchorwoman jabbering on about a Jane Doe. Behind the shoulder of her royal blue blazer was a head and shoulder shot of a pale woman in a leather jacket. The slightly blurred photo was magnified till it was four times the size of the reporter's head. Goggling the TV, Wade heeded every word. Even with wraparound shades on, the attractive biker wanted for questioning looked familiar to him. Wind had tossed her curly raven hair beneath her maroon, paisley-patterned half-helmet.

"I don't believe it!" Wade exclaimed as his widened eyes recognized Jane Doe. "Only one woman wears a helmet like that—Sonya McCall."

While riding her Harley, Sonya had looked at the FOX News helicopter seconds before it had been shot down. The image of her had been taken from footage that had been filmed by a camera operator in the rotorcraft and sent to the news station.

"Sonya who?" Jackie asked. "The TV lady just said her name is Jane Doe, stupid. What are you talking about?"

"Hang on, darling, I need to hear this."

Ten minutes later, Wade moved to his garage for a private conversation. A lawn chair was unfolded and he plopped down in it. Then he fingered the touchscreen of his smartphone until it read

CALLING LEVI. After four rings, his leader picked up.

"Why are you calling me so late, Wade?" Levi's tired voice carped.

"I'm sorry, boss. I just need to know one thing. Have you crossed the border yet?"

"Yeah. We're staying at a hotel in Chihuahua. We'll reach Manzanillo tomorrow. What's going on? Are you not keeping things under wraps in Sacramento?"

"There's nothing wrong here, boss. Our drugs are yielding more profit than ever."

"That's what I want to hear. That's why I left you in charge of the business. And when I get back, I'd better not find—"

"Sonya's not in Mexico." Seconds of silence assured Wade the boss understood.

"What are you talking about?"

"I mean, your ex-girlfriend made the news, boss. The authorities are calling her Jane Doe. They don't know her real name and probably never will; the whole time she was with us, she managed to avoid getting a criminal record. I wish there was a way for me to tell the cops who she is without being traced, but as you know, our whole team has too much to hide."

"Get to the point!"

"She was helping some nerd named Radisson or something evade the cops."

"Radisson? Who is he? Her new boyfriend?"

"I don't know, but he's one of the most wanted men in the country. Since Sonya was helping him, they showed her picture on TV right before his and now she's wanted for questioning too. Since she was wearing shades, the picture won't do anyone much good. Anyhow, she was last seen near Denver with about a dozen—"

"Denver? What is that dumb broad doing in Denver?"

"I don't know, but your old license plate must have been on her Harley."

"Why do you say that?"

"Because, now *you* are wanted for questioning too. After they showed the pics of her and the nerd, they showed yours and said that her bike belonged to *you*."

Wade winced at Levi's words of fury.

"What? What! I'll kill her! That stupid woman is dead! *Dead*!"

"Boss, please, you have to forget about her. Lay low in Mexico for a while."

"Why would I do that? You think I'm giving up now? You think the fact that the cops want to question me again changes anything? Sonya is still dead when I find her!"

"She's untouchable."

"I'll see about that when I find her!"

"She's mixed up with Chrome Falcon."

"Who?"

"Some terrorist-paramilitary-something group. We're no match for them. Not even the U.S. military can bring them down. What makes you think *we* can? Besides, since these terrorists rescued her and the dork from the cops while your tag was on her bike, the cops think *you* are mixed up with the terrorists too. In other words, the authorities want you in their custody now more than they ever did before."

More silence as Levi pondered this. "I don't care. I've been evading police my entire life and I've gotten quite good at it. I'm coming back across the border tomorrow."

"Why, boss?"

"Why? Why do you think, dumbbell? I have a mission to finish—the death of Sonya Meadows!"

"You mean Sonya *McCall*."

"Whatever! I've waited three damn years to put down that double-crossing whore, and I'm not waiting anymore! Now, let me sleep!"

CALL DISCONNECTED blinked on the screen of Wade's phone. "Fine with me, boss, you hotheaded lunatic," he sniggered. "You will get yourself killed and *I* will become the new leader of the Screamon Demons."

CHROME FALCON COMMAND CENTER

At 9:05 A.M. the next day, Colonel Epperson sat alone in a plush conference room where he savored an omelet stuffed with sausage, mushrooms, jack cheese, and avocado. Near his plate was buttered wheat toast on a saucer and a glass of tomato juice. His scarlet beret was also on the glass table instead of covering his gray crewcut. Left of his cap was his smartphone and the remote for the sixty-inch TV fixed to the wall at the other side of the table. The can lights rimming the oval room's ceiling had been dimmed so he could see the screen better.

On the TV was a press conference. The president verbally danced around questions about how Chrome Falcon would be dealt with. The high-tech radicals were the culprits of numerous bombings that had been transpiring all across the U.S., and every upright citizen was fed up with it. Epperson's confidence swelled as he chuckled at the indecisive replies of America's commander in chief. While trying to appear confident before the media, he seemed acutely troubled.

"Colonel, the prisoners are here, sir," the overhead intercom said.

"Enter," Epperson replied, turning off the TV.

The door to the colonel's left was opened by a masked trooper called Sergeant Wits. Trey and Sonya, both in handcuffs, followed him through. The second and last trooper to enter was Sergeant Arch. Like Wits, he was armed with a tranquilizer gun that somewhat resembled an ancient German luger. The troopers had wanted to keep their assault rifles instead, but the colonel wouldn't allow it. Even if the prisoners tried to fight or run, they were still far too valuable to stop with lethal weapons.

When the woman paused to scan her surroundings, she nearly lost her balance when Arch pushed her. "Hey!" she spat, glaring over her shoulder at the trooper's tinted goggles.

"Hey, what, missy?" he countered through his face mask in the disguised voice. The gun's cold muzzle was pressed to her neck above her jacket collar. "You don't 'hey' anyone holding one of these…unless you want a one-hour nap."

"Sergeant, be nice," Epperson chided mildly around a mouthful of egg. While looking at the captives, he gestured to the seats across the table from his. "Come sit down, you two."

The Jewfroed genius and biker woman warily moved to the table's other side to be face-to-face with the colonel. They pulled back and sat in two upholstered, roll-around chairs, setting their cuffed hands on the table with a *clink*.

The British man regarded their fatigue-reddened eyes and displeased lines of their mouths. "You didn't sleep well, did you?" he sighed, spearing the last of his omelet. "Still not over your collywobbles about this place? Most unfortunate. One way or another, you will need to get comfortable around me and my people." He eyed them thoughtfully as he chewed. "Well, how about some breakfast? I can summon a waiter to bring you a menu." The tousled-haired couple said nothing. "Something to drink, perhaps? Want to watch the telly?" More silence. "Suit yourself." He let his fork clatter noisily on the elegant plate to stress his displeasure at having his hospitality rejected.

Still gripping their nonlethal guns, the troopers exchanged looks and shook their heads at the prisoners' choice.

"Very well, Mr. Radisson," Epperson continued. "Let's just get to the only relevant question: why have you been brought here?"

He cleared his throat. "Do you remember that frightfully fancy gismo you created three years ago and then…rashly demolished like a bleedin' tosser? The VV1?"

Trey's large gray eyes grew larger, not noticing Sonya's puzzled face. "What? The VV1? You know about that?" he said, half wheezing from disbelief. "How is that possible? I told no one but…my *ex-fiancée*."

Epperson smiled through his beard, then chuckled. "Lieutenant?" he called out, facing the room's only entrance. Wits moved aside as Arch opened the door.

Trey immediately recognized the face of his Filipino ex—Zuri Navarro.

She strode in the room, wearing the same style of dress uniform as the colonel. The main differences were gender-related: high heels and a tie tab instead of a tie. The pupils of the falcon eyes embroidered on her sleeves were as forest green as the beret atop her tied-back hair.

The former inventor swiveled his chair to face her as she set a briefcase on the table and stopped four feet away from him. He thought of all the time he'd been hunted by this heinous paramilitary group. How they'd murdered innocent people just for getting in their way. How they'd utterly devastated his reputation with the authorities. How they meant to force him to work for them—the last thing he wanted to do.

He'd never guessed this vile, opportunistic woman and her big mouth were the cause of it all. The more he thought about it, the angrier he got.

"It's been a long time, hasn't it…Trey Radisson?" she sneered, doffing her beret and tossing it on the table.

"Indeed…Zuri Navarro," he replied almost without voice, still scarce believing what he was seeing.

Her arms went akimbo. "I would appreciate it if you addressed me as *Lieutenant* Navarro. I think I've earned it."

He eyed the carpet, shaking his head and chuckling. "I get it, I get it. Just because I destroyed my VV1 instead of using it to make you and me rich with it, you dumped me and sided with these... people so I would be forced to produce another VV1, right?"

Zuri shrugged one shoulder. "There was a lot more to it than that, but for the part you're talking about, I guess I'm guilty as charged. However, I would rather be guilty and rich than innocent and poor. Maybe once you get over your negative feelings about me, you will come to your senses and appreciate the idea of being on the winning side. Because, that's what Chrome Falcon is—the winning side. And with your invention, we will be *completely* unstoppable."

Sonya's sable mane flew as her head spun to face Trey. "Jiminy Christmas!" she exclaimed. "What the heck did you invent?"

"Just a stupid invisibility device," he said nonchalantly, ignoring the way she gaped at him in response to his words.

"You didn't know that?" the colonel said, eyeing Sonya. "*You*, his so-called science partner?" He could tell by how she looked down that she wished she'd kept her trap shut. "You know *nothing* about science, do you? I may dispose of you sooner than I thought." His words quickened her pulse.

Trey felt compelled to speak with no delay. "Sir, please reconsider. It's true, she's no scientist. But I think far more clearly in the lab when I know I have her to come home to."

No one had noticed the third officer enter the room. The burly man's stature was four inches shy of his seventy-eight-inch leader, Epperson. Trey regarded the officer as he tossed his blue beret on the table and strode up to Zuri's back. His burly arms, threatening to tear the sleeves of his dress coat, encircled the waist of the petite woman who was half his size. Drawing a grin from her, he planted a noisy kiss on her cheek. Neither of them noticed the colonel shake his head before answering a call on his smartphone.

"Stop," the lieutenant tittered. "Not in front of the...newcomers. Where have you been all day, anyhow?"

"Where I go for hours *every* day, babe," he replied in a high, scratchy voice. "I was at the gym, pumping iron. Then I got a shower."

"You might need another one if you don't control yourself."

Trey and Sonya studied the officer's tan triangular face, which habitually bore a smirk. He kept his jet-black hair gelled in spikes. His jade, wide-set eyes regarded Trey with ridicule as he rested his chin on the Filipino woman's shoulder—an act that would remind some people of a dog raising his leg.

"So, sweets, is this the nerd you dated before me?" the officer taunted.

"Trey, this is Captain Ferch." Zuri presented the man embracing her. "He's my—"

"New squeeze, boy-toy, whatever you want to call it," Trey cut her off.

"I heard you're some kind of genius," Ferch scoffed. "You can't be that bright to let *this* sexy mama get away." He let go of Zuri after facing Sonya, looking interested. "But, I admit, your *new* chica is rather bonita too. She reminds me of one of the many virgins who became single moms after they met me."

Zuri teasingly slapped her lover's arm. "You're so bad."

Rolling her eyes, the biker saw little point in telling the randy gym rat that she and Trey were not dating.

"Did you see that, girl? She rolled her eyes at me," Ferch observed aloud, pressing his nose to Zuri's cheek as he held her against him again. "But I bet deep down, she would like to be *you* right now."

"I'd rather get a Pap smear with a rake," Sonya huffed, reversing his smile and making his girlfriend cringe. "I'm not into lowlifes like you who keep their brains in their pants instead of their heads."

"You got some nerve talking to me like that!" Releasing the petite lieutenant, he strode closer to Trey's "girlfriend," trying to appear menacing. The cuffed woman didn't even blink and decided the captain was even more revolting than the most promiscuous jocks she'd known in high school.

"Focus, babe, focus," Zuri cooed with her hands on his chest. "We need to make Trey *and* his woman feel somewhat at home here. The mission depends on it."

"Fine." He returned his attention to the man in cuffs. "You'll like it here with the Chromes, Trey. You'll be totally safe from cops just like *I'm* totally safe from paying child support." He put a hand on Zuri's shoulder. "No one knows we still exist. Not even the U.S. government knows."

"Maybe that would please me if I was actually a criminal," Trey ground out.

Epperson finished his phone call and set the smartphone down on the transparent table. Then he faced the lieutenant's beau, looking annoyed. "Captain Ferch, why exactly are you here? This meeting has nothing to do with—"

The PA system silenced everyone in the room.

"Attention, all personnel. Attention, all personnel. This is General Casprite. All colonels will report to my conference room in fifteen minutes. I highly encourage you all to bring at least one subordinate to the meeting," a male voice boomed in American English.

"Blimey," Epperson groused, doing a face palm. "The commander's bloody timing gets worse every week."

"Commander?" Trey inquired, curious. "Is he the top general of Chrome Falcon?" *You know, your version of Hitler?*

"He's the *only* general...so far." The colonel stood, meeting eyes with Ferch. "Captain, come with me."

"What for?" Ferch griped. "Those stupid meetings last over an hour."

"Enough of your rubbish! If you ever want to promote, you will attend the bloody meeting like a good chap so you can learn something. Besides, you obviously need time apart from Lieutenant Navarro. Now, let's go, you lascivious dolt!"

Ferch groaned. Like Epperson, he donned his cap as he followed him out.

Why don't they just use this *conference room?* Trey wondered, a bit sorry he wasn't getting to meet Chrome Falcon's top commander. *In fact, how many conference rooms does this base have? And why do I want to meet General Casprite? Certainly not to praise him. Maybe I want to know who to despise for starting this vile organization—this cancer infecting America!*

"May I please use the restroom?" Sonya asked the lieutenant with a softer voice than she'd used earlier. "I really need to pee."

"I don't know," Zuri replied, looking at her broodingly. "Maybe I'll allow that if you behave yourself. Do you think you can do that?" Sonya nodded. "Fine." The petite officer pointed to the pair of troopers by the door. "Go with one of them."

The biker eyed the maroon carpet as she timidly neared Arch and Wits, keeping her cuffed hands down to appear nonthreatening. As Wits opened the door, Arch put the tranquilizer gun to Sonya's back.

"No sudden movements," he warned and followed her out. She nodded and kept walking, doing her best to appear scared. A few strides down the hallway, her long eyelashes flicked up as she listened carefully to a base-wide notice.

"Attention, Sergeant Frosty Team. Your flight leaves in forty-five minutes," a female voice reported from the PA system.

Trey could not recall a time he'd exhausted his self-control as much as he did in the plush conference room. Albeit he'd never been a violent person, all he could think about was how good it would feel to strangle his soulless ex-fiancée, or to repeatedly clobber her skull with a fire extinguisher he saw bracketed on the nearby wall. But, handcuffed or no, he dare not make any threatening movements, lest the trooper use his tranquilizer gun on him.

Instead of attacking Zuri, he eyed the nearest wall—a row of nine floor-to-ceiling panels between polished walnut pilasters. Only the three centermost panels were not made of sheetrock; they were canvas screens displaying scenic landscapes since the room was not allowed to have windows—like the rest of the base. Every thirty seconds, the images changed. He might have noticed the display sooner if not for his discourse with the officers.

Zuri took note of where Trey's eyes were focused as the depiction faded from Niagara Falls to Machu Picchu. "Lovely, isn't it? I hope to go there with Dylan someday," she said.

"Dylan? Is that your boyfriend's first name?" Trey queried.

"It is."

"I see. Well, don't get your hopes up too high. My money says that Dylan will be with someone else before long. If what he said about his sordid past is true and he really *does* have a lengthy list of past lovers, how can you be dumb enough to think you'll be his last?"

She shrugged. "Maybe I *won't* be. It doesn't matter."

"Well, what about all the innocent children Dylan made all over the place? Do their lives matter? Haven't you realized yet that your idiot boyfriend can't go one minute without proving what a vile degenerate he is? That's what we should call him: Dylan the Degenerate. Would you agree that shoe fits?"

"That's enough!" She looked ready to hit Trey.

"I'm just telling it like I see it. There's no need to get so mad."

"You don't know Dylan the way I know him, so, shut your mouth! Anyway, what are we discussing this for?"

Of course she's offended by my questions and remarks, he thought, somewhat amused. *She enjoys her phony relationship more if she ignores her conscience...if she has one. I doubt it. I'm not sure who's dumber—Dylan or anyone who would rise to his defense.*

"We didn't bring you here to discuss my relationship!" she carried on. "I don't need your forgiveness either! If you go the rest of your life hating my guts, it doesn't matter to me at all. All that matters is that you do what you were born to do—create the VV1. You have a talent that should not go to waste. So, *use* it...for the benefit of the Chromes. We are your only salvation. You might as well learn to like us."

"How can I like *anything* about the Chromes when they murder innocent people?"

"Maybe you need to desensitize yourself. Don't be so uptight about murder. It's just business. People kill every day."

Trey sighed and shook his head. *This topic is getting me nowhere. Time for a subject change. And I know just the one.* "Tell me something, Zuri. Where does Chrome Falcon plan to be in say...ten years?"

"In control of this entire preposterous nation...and then some," she answered smugly.

This nation? What is *"this nation"? Is it America? It must be. There's only one way to find out.* "What's so preposterous about America?"

"There's too much freedom. People will *never* be ready for freedom."

Got you, you dumb broad. So, it is *true—CFCC is hidden somewhere in the U.S. I should keep her going before she realizes her slip of the tongue.* "People will never be ready for freedom? Why do you say that?"

"If this is such a great country, why does it have five percent of the world's population and seventy-five percent of the world's lawyers?"

It's America, all right. He needed a moment to find a way to counter such a valid point. "Well, *I'm* ready for freedom. I never needed a lawyer until you Chromes messed with my life."

"Well, not everyone is like that."

"What state are we in?" *Come on, Zuri. Let it slip.*

"Nice try."

Damn. "Come on. Who will I tell? I'm sure I don't have a prayer of escaping this place. I'm just curious what state we are in."

"None of your business!"

Trey felt the cold steel of Sergeant Wits's tranquilizer gun against the back of his neck. He slowly turned his head to face the trooper, surprised to see him suddenly so near him.

"She told you to shut your mouth," the sergeant warned. "If you don't, I'll do it for you."

As Wits walked back to the door, Zuri turned away from the captive while replying to a text on her smartphone.

I'll go fishing later for info I'm not supposed to know, Trey opted.

Lines of engraved text centered in the transparent tabletop caught his attention. He peered closer, noticing white paint filled the letters etched meticulously into the glass.

CHROME FALCON CREED

WE ARE SOLDIERS OF THE CHROME FALCON FORCE.
WITH THE GLEAM AND RESILIENCE OF CHROME,
AND THE SPEED AND SIGHT OF A FALCON,
WE ARE A FORCE TO BE RECKONED WITH.

YESTERDAY, OUR HUMANITY HINDERED US.
MORALITY AND GUILT SLOWED OUR PROGRESS.

THEN, WE SHED SUCH TRIFLES TO BECOME SOMETHING BETTER.
WE HONOR GENERAL CASPRITE FOR OPENING OUR EYES.

TOMORROW, WE WILL EXPAND OUR DOMAIN.
WE WILL DRIVE FREEDOM FROM THE WORLD TO MAKE IT BETTER.
WE WILL HUMBLE THIS PLANET, NO MATTER HOW LONG IT TAKES.
SAVE YOURSELF AND SUBMIT TO OUR BELOVED COMMANDER.

OUR MISSION IS TO CONQUER AND ADVANCE ALL REGINES.
TO TAKE INDEPENDENCE FROM MILLIONS WHO ABUSE IT.
WE WILL SHOW NO MERCY TO THOSE WHO NEVER EARNED IT.
WE WILL POLICE THE WORLD PROPERLY WITH AN IRON FIST.

WE WILL PROTECT ALL WHO WILL JOIN US.
WE WILL SLAUGHTER ALL WHO ARE AGAINST US.
NONE WILL DERIDE US, DEFY US OR EVEN IMITATE US.
WE ARE UNSTOPPABLE AND WE WILL WIN EVERY TIME.

Trey mulled over the creed for a moment, then snorted. *That has to be the stupidest thing I've read in years.* He perused the fourth paragraph again. *I wish the moron who worked so hard to etch all this noise was here; I could see his face as I told him he spelled "regimes" wrong.*

✞

Sergeant Arch leaned against the wall a foot left of the ladies' room. *What's taking so long*, he thought and rapped thrice on the door.

"Time's up, lady!" he bellowed through his mask. There was no reply. "Are you about done or what?" More silence. The door was pushed ajar. Across the floral-patterned mosaic floor, the trooper saw the woman's feet in the nearest stall with the heels inches from the toilet.

How long has she been sitting in there?

"Hello?" Nothing. "I know you can hear me!"

Losing patience, Arch pushed his way inside, holding the non-lethal gun ready. He normally wouldn't invade the ladies' room, lest his friends think he was some kind of sicko. They would laugh at him and remind him of how the Internet offered far easier ways to ogle half-naked women than public bathrooms.

As the door swung closed behind him, a pair of lavender-socked feet soundlessly followed his field boots.

He strode up to the stall's steel door, eyeing the toes of the black boots behind it. "I said *time's up*!" he boomed, only to be ignored again. His gloved fist pounded on the door—an act that unexpectedly swung it open.

There were no legs in the boots.

If not for the shock of his discovery, he might have also noticed what was next to the toilet—a plunger with no handle.

Even with cuffs on, Sonya's adrenaline-fueled swing was a direct hit. She clubbed the back of the trooper's knees with the plunger handle. She'd wanted to go for his head or face, but they were too well-protected.

Arch fell backward, lying supine.

She wasted no time stomping down on the wrist of the hand holding the gun, keeping it immobile. Then, with the stick, she smacked the man's groin. Moaning in agony, he cradled the new pain with his only free hand. As her hair swayed in front of her gnashing teeth, she struggled to tear the air pistol from Arch's grip. When it was finally hers, she aimed and fired with a hollow *SNAP!* The last thing the trooper saw before the world turned black was the fluffy scarlet end of the sedative dart lodged in his thigh.

Trey eyed the black leather briefcase atop the glass table as Zuri turned its two trios of gold dials to the right combination.

"Go see what's keeping Arch and the female captive," she ordered Wits. "I'll be fine."

"Are you sure, ma'am?" the sergeant asked. Though the prisoner appeared to be nothing more than a harmless techie, he was still larger than the lieutenant, and his handcuffs were not behind his back.

"Yes, I'm sure." Zuri raised the hem of her dress coat, showing the trooper a small Glock holstered by her hip.

The sergeant exited the conference room, and the briefcase's latches popped open. Trey noted the dials' position: 3-1-2 on the left, 9-7-8 on the right. The petite lieutenant raised the lid, exposing a fortune of stacked bills with Franklin's face on all of them. She beckoned Trey closer, amused by the look in his bulging eyes. Goggling the money, he rolled his seat up to the leather container.

"Let me guess: this cash was stolen from a bank, right?" he asked. "I heard on the news that you people do that sort of thing."

"Well, we can't pay our troops with *checks*, can we?" Zuri replied coolly. "It's true, we make many withdrawals, using assault rifles instead of pens. However, this particular dough came from one of our drug lords who turned disloyal. So, we had him shot in the head and took possession of everything he had."

Now you psychos are involved with drugs? "How much is that?"

"Just a million—less than one percent of what we keep in our vaults. And that's not the only thing in this briefcase." She pulled a black felt pouch from a pocket inside the briefcase's lid. When she handed it to him, he took it, guessing it weighed between one and two pounds. He allowed a third of its contents to spill out. Sparkling diamonds, a quarter-inch in diameter, clattered across the clear table. "That's worth about two million."

"Huh." He held a sparkly rock near his engrossed eyes.

"Like what you see?" She smiled and leaned on the edge of the table. "Of course you do. Who wouldn't? And this is only the beginning if you work for us." Her monolid eyes watched his attention bounce back and forth between the cash and jewels. "When you go to bed tonight, ask yourself this: would I rather be rich…or dead? Life is already too short."

He regarded her a moment with uncertainty before returning his attention to the wealth. Thoughts of a different future flitted through his mind—a future with endless travel opportunities and no more tedious work.

"All we want in return, Trey, is that VV1. We *need* the VV1. The Green Gates are becoming too expensive to operate."

What a tempting offer, he thought. *But I don't like who's making the offer. The sole reason I destroyed the VV1 was to keep it from people just like the Chromes.*

She checked the time on her smartphone, an act that drew Trey's attention from the diamonds. "Is your boyfriend texting you?" he asked her.

"No, I'm making sure I have enough time to get to the dining hall before they stop serving lunch. Then, at 1400, I have an execution to attend."

Trey gaped at her. "A— A what? Execution?"

"Yeah. One of our sergeants from—"

Their heads turned when the door opened and the trooper returned.

"Any problems, Sergeant?" Her question was answered with a

headshake. When she faced Trey, the trooper furtively rounded the end of the table to approach her from behind.

"As I was saying, one of our sergeants from the Middle East wouldn't keep his unwanted paws off a female corporal, despite already being warned twice before. General Casprite has discovered that sort of thing is far less common around here when the penalty is a firing squad, especially when the entire base is there to watch. Maybe the *American* military shou—"

SNAP!

Feeling the sting in her right hip, she spun. The masked trooper was two feet from her, regarding her livid face. She took a confused glimpse at the fluffy red dart in her backside, then its source—the air pistol in the sergeant's hand.

"What the hell? Did you just...*shoot* me?" she hissed, gripping her smaller—but lethal—gun. In response, the soldier held the tranquilizer gun inches from her left eye as a warning to keep the Glock in its holster.

She couldn't lift the light weapon, anyway; the dart's anesthetic fluid was already taking effect. As her slanted eyes fell closed, her knees buckled. No one bothered to save her from sprawling to the carpet.

Trey's disbelieving eyes went from Zuri's comatose body to the trooper, whose goggled helmet read ARCH instead of WITS. The sergeant set the air pistol on the table and doffed the helmet and face mask in one piece, exposing a wild mane of long black curls. The lab genius grinned from ear to ear as he recognized Sonya. To him, she looked a bit odd in the loose black jumpsuit.

"I found these in the pocket of the moron who wore this uniform before me," she said merrily, dangling the tiny keys to their handcuffs. She used them to free Trey's hands and put the cuffs and keys in a thigh pocket. "*My* cuffs are on Sergeant Stupid. We'll need *yours* for Sergeant Stupider. They're both sleeping under the sink in the ladies' room."

Her focus went straight to an ancient coffee table against the wall on the other side of the room. The legless antique was as flat on the bottom as the top, with spindled columns on each corner and a cabinet in the center. The latter would prove itself useful.

She hastily put the sleeping lieutenant's beret back on her head, not caring that it was crooked and covered her eyes; if the cap was left in sight, people would wonder where its owner had gone. With both hands, Sonya grabbed the officer by the ankles and dragged her lifeless form across the floor toward the table. Halfway there, the lieutenant's pistol slipped out of its loose holster.

"We have an hour before Colonel Clod and Captain Cretin return," she explained without stopping. "But the *plane* leaves in a half hour." Once she reached the coffin-size piece of furniture, she opened the empty cabinet and stuffed Zuri's petite body inside. Then the carved doors were closed. "If we don't leave now, I seriously doubt we'll find another opportunity."

Sonya spun the table around on the carpet—an action made easy by the many months she'd spent pumping iron at her late grandmother's house. The back of the table faced the room as its cabinet doors were against the wall. Once the Filipino woman's hour-long nap was over, she would find herself trapped and waiting for anyone to come within earshot of her muffled shrieks for help. Trey thought it a shame he wouldn't be around to see Zuri's incensed face once she was rescued.

Sonya took a seat atop the coffee table, seemingly enjoying her victory over the lieutenant. This further amused Trey, even though she'd only sat to catch her breath. Everything she'd said and done after returning to the conference room amazed him.

"I remember hearing about the flight," he said, recalling her last words. "Is there a disguise available for me too? And maybe a gun?"

"Yes. They're in the ladies' room on Sergeant Stupider. I had no trouble taking him down since I looked just like his friend." She got up and hastened over to Zuri's pistol to stuff it in an empty pocket. "I don't know how many darts the tranquilizer guns carry. I've already used three of them. So, we'll take your ex's Glock as backup."

When the wealth of the briefcase caught her eye, she froze.

"Wow!" she wheezed, no longer angry about the cash stolen

from her yesterday. "I don't know where the plane is taking us, but I'm sure we could use *this*. Pack it up, quickly."

"Will do." Trey's hands blurred as he put the diamonds back in the felt bag with the others. The bag went in the cash-filled briefcase, which he closed a second later. "Okay, I'm done." He noticed Sonya reading the Chrome Falcon Creed incised in the table.

"That has to be the stupidest thing I've read in years!" she sneered.

"My thoughts exactly. I could feel myself losing IQ points when I read it."

"Let's go get *your* uniform." She donned the helmet and took up the dart gun. Briefcase in hand, Trey followed her out and wondered if he was falling in love. Last night, they'd been too nervous to sleep on the cots in their holding cell. Therefore, they'd passed the hours faster by getting to know each other better. However, none of their exchanged words gave any hints she was *this* tough and fearless.

✞

"Arch" stood by the ladies' room, facing right where the hallway formed a T with another corridor. A trio of officers came into view, chatting about having old computers replaced. Sonya was happy to note the men kept strolling the same way, showing no interest in the direction leading to her.

She turned to face "Wits" as he came out of the restroom like a reflection of her, except for the briefcase in his hand.

"How does it fit, Trey?" she asked in a muffled version of her real voice. Rather than answer, Trey flipped a switch on her helmet's face mask. "What?" She noticed the change in her voice. "Oh, that. Good catch."

"It fits fine," he said in the same disguised voice. "Let's go."

They moved further down the bright hall from the conference room, recalling the ways they'd turned to get there. Minutes later, they were following another pair of masked troopers, both armed with scoped assault rifles like almost all the troopers carried. Seconds later, the pair pushed through the door to the men's room.

"We need their guns to complete our disguises," Sonya said. "Once we're inside, you guard the door."

Trey nodded and followed her into the restroom.

To their left, both rifles were unattended atop the sink-studded counter. At the row of urinals on their right, the troopers stood unarmed as they relieved themselves. Trey stood with one boot against the door, while Sonya crouched briefly to verify the stalls were unoccupied. Then, she slinked up to the unsuspecting duo and fired twice. They both went down with a sedative dart in the back of one thigh.

"Guard the door while I hide them," Sonya instructed.

Before exiting, Trey went to the sink to arm himself properly and drop his non-lethal pistol in the trashcan. Then he reached up to grab the arm of the door's self-closing device. Without touching the possibly unclean handle, he opened the door, noticing Sonya had paused to give him a puzzled stare.

"Germs," he explained before going out. He waited outside the restroom as his rescuer swiftly installed the comatose bodies atop toilets and secured their stalls. Ten paces down the corridor were closed doors to a lecture hall. From behind the double doors, he heard over fifty voices quoting the Chrome Falcon Creed. *More IQ points going to waste*, he thought.

Minutes later, Trey and Sonya found the familiar cavern filled with Chrome Falcon worker bees. The disguised duo felt their hearts hammering as their anxious breathing turned loud in the confines of their helmets.

"Just walk like you own this place," Sonya said.

They strode abreast across the causeway. Their course led them past numerous officers, maintainers, and other troopers, all chatting and heading for their next tasks. Trey did his best to mirror Sonya's purposeful stride, unaware of the extreme nervousness she hid so well. Despite his fascination with the high-tech atmosphere, he willed himself to keep facing ahead and act like he was here for a reason. Before long, the door leading to the subterranean runway was fifty yards ahead.

"What have you got there?" a captain queried, stepping in their path.

Just as their pulses were starting to calm, the nosy officer hiked them back up.

"Sir?" Sonya replied, very thankful Trey had flipped the switch to hide her feminine voice. She'd understood the man's question, but hoped to buy time to fabricate an explanation.

"I've never seen a pair of troopers walking around with a briefcase before. What's in it and where are you taking it?"

What should I do? she thought nervously as one hand moved an inch closer to her weapon's safety switch. *I don't want to kill him and raise panic around me. How will Trey and I get to the plane then? I must say something. But what? If he makes us open it and sees the money, we're finished.*

"We don't know what's in it, sir." Trey lied. "It belongs to the science team and they told us not to open it." He was amazed by his own calm.

"The science team?" The captain snorted and rolled his eyes. "Well, you dunces are going the wrong way."

"That's because they need us to get rid of it. It needs to go on the plane before takeoff."

Wow! How did I come up with that hogwash? he thought.

"Well, hurry. They're about to leave."

Yes! He raised a saluting hand. Sonya saw it and mirrored the gesture a half-second later. The captain returned their salutes and moved on. For twenty paces, Sonya shot Trey admiring glances, impressed with how superbly his silver tongue had gotten them out of the bad spot. Trey, on the other hand, counted only two times he'd used that gift. The first time was during his last night at work in San

Antonio. He was not proud of himself for that and hoped his former colleagues, dishonest or not, were alive and well.

The two "troopers" reached the door to the runway cavern. Trey peeked through, finding himself at the ten o'clock position of the gloss-black cargo plane. It was less than ninety feet away, facing the way it had come from half a day ago. He observed the half-circle of windows above the nose. A light had been left on in the cockpit, making it obvious the pilot and copilot were not inside yet. Trey spied them after putting his head further through the door.

They were beyond the port wing, standing near a heavily laden aircraft pallet with a trio of troopers: Tricks, Frosty, and Skewer. The five men formed a C around the cargo, with four of them showing their backs to the distant personnel door and the fifth—a trooper—had his side to the door. Trey realized the fifth guy could no more detect motion to his side than *he* could—not with the helmet on. The quintet stayed busy reading off numbers stenciled on the pallet's wooden boxes, putting checkmarks on a clipboard or securing the pyramid of cargo with tie-down straps and a net.

Between the wing's two engines, Trey saw a way in the jet—the lowered ramp. *Now or never*, he warned himself.

Sonya stayed in his wake as they skulked up to the forward landing gear, verifying no heads turned in their direction. Then they sidled along the length of the fuselage, using it to keep all but their legs out of the Chromes' view. Fortunately, their boots and jumpsuits blended well with the granite wall a stone's throw behind them. They reached better seclusion at the starboard landing gear. By peeking around the immense tires, they determined their position relative to the crew. If they kept their heads low and stayed quiet, they could reach the ramp without being seen.

The copilot called out more numbers, and the duo tiptoed further toward the tail until they were waist-high with the ramp. If they moved further back, the fuselage would leave them entirely exposed.

Sonya slung her rifle across her back and slowly assumed a prone position on the ramp's right edge. Crawling like a lizard, she soundlessly inched up the incline and entered the plane, keeping her head down so the left edge would not betray her location. With his heart racing, Trey did the same.

After crawling far enough inside, they stood and leaned against the port wall that shielded them from view more effectively. They began to consider where in the already loaded cargo they should seek seclusion—

—and froze at the next words spoken outside.

"What do you mean?" the copilot groused.

"That last box you called off is not here," one trooper said ruefully.

"Are you sure?"

"Positive."

"It must still be in bay four," another trooper added.

"Well, go get it!" the pilot ordered. "Thank you very much! You fatheads have delayed our flight by at least fifteen minutes!"

Feeling chills run down her spine, Sonya doffed her helmet so Trey would hear her whispered words. "Do you realize what this means?" she said softly as panic sweat glazed her face.

Trey nodded, and then removed his own helmet. "I believe I know exactly what it means, but let me hear your version."

"The general's meeting is going to end in about fifteen minutes. The colonel will see everyone gone from the conference room. Then, he will alert the whole base that we're missing and they won't let anyone leave, including the pilots of this plane. They'll tear this place apart looking for us."

Her next bloodcurdling thought was of Epperson's last words to her: *"You know nothing about science, do you? I may dispose of you sooner than I thought."*

Like Sonya, Trey grew winded from fright as they heard the footfalls of two troopers leaving to fetch the missing box and stall the jet's departure.

"Stop! I found it," the third trooper called out.

The stowaways let out a heavy sigh of relief.

"This is not how we stack boxes, you morons!" The pilot scowled. "You are supposed to make sure all the numbers are showing! How many times do I have to say it? Now, get this pallet on the plane! Hurry up!"

Trey followed Sonya as she re-donned her helmet and sought a hiding place somewhere in the jet's freight.

NEW MEXICO

In one of the state's most desolate regions, no witnesses were present to see the mammoth cargo plane soar west the instant it materialized. The aircraft's source was an immense energy field that buzzed and rippled between two black columns fixed to the dry face of a cliff. Thirty seconds later, the Green Gate shut down.

The black jet's landing gear retracted as it climbed higher. Inside, Trey and Sonya were alone in the full cargo hold without helmets on, famished and tearing into a box of MREs they'd found under the net of the third cargo pallet. Filling the box were ten brown packets half the size of a shoebox.

"What are these?" Sonya asked.

Trey recalled references to the meals when one of his past coworkers at Envisiocom developed a new method of preserving food. "They're called MREs," he told her. "That's an acronym for 'meals ready to eat.' Very popular with the military, I've heard."

"Nice." She took the first one that read VEGETARIAN on the front. "Nope." She discarded it. "No." CHICKEN AND NOODLES followed. "Hah! I don't think so." CHILI AND MACARONI was chucked much further. "Now, that's more like it." She took the one labeled BEEF RAVIOLI and took a seat on a bench jutting from one of the plane's curving, ribbed walls.

Trey showed no interest in the BEEF ENCHILADA or PORK RIB MRE after finding one labeled MEATBALLS IN MARINARA. He sat beside his rescuer and, like her, raided his well-packaged meal.

"What is this?" Sonya queried, showing Trey her flameless ration heater.

"Huh?" Eyeing the small plastic pouch in her hand, he recalled a program he'd seen about life in the U.S. Army. "I think that's for heating the food. You have to put your entree packet in there and add water. The chemicals in the bag sort of react to the water and—"

"I'll pass." She tossed the green pouch away. "I would rather eat it cold than put it in chemicals." The largest packet enclosing her entree was taken from the MRE, followed by a packet with a plastic spoon. She tore into both and began shoveling the ravioli into her mouth. The increasing elevation annoyed her as her ears popped on every swallow.

Trey savored his cold meatballs the best he could and glanced nervously at the closed door leading to the rest of the plane. "I hope none of the crew comes back here," he mused aloud.

"If they do, I'm not afraid to use this," she assured him, patting the assault rifle she'd set on the bench inches from her hip. "Are you afraid to use yours?"

He eyed the weapon he'd left atop one of the two dozen boxes on the nearest pallet. "A little. I've never fired a gun in my life. They're just not my thing."

Nodding her head, she chewed the last of her ravioli while tearing into a smaller packet of vegetable crackers. "Nothing wrong with that. I'm a little surprised we got away from that place so easily. Aren't you?"

"Not really. As far as I can tell, Chrome Falcon is a fairly new organization. So, they still have a lot to learn. Plus, we were clearly in all the right places at the right times."

"Well, I thought you were brilliant—the way you handled that nosy officer who blocked our path and pestered us about the briefcase."

"I appreciate that. You did well too, getting us these stupid uniforms."

"Thanks." She devoured the crackers and squeezed a packet of cheese spread into her mouth. Trey did the same with a packet of peanut butter and then spied a pack of twenty-four water bottles on one of the pallets. He tore two free and handed one to Sonya. "Thanks. I'll trade you my M&M's for your Skittles," she said.

"Okay. I like M&M's better anyway." They made the exchange and swigged the water. "I guess I'll save this for later." He pocketed a packet of nut raisin mix.

"I wonder if I have one of those," she thought aloud, dumping out the rest of her MRE. "Don't need *this* garbage." A packet of instant cappuccino powder was dropped atop the pile of trash they'd made by their feet. "These will do." She shoved an apple-cinnamon energy bar and pretzel pack into her thigh pocket. From the same pocket, she pulled out a pair of handcuffs and their key. "Oops. We forgot to cuff Sergeant Stupider."

"Oh, well, he's no threat to us now."

"That reminds me, how did you ever get involved with that psychotic Filipino woman? Until today, I always thought all Filipinos were nice."

Sighing, Trey shook his head. "I'm not sure. I don't even want to think about Zuri."

"I don't blame you. Let's think about something else." Her azure eyes scanned the tons of payload. "Like…what do you think all this stuff is for?"

"My first guess: the Chromes are trying to get a second base established."

"Or a fourth, or fifth."

"Let's hope not."

"The other base must be where this plane is going, right?"

"I guess. It would be nice if there were some windows in these walls. Wherever we're heading, I hope it won't be impossible for us to sneak away."

"What if it *is* impossible?"

He eyed the small console on the wall that controlled the cargo ramp. Then he studied other objects in their surroundings. "We should get off this plane *before* it lands." Sonya's gaze followed his pointing finger to a crate on another pallet. Stenciled on the side of the box over a serial and model number was PARACHUTES.

"My adrenaline is up again," she said tensely. "I've never used a parachute before."

"Nor have I, but we have to."

"I want to bring my Harley." She stood and side-shuffled past two laden pallets, finding her motorcycle at the front of the cargo hold. "Maybe some other stuff." The net was unbuckled from the first pallet as she examined the boxes beneath.

"Is the Harley really necessary?" Trey moaned, having no desire to mess with the heavy two-wheeler. They needed food and weapons much more. Also, once they were on the ground, they could just *buy* a means of transportation—one that would help them blend in better.

"I'm sorry, but I *love* that bike." She remembered being near Lake Tahoe three years ago, barely escaping from Brock Laxdal. The way she saw things, the Low Rider had saved her life and deserved better treatment than being abandoned on the terrorists' plane.

"Fine." *No time for an argument.* "We need to find out what else the Chromes are keeping in here. And we need to do it quickly. Then we need to build our *own* pallet. We'll replace everything on the last platform with stuff that *we* need."

"Starting with your ex's million-dollar briefcase."

"Right. *Three* million, not just one million."

"Very nice."

✞

Forty-five minutes later, the pallet was complete with a net and multiple tie-down straps securing the load. Sonya had done most of the work on the pallet, uncertain half the time of what Trey was up to.

She finished tightening the net's buckles, noticing the scientist now working with wires he'd exposed on the ramp's three-button control panel.

"Whatcha doing?" she queried, weaving up to him through various obstacles.

"Rewiring this console," he replied. "If this works, I will have total control of the loading ramp while the pilot unknowingly has none."

"Wow. How's that going?"

"I think I'm almost done."

Sonya studied the control panel. Two plastic conduits branched off from it. The first one ran along the wall to the back of the plane and entered the floor near the hinge of the closed ramp. The other pipeline, secured to the same wall, led to the front. She could think of no purpose for the tubing other than to protect wires that fed power to the rear opening. Common sense told her the second conduit was for giving the pilot control of the ramp.

"Couldn't you just cut this?" she suggested, pointing to the second pipe.

Trey paused the rewiring to give the plumbing a few once-overs. With a headshake, he showed resentment toward his time-wasting oversight. "You're absolutely right," he admitted. "Instead of the hard way, let's do this the *smart* way. While I put these wires back how they were, can you find something to sever that link?"

"Sure." She ransacked the drawers of a composite tool kit until she found a set of bolt cutters. With the heavy instrument, she pinched the conduit.

SNAP!

The pipeline and wires inside were cleanly cut. Trey completed his work on the console two minutes later.

The two stowaways donned parkas, gloves, and their helmets. They'd found hoses to link their headgear to small air tanks strapped to their backs beneath their parachutes. Sonya was slightly annoyed from not finding her backpack of cash, albeit it paled in comparison to the briefcase's contents. Then Trey drew her attention to a more relevant matter.

"Cuffs?" he told her.

They both removed one glove and flanked a vertical pipe on the wall with their exposed wrists. They weren't sure of the conduit's function, but could tell it was solid enough for their plan. The cold handcuffs were closed, one on his wrist, the other on hers. The short chain connecting the restraints went behind the steel pipeline so they wouldn't be sucked out when the plane depressurized; they didn't entirely trust the strength of their grip under such extreme circumstances. As they re-donned their gloves and gripped the metal tube, their nervous breathing was loud again in the confines of their helmets.

"Where is the key to these cuffs?" he asked her. She frantically searched her jumpsuit, raising his pulse as much as hers. Then she showed it to him. Letting his helmeted head fall against the wall, he let out a sigh of relief. "Good. Hang onto it for dear life." She nodded, putting it in a breast pocket and zipping it. "Ready?" Another nod.

The bottom button was pushed.

All the trash from their MRE lunch instantly vanished. Wind whistled through the cargo hold with tornado-like ferocity that raised their feet off the floor and aimed them toward the tail. They looked beyond their boots where the lowering ramp revealed a majestic sapphire sky filled with sun-gilded clouds thirty-two thousand feet above sea level. Tarps flapped beneath nets securing the loads as shipment paperwork fluttered loose from the freight.

In the compartment ahead of the plane's cargo hold, Tricks, Skewer, and Frosty observed the oxygen masks dropping and dangling from the ceiling. In response, they all ripped their helmets off so they could put on the life-saving devices.

The cockpit was loud with a warning buzzer as two more masks were donned and the copilot beheld a screen at his two o'clock position. A lighted diagram of the jet showed a flashing red square inside the fuselage near the tail. Further down, RAMP OPEN flickered continuously on the screen. To no avail, the copilot repeatedly pushed a button to close the ramp.

"What's going on?" the worried pilot shouted over the buzzer. "Are we losing pressure in the tail?"

"Yes! There's a malfunction with the cargo ramp!" his comrade explained.

"Close it!"

"I *can't* close it! Dive! Dive *now!* Get us to ten thousand feet, *fast!*"

Four turbine engines shrieked as the massive aircraft plummeted. The stowaways' feet were back on the floor as the pressure in the tilting hold equaled what was outside. The handcuffs saved them again—this time from somersaulting against their will to the front of the jet. While their surroundings shivered from turbulence, they shivered from the altitude's freezing temperatures. Sonya threw her free arm around Trey, anxious to get warm. He gladly returned the half-embrace, knowing it would not have helped if they'd not found the parkas.

The three minutes it took for the jumbo jet to reach ten thousand feet felt like hours. When the right altitude arrived, the airplane leveled out and the engines' pitch dropped.

"Get these cuffs off, quick!" Trey insisted. "Now that we're in breathable air, the crew will likely come back here to investigate—with assault rifles in hand."

Sonya fitted the key to both holes, freeing them. She followed Trey to the last pallet, which sat two feet from the lowered cargo ramp. The only thing keeping the aluminum platform from falling out was a pair of stoppers set in twin, rollerized tracks that ran along the floor to ease cargo loading.

Boarding the platform, the stowaways were happy to see land instead of sea through gaps in the clouds, albeit they'd included an inflatable life raft on their pallet. Still, the world was frightfully far below. Doubts of surviving the drop began to fill their minds.

Sonya grew annoyed by how the passing seconds of hesitation worsened her fear. "Come on!" she snapped, taking a stopper handle. Shiny rollers spun as the steel safety device was removed from them. Gripping the net that secured the pallet's load, the duo steeled themselves for the drop. They took deep breaths as Sonya pulled the other stopper and chucked it away in one movement.

They two-handed the webbing as the platform glided backward. Once it was halfway off the rollers, it tilted, landing on the ramp's rollers—where it didn't stay long.

Two hearts raced as the pallet exited the plane and plummeted.

Fifty feet later, a motion sensor signaled devices fixed to the platform's corners. In the same fraction of a second, four parachutes deployed from every corner, keeping the pallet level as it continued to drop at a much slower rate. The chutes on Trey's and Sonya's backs were only there as a precaution.

Sonya glimpsed the big black aircraft leaving them behind. Keeping one hand on the netting, she doffed her helmet, wanting Trey to hear her next words. She tucked the helmet under the mesh and leaned closer to him as the roaring wind tossed her hair.

"These parachutes may be saving us from gravity, but they won't save us from the Chromes. We're sitting ducks. The plane could turn around and waste us with its cannon, like it did that news helicopter yesterday. What's to stop it from doing that?"

Trey did with his helmet what Sonya had done with hers. Then he pulled a small black remote from a breast pocket of his jumpsuit. "Just this," he replied, flipping a switch atop the remote near its short antenna. On the face of the controller, ARMED appeared on a tiny screen. Further down was a square red button. When he pushed it, they heard a *click!* The screen went blank for half a second before it displayed DETONATING.

When they returned their eyes to the departing cargo jet, they felt the heat from chains of explosions that thunderously devoured the whale-like aircraft from tail to nose, fuselage to wingtips. Hundreds of twirling fragments flew as yellow blasts expanded, turning orange, then red, then black. Despite the noon light, the fourth of July had nothing on the spectacle.

After eyeballing the flaming debris raining from the growing cloud of smoke, Sonya beamed at the man responsible. "What is that thing you're holding?"

"The remote to a bomb I found when we were exploring their pallets," he explained in an elation-filled tone. "I set the bomb on the second pallet, which was mostly loaded with explosives."

"Very nice! How did you know how to work it?"

"I read the instructions."

She showed him the palm of one glove, cuing him. The remote, no longer having a purpose, was chucked away so he could high-five her.

Slowly dropping into a sea-like cloud layer, the pallet and its parachutes disappeared. When it emerged from the bottom, the platform's two passengers saw civilization beneath them. For two minutes, they basked in the view, exchanging guesses about which big city they were about to land in.

With a *CLACK!* the pallet came down on the roof of a high-rise.

DALLAS

The two-year-old building was called the Olivine. Clad in thousands of teal glass panels, the four-star hotel was a bundled tube structure, similar to the Burj Khalifa in Dubai. Albeit the highest cylindrical tube-unit, where the pallet had landed, did not exceed seventy-one floors, the lavish skyscraper was a true marvel on its block.

None of this was yet known to the pair on the roof. All they saw were antennas, satellite dishes, ventilators, air-conditioning units, smokestacks, and drainage vents cluttering a vast circle of pavement. In the center of everything was a concrete cube, seven feet high and wide on each side. Recessed into the cube was one steel door—the only way off the roof.

The duo stepped off the loaded pallet, shrugging off their parachutes, air tanks, and parkas. As Sonya drank in the breathtaking view of the city, Trey began rolling up the platform's four parachutes and stuffing them back in their sources—he detested them waving in the wind like flags, as if announcing his presence.

"Where do you think we are?" she asked.

"I don't know," Trey replied, glimpsing three directions. To the north, he saw the globe atop Reunion Tower. "Actually, I *do* know. We're in Dallas, Texas."

"Texas?"

"Yeah. That's the Hyatt over there." Trey pointed at the tower—the most significant feature of the other high-rise hotel. During his youth, his father had used a week of vacation time to bring the whole family to see the highlights of Dallas—mainly Six Flags. The Hyatt was where they'd stayed every night of the week.

"Never heard of the Hyatt."

"Well, this building we're on must be new; I don't remember anything this big being south of the Hyatt last time I was here."

"What *is* this building? Another hotel?"

"Probably." He started rolling up the last parachute. "Can you go downstairs and see? If this is a hotel, you should get us rooms till we figure out what to do next."

"Why me? I— Oh, I forgot; your face is all over the TV."

"Exactly. Before you go, grab some cash from the briefcase."

"Okay." After pulling the briefcase through the net, she studied the gold dials. "What's the combo?"

"Uh…three-one-two on the left, nine-seven-eight on the right… I think."

"You think?" she scoffed, spinning the dials. A sigh of relief escaped her lungs when it popped open. She took out a bundle of Franklins. "Be right back."

"Okay. Turn your jumpsuit inside out. You have to hide the evidence that it belonged to a Chrome Falcon trooper."

"Turn it inside out? In front of you?" She scoffed at the idea. "Forget it, Trey. I'm not showing you my underwear."

He rolled his eyes. "I meant in the *stairwell*. I doubt it gets used much this high up. Now, please, go in there and turn that stupid jumpsuit inside out."

"Forget the jumpsuit." She opened the left saddlebag on her Harley and pulled tattered jeans, her tie-dye T-shirt of six blues, and a zippered leather case.

"Even better." He wasn't sure what the third item was for.

✞

With his own jumpsuit inside out, Trey sauntered laps around the roof with only the view of Dallas to take his mind off the boredom. He'd been waiting nearly a half hour for Sonya to return. When his stroll brought him near the pallet again, he paused, letting the wind flutter his jumpsuit and flaxen shock of curly hair.

Should I search these boxes again for anything resembling a transmitter? he asked himself, hoping the Chromes had no way to track their location. *Was my search ten minutes ago thorough enough? I think it was. I wonder if the Chromes have a satellite above the Earth that could find this pallet.* He mulled over this last possibility as he eyed the blue-and-white arch of the sky.

CLACK!

The door's push-bar startled Trey. He spun, finding Sonya back on the roof. As the door closed behind her, he decided her worn-out jeans and outdated shirt were still a significant improvement over the loose jumpsuit she'd worn earlier.

"I had to disable the lock on the inside of that door," she said, strolling up to him. "I guess the hotel staff doesn't want people up here."

"I see," he replied, observing a two-foot-high wall that rimmed the roof. It offered meager prevention against suicidal jumps. *Why waste the concrete when you can just lock the door?* "How'd you disable the lock?"

"With this." She showed him the small leather case she'd taken earlier from her Harley. "It's my dad's lock pick kit. He was a locksmith, I was his little helper, and after he died, my lawless years helped me hone my skill."

"I see."

"Sorry about the accommodations, but I could only get one room."

"No problem." He'd never shared a hotel room with a woman before and didn't want to admit the idea of it intrigued him a little.

"The front desk won't let you have your own room unless you show them a photo ID. And we both know that's not possible since the media made you infamous."

"Right. Any good news?"

"Yes. The room has two queen-size beds. When we need privacy from each other, there's always the bathroom, right?"

"Right." Trey took up one of the two helmets from the pallet after unplugging the air hose from it; he would need it to hide his face on the way to their room. "What room are we in?"

"Room 5212. It's in *this* tower, nineteen floors down."

"Good. Let's take the stairs all the way there. What's the nightly rate?"

"Two hundred and twenty." She took up the cash-filled briefcase and followed him to the stairs. "I know we could have easily afforded a suite, but I think we should conserve this cash."

"Agreed."

They started down the concrete steps and fluorescent-lit landings.

"What shall we do while we stay here?" she queried, her voice resonating through the stairwell like they were in a cave.

"I don't know yet," he answered, donning the helmet. "Maybe prepare ourselves for our next encounter with Chromes. If we're lucky, there won't be one."

After a long shower, Trey was in a white bath robe of Turkish linen, sleeping peacefully atop the covers of his bed for three hours. His deep slumber was interrupted by the *click* of the door opening. He sat up, scarcely recognizing the tall, pale woman who came in, wearing brand-new clothes from neck to feet. Above Sonya's nape, most of her curly raven hair was rolled up neatly into a large bun. Over her eyes were black, oval-lensed shades. She wore a forest-green dress coat that hung to her upper thighs. Exposed by the open coat, a tan T-shirt read PRAYER WARRIOR in black Nyala text. Beneath the tucked-in shirt were skintight jeans with a pewter-studded belt that matched the walnut shade of her hiking boots.

"I think I'm done shopping for today," she said, collapsing the handle of a new roll-around suitcase.

"Get me anything?"

"Simple men's clothes, fake glasses, fake mustache, hair dye, you know, the usual stuff." She doffed the wool coat and turned to hang it up in the closet, revealing Zuri's Glock tucked down the waist of her black denims. "Now you can throw away that stupid jumpsuit." She removed the sunglasses and pistol from her person and set them on the nightstand. Trey eyed the gun for a minute, wondering where the nearest shooting range was.

"Oh, I forgot. Where is the 'Room Occupied' sign?"

"It's right where it should be—hanging outside our door, where it will stay until we check out of the Olivine, whenever that will be."

"Good. We don't need a maid coming in here every day and possibly seeing me without my disguise on."

"Or finding the helmet you hid in the closet. Or seeing the firearms I plan to bring down later from the roof."

✞

For the rest of the day, the pair watched TV and ordered room service—with Trey hiding in the bathroom when the food arrived. On the second day, they colored his yellow Jewfro as black as Sonya's hair. She did most of the work with the hair dye and admired the results as they gazed in the bathroom mirror together, exchanging smiles. To some extent, they thought they looked like brother and sister.

Later, they made three trips to the roof to fetch three of the four wood containers on the pallet and take them down to their room. As they carried the heavy, suitcase-sized boxes down the stairs, they were thankful the trunks had rope handles on each end.

Following a fourth visit to the roof, the aluminum platform was, with great difficulty, slid out of sight atop the cement block with the access door. The nets, tie-downs, other helmet, Sonya's Harley, and the last box were hidden beneath a tarp behind an AC unit.

Like the containers taken to room 5212, loaded guns and extra ammo filled the one by the Low Rider. They left the trunk in a corner that would be of no interest to any maintenance man who might have work to do on the roof. In case Trey and Sonya ever needed to arm themselves and couldn't get to their room for some reason, they now had an alternate gun stash.

The bike was left under the same tarp as the guns since Sonya felt it would be safer there than the parking garage. They had more than enough cash to rent a car.

Daily, the odd pair watched TV, happy to see Trey Radisson was not big news for long and that no one knew the name of his "accomplice" or what her eyes looked like. For weeks, they dined out, went to movies, amusement parks, and fall festivals, using a rented Chevy Malibu, which only Sonya drove; if they were ever pulled over, they couldn't have the cop asking to see *Trey's* license.

Albeit he was no fan, Trey wore his new Dallas Cowboys ball cap every time he left the room. He also never forgot to put on the fake mustache and glasses with lenses that were like windows—neither concave nor convex.

Trey often let Sonya drive him to the nearest shooting range. She familiarized him with firearms and helped him hone his marksmanship while keeping her own from getting rusty. In her opinion, the first week was the most trying since the gentle genius had never used a gun before. Once he became comfortable with the single-shot firearms, they found an isolated spot outside town for him to try the Uzi.

Visiting nearly every jeweler in Dallas, they sold a few diamonds at a time since selling the entire bag in one place would look suspicious. Sonya had the precious stones' value put on her debit card since she and Trey didn't want to become entirely dependent on the cash-filled briefcase. Once they ran out of rocks, they went to an ATM where Sonya did a balance inquiry on her checking account. The screen displayed $944,736.34. She smiled from ear to ear, never before seeing her balance so high. Last time she'd checked, it was just under four thousand.

"Don't worry. I won't forget that half of this is yours," she promised Trey, who stood next to her, eyeing the number.

"Thank you. Too bad this is less than half of what all the stones were worth. Still, the jewelers have to make a profit, don't they?"

"Yeah. Are you sure your account is frozen?"

"I'm *not* sure. But if I test my card, I'm *very* sure it will give away our whereabouts to the authorities."

Six days a week, they went to the Olivine's gym, which was surprisingly large, even for the high-rise hotel. They warmed up their limbs with some racquetball, and then headed straight to either the weight room or cardio room. Every Monday, Wednesday, and Saturday, Sonya did crunches and pumped iron for at least an hour. Every Sunday, Tuesday, and Thursday, she used a treadmill for the same amount of time. No matter what she did, she always encouraged Trey to do the same.

For him, the hardest challenge was getting used to the kind of exercise that left him drenched in sweat. In San Antonio, he'd rarely gone to the gym and, when he did, it was only for a mild thirty-minute walk on the treadmill to help settle a heavy meal. Each time he thought about quitting at the Olivine, Sonya reminded him of the extremists, who were most likely scouring the U.S. for the two of them every day. Therefore, he pressed on with the exercises, wanting to be faster, stronger, anything to raise his chances of escaping the Chromes if they found him again.

After Sonya cajoled him into her workout routine, he was sore every day, but sleeping quite well each night. The more he adhered to her sequences on cardio and resistance training, the more he wanted to repeat them the following week. Noticing the energy increase provided by his developing muscles, he wondered why he'd waited so long to take fitness seriously.

Most of the Olivine's male gym rats—and even a few of the females—shared Trey's second hardest challenge: keeping his wandering eyes off Sonya's chiseled abs and shapely muscles. As much as Trey adored the sight of his free personal trainer in yoga pants and a sports bra, he still felt compelled to ask her to wear a large T-shirt over them. She honored his request, knowing he needed no distractions. They both needed their physical prowess as high as possible.

Every evening, they checked the hidden goods on the roof to make sure they'd not been disturbed. Afterward, the offbeat duo would occasionally practice self-defense moves—Sonya being the teacher, Trey the student—and watch the sun go down before leaving the roof and returning to their room.

After a pleasant afternoon at the Six Flags theme park in Arlington, Trey and Sonya were astride the latter's motorcycle as she headed back to the Olivine. Traffic turned more congested as they neared the center of Dallas.

"This is so weird," Sonya thought aloud.

"What's so weird?" Trey replied.

"I think we have an airborne foe following us."

Trey looked behind them. Over the orange disc of the setting sun was the black form of a nearing cargo plane, no different than the one Chrome Falcon flew.

It was flying directly toward them.

"Oh, great!" he groused, becoming a nervous wreck. "They found us again! Step on it!"

The speedometer climbed from fifty to seventy as the roaring Harley snaked through other motorists down a canyon formed by the street and buildings. The jet came closer, dropping in speed and elevation.

"Waste that plane!" Sonya ordered, holding up the back of her leather jacket and T-shirt with both hands as her ride effectively steered itself. Trey looked down at her exposed lower back. Where flesh and bone should have been, he saw a gleaming metal spine, circuit board, wires, hoses, and hydraulic actuators. Jutting from the machinery was the grip of an Uzi.

“You’re not human?” he gasped.

“Long story! Just take the bird down!”

After he pulled the machine pistol from her body, she tugged her clothing back in place. He spun on the passenger seat to face backward, not sure how he turned so easily without falling off. The safety catch was taken off and he held the Uzi upward, putting the jumbo jet in his iron sites. Despite having four turbine engines, the aircraft was somehow able to do the impossible—keep the distance of a football field between itself and the speeding two-wheeler.

A thirty-millimeter cannon fired from where the plane’s front landing gear should have been, brutally raking the street below. Vehicles and chunks of pavement exploded in the cycle’s wake. Trey returned fire, dazed by the way the daring pilot kept the jet’s wingtips only a few yards over the roofs of the five-story structures flanking the four-lane street. Seconds later, he’d fired off over eighty nine-millimeter slugs, not sure why he didn’t need to reload.

A car-size blast below the aircraft’s nose announced the feat of Trey’s marksmanship; he’d miraculously disabled the jet’s only weapon. Smoke trailed from the ruined cannon as it spun in three circles and slowed to a halt. The Low Rider flew past a twenty-story building. Without enough time to avoid the obstacle, the plane ripped most of its left wing off on the passing structure, demolishing windows and columns on the seventh and eighth floors. While awed by the scene, Trey guessed the trigger-happy pilot had been too distracted by the cannon’s impairment to see the building coming.

Dropping below the rooftops of even the shortest structures, the jet entered the street—a street too narrow to accommodate its other wing, which was torn completely off and left behind. The ruined cannon was crushed beneath the weight of the fuselage. Thousands of sparks were produced by the aircraft rasping across the blacktop as flames quivered where the wings had been. Cars, streetlights, and traffic lights were knocked aside by the fuselage’s nose as it slid past higher structures and closed the distance between itself and its target.

The Harley raced under a trio of third-story skywalks that linked high-rise buildings flanking the avenue. Seeing the unstoppable remains of the cargo jet coming with more momentum than a wrecking ball, business people shrieked, dropped paperwork, and evacuated the enclosed walkways. The fuselage didn't slow as it plowed through the first, second, then third obstacle with deafening severity that produced vast clouds of glass shards. By the thousands, crystal fragments chimed and skipped across every square foot of pavement between the Low Rider and aircraft.

More glass crumbled as Trey's Uzi sprayed across the cockpit's half-circle of windows; he hoped something else might explode from the shots and slow the plane. The nine-millimeter rounds collapsed more than enough tinted glass to expose the pilot—a Filipino woman.

Lieutenant Zuri Navarro.

Gnashing her teeth, she eyeballed Trey with unimaginable rage. Just as she took aim at him with her own loaded Uzi, a blast in the cockpit vaporized her. The remaining glass was dislodged as fire fluttered from all the jet's windows. Another much larger explosion broke the aircraft in two. The colossal tail tumbled behind and wrecked the face of another building.

Like a gargantuan torpedo, the wingless remains of the plane kept coming toward the fleeing duo astride the bike as they zigzagged around more motorists who didn't clear the street soon enough. Feeling the heat from the flaming cockpit, Trey watched in horror as the tip of the fuselage came within yards of his ride.

Yards became feet.

Feet became inches.

Then—

—he sat up in bed, winded and soaked in perspiration.

His head spun left where his bulging eyes drank in the real Dallas through the floor-to-ceiling window of the dark hotel room. Sparkling fifty-two floors below was a sea of city lights.

"Trey?"

He turned right, barely seeing the other queen-size bed where

Sonya—the *real* Sonya—was tucked in. Her motorcycle had never left the roof. And she was certainly no robot.

"Oh, thank God," he wheezed, letting his head fall back on the pillow. He replayed the bad dream in his head, recalling other moments that clashed with reality. Once he identified five of them, his thoughts returned to Sonya.

Why was she a robot in my dream? he wondered. *Was that inspired by her body's perfection? Maybe. If I could build a robot and had a reason to make it female, I suppose I would make the body as flawless as hers. It would definitely sell better.*

"Let me guess," Sonya said in a raspy, fatigued voice. "You had a bad dream about the Chromes, right?"

"Bingo. I'm sorry I woke you."

A deep yawn escaped her mouth as she eyed the blue digits on the clock atop the nightstand between their beds. It was 4:37 in the morning. "It's okay; we are free to sleep whenever we want, you know." She recalled an event she wanted to tell him. "I had a bad dream myself about those high-tech monsters a couple nights ago. It was like I was looking a year into the future, or something. I was off-roading on my bike near the Rockies, I think. As the sun was going down, some military base on the horizon was getting annihilated by missiles or something. They seemed to just come out of thin air. I didn't realize they were being fired from three invisible choppers… until they turned visible."

Trey pondered the tragic story. "Sounds familiar."

"Familiar to what?"

"To the nightmare *I* had three years ago, just before I destroyed my VV1. So, what happened next in your dream? Anything?"

"Yes. The choppers flew past a mountain. Then the peak was hit by some kind of light beam from the sky. I don't know if it was the power of God, or what, but it drilled all the way through the mountain. After that, the helicopters lost power and crashed. It was like they were being controlled from someone inside the mountain—someone God wanted dead."

Her friend chewed this over. "What do you think all that means?"

"Maybe the Chromes' command center is inside a mountain. I just wish we knew *what* mountain. I think God is going to stop Chrome Falcon somehow. And I also think you should never, *ever* reinvent that cloaking machine."

"Believe me, I won't. I don't have a clue why I was given the ability to create that stupid device. Maybe someday God will tell me why."

"You're a genius, Trey, but I don't blame you for getting rid of it. Can you imagine where the world would be now if you had kept it?"

"I'd rather not imagine that." He sat up to admire the view of Dallas again. "I hate thinking about that stuff…almost as much as dying. I would have died in that dream I just had if it had been real."

Sonya considered his words. "You fear death a lot, don't you?" She beheld the silhouette of his nodding head. "Why?"

"I don't know." He felt his eyes starting to well. "I guess I'm a coward. I hate the unknown. I don't know what will happen when I die. I don't know how painful it will be. And what scares me the most is knowing it's…inevitable." With the corner of his blanket, he wiped the moisture from his eyes. "You must think I'm pretty pathetic."

"Not at all. Cut yourself some slack. You're a scientist, not a Navy SEAL. Besides, I've had fears like that too."

"But no more, right?"

"No more."

"How?" He faced her, even though the darkness made her face nearly impossible to see. "How are you like that? How are you so fearless?"

"I know I'm going to Heaven when I die. I'm a devout believer in God."

Trey recalled a few pleasant Sundays during the first twenty years of his life. "My parents are the same way. I wish *I* was. It would be nice to lose my fear of death."

"Who says you can't be a believer?"

"I don't know. Ever since I went to the California Institute of Technology and pursued my love for science, I became so focused on what *I* could make possible, I lost focus on what *God* can make possible. But I still recall the people in church who sang hymns with their eyes closed and hands in the air. I want to feel what they felt. I want to feel connected…but I don't know how. I never did." He let his head fall back on the pillow and eyed the ceiling.

"Will you go to church with me this coming Sunday?" Sonya asked.

He considered this and beamed. "I'd love to. Where?"

"Don't know yet. We'll find a place. I know I've said this before, but we should also find an apartment soon. I don't like how fast our money is going at this fancy hotel."

"Yeah, I know."

Their first encounter near Colorado Springs returned to his mind. Then he recalled the time in Denver she'd warned him to exit the limo and get on her bike before the cops caught up with him. The next day, she'd rescued him from CFCC. She'd saved his hide three times and done things for him no woman had ever done. Ever since they'd landed in Dallas, her company had done nothing but make him a better person. He'd never known anyone like her. She was beautiful, tough, and entirely devoted to his well-being.

He sat back up and switched on the lamp so he could see her better.

"What's with the light?" she carped, squinting at him.

"I just wanted to look at you."

As her mind digested the slightly awkward moment, her deep blue eyes flicked to various objects in the room before returning to his gentle gray gaze, filled with deep admiration for her. "O…kay."

"You've been so good to me. And you saved my life more than once."

She briefly pointed a finger at him. "Let me remind you that *you* also saved *mine*. The Chromes were going to execute me…until *you* spoke up. And if not for you and your genius ideas, I would have probably never escaped from that plane…or that nosy officer who stalled us on our way to the plane."

He nodded. "I hope we can keep dating, if that's what you call what we've been doing all this time."

"Absolutely. I've never had this much fun in my life. But we're still just friends. *Best* friends, actually." She sat up in her bed. "Before we become more than that, I need to see if we're *still* best friends in a few months or so. I've made too many mistakes in my life already. Besides, I promised my dad that if I ever meet Mr. Right—who might be *you*, by the way—I would not share a bed with him until he married me first. I already feel like I'm in the wrong, sharing a room with you."

"I completely understand." He eyed the TV as she took the remote, turned it on, and started flipping channels.

"Sorry for putting conditions on our friendship, especially with my best friend."

"Don't be. It makes me respect you more. You're just…amazing. If I *do* have a chance of being more than a friend to you, I'm willing to wait a *decade* for it."

This earned him more than an ear-to-ear smile from her; she was also blushing. No man had ever told her anything like that.

"And that makes *me* respect *you* more," she replied, feeling warm and fuzzy inside. "Maybe this Christmas we should find mistletoe to stand under."

"Okay, but it won't be easy for me to wait until then."

"Me neither. If you continue to be really good to me, it might be sooner."

When she changed the channel again, what appeared next on the screen was *The Xavier Fenderson Show*, a talk show that started two years ago.

"Change it, quick!" Trey groaned.

"I've never heard of this show," Sonya said, flipping to a televised museum tour. "Is it that bad?"

"I can't stand Fenderson and his absurdly ignorant thoughts on current world events. It's bad enough that idiots think they have a lot to teach us. It's even worse that we can't keep them off the TV. And what in the world is this?"

"I don't know."

The screen showed an elderly man in a three-piece suit wandering through an exhibition hall. He paused in front of a globe of the earth that stood twice his height. Then he faced the camera to speak.

"This globe brings me to my next point," he said eloquently. "Isn't it odd how every atheist in the world believes that someone, *someone*, created this model of the earth...yet they *don't* believe anyone made the *real* earth?"

"Wow! I think that guy just disproved evolution," Trey thought aloud.

"Yeah," Sonya agreed. "I think I'll remember that thought-provoking sentence for the rest of my life."

Two minutes later, the show ended so a yawn-inducing nature show could begin.

Sonya flipped to the next channel. It featured amusing video clips from the Internet. She couldn't remember the name of the show, but decided it would do. For several minutes, the duo laughed at the lengthy collection of fail videos and the host's thoughts on each one. Then a series of cat clips came on. Toasters, balloons, water sprinklers, remote-control cars, and other things frightened the skittish felines. One tabby ran from a plastic bag hooked on its tail. The orange cat reminded Trey of his youth.

"My mom once had a cat like that." He sighed, remembering the main reason he'd left his home in San Antonio—to go see his parents. "Man, I miss her and Dad."

Sonya gave him a sympathetic look. "At least you still have family."

"That's true." He recalled their second week in Dallas when she'd told him what had happened to her family. Her mom deserted her and died of lung cancer. Her dad died from riding his motorcycle drunk. Her grandma passed away months ago, making her the only living member of her family. "I'm sorry to bring that up. You probably don't want to hear me carry on about things you miss having."

"No, that's okay."

"I'm nearly going crazy, forcing myself to stay off phones and computers."

"It must be very unnatural for a techie like you."

"Indeed. I can't remember being away from a computer this long."

"Did you use social media much?"

"Not really." He thought of Vyron Truax from his days at Envisiocom. "I once had a friend who told me that the more you use social media, the more you become socially incompetent."

"That's true."

"I *would* use it now if I could…just to see how my family is doing. I keep wondering how much the press and authorities have been harassing them…over me. I hope it hasn't been much. They must be worried sick about me."

"I'm sure they are, but it's imperative you not contact them in any way. Not yet. The cops probably rigged their phones to trace every call they get."

Facing the window again, he sighed and nodded. "I know. And I'm sure they gave their computers, email accounts, and Facebook accounts similar treatment." He eyed the northwest skyline, haloed by the lights of Dallas. Somewhere beyond it was Winter Park, Colorado, where his beloved parents lived. Cherished memories from the first twenty years of his life passed through his mind. Then he eyed the sooty sky above, filled with dark purple clouds. There, he imagined the kind eyes of God looking down on him. Knowing the Creator could read his thoughts, he focused on the most appropriate ones he could think of.

God, I haven't talked to You in weeks. Please forgive me for that. Please forgive me for many things. You know what they are. I am in desperate need of Your help now. I'm tired of being a runaway. Please help me find a way to see my family again.

Days later, on the Olivine's highest enclosed floor, Trey and Sonya sat at a booth-style table in the sumptuous Vista Steakhouse, where they adhered to the establishment's business-casual dress code. Grandiose chandeliers and burgundy, tassel-lined drapes hung from the high, coffered ceiling. The ritzy eatery was further graced with potted greenery, floral-patterned woodwork, and rococo-framed reproductions of William-Adolphe Bouguereau's most varicolored paintings. A well-dressed pianist deftly played a number of melancholy and rousing songs on a polished grand piano. None of the waiters or other diners had any idea Sonya's Harley was on the roof just above them.

"One Heineken and one ice tea," a black-and-white-clad waitress announced with a German accent. She neared their table and set the glass and green bottle down on the maroon tablecloth. The couple's focus was on a broad window within arm's reach of their seats. Through the glass they saw a seventy-story-high view of East Dallas—a sight that had inspired the restaurant's name.

"Thank you," Trey replied as he and his date turned to their cold drinks. Then he read ASTA on the woman's nametag. "Where are you from, ma'am?"

"Germany."

He recalled a few things his father had told him about his travels in Europe. "Is it true that you can get a steep fine for spitting on the sidewalk in Germany?"

"That's right. When it comes to germs versus Germans, the Germans win every time."

"I believe it." He and Sonya chuckled at Asta's witty remark.

"I'll be back soon to take your order…unless you need more time, of course." The waitress strode away to attend other tables.

"That view is distracting, isn't it?" Sonya said, returning her attention to the window while gripping the top of her beer and twisting.

"Indeed."

"We can see East Dallas from here and *West* Dallas from our room." Gritting her teeth, she twisted harder at the bottle. "Man, that lid is really on there. Can you get it off?" She held the Heineken out to him.

"What lid?"

For the first time, she looked at the uncovered mouth of the bottle. "Oh. I'm retarded." She took several swallows.

He pensively eyed her droplet-covered bottle after she set it down. It was already half empty. "Sorry for asking, but you being a Christian and all, I didn't think you drank alcohol anymore. We've dined together for weeks and this is the first time I've seen it."

"It's my birthday today, Trey," she shot back. "You know that. Besides, I haven't had one in years. I think I've earned it. Not only am I rich for the first time in my life, but I'm sharing a table with the best friend I've ever had. So, I want to celebrate."

The smile lines flanking his large nose became more apparent. "Yeah, me too."

They focused on their menus. By the time they placed their orders, the Heineken bottle was empty. An hour later, Trey had eaten a Caesar salad and filet mignon with a side of sweet potatoes. Sonya had finished her beet salad and parmesan-crusted chicken with asparagus—and fifth beer. As she amused him with wild stories from the first fifteen years of her life, his reminders to keep her voice down became more frequent with each drink she had.

He wasn't sure which story he liked best. The ones that stood out included the time she'd said, "You're not dead! You're faking it!" at a funeral, "Where's the little diaper?" when she and her father were gazing at the stars, and "Wake up, Grandma!" during a church service. Then, as Iza drove them home, she ran over an empty donut box, which stayed stuck to the bottom of her Subaru for three miles.

Then came her school shenanigans. She'd launched a rubber band from the back of the bus, popping a fat boy in the back of the neck. So, he turned around to beat another boy sitting behind him. In a science class, the teacher had the students dissect starfish, but Sonya was more interested in wearing her starfish's five arms on the fingers of her left hand.

"And during my sophomore year in high school," she continued, "the head cheerleader was a senior named Madison. Her boyfriend, Tyler, was also a senior…and a stupid pervert. Even though he was dating the most popular girl in school, he still wasn't satisfied and started flirting with *me*. When Madison saw this, she assumed I encouraged it. She stomped on my toes and ran off like a little coward. The next day, I stuck a maxi pad to her backpack and let her walk down the halls with it. We changed classes three times that day before she noticed it. For the rest of the week, she was the laughingstock of the school. But the week after, she found out I did it and dumped a bottle of honey in my locker."

Trey shook his head in disgust. "And she thought she would get away with that?"

"Of course; she was a wishful-thinking moron. Wishful thinking tells *millions* of people that bad choices will make them feel better. It's been that way for centuries."

"True. How did you respond?"

"At the next basketball game, I sniped her with my dad's paintball gun while she and the other cheerleaders were doing a dance routine at halftime. It was the most humiliating night of her high school life. I'm still amazed I got out of the gym without being caught. Since I was wearing a mask, I heard later that Madison assumed I must have been one of her many bitter ex-boyfriends."

He barely suppressed a laugh. "Sounds pretty wild."

"That wasn't wild. Wild would have been me wearing nothing

but rollerblades and skating past rush-hour traffic while talking on the phone with my grandma. Wild would have been—"

"I get the point," he silenced her, showing her the palms of his hands. Then he gave the nearest tables a concerned once-over, noticing a few heads had turned. "Geez, will you keep your voice down? I don't know where you get these ideas from, but I hope it's not your own experiences."

She smiled at him. "You'll never know."

"I can't help but wonder what made you so feisty."

"My dad was Irish, my mom Colombian."

"That explains a lot."

"Wait till you hear about my *junior* year. I was at the prom and— Did you go to *your* high school prom?"

Trey shook his head. "No one would go with me."

"Oh, I'm sorry."

"I'm not. To me, the prom looked like nothing but a chance for poor kids to imitate rich kids. I've had a lot of coworkers who lived the same way. I never understood poor people who pretend to be rich. The reverse makes more sense."

She eyeballed him with keen admiration. "You hit the nail on the head…with a *sledge*hammer."

"Anyhow, go ahead with your prom story."

"Okay, so, there was thi—"

Four waiters interrupted her as they gathered around the table, singing "Happy Birthday" and clapping for rhythm. She drew multiple grins as she bobbed her head to the song with enough intensity to loosen the bun above her nape and let her hair fall free around her shoulders. As one waiter tied a balloon to the coat hook fixed to the side of Sonya's seat, another set a dessert on a silver-rimmed saucer in front of her. A single candle burned atop a slice of seven-layer chocolate cake.

The waiters gave a light applause and departed. Grinning, she watched them head for the kitchen, then returned her gaze to her best friend. "Your idea?"

"The cake was. Not the song or balloon."

She reached across the table to squeeze his hand. "Thank you. That was very sweet." Liking the way his hand felt in the warmth of hers, he beamed, unaware she was about to ruin the moment. "Hey, wanna see something really cool?" She reached for the plastic holder between the salt and pepper shakers and took a packet of coffee creamer. The packet was given a few shakes and torn open. "I used to do this in McDonald's when I was a kid." She sprinkled some of the powder on the lighted candle, creating a fleeting fire over it. The brief roar of the flames turned a few heads, including Asta's.

"Will you stop that?" he groused, trying to keep his voice down. "You don't want to get thrown out of this place, do you?" For half a minute, she shivered with intense voiceless laughter. "No more beer in public, okay?" This only prolonged her bout of hilarity. When she held the pack over the candle again, he blew the flame out.

"You jackass!" she flared, throwing the packet at him. The smoking candle followed. "Now my wish won't come true." She speared the cake with a fork, unconcerned with the coffee creamer sprinkled on it. Her response to the first bite was an exaggerated moan of approval.

Once the cake was gone, she took Trey's steak knife and twisted around to see her balloon. The Algerian text on the green globe read: HAPPY BIRTHDAY FROM THE OLIVINE'S VISTA STEAKHOUSE. She sliced the string free from the coat hook as her free hand kept it from floating away. Then she bit down on the knotted valve and stretched it. While her left hand pinched the top of the valve, the blade in her right hand sliced it just above the knot.

"What are you doing now?" Trey scowled.

The balloon hissed as Sonya let some of the helium escape—directly into her lungs. Then she held it aside so she could see her table companion as she spoke.

"I saw a saw in Arkansas. It could out-saw any saw I ever saw."

Heads turned again to the source of the unnaturally high-pitched voice. With both elbows on the table, Trey did a face palm with both hands. He didn't even watch as his friend inhaled on the balloon again, intending to deflate the entire rubber globe in one breath.

When it was half the size of a minute ago, three onlookers saw her go saucer-eyed, then cross-eyed. When she blacked out, the balloon escaped her grip, flying to the next couple's table. Losing the last of its helium, it plopped into the wife's bowl of clam chowder, bringing an unbelieving look to her face.

At the same time, Sonya's upper body tilted left, letting her head thud against the window. Trey looked up, seeing her closed eyes and fallen jaw through a tangled web of her raven curls. She'd gone completely still.

"Sonya?" he uttered, growing concerned. "Sonya, are you okay?" Asta watched nervously as he moved to the birthday girl's side of the table. "Sonya?" He and the waitress started fearing the worst, and he gripped her shoulders and pulled her forward—

—then her eyes flew open, drawing a gasp of relief from her date and a few observers.

"That was…awesome!" she crowed, smiling. "I totally fainted from that!"

Trey cupped her face in his hands, making eye contact. "You gave me quite a scare, Sonya. Are you feeling okay?" She nodded with a lightheaded grin. "Can you sit still and pause the shenanigans while I go use the restroom?"

She combed her fingers through his dyed curls. "Whatever you say."

"Okay, I'll be back." He stood and strode past Asta. "Check?"

"You got it," the waitress answered, setting a leather booklet on the table.

As Trey weaved through well-dressed couples seated at other tables, he spied the restroom sign ahead and muttered his next thought to himself. "Tomorrow I'm eating alone."

The following evening, Trey sat alone at a table in a Mexican restaurant where he enjoyed a black bean enchilada dinner. He could tell by the good food and pleasant atmosphere why the place had received decent ratings on Google. But it paled in comparison to where he'd eaten yesterday. No matter how great a place the Vista Steakhouse was, he doubted he would ever dine there again; it would only remind him of Sonya's embarrassing behavior, which drew unwanted eyes to both of them. Customers had clearly wondered when he would leave and take Miss Loud Mouth with him.

He wasn't as angry with her now as he was last night. Replaying some of her drunken silliness in his brain did not have the same effect on him now that it did four hours ago. Instead of upsetting him, the memories were now making him grin.

Hearing simulated flatulence to his right, he turned to see a father of three at a nearby table. He had two sons and one daughter, all in elementary school. The trio of siblings, bored with waiting on the food to arrive, made fart sounds with their armpits, drawing smiles from their dad as he sipped on a Coke.

"Mine's louder than yours!" the little girl bragged, still flapping her left elbow.

"Nuh-uh!" her younger brother countered, trying to prove her wrong.

"We got nothing on Dad," the older boy said. "And he don't

even need his arm."

Trey found himself as amused as the father. Until then, he thought only boys did this sort of thing, not girls. Then he noticed the uptight-looking mother returning to the table after a trip to the bathroom.

"Stop that!" she barked, silencing her whole family. As she sat down, she backhanded her husband's shoulder. "I leave you alone with the kids for five minutes and this happens? Quit laughing!"

Still grinning, Trey returned his focus to his half-eaten dinner. He wished Sonya was there to see the offbeat family. Then came thoughts and questions that filled him with regret.

Why did I come here alone? Why did I sneak out of the room and call a cab while Sonya was in the bathroom? Why did it take me this long to feel ready to forgive her?

While she wasn't sleeping or puking that day, Sonya repeatedly made one thing clear: she truly regretted downing all the Heinekens and needed to be reminded why she'd given up drinking. She's been miserable all day from her overindulgence. Trey could not fathom why he felt the need to protect himself from another recurrence. If Sonya ever got smashed again, it would not be for a very long time. Trey had not had dinner without her for weeks—and didn't want to again. To him, it just wasn't the same without her.

"Trey?"

His fork fell from his hand, clattering noisily on the plate.

What the...? Who just said my name? What's going on? No one knows who I am...except Sonya. And that was not her voice. This can't be good. Not good at all!

Through his fake glasses, he slowly gazed up the olive slacks and charcoal dress coat of the person standing near his table. At the top of the figure was the unfamiliar face of a black woman with neatly cornrowed hair hanging in multiple braids that grazed the shoulders of her wool coat. Frameless, narrow-lensed glasses complemented her friendly gaze. She appeared to be in her late forties or early fifties. Trey was unsure of how to describe her caramel-colored face other than very intelligent looking.

"Um…I'm sor— sorry?" he stammered.

Smiling, she took a seat in the booth across his table, eyeing him with esteem. "Trey Radisson. It's really you," she said sunnily.

That's it. I'm dead.

He lightly touched beneath his beaklike nose, thinking his false mustache must have fallen off. It was still there.

"That disguise may fool most people, but not me."

His heart raced as he shot glances around the restaurant, expecting to find others watching him. There were none.

"Relax, Mr. Radisson, I'm alone. Just don't run off before you hear me out, okay?"

Closing his eyes, he took a few deep breaths to calm his nerves before speaking. "Ma'am…who are you?"

"Nova Krenshaw, FBI."

"FBI?" He was certain this was the beginning of his freedom's end. "You're not going to arrest me?"

"No…at least not yet. And I'm taking a huge risk with my career by not apprehending you right now. You see, Trey, I'm— May I call you Trey?" He nodded slowly. "I'm not always as by-the-book as I'm expected to be, because I keep something in mind that most people in my line of work do not. Do you know what that is?"

"Uh…I give up. What is it?"

"No one is perfect. No one…including those controlling our news and laws. There are two sides to every story. I've already heard the media's side. Would you mind sharing *your* side with me?"

Trey could scarce believe this was happening. After all the time he'd spent hiding from the misled authorities, someone with the power to take his freedom had identified him. But, instead of taking him in, she was showing him mercy and giving him a chance to explain himself. He knew next to nothing about Nova Krenshaw, but already had immense respect for her.

The time in Colorado Springs flew through his brain. "Okay," he began. "In Colorado Springs, Chrome Falcon was not trying to *protect* me from the cops; they were trying to *capture* me, and the cops got in their way." The Denver scene was replayed next.

"Go on," Nova urged him.

"In Denver, they tried again to capture me…and succeeded. I know it looked like they were helping me *escape* justice…but that wasn't the case. Then they took me to their base and…" *It might be best to not mention the VV1. At least not yet.* "And…told me I had a choice: work for their science team or…be executed. Then I escaped. I was a stowaway on their cargo plane." He wasn't ready to bring Sonya into the story yet. "I jumped out with a parachute when the jet was over Dallas…but not before setting up a bomb."

"So, *you* are the one responsible for destroying that aircraft."

"Guilty as charged." *And proud of it too.*

"I know all about the bird. I was sent to this city to investigate the wreckage and search for other signs of Chrome Falcon. So, you have never worked for the Chromes?"

"Never." He stressed his words with an exaggerated headshake. "Definitely not."

"I believe you."

"You do?" *How is my account of what happened enough to convince her so fast?*

"Of course I believe you; I already questioned your coworkers in San Antonio. Albeit they were not happy you left them to the mercy of that disgruntled employee, they still spoke highly of your work ethic. They told me you were too much of a workaholic to have time for AA meetings, much less meetings with the Chromes."

"Really?" Knowing why the agent believed him, Trey felt terrible for not helping out his colleagues during his last night at Almighty IT.

"My team and I also searched your house and phone records. We found absolutely nothing to connect you to the Chromes. However, I have unfortunate news. The San Antonio Police are charging you with obstructing justice. As you know, you could have helped them with that hostage situation, but you didn't. You're also being charged in Denver for evading arrest."

"I'm sure I am," Trey sighed, cupping his forehead in his hands. The past had caught up with him and had his pulse back up. *What was I thinking? Why was I so stupid?*

"So, why *did* you run from the cops in Denver?"

"To save them from dying in the line of duty." When the Fed's puzzled look cued him to explain, he recalled the rationale he'd thought up on the way to Denver. "A cop in Colorado Springs died because of me. I didn't want more in Denver to be killed. Let's say I *had* allowed myself to get arrested. Once the Chromes discovered my location—which I knew they would have, as high-tech as they are—they would have murdered as many cops as they had to just to get to me."

"That's very noble of you. Now, let's talk about your smartphone for a sec. We traced its GPS and found it in the backyard of some resident of Denver. That wasn't *your* idea to leave it there, right?"

"Of course not. The Chromes tossed it out of the plane, not me."

"I believe you. Since you were nowhere near your phone, the government has tried other ways to track you down. Your driver's license is suspended, your credit cards are frozen, and there are people waiting for you to try to use one of your cards or your email account so they will know where you are. I must admit, you've done an incredible job staying off the grid. How have you survived all this time?"

He shrugged. "I'm just that good, I guess."

"I bet you had help from that biker woman that no one can identify, right?"

"I won't confirm or deny." Feeling backed into a corner had thoroughly killed his appetite. He did another two-handed face palm.

"I have the power to expunge all the charges against you and put your life back the way it was…if you're interested."

He slowly raised his head, peering over his fingertips at the Fed. Her eyebrows flew up as she cocked her head and peered over her glasses, as if telling him she meant every word. "You can do that?" he asked in a scarcely audible voice.

"Indeed. Not only do I have friends in high places, but in the FBI, I'm *also* in a high place. My people and I can protect you from the Chromes…*and* we can clear your name in all fifty states."

He continued eyeballing her, still wondering if she really could—and *would*—do all this for him. *Is this a trick? It all sounds too good to be true.* "I…I don't know. I…" Ashamed of his stammering, he just sighed.

"I get it, Trey, I get it; you need time to think about it. You don't trust anyone right now, and I don't blame you. If you decide you want my help, meet me at the food court in the Galleria Dallas."

"The Galleria Dallas? I've never been there before. Are you sure it's not called the Dallas Galleria?"

"It *should* be called that…in my opinion. Don't worry; it's not hard to find."

"Uh…okay. When do you want me to meet you there?"

"Friday evening at eight." She gave his hand a friendly squeeze. "I know you'll make the right decision."

Nova stood and, in no particular hurry, headed for the exit. Trey's eyes never left her till she pushed her way out the door and disappeared from view. The offer she'd extended to him replayed in his mind again and again.

It was Wednesday; he had two days to decide if he should meet up with her. He wondered if the FBI agent was the answer to his prayer—to see his beloved parents again. He couldn't imagine how this could be done without government aid.

Then he imagined other agents charging in to arrest him after getting confirmation from Agent Krenshaw that they'd found the right person. But it did not happen, even after five minutes.

Is anyone waiting outside for me?

He thoroughly studied his hand—the one she'd squeezed. There was no evidence she'd planted any sort of tracking device. Then he paid the check and cautiously exited the restaurant, glancing in all directions outside.

Someone must be watching me. As much as the government wants to find me, surely Nova has better sense than to let me wander off without a tail.

It was too dark to see which cars in the parking lot were occupied. He saw nothing suspicious at the tire shop next door or the auto glass shop the other way. Feeling the chill in the air, he zipped up his jacket and glanced both ways as he neared the four-lane avenue. Cars and trucks sporadically roared by, showing no interest in him. He found no one across the street watching him. After scanning what was further away—an apartment complex, discount store, and liquor store—he decided he'd searched long enough.

Time to call a cab.

Then he turned skyward to the star-filled blackness. He wondered if there was a satellite camera somewhere up there and if it was zoomed in on his face.

Way to go, Trey, you moron! If you're being watched from orbit, you've just made your identity clear by gazing up.

The new smartphone Sonya had loaned him jarred him from that thought as it chimed in his pocket. Weeks ago, she'd bought two phones under her name to keep Trey undetectable. He pulled it out to read her text.

where r u? sorry how I acted last night I swear I wont drink again pleez come back 2 the olivin miss u ☹

He typed up a reply and hit send.

On my way. You won't believe who I just ran into.

CHROME FALCON COMMAND CENTER

Two bored corporals sat before a bank of video monitors, watching six drones complete their sweep of zip code 75207. With their right elbows propped up on the console and heads resting in their right hands, they looked like twins from behind.

"I'm sick of this," Corporal Wells griped. "We've been searching this stupid city for weeks and found nothing! Do you know the point behind any of this?"

"Not a clue," Corporal Savage replied. "Don't worry. We only have fifteen zip codes left to cover. Then we can move on to more interesting tasks."

"Yea, I know, but the least Captain Ferch can do is tell us why. If we detected no signals from the wreckage, why search the rest of Dallas?"

"Maybe the captain thinks some traitor jumped out of the plane before the plane blew—a traitor who didn't know he was carrying a transmitter."

"No, *two* traitors. Aren't we searching for *two* signals?"

"Oh, yeah, you're right. I wonder who the turncoats are."

"Not as much as you're wondering what the new chick in our squadron is like in bed."

"Give me a break." Savage slapped Wells on the shoulder. "You know what a fine piece of eye candy she is. And it won't be long till I see the *whole* piece."

"Yeah, in your dr—"

An echoing *bleep* interrupted Wells, drawing his attention. Something blinked in red at the top of the lower left monitor: SIGNAL FOUND.

"Well, it's about time." Wells huffed. "Drone four has got something."

"This crap is finally over!" Savage cheered, giving his comrade a high-five. After he twisted a knob on his console, NIGHT VISION ENHANCED: 100% flickered at the bottom of the same screen for three seconds. The drone's camera offered a sharper view of a bundled tube structure.

"It's gotta be coming from there."

"I know. Hang on." Savage took the drone off autopilot and flew it closer to the multi-cylinder building. Another SIGNAL FOUND appeared under the first. "Yes! Damn, we're good!" Seconds later, the text on the screen changed from red to orange to yellow. "Both signals are getting stronger." When the yellow text turned green, two white dots blinked on the structure, showing the precise locations of both transmitters.

FRIDAY

A weather report on TV reported snow in the Dallas area. Sprawled across the top layer of his bed, Trey rolled his head on the pillow to face the dark window. A floodlight outside made the falling flakes obvious.

"I think windows inform me on the weather faster than weather *men*," he thought aloud.

"I think so too," Sonya agreed from the other bed. Feeling thirsty, she got up to get a glass of water.

The next thing to catch Trey's eye was the time on the clock—7:21 P.M. "Okay, I think we'd better go." He got up to don his sneakers and started lacing them. "You'll still drive me to that shopping mall, right?"

The question paused her hand that reached for a clean glass on the bathroom sink. She recalled his story of his encounter with the FBI agent. *What if that Fed is not really a Fed?* she thought. *What if she's really a Chrome? Wouldn't a* real *Fed have busted Trey without delay? I've never heard of the FBI having such open-minded leaders. It's gotta be a trick! A trap! Jiminy Christmas! Why did I not think of this until now? Forgive me, Trey.*

"What's wrong?" he asked her.

She slowly turned to eye him pensively. "I don't think you

should go meet that agent."

"You what?"

"It just doesn't seem right. I think it's a trap."

When his shoes were tied, he stared at her with annoyed disbelief. "I thought we agreed I should do this. Now you're having second thoughts?" She nodded. "Well, thirty-nine minutes before her specified time is a hell of a time for that." He pulled on his jacket. "There's no time to call a cab. So, let me have the key to the Malibu since you're forcing me to drive with a suspended license."

After taking the rental's key off the sink and shoving it down a back pocket, she moved toward the room's exit to block his path. "Stop! I just think—"

WHUMP-WHUMP-WHUMP-WHUMP-WHUMP-WHUMP!

They turned to the sound's source—a CF Gunship!

It came into view, halting its descent to hover right outside their window. Then a searchlight came on, causing the room's two occupants to squint as their hearts raced with extreme fright.

Vying to stay out of sight, Trey boldly neared the window and yanked the drapes shut.

"On second thought, maybe you *should* go!" Sonya declared, snatching her coat and hiking boots. "We *both* should!"

Trey meant to open the closet with the hidden arsenal so he and Sonya could arm themselves. The next event changed his mind, showing him there was no time.

The chopper fired a gas canister through the window, producing a starburst of cracks in the glass. As big as a soda can, the olive drab cylinder bounced off a wall and rolled across the carpet, spewing sedative fumes.

Like Trey, Sonya held her breath and pinched her nose closed as they vamoosed room 5212, letting the door shut behind them. In a full-out sprint, they headed down the curving lamp-studded hallway for the bank of elevators.

"Do you think the 'Fed' has anything to do with this?" Sonya asked, not slowing.

"No, but I'll change my mind about that when we get to the mall and don't find her waiting for me," he replied.

"*If* we get there!"

Seconds later, a room with six pairs of copper lift doors came into view.

DING!

The pair froze before entering the room's broad passageway.

"I bet that's them," Trey panted. "Come on!"

They spun for the door to the stairwell and pushed through, thankful it was only eight yards away. Not wanting to wait for the self-closing device to do its job, Sonya shoved the steel door back in place, holding down the button over the handle, lest the latch click and give away their position. A familiar voice barked from the hallway.

"Corporal, guard the lifts! Sergeant, come with me!" Captain Ferch ordered in his high, scratchy voice.

The couple ducked below the small window set in the stairwell door as the armed officer and sergeant blurred by. From head to toe, they were dressed in black like SWAT team members. They wore open-faced helmets, flak vests, fatigues, and combat boots, but no insignias.

Sonya put on her coat and boots faster than she thought possible. "I remember *that* voice," she scoffed, catching her breath. "Mr. Brains-In-His-Pants has come for revenge."

"Yeah," Trey agreed. "So much for the elevators."

"We can go down one floor and *then* take the elevator."

"No, no. There's gotta be more Chromes on the first floor expecting us to do just that. Let's take the stairs all the way down and—"

From four floors below, the footfalls of two winded men in the stairwell reached their ears. "Come on!" one of them huffed. "We can't let them get off fifty-two!"

Sonya glimpsed the painted *52* on the wall next to the door, reminding herself of what floor they were on. "Not down; *up*," she corrected in a whisper. "We need what's on the roof." They tiptoed with haste up the stairs.

✞

At the door of room 5212, Sergeant Clout followed Ferch's example and put on his gasmask. With a twelve-gauge shotgun, the trooper fired three rounds at the polished pine door, blasting away everything between the doorframe and keycard reader. The captain kicked the entrance open, letting fumes from the gas canister escape into the hallway. Then he moved to the side in anticipation of the room's occupants being armed—a likelihood he'd not bothered to convey to his subordinate as he let him scour the room without caution. The officer's right gloved hand held a tranquilizer pistol ready, and he eyed a beeping tracking monitor strapped to his left arm. Displayed on the tiny screen was 3 METERS.

"They're not in here, Captain," Clout reported after checking every possible hiding place.

"I should break that stupid nerd's oversized nose the next time I see him," Ferch grumbled to himself. "No one traps my girlfriend in a coffee table and gets away with it!"

When the trooper exited the room, his superior's tracking monitor beeped faster, showing 0 METERS. "Here it is, sir," Clout said, handing Ferch the source of the signal—the goggled helmet that had belonged to Sergeant Wits. "It was in the closet."

Enraged, the officer strode in the room and ripped the padded lining out of the helmet. The next thing he pulled out was a transmitter the size of a credit card. After throwing down the helmet, he dropped the black card on the carpet and stomped on it, causing a tiny red light to stop blinking. Then his attention went to the broken window.

The rotorcraft's xenon spotlight made him squint when he swiped the curtains open. He pulled a handheld two-way radio from a pocket in his flak vest and held it to his mask while pressing the *PTT* (Push-To-Talk) button.

"Fal Three, report," he ordered in a muffled voice.

"We still have a strong signal from the roof, Fal One," the radio's speaker boomed back. "But we just lost the other one we were detecting behind a window on the fifty-second floor."

"That's because I just smashed the transmitter, idiot!"

"Is that you in the window, sir?"

"Of course it's me! Now, get that light out of my face!" The copter's searchlight was switched off. "Did you see anything before I came in here?"

"We saw the drapes shut, but couldn't ID the target."

"You morons flew too close to the window and scared him off! You don't need to hover that close just to fire a gas canister through a window. If not for your mistake, he and the girl would be sedated and in our control again. You really messed up!"

"Sorry, sir."

"You *are* sorry! Now hold your position! Fal Six, report!"

"The other helmet and girl's bike are still on the roof," a different voice said. "I think they're a diversion."

"Rog. Stay there in case they show up." Ferch returned the radio to his vest. He and Sergeant Clout bolted down the hall for the elevators.

Wearing headphones, a petite Asian maid headed for the propped-open door of a room she'd finished cleaning. She'd not heard the shotgun earlier over the sounds of her vacuum cleaner and hip-hop music turned too high. She rolled her housekeeping cart back into the hall so the door would close, not knowing about the racing duo whose path she was blocking.

They collided with the cart and fell atop it, scattering trash and towels across the carpet. The maid gasped and turned to see if anyone else was coming. Then she saw the smoke from room 5212.

"Fire!" she shrieked and ran for the nearest pull alarm.

"Don't even think about it!" the captain roared, standing back up. He shot the tiny woman in the back with a soporific dart. She collapsed a few feet from the alarm.

Ferch and Clout arrived at the bank of elevators where three more troopers were waiting. "You didn't see them on the stairs, did you?" Ferch asked the wheezing pair from the stairwell.

"No, sir," the taller one gasped.

"What's wrong with *you* two?"

"My apologies…Captain," the shorter one panted. "But we just climbed…fifty-two floors…as you ordered. We're just—"

"Yeah, yeah, yeah! Shut up and listen! Trey could be anywhere." He poked the *Down* button on the elevator call box and, like Clout, pulled off his gas mask. "Let's get downstairs and guard every way out of this building. Remember, if you see Trey, he lives. His girlfriend dies."

✞

Fal Six was the call sign of Sergeant Sly. Gripping an assault rifle in both gloved hands with a tranquilizer gun holstered at his right hip, he puttered about the Olivine's highest rooftop. He was a bit intrigued by the architecture of the four-star hotel—a cluster of connected cylindrical towers. Though most of the towers were equal in width, some soared up to thirty stories, some forty, two at fifty, one at sixty and the tower he stood on was seventy floors, not counting the roof level.

As he paced back and forth, he occasionally shot a glimpse at what was set in the concrete block—the door that led to the only way on or off the roof.

Sly doubted Trey Radisson or his "girlfriend" would come up here; they would be trapped. He decided Captain Ferch was a moron for making him wait up here in the cold. Sly wanted to be in his cozy room at CFCC, browsing adult sites, and chatting with underage girls. He never wanted to be picked for this assignment; it seemed pointless since Ferch never told his people enough—not even what made the man they were after so important.

The sergeant looked beyond the stairwell's cubical housing at the farthest AC unit—the hiding place of the Harley and two helmets. One helmet belonged to a Sergeant Arch, who he barely knew, and the other was a faceless half-helmet for a woman. These items were right next to a boxed arsenal. Perhaps he should be guarding that in the off chance the odd couple came up to the roof with the intent of arming themselves.

As he crossed the roof to where the goods were hiding, he watched tiny snowflakes fall by the hundreds past floodlights studding the low wall that rimmed the rooftop. When he was five strides away, he barely heard the rotorcraft's *WHUMP-WHUMP-WHUMP!* Curious of what his comrades in the aircraft were doing, he turned right, putting his back to the stash of guns. Ten strides later, he bent slightly over the wall to look down. A red halo showed the path of the chopper's six-bladed rotor as it hovered nineteen floors below. Underwater lights revealed the Olivine's heated pool on the roof of a shorter tube-unit eleven floors below the copter.

I wonder what will happen if I spit from here. Will it land on the gunship, or will it miss and land in the pool?

He tried it, hocking and spitting hard enough to know it would not graze the windows on the way down. With an amused grin, he watched the mucus plummet, expecting it to land in seconds. If it made it past the rotor, it would land directly on the copter's canopy. Sly puckered his lips and whistled from a high to a low note, mimicking the sound of a bomb dropping. Though it was dark, he was certain his spit had landed where he'd meant for it to.

"Splat!" he cheered and let out a chuckle.

KA-CHAK!

"Drop it!" a tough female voice ordered.

Sly slowly turned. Standing four feet away was an attractive woman with long sable curls—the same one Captain Ferch had showed the team a photo of with orders to kill. *Can we violate her first?* he'd wanted to ask after seeing her picture.

He felt stupid for failing to notice her tiptoe up to him. She'd also taken a twelve-gauge shotgun from the arsenal he'd been foolish enough to turn his back to. Albeit she had the weapon aimed directly at him, he was overconfident enough to make a third mistake—he raised his own gun, believing he could fire off a shot before she did.

BOOM!

A hollow-point slug from Sonya's shotgun pounded the center

of Sly's flak vest. He soared backward over the two-foot-high wall and another twelve feet beyond, arms and legs limp in the wake of his flight. Losing his grip on the assault rifle, he plummeted, unable to scream from the shot that had collapsed his lungs.

Moving closer to the low wall, Sonya watched indifferently as the man fell, taking the same course his spit wad had taken. She whistled the way he'd whistled. Then he met his macabre end on the gunship's main rotor.

"Splat," she said in a bored voice as a horizontal ring of blood expanded and splashed across windows.

Trey strolled up next to her and observed how most of the sergeant continued to fall in pieces and foul the pool. "Look what you did," he chided jestingly and shook his head. "I guess no one will be swimming tomorrow."

"Nope. If only we had an RPG up here so we could crash that human blender."

"Uh-huh. Let's go settle for lighter weapons and get out of here."

✞

The chopper's two-man crew gaped up at the crimson mess on their canopy.

"Was that who I think it was?" the pilot queried, turning on wipers and washer fluid so he could see clearly again.

"Fal Six, come in," the gunner said in his helmet's built-in mic while holding down a *PTT* button. "Fal Six, do you copy?" He sighed, slapping his console. "Well, that just sucks!"

"It *was* him, wasn't it?"

Scowling, the gunner turned around to face him. "Nooo, it was the Kool-Aid guy!" He faced forward. "Halfwit."

"Don't make me come over there!"

"Fal Three, report," Ferch's voice demanded in their earpieces.

"Fal One, I think we lost Six," the pilot replied in his own mic. He flipped the searchlight back on and raised the gunship's collective lever so it would ascend. "We will investigate the roof."

"Rog. The targets had to have gone up there and armed themselves. Proceed with caution and report your findings."

"Copy that."

Seconds later, the helicopter had climbed high enough to see the roof. As the spotlight shined on the wrong side, Trey pulled open the stairwell door for his "girlfriend." Then he bowed and ushered her through with a sweep of his arm. Wearing her maroon half-helmet, she accepted the offer—atop her roaring Harley.

She cautiously descended the steps to the landing half a floor down. Snowflakes drifted through the slanting beam of the searchlight as it moved to Trey's location. He waved to the gunship just before going down the stairs and letting the door close behind him.

Much to the gunner's delight, the scientist appeared to be wearing Sergeant Arch's helmet. A tracking device on his console confirmed it, showing a distance-in-meters number increase every two seconds.

"Was that the scientist?" the pilot asked.

"I think so," the gunner replied.

"Well, that's just swell! He got away from us again!"

"Not quite. He's wearing that trooper helmet—the one he'd left up here. I'm detecting movement."

"You're kidding. Why would he wear that?"

"I doubt he knows we can trace it and he's probably wearing it for protection."

"Protection?"

"From falling. He must be trying to escape from here on the back of his woman's motorcycle. See if the bike is still up here." The copter flew back to the other side of the roof, shining the light where the Low Rider had been. "I knew it! She's been up here too. I bet it was *her* who offed Fal Six."

"Probably. The captain did say that she's one tough piece of eye candy."

"That's why she must die; she's making it too hard to recover the lab geek."

"Fal Three, what have you got?" their earpieces said. "Did you find the scientist?"

"The next best thing, Fal One," the pilot answered. "Check your tracking monitor. He was dumb enough to put on the other helmet."

"Excellent! Seal off every street that leads away from this high-rise."

"How, sir?"

"Think, idiot! Use your rockets! Blow things up!"

"I'm on it, Fal One," the gunner said with a malicious smile.

✞

Agent Krenshaw was at the north end of the city, strolling through the crowded Galleria Dallas. Passing a chic department store, she weaved through Christmas shoppers and boarded an escalator that would take her to the mall's second level. After that, she would need to go up another floor to get to the food court. For the last hour, only one thought was on her mind: *Trey Radisson, please don't let me down.*

Accordion music blared from her smartphone, startling her. She took it from her pocket and eyed the screen, reading CLINE CALLING. *What does my second-in-command want now?*

She swiped the screen to answer. "What is it?"

"Trouble at the Olivine," a male voice replied. "The Chromes have sent a chopper over here, most likely to find Trey. I don't know how they found out he's staying here, unless they have satellites too."

Stunned by the news, Nova nearly tripped at the top of the escalator. "You've got to be kidding me! This is happening now? Right…*now*? I can't believe this!" She sighed, trying to decide the best course of action. "Call the Army National Guard!"

The pianist in the Vista Steakhouse stopped playing as dozens of screams filled the air. The odd couple on the Harley zigzagged through occupied tables.

Man, did I make a wrong turn or what? Sonya thought as a waiter jumped out of her path, dropping his cluttered platter. *I should have learned the layout of this floor better. Now, where the hell are those stupid elevators? I might have remembered if I didn't get wasted last time I was here.*

All eyes were on the biker woman and her unidentifiable passenger as they glanced in every direction for a way out of the elegant restaurant. The only time they'd been on this floor was on Sonya's birthday. For fitness reasons, the duo had always taken the stairs each time they'd gone from their room to the roof and vice versa. Now that they had the Low Rider, they weren't about to take the stairs down the entire tower. Going down one floor was hazardous enough, but they had no choice since this was the highest floor the elevators reached.

Sonya slowed the motorcycle to a stop, bumping over a messy table with tip money instead of customers. The engine idled as soiled dishes crashed across the carpet. Then she turned to the nearest diner—an overweight man in an expensive suit.

"Can you tell me where the elevators are?" she asked casually. Like every member of his shocked family, the obese customer slowly raised a finger to her ten o'clock position. "Thanks."

Shrieks, spills, and crashes carried on as the two-wheeler gunned toward the exit, passing more tables. Feeling too hemmed in, one acrobatic waiter jumped, grabbing a chandelier to raise his entire body out of the Harley's path. Once the bike went by, he painfully learned the decorative light was not made to support his weight.

Still feeling parched, Sonya swiped a woman's glass of ice water as she rode past her table. Without slowing, she chugged the cup, spilling half of it on her face and jacket.

Just before they reached the propped-open double doors of the restaurant's main entrance, Trey waved at the dazed waitress who'd served them on Sonya's birthday.

"And I thought her *last* visit was bad," Asta mused aloud in German when she saw the biker's face.

✠

The chopper's gunner armed the weapons. A roll-up panel on the front of the octagonal munitions pod rose, exposing a launcher loaded with thirty-six rockets. Three red bars came together on the targeting screen, forming a flickering triangle that produced an echoing bleep. He was locked on his first target—the base of Reunion Tower at the Hyatt Hotel. The button to fire was pushed repeatedly, sending down explosive projectiles that blasted the east face of the tower's base.

Wineglasses trembled in the revolving restaurant atop the observation tower. Well-dressed diners gaped in all directions as they felt the tremors from the copter's rockets. When the vibrations ended, waiters stumbled on the carpeted floor, feeling a change in the pull of gravity. Furniture slid, screams filled the air, and the picturesque night view of Dallas tilted sideways.

The decades-old landmark toppled east. It came down with deafening ferocity, producing an immense dust cloud. The helicopter's two-man crew let out triumphant laughter. With the north end of

Hotel Street blocked by the tower's debris, they searched for more objects to destroy and block other ways leading from the Olivine.

✞

"But, Mom, I want ice cream *now*!" a five-year-old whined as she waited with her parents on the Olivine's forty-seventh floor.

"Knock it off, Danica!" Her father scowled. For the second time, he pushed the already lit *Down* button for the elevators.

"The ice cream is downstairs, sweetie," the mother said. With a chime, the indicator over the nearest elevator showed a flickering down arrow. "Okay, let's get on this one." The family approached the copper doors as they parted—

—and revealed a couple astride a rumbling Harley. The shocked trio froze, scarce believing what occupied the lift.

"Uh…we'll take the next one," Danica's father said. The odd duo in the elevator car nodded as the doors slid closed.

✞

"This is a mistake," Sonya said, punching the *3* button, albeit the *L* for Lobby had already been poked by her passenger. "I forgot what you said about the Chromes—there probably *are* more of them waiting for us on the first floor."

"Oh, yeah, I *did* say that, didn't I?" Trey sighed, shaking his head at his slipup. "You probably just saved our lives by remembering. But how will we escape from the Olivine on the third floor?"

"You don't want to know."

"I believe it. Tell me again why we're on this bike?"

"To get us to the Chevy faster."

"Uh…okay, I guess that makes sense. I just— Oh, crap!" Thrice, he deliberately thumped his helmeted head on the lift's mirror-paneled wall.

"What?"

"We left the briefcase full of cash in the room."

"Crap!" Sonya cringed and copied his show of frustration, producing more cracks with her own helmet. "Oh, well, it's not like we had a way to carry it, did we? I guess the Chromes have the briefcase now!"

✞

"Crap!" Captain Ferch roared, waiting with Clout in the ground floor's bank of elevators.

"What is it, sir?" the sergeant asked.

"We forgot to look for the briefcase when we were in Trey's room!" He slapped the top of his faceless helmet, ignoring the passersby who wanted to take the lifts and changed their minds after seeing the two men's weapons.

"It's been over a month. They've probably spent whatever cash was inside."

"That wouldn't be likely, according to Lieutenant Navarro." He noticed the meters decreasing on his tracking monitor as the beeping increased. "Hang on. Here they come. I'll sedate Trey, you kill the girl."

"Yes, sir." With a *K-CHAK,* the sergeant readied his twelve-gauge to fire. While his superior held the dart gun ready, they neared the only elevator displaying a decrease in floor numbers. Their hearts raced with anticipation as they observed the countdown glowing light blue on the lift's indicator: 5…4…3…2…1.

DING!

Engraving-smothered doors divided, showing an elderly man and his thirty-something-year-old son. They both wore midnight-green jerseys. The two fans of the Philadelphia Eagles had a full weekend planned, which included watching their favorite NFL team take on the Dallas Cowboys on Sunday. They'd not expected to have guns pointed at them.

As they raised their hands in surrender, a frustrated sigh escaped Clout's mouth. His annoyed commander—a Steelers fan—showed his irritation differently.

"Get new shirts!" he snarled at the fear-frozen pair.

"And new pants!" his subordinate added, noticing wet spots on their jeans.

Lowering their guns, they spun to find another elevator, letting the doors behind them slide close. Wanting to change and call security, the Philly fans pushed the button for their room's floor. Ferch and Clout flanked another lift coming down.

✞

On the third floor, the Harley exited the elevator, turned right, and revved across the carpet. As people scurried out of her way, Sonya kept the bike's left handlebar within arm's length of floral-patterned glass railing. Behind the five-foot-high barrier was a view of the lobby two floors below. Several yards ahead, the multihued rail curved into her path and ran another twelve feet before connecting to a wall, leaving her no apparent way out.

Instead of slowing, she fed maximum throttle to her powerful engine, deciding it was time to put her weeks-old escape plan to the test.

"Hang on!" she warned loud enough for Trey to hear. His heart raced and he tightly gripped her waist, not sure what her plan was. He hoped the ending would justify the fatal-looking beginning.

Stained glass shattered from the Low Rider's passage through the railing.

Trey wouldn't watch as the bike turned airborne, grazing an ornate brass-and-crystal chandelier. Below, a trio of new guests entered a sumptuous revolving door and froze to eyeball the motorcycle overhead. Above the hotel's gyrating main entrance was the couple's way out—a lavish translucent fanlight, colored mostly like a peacock's feathers and large enough for a car to pass through.

I may never forgive myself for ruining this, Sonya thought.

Outside, heads turned as the roaring Harley blasted through the semicircular window, wrecking Algerian capitals that spelled OLIVINE in pineapple-hued glass. The two-wheeler flew down in a half arc before landing atop a parked limo. Every tinted window of the sedan crumbled as the seven-hundred-pound machine collapsed the roof and rolled off the hood.

Grateful they'd already exited the stretched Rolls-Royce, the chauffer and his snobbish passengers watched the motorcycle's departing taillight in utter shock and disbelief. Like other onlookers, they paid no attention to the glass shower behind them as the exquisite window's remains disintegrated. The odd duo drew more stares as their ride weaved through stopped and slowing cars coming for valet service.

Ferch had heard the sounds from the Harley and shattered window when his tracker's beeping slowed. He dashed for the crowded lobby with Clout in his wake. While the captain glanced left, a bellhop unknowingly rolled a loaded luggage cart into his path. He ended up in a pile of suitcases, and the handheld radio slipped from his grip. He watched in dismay as the communication tool flew through the air and splashed into the hotel's indoor fountain.

The sergeant ran into the shallow pool and snatched the radio from the water. Static crackled from the device when he tried to transmit.

"Fal Three, come in!"

He noticed the five-inch whip-style antenna was loose and screwed it down the rest of the way. After checking the channel selector and volume knob, he pushed the *PTT* button twice more, demanding a reply. Nothing. The radio was ruined.

Rage and incredulity creased Ferch's face when he met eyes with Clout, who shook his head. People backed away as the large man shrieked at the top of his lungs, getting back on his feet while kicking luggage away. The bellhop showed concern and tried to voice an apology, only to be bashed in the jaw by Ferch's gloved fist. With ringing in his ears, he could scarcely hear the words from the man who'd punched him down.

"I swear, if I get one more cart shoved in my path…"

"Come, Captain!" the trooper urged with one hand beckoning him, the other dropping the useless radio. "Fal Four and Five have radios. Let's go outside and find them."

They rushed for the exit, but could not get out at first; they had to jostle through panicky guests and malfunctions with the oversized revolving door.

✞

After leading Sonya and Trey half a lap around the Olivine's immense outdoor fountain, the driveway formed a T with Hotel Street, where they stopped. To their right, a quarter mile south, the CF Gunship created another roadblock by blowing the Houston Street Viaduct to pieces. Sonya headed north where the street crossed Reunion Boulevard a stone's throw away. Beyond the red traffic light and a few halted cars was the cloud of destruction where Reunion Tower had fallen across the street. To make matters worse, Reunion Boulevard was a one-way street going east through a nearby tunnel—which the chopper had already collapsed.

Sonya took the only option—to turn left and go the wrong way between two of the four lanes, all crowded with traffic. Thankful none of the cars were moving, she and Trey squinted from the numerous headlights they passed, praying no one opened a door.

The biker glanced at her glowing gauges, noting with ire that the fuel needle indicated a nearly empty tank. "You've got to be kidding me!" she hissed.

✞

The battle chopper's pilot cackled as a few cars slipped through the crack the gunner's projectiles had made across the bridge. In seconds, over a hundred feet of traffic was built up on the Houston Street Viaduct. A touchscreen in the cockpit displayed an outline of the rotorcraft in neon green. Inside the copter's eight-sided weapons pod was the turntable—a circle divided like a pizza. Most of the ten slices displayed ROCKETS: 36. Three other portions were occupied with something else. One showed twenty-millimeter rounds at one thousand, another showed a flame thrower at full, and the gas canister count was twenty-nine.

The armed wedge at the fuselage's nose had turned dark red, showing a rocket count of zero. Pushing a button to rotate the table, the gunner swapped the spent launcher with a full one.

"Hey, hey, bogey at our three o'clock!" the pilot warned, eyeing the lights of the nearing aircraft to his right. "Is that a police or media chopper?"

"Who cares," the gunner replied, tapping a different slice on the touchscreen. "It's about to be a *dead* chopper."

A launcher on the gunship's right side armed as the front one disarmed. Outside the rotorcraft, the front panel of the munitions pod closed as the right one opened. The gunner locked onto the target and fired. They both turned their heads right to watch the rocket hiss away and close in on the hovering news copter. It exploded, putting the duo into a fit of laughter.

A loud bleep on the console turned the gunner's attention to the tracking monitor's screen. Displayed in red, the words SIGNAL LOST faded his smile. "Uh-oh."

"What is it?" the pilot asked.

"Trey is out of range. He and the girl must have found a way past our friends and escaped the hotel."

"Using what street?"

"I don't know. Is there some street we haven't blocked yet?"

"Well, we have *this* side covered. Let's check the other side again. They must have gone the wrong way down a one-way street. Didn't I tell you to block those streets as well?"

"My bad."

The gunship made a U-turn and thrummed north.

✞

Watching Fal Three fly by, Ferch and Clout ran full tilt across a half-filled parking lot. They jumped a black chain-link fence and crossed a narrow sward of grass studded with leafless trees that were decked with Christmas lights. Just beyond the row of sparkling oaks was what the pair sought—a glossy black eighteen-wheeler they'd spied from the lot. Hazard lights blinked on the unlabeled big rig, parked in the slow lane of Stemmons Service Road. Its right wheels were against the curb that bordered the tree-lined turf between the street and fence.

"Sir, we've been trying to reach you," a sergeant in the same SWAT-like garb said as he exited a Humvee parked behind the tractor-trailer.

"I lost my radio, okay?" Ferch spat. "Give me yours." He ungratefully took the communication tool from the man's hand and pressed the *PTT* button. "Fal Three, report!"

"Trying to re—" Static cut off the pilot's voice.

"Come back."

"Trying to reacquire target, Fal One," the pilot repeated nervously.

"What do you mean? Use your tracker, stupid!" Ferch checked his own tiny screen, reading that the signal was gone.

"We lost the signal, sir."

"What? You too? Well, you find that signal or you're dead meat! It took over two months for us to find it, you know! And once you get it back, don't let it out of range again! Understand?"

"Copy, Fal One."

Ambling up to the captain were two more men in flak vests and helmets—a pair of corporals in charge of the sleek semi. "Orders, sir?" the taller one said.

"Hang on," Ferch replied and raised the radio to his mouth again. "Fal Two, this is Fal One. Prepare to launch. I'm riding with you."

"Copy, Fal One," a woman's voice answered.

The forty-foot trailer's roof was a recessed pair of roll-up doors that faced skyward and opened in the center. Two chains of steel slats slid apart—one backward, one forward. The trailer's interior was exposed to the dark, flake-filled sky. All eyes were on the big glossy box as tiny rollers at both ends of the door slats rumbled loudly across a pair of tracks. A metallic thump announced the process's completion.

Hydraulics moaned and a small Eurocopter with a collapsible rotor slowly emerged from the trailer. The fantailed aircraft was as glossy black as the battle chopper and ground vehicles and, like the gunship, had the Chrome Falcon emblem on the tail boom. Interior lights showed an attractive blonde lieutenant in the cockpit. She donned a headset and hurried through her preflight checklist. The platform supporting the Eurocopter completed its ascent to the roof with a *CLACK!*

"Listen up!" Ferch ordered, handing the two-way radio back to the Humvee's passenger, not sure why the driver was still sitting behind the wheel. "After I help Fal Three find the signal, I will report the scientist's location to you. Then you need to catch up with him and get him back in our custody. Nobody, I repeat, *nobody* shoots his girlfriend until she stops her bike; we can't have Trey falling off and getting hurt or, worse yet, getting brain damage. Don't forget, his brain is the key to Chrome Falcon's ultimate victory. Understand?"

"Aye, sir!" the four troopers chorused.

Good, they are buying the same crap the colonel had told me, Ferch thought.

He recalled other words from Epperson: "Captain, you are all mouth and no trousers! If you want to prove me wrong, you will assemble a team and reacquire the scientist. If your mission succeeds, a promotion to major is in store for you."

As Ferch scaled ladder rungs on the back of the trailer, his subordinates returned to their vehicles. With nowhere else to go, Sergeant Clout got in the Humvee's backseat. The Eurocopter's three-bladed rotor extended and began gyrating as the captain climbed in with the pilot, swapping his helmet for a headset.

Glancing in all upward directions for any sign of the gunship's lights, Sonya squeezed the trigger of the gas nozzle, refueling her Harley-Davidson. Trey came out of the gas station, holding a pair of wraparound sunglasses he'd bought inside.

"Now, why do you need these things at *night*?" he asked, handing the shades to her.

"So the wind won't tickle my eyes," she explained, slipping them on beneath her half-helmet. She saw her companion sigh and let his head hang. "What?"

"We forgot the Chevy."

"Well, we can't go back for it *now*, can we?"

He puttered around, throwing his arms out to his sides. "I still don't get it. How did the Chromes find us when not even the cops could? We were so careful to stay off the grid."

"I have no idea." The nozzle clicked off, affirming a full tank. She hung it up and mounted the Low Rider. "Let's go. The fastest way to the galleria is north on the interstate."

As the Harley's engine roared to life, Trey climbed on and put on the helmet—which he would have undoubtedly left behind had he known about the transmitter under the padded lining.

They headed east on the divided Continental Avenue, waited out a traffic light at Stemmons, and made a left to get on the northbound lane of I-35.

Fal Four and Five—the Humvee and eighteen-wheeler—had arrived at Continental from the south with the intent of turning west once the light turned green. They changed their minds when the pair on the motorcycle appeared in front of them.

"Is that them?" the military truck's driver asked.

"According to my tracker, it is," the passenger replied.

"Go! Hurry!" Sergeant Clout insisted from the backseat. After five more motorists flew by, the all-terrain vehicle ran the red light with the rig staying close behind. "I never thought we would find them before the choppers. Give me the radio." The sergeant in the front passed it to him. "Fal One, Fal Four."

"Go, Four," Captain Ferch's voice answered.

"Target sighted at Stemmons and Continental. We're tailing them north on I-35. Request assistance."

"I copy, Fal Four. ETA, two minutes."

"This is Fal Three. ETA, *one* minute," the gunship's pilot said.

"Stop trying to one-up me!" Ferch bristled.

"Not my intention, sir."

"Better yet, Fal Three, get half a mile ahead of the target, preferably without being seen. Then, make some roadblocks."

"I copy, Fal One."

"Fal Four and Five, once the target stops moving, drug Trey and waste the girl."

"We copy, Fal One," Clout replied.

✝

Sonya kept the Harley at the speed limit, glancing around for helicopters every few seconds—an action Trey could afford to do more often. Traffic passed them as they remained in the slowest of the six lanes; the dark green signs showed the exit for the Dallas Tollway was not far. The single lane later branched off and continued across a lengthy bridge, keeping them heading north to the whereabouts of the galleria.

Yards ahead of them, a white Wrangler followed a red Grand Cherokee. Both jeeps were cruising at five under the speed limit, testing the biker's patience.

"Move it!" she groused, wishing the long overpass offered more than one lane.

"Can't you jeepers creepers go any faster?" Trey thought aloud, unaware the jeeps were filled with people dressed up for a horror movie convention. Two occupants were in Creeper costumes.

Sonya gave the snow-filled night a worried once-over, searching again for any sign of the rotorcraft beyond the passing structures and billboards. Nothing yet. Then the tollway returned to the ground to connect with two more busy lanes.

"Finally," she sighed, swerving her Harley into the center lane to pass the two jeeps. The tailing Humvee and tractor-trailer did the same, maintaining enough distance to keep their targets from turning suspicious.

For the first time, Trey saw the Eurocopter. It flew high above them and moved in the same direction. *Is that the Chrome gunship?* he thought. *Can't be. Too small.*

The next speed limit sign read 60 M.P.H. Sonya sustained sixty-five, her two tires steadily following the wet pavement's blackness, broken by yellow pools of illumination from the sodium-vapor streetlights lining the tollway.

A bright orange blast several cars ahead made the couple squint.

Dozens of brake lights lit up as traffic slowed and drifted right to avoid the unknown tragedy. Sonya did the same. Like all the curious drivers, she slowed as she passed where the explosion had transpired. A pickup in the fast lane was upside down and on fire.

Another motorist a quarter mile north ended in a fiery burst.

"What's causing that?" Trey asked himself. The answer came out from behind a billboard advertising a dental clinic. For the third time, the CF Gunship fired a rocket at the traffic ahead—another attempt to block Sonya with wreckage.

Then the Eurocopter's searchlight came on, shining directly

down on the Harley and sending chills down the spines of its two riders.

"Now the enemies have *two* choppers!" Trey reported.

"I know!" Sonya scowled, rolling her eyes.

In response to the fire ahead, more brake lights came on in all three lanes. Sonya decided she'd had enough; this was no time to keep her driving legal. She swerved the Low Rider onto the highway's shoulder—the safest place to accelerate, albeit the concrete barrier was under three feet from her right handlebar.

"Don't let them get away!" Ferch bellowed in the radio. The pilot seated next to him thought he was talking to her and did her best to put the bike back in her searchlight.

"I copy, Fal One. Fal Five, will you take the lead in the shoulder?" one of the Humvee's passengers said.

"Roger," the tractor's passenger replied.

"What?" the driver, Corporal Roger Stansell, said as he moved to the shoulder.

"Nothing, Roger." The other corporal rolled his eyes.

Shifting up through the gears, the semi passed the Humvee while keeping the gap between itself and the motorcycle from getting any wider. The all-terrain truck stayed in the wake of the big rig as they sped past slowing civilian vehicles, missing them by inches. Mounted on the tractor's bumper was a titanium push plate that pointed forward in the center like a double-bladed snowplow. The indestructible plate occasionally pounded aside motorists coasting near the shoulder.

Hearing steel bend and glass shatter, Trey looked over a shoulder just in time to see the eighteen-wheeler take out a fifth car seconds after the fourth one. More shudders hit him when he realized the trucker would have no reason to drive that way—unless he or she was taking orders from Captain Ferch.

Trey switched on the speaker of his mask, keeping one arm around Sonya's waist. Then he gave her the bad news. "The Chromes have a big rig too! It's right behind us!"

"I see it! I see it!" Sonya retorted, glaring at her rearview mirror.

The tractor's blinding headlights and orange marker lights were gradually coming closer.

"Can't you outrun them?"

"Not likely!"

"Why not?"

"My transmission is garbage; I'm stuck in third gear again!"

✞

Thirty cars ahead, a bearded restaurant manager was behind the wheel of his white Toyota Highlander. He was too focused with texting his mother on his smartphone to notice anything odd in the heavy traffic beyond the Nissan Rogue in front of him.

"Dad, I wanna see Santa!" his four-year-old demanded from the backseat.

"Be patient, Cody," the boy's overweight mom said from the front without looking up from her own phone. "We'll get there."

"So, what do you kids want for Christmas?" the father asked. "Your grandma just now told me she'd like to know."

All heads turned when Sonya's Low Rider revved by.

"I want a Harley!" Cody announced.

The mom's rearview mirror snapped off from the tractor's passage, shocking three of the four family members. After the attached forty-footer passed, so did Fal Four.

"I want a Humvee!" Cody's six-year-old brother declared.

✞

Fal Three's pilot flew the gunship a quarter mile ahead of the Harley, not sure how its riders and the pursuing ground units managed to get by the gunner's handiwork. Then they heard from Fal One.

"Keep firing, Fal Three!" Ferch ordered. "You can do better than this! Trey and his chick should have been blocked over a mile ago!"

"I copy, Fal One," the pilot responded as the gunner reacted by targeting the overpass of Mockingbird Lane. A chain of rockets zipped down, blasting away at the bridge. Most of it collapsed into a pile of concrete chunks, letting traffic fall into the tollway's north-bound lane and add to the roadblock.

Sonya saw the damage just in time to exit the tollway onto Roland Avenue. The semi and Humvee stayed behind her Harley as it neared Mockingbird, now backed up with motorists who'd planned to cross the bridge till Fal Three changed their plans.

At fifty miles an hour, the cycle roared through a three-foot-wide gap formed by the back of a Subaru and front of a Nissan. Both cars were sent spinning by the unstoppable big rig bullying through the intersection. The Humvee's driver didn't slow either and liked how effectively Fal Five kept his path cleared.

With the Eurocopter's searchlight back on them, the pair on the bike followed the single lane that put them back on the tollway.

✞

"Bogey at nine o'clock!" Fal Three's gunner announced. The pilot slowed the copter and turned left, sighting another news helicopter without enough lights on to be identified. "Targeting bogey. Still targeting."

"Hurry up!" the pilot insisted as the aircraft came too close for comfort.

"Still targeting bogey. Firing!"

The side of the weapons pod launched another rocket, reducing the whirlybird to plummeting, flaming wreckage.

"Fal Three, what's this I hear about a boogie?" Ferch inquired in their earpieces. They could not contain their hilarity for over ten seconds as the gunner realized his *PTT* button was stuck. "Shut up! Shut up! What are you laughing at? Tell me about the boo— The bogey! Tell me about the *bogey*!"

"Boogie destroyed, sir," the gunner replied, drawing another fit of amusement from his comrade behind him. Then he slapped his *PTT* button till it popped back out and stopped transmitting.

"You two better get serious about life! I'm not kidding!"

"Copy, Fal One," the pilot said and continued north, knowing he was supposed to be ahead of the target, not the other way around. Seconds later, another overpass came into view—one that offered no exit. The gunner locked onto the bridge and then took his hand away from the button to fire; the Harley had already reached the tunnel with the Eurocopter and two ground vehicles still after it.

"Fal Three, will you hurry up!" the captain boomed. "This is taking way too long. Don't you know the gate team near Ennis is waiting on all of us?"

"I *am* aware of that, sir."

"Then get half a mile ahead of the target and keep obstructing the road, like you did earlier! What's the matter with you?"

"Copy, Fal One." The pilot accelerated the gunship. "I didn't think the target would get around that last roadblock. Where do you think they are going?"

"I don't know and I don't care! I don't want to hear any more stupid questions! Stop the target, *now*!"

✝

Sonya steered her Low Rider in a serpentine path around another dozen slower motorists before exiting on Walnut Hill. She'd had enough of the tollway; not only did the confining walls offer few escapes from the enemy's makeshift roadblocks, but it was too obvious which direction she was headed.

More red lights were unheeded as more cars and trucks were rammed or sideswiped by the semi and military truck, still in hot pursuit of the Harley.

"My bad!" Sonya apologized after every auto mishap.

The northbound chase carried on Preston Road with occasional detours enforced by the gunship's projectiles. With the aid of side streets, parking lots, sidewalks, and people's front and backyards, Sonya bypassed every obstacle. She was fully aware the Chromes couldn't kill her without possibly killing her precious passenger—the whole purpose behind their mission in Dallas. As long as she stayed in motion, she was safe. She would feel much safer if she ever managed to outrun the relentless foes. However, as long as her ancient motorcycle remained stuck in third gear, it would not be fast enough to lose the tailing ground units, much less the Eurocopter.

Two miles later, Sonya's evasive maneuvers paid off with the aid of an extensive wreck involving a commercial eighteen-wheeler that had jackknifed.

"*Not* my bad," she said while skirting the smoky accident. She used it to make her next turn a mystery to the Chromes on the ground, already preoccupied with three squad cars from the Dallas P.D. with wailing sirens and flashing lights. Instead of obeying their demands to pull over, Fal Four and Five slowed down, uncertain of where to go next. They radioed Fal Three for help.

✞

Shrieking at the top of her lungs, the Eurocopter's pilot lost focus on the two-wheeled target after nearly colliding in midair with a police helicopter. The two aircraft's main rotors grazed each other with a sharp *CLANG!* Ferch hung on as the small rotorcraft nearly spun out of control. Then he called for assistance.

Heeding the captain's next order, the gunship's two-man crew turned their attention to black-and-white targets, both airborne and on the ground.

Sonya found Preston Road again after being lost in a residential area for nearly five minutes. Seeing no sign of her pursuers, she pulled the Harley over onto the sidewalk across the divided street from a Tex-Mex restaurant. Noxious black smoke flowed from the tail-pipe—a sign the bike had been redlining too long. As the hot engine idled, Sonya took her smartphone from a pocket to speak into it.

"Directions to Galleria Dallas," she enunciated. Limning her features, the screen responded to her words by showing a road map with a highlighted route connecting the blue dot of her position to the mall. The correct course was short and involved only three roads: Preston, Alpha, and Noel.

Smiling, she looked over her shoulder at Trey. "We're almost there." He nodded his helmeted head.

The bike's steaming engine stalled and shut down.

"Come on! Not now!" she flared, pocketing the smartphone. She turned the key and listened to the bike make an effort to heed her command.

WHUMP-WHUMP-WHUMP-WHUMP-WHUMP-WHUMP!

Trey's heart raced again when he heard the nearing rotors. He faced behind them, seeing the Eurocopter's xenon spotlight shine on the road a quarter-mile south.

"How do they keep finding us?" he asked in utter disbelief, not knowing the answer to his question was atop his head. "Come on!

Get this thing started!" He gave Sonya encouraging pats on the back. "They're coming!"

"I know!" She twisted at the ignition again and again.

Her passenger turned around again, finding the searchlight only two football fields away. Not far behind the pool of light were the familiar orange marker lights studding the eighteen-wheeler's roof. Next to the tractor's headlights, the high beams came on. Smoke belched from the exhaust stacks as the rig lanced directly toward them.

"Sonya?"

"Shut up!"

The Harley's engine continued to protest.

Seconds later, more vivid light bathed the two-wheeler. The searchlight's flake-filled beam slanted down from the hovering Eurocopter like a condemning finger of God. Chilled by the rotor wash, Trey strove to keep from slipping into a panic. As the aircraft thundered closer, the tractor-trailer halted two car-lengths away. Hearing the loud hiss of the airbrakes and the grind of the idling diesel engine, he considered dismounting the Low Rider and fleeing back into the neighborhoods, hoping Sonya would follow him. He squinted up at the small chopper, using a hand to block out the searchlight and find other features. He could barely see the right door open and Ferch leaning out to aim a pistol at them.

A tranquilizer dart missed, lodging itself in the top case behind the passenger seat.

Another, fired too high from the semi's passenger, glanced off Trey's helmet. Nearly losing bladder control, he doubted their next shots would miss. Then he would be in their custody again at CFCC. And they would be far less hospitable than last time since he was responsible for what had happened to their multimillion-dollar cargo plane. They would likely torture him till he produced another device for them. Then, once they knew how to operate it and make more of them, they would discard him like a bag of garbage.

Sonya, his best friend and the most remarkable woman he'd ever known, would be dead much sooner—in seconds, probably. After all the trouble *she'd* caused the Chromes, nothing would stop them from ending her life. She was far worse than useless to these high-tech savages; she would do anything to keep the man they wanted most away from them.

Her bike's engine revved back to life.

Trey hung on as their ride lunged forward, putting another black cloud in its wake. Splitting lanes, they neared the next red light and waited for a break in a service road's eastbound traffic. When a gap came seconds later, they crossed a bridge over an interstate.

Motorists cursed at the Harley as it passed them illegally. Then the black eighteen-wheeler gave them bigger things to complain about. The Humvee caught up and tailed the semi, following the path it sliced in the heavy traffic.

The Eurocopter also caught up, shining its searchlight on the two-wheeled leader of the destructive procession. Not far behind was the gunship.

After flitting by a bridal store, fitness center, and donut shop, Sonya failed to heed another red light. Nearly getting T-boned by an articulated city bus, she made an illegal left turn onto Alpha Road.

With a thunderclap, the semi rammed the same passenger vehicle, cannonballing through the pivoting joint and protective bellows that linked the front to the back. Roaring between the spinning halves of the elongated bus, the rig made the same left on Alpha.

Signs and bus stop shelters were taken down as the tractor-trailer stayed under five car-lengths behind the Harley. Half the vehicles passed by the Low Rider were rear-ended by the steel juggernaut and left on the sidewalk and center divider.

At Noel Road, Sonya turned left again and raced south in the wrong lane. Fal Five and Four did the same, but fell behind as their prey regained fourth gear. Sonya slowed when she noticed a ritzy department store on her right and decided it would be her way inside the Galleria. The original plan was to leave the Harley in the parking garage, walk inside the mall, and find the FBI agent on foot. However, with Chromes after them, the pair couldn't afford to leave their ride.

People moved aside when the bike turned off the road and coasted up to the entrance. Once it stopped, Trey instantly realized where he came in. He took his right foot off the passenger footpeg long enough to kick the handicap-access button. Glass double doors swung open for them. Another pair further inside did the same.

With the aid of the Eurocopter's searchlight, the pair in the eighteen-wheeler saw the Harley from a distance as it disappeared inside the store. The driver, still in the wrong lane of the quiet street, slowed to a halt. The store's arched entrance was at the semi's three o'clock position several yards away. The small chopper took the light off the entry and flew off somewhere.

"Now what?" the tractor's passenger said. As the driver shrugged his shoulders, they heard Ferch's voice on the radio.

"Fal Three, Fal One."

"Go, Fal One," the gunner answered.

"Put a hole in the skylight. I'm going in."

"Sir?"

"Just do it!"

"I copy, Fal One."

Troopers in both ground vehicles exchanged disbelieving looks.

✝

More rockets hailed down from the big war chopper and exploded across the immense skylight. Screams filled the shopping mall, and people on the ice rink skated off to safety, avoiding a hail of plate glass and steel framework. A towering Christmas tree stood in the center of the rink, pointing at the edge of the great opening Fal Three had produced in the crystal ceiling. As most the locals panicked and ran for the nearest exits, the bravest were curious enough to stay and gawk at the hole in the glass roof.

Satisfied with Fal Three's work, Ferch faced the pilot in the seat next to his. "Take us down inside that hole," he ordered. "Right now!"

"Are you out of your mind?" the lieutenant bit back, glowering at him. Like any rational chopper pilot, she doubted the mall offered enough space for safe navigation.

"I said *now*, stupid broad!" He drew a concealed .45 and held it to her forehead. "The guy we're after holds the key to Chrome Falcon's future! Now he's gone inside that structure! If he gets away, it will be *your* fault! When my people fail my missions, they don't live to tell about it! Do you get it?"

She continued eyeballing him with disbelief. When he thumbed down the gun's safety switch with a *click*, she nodded. He took the pistol away and watched her navigate till they were above the skylight's jagged opening. She lowered the collective lever so the rotorcraft would descend. Her commander did not see her malicious smile.

✞

Through the side windows of the idling Humvee and eighteen-wheeler parallel parked on Noel Road, five men regarded the glass-and-steel entrance of the chic department store. Three pairs of double doors were set beneath a great arched window.

"Fal One, Fal Five, what are your orders?" the tractor's passenger asked his two-way radio.

"What do you think they are?" the captain's voice replied acidly. "Get in there and reacquire our target! And I don't mean on foot!"

Shocked onlookers at the jewelry counter watched Sonya once again struggle to bring her motorcycle back to life. Then, all heads turned to the earsplitting crash from the store's entrance. Glass doors and most of the window above them came down stridently from the semi's passage. Then the inner doors collapsed as the big rig bull-dozed into the store at forty miles an hour.

More dark smoke belched from the Harley's exhaust muffler as the engine revived itself. Trey held on tight, and Sonya, with a roaring blast of rpms, rode her cycle deeper into the swank department store. With frightened shoppers hurrying out of their path, they zipped down linoleum walkways flanked by racks of expensive clothing.

Several yards behind them, the jewelry section was abandoned by shrieking employees who saw what was coming next. Like a derailed train, the eighteen-wheeler charged through the display counters, demolishing everything with deafening ferocity.

Finding where the store ended and galleria began, Sonya steered her rumbling ride directly toward it. She had to zigzag through people fleeing the opposite way—locals who assumed the entire shopping mall was about to collapse after they'd seen much of the skylight disintegrate. Everyone ahead of the biker obeyed her constantly beeping horn and bellowed demands to get out of her way.

Synthetic greenery and Christmas lights were coiled neatly

around every foot of railing that stood one floor above the ice rink. When the bike neared the decorated barrier, what Sonya saw next made her and her passenger saucer-eyed. The brakes were applied so hard, the motorcycle slewed sideways, almost falling over.

The Eurocopter was descending a stone's throw in front of them, nearly grazing the Christmas tree with its main rotor. Sonya and Trey recognized the large man seated next to the pilot. Ferch had gone completely mad. No one in their right mind would keep their aircraft in pursuit of their target if the chase had moved *indoors*.

Trey had enough of this and decided it was time to stop running from these problems and end them once and for all. Moreover, he was utterly humiliated by the lengthy path of destruction across Dallas. What the Chromes had been willing to do to innocent civilians just to try to reclaim him made his blood boil.

His fear evaporated as he recalled what was under his jacket—something he'd taken when he was on the Olivine's roof. He was now more emboldened than he'd ever been. Sonya had not trained him at the firing range or in the isolated forest for no reason.

Time to put my new skill to the test, he thought.

"I got this!" he assured Sonya after shoving off his stifling helmet and letting it bounce across the floor. Beads of sweat flew as he shook his head, tossing around his soaked shock of dyed hair. Then he pulled an Uzi from his jacket and clicked off the safety. As he'd suspected, it was easier to see the iron sights without the helmet on. The small rotorcraft turned to face them. He leveled the weapon at it.

Gnashing his teeth, Trey sprayed the cockpit's windows with nine-millimeter bullets. Through cracked glass, he saw the two occupants duck behind the instrument console. They clearly were not expecting this; the entire time their quarry had fled from them, he'd never once revealed he was armed. The pilot made the chopper elevate to a safer position.

"Shoot the other way!" Sonya warned, pointing.

Her passenger turned his head from their left to their right. He found the semi exiting the store and rushing directly toward them, blowing its shrill air horn at the oblivious group of shoppers who stood in its path to gawk at the Eurocopter. Trey's right hand snatched the machine pistol's grip from his left. Then he zeroed in on the driver.

RAT-TAT-TAT-TAT-TAT-TAT-TAT-TAT-TAT!

Behind the ruined windshield, the trooper took multiple rounds in the face and gave up his last breath. Gloved hands fell from the steering wheel as the body slumped forward, still holding down the gas pedal. The corporal in the passenger seat, no longer interested in sedating Trey, dropped his nonlethal gun and tried to reach the brake, despite his lack of time.

The runaway eighteen-wheeler was two seconds from T-boning the Harley. Sonya throttled forward to safety, getting out of the rig's path. Without slowing, the tractor crashed through the bedecked metal-and-glass railing surrounding the view of the skating rink. The forty-foot trailer followed, nearly scraping its roof on the landing skids of the ascending Eurocopter.

As half of the lighted railing winked out, all eyes were on the monstrous vehicle. It made an earsplitting spectacle of itself, falling grille-first on the ice one floor below. Inside the truck, the shrieking passenger's helmeted head went through his half of the divided windshield, breaking it and fatally cutting his throat on glass. The trailer uncoupled itself from the tractor and thundered down beside it as it stood for three seconds on its smashed-in nose. Then the huge truck toppled forward with its spinning tires in the air.

On all three levels above the rink, spectators were leaning on the railing to ogle the semi. After it stopped moving, all eyes returned to the noisy rotorcraft, now hovering even with the third floor. More riled than ever by the slugs that had barely missed him, Ferch dropped his tranquilizer gun—a pathetic weapon to use on anyone armed with an Uzi. He slid open the window in his door to train his .45 down on Trey's head. He still believed the scientist had trapped his beloved Zuri in an antique coffee table. Plus, he was still embarrassed by all the events in the Olivine—Fal Three scaring Trey from his room before he could get there; carts being shoved in his path, *twice*; the time he'd dropped his radio in the fountain; the hindrances that included the panicky guests and faulty revolving door.

As if all that wasn't bad enough, the lab geek had evaded him and his men for over thirty minutes. The maneuvers Trey's "girlfriend" had made with her bike were notably slippery. If not for this, Ferch and his team would have completed their mission by now. Instead, they'd made themselves the most heinous and destructive creeps to ever pass through Dallas.

The livid captain couldn't take any more of this. He no longer cared about the mission. He didn't care about impressing Colonel Epperson or being promoting to major. He just wanted these "lovebirds" dead.

The first shot from the .45 missed Trey's head by a handbreadth. After a brief shudder from the close call, he dismounted the Low Rider to aim more effectively. Then he pointed the Uzi skyward and returned fire till the twenty-five-round clip was empty. The officer cowered inside the aircraft as nine-millimeter rounds shattered more glass and raked the fuselage. Before reloading, Trey moved back from the rail so the edge of the second floor blocked him from the Eurocopter's view. Pushing the magazine-release button, he let the empty clip fall, pulled a fresh one from his pocket, and slapped it into the machine pistol's handle. Prepared to fire, he returned to the spot where he'd spent his last clip and looked up. When he saw the pilot's next action, he decided to save his ammo.

"What are we doing up here?" Ferch bellowed. "Take us closer to the target!" He turned to verify the pilot understood.

She was gone.

Her wide-open door was four feet over an escalator.

"Where did you go?" her commander shrieked as his skin crawled with indescribable terror. "Get back here, traitor! I can't fly this thing!"

Not wanting to upset the rotorcraft, he climbed awkwardly around the cyclic stick for a better view through her door. Being a large, clumsy man in a confined space, he accidentally stepped on a pedal to slow the tail rotor. The fuselage began to turn counterclockwise, briefly giving him a better view of the escalator. He spied the pilot sprinting down the descending steps and off to a new future.

For weeks, she'd secretly grown more and more fed up with her stressful life of service to Chrome Falcon. When her short-fused, psychotic captain had put a gun to her head, it was the straw that broke the camel's back. To her, the higher pay was just not worth it. Plus, this could be her only chance for successful desertion—a crime General Casprite deemed punishable by death.

Alone in the revolving chopper, Ferch got one more glimpse of the blonde lieutenant, now disappearing around a corner. She knew she'd never be caught; the Chromes would always have their hands too full to concern themselves with her. But *he* would concern himself with her. She'd just left him to die, making herself the new target of his fanatical wrath.

He meant to jump onto the escalator, as she had, and go after her till he was near enough to put a bullet in her skull. However, it was too late now; during his hesitation, the Eurocopter had drifted too far from the stairway and was now spinning out of control.

The tail boom brushed the artificial pine tree. At that instant, the enclosed rotor sucked in strands of Christmas lights. Eruptions of sparks announced the end of the rotor's serviceability. With the tail system no longer stabilizing the small aircraft, the fuselage twirled faster and faster. The rudder and main rotor blades grazed and bounced off balconies, escalators, rafters, and skylights, sending bystanders on the top two floors running for cover.

Dizzy from the chopper's uncontrollable spin, Ferch made a decision: if he miraculously survived the imminent crash and could still walk, the first thing he would do is hobble into the nearest department store and steal more underwear.

After producing more bursts of glass and sparks, the gyrating airfoils scraped enough objects to lose their shape. With a stalling engine, the Eurocopter dropped to the ice rink below, demolishing itself next to the semi's remains. Ferch was still inside the downed aircraft with injuries that gave him only minutes to live. The exploding fuel tank gave him even less time.

✞

Like the stunned patrons, Trey's protruding orbs had never left the rotorcraft. He couldn't decide if the crash was more or less amazing than the one he'd seen near Colorado Springs.

"Trey, get on!" Sonya yelled.

"Yeah, yeah," he groaned, switching the Uzi's safety back on before returning it to his jacket. Then he climbed back on his seat. "Why so pushy?"

"*That's* why!"

His gaze followed her outstretched arm and pointing finger to the department store's broad entrance. The black Humvee had caught up and was coming for them.

Fal Three hovered over the Galleria Dallas, awaiting orders from Fal One—orders that would never come. The concerned pilot maintained distance as he circled the gunship around the breeched skylight. Without success, he and the equally worried gunner tried both visually and with the radio to determine Captain Ferch's status.

A low-fuel buzzer blared on the console, keeping their attention off three more inbound aircraft. As a result of Agent Krenshaw's order to contact the Army National Guard, a trio of the most advanced Boeing AH-64 Apaches approached the shopping mall. Inside the first attack helicopter, the pilot spoke into his helmet's mic.

"Stinger Command, this is Stinger One. We have visual on the hostile. It looks like it's alone, but it's left an enormous path of destruction. Civilian casualties may be in the triple digits and rising."

"Rog, Stinger One, you are clear to engage hostile," his earpiece said. His gunner also heard the authorization. Weapons were armed, the CF Gunship targeted.

A Sidewinder missile launched from the lead Apache and soared straight for the unaware target four hundred yards away. The projectile breached the front-right wall of the weapons pod, stopping with its warhead section beneath the cockpit. The blast ended the lives of the pilot and gunner as instantly as it fragmented the canopy. Then, what was left of the helicopter's own ammo ignited. A chain of explosions formed a brief C around the flaming cockpit, consuming the entire pod. A second later, the engine blew, causing the main rotor to pop free from its mast and fly skyward.

The flaming fuselage dropped into the parking lot, drawing gasps from onlookers as it crushed four empty cars of hapless Christmas shoppers—a small price to pay to prevent dozens more lives lost. Once the burning wreckage stopped rocking, the six-bladed rotor came down, as if performing a coup de grace. It landed vertically and stood in the midst of the flaming ruins like a ninja's throwing star, producing more voices of shock. As the lighted tips waned, the tail rotor slowed to a halt.

✞

With the Humvee trailing them, Sonya's Harley carried her and Trey deeper inside the galleria. While rocketing down the mall promenade, they flashed past a variety of upscale stores that sold home furnishings, clothing, shoes, jewelry, lingerie, beauty products, and leather goods. There were citizens who'd heard the clamor from the skating rink, but had not been near enough to perceive a reason to evacuate the shopping center. These people scurried aside when they saw the motorcycle and military truck coming their way—two things they'd never imagined would ever be inside the elegant mall. Once the two vehicles passed the shoppers, curiosity drove many of them to walk in the same direction.

The Humvee was only two car-lengths behind the Low Rider, demolishing every bench, trashcan, and temporary sales counter the bike zigzagged around. Then, Fal Four's prey rounded a large planter filled with topiary trees and neared a luxury department store, which marked the north end of the galleria. Finding nowhere better to go, the duo boarded an escalator while still on the Harley. Knowing the Humvee would not fit between the rails of the moving stairway, the driver floored the brake pedal. All-terrain tires squealed, producing skid marks across the tile floor. The bumper stopped within inches of the rubber rails.

Shocked patrons on the ascending steps turned to see the spectacle below and tripped once they reached the top. More witnesses gaped from the escalator's descending twin. With her hiking boots on one of the ridged steps, Sonya kept the heavy motorcycle balanced. She held the brakes down tight so the bike wouldn't roll back down the stairway that slowly carried them out of Fal Four's reach.

Uzi in hand, Trey climbed off the passenger seat and exchanged odd looks with a group of teenagers on their way down. Then he saw both front doors and one back door swing open on the Humvee below. Gripping their tranquilizer pistols, the driver and front passenger got out. For protection, they stayed behind the open doors of the all-terrain truck as they reached around to aim their guns upward at Trey.

He aimed downhill and fired first.

RAT-TAT-TAT-TAT-TAT-TAT-TAT-TAT-TAT-TAT-TAT-TAT-TAT!

Every spectator screamed and ducked as the slugs bounced off the Humvee's shield-like doors and bulletproof windows, leaving the troopers unscathed. Then Trey found better places to shoot. He trained the machine pistol just below the driver's door.

RAT-TAT-TAT-TAT!

Then the passenger's.

RAT-TAT-TAT-TAT!

Dropping their nonlethal weapons, both men collapsed with bloody holes in their boots from the nine-millimeter bursts. With no interest in completing the mission, they rolled around in agony on the tile floor and decided they were more than ready to go to prison as long as their injuries were treated first.

The back door closed as fast as it had opened.

Sergeant Clout had also lost concern for the op. He was now resolved to not leave the security of the Humvee till the armed scientist was out of sight.

A few considerations flashed through Trey's brain. *What if Krenshaw didn't make it to the Galleria for some reason? What if Sonya and I have to leave this mall the same way we came in? If we do, that Humvee could still follow us. The man in the backseat could drive it. Unless...*

He aimed for one of the tires.

RAT-TAT! CLICK!

The second magazine was empty. And he'd not brought a third.

Oh, well, I think he's too scared to follow us anyhow.

"Very impressive!" Sonya hailed, also recalling Trey's marksmanship near the ice rink. "I'm glad I taught you how to shoot."

"That makes two of us," he replied, dropping the spent Uzi. It clattered noisily on the ridged steps.

When the Harley reached the top of the escalator, Sonya walked it forward a few feet and gave Trey a moment to climb aboard. Leaving another noxious black cloud behind, the Low Rider roared on, passing a fashion store and athletic footwear retailer. Then the biker's passenger patted her on the shoulder.

"What now?" she huffed.

"Stop at that map ahead," he told her.

The bike slowed to a halt next to a lighted display of the Galleria. Without getting off, Trey studied it a moment. *"Meet me at the food court,"* Agent Krenshaw had told him. Then he found it on the third floor, only it was called the Food *Place*.

"We need to go up one more level."

Sonya throttled ahead and put them on another escalator. Seconds later, they found places that served wraps, cheesesteaks, burgers, shakes, chicken fingers, and pizza. The varied chain of restaurants surrounded clusters of tables. As Trey scanned the tables, every diner—except the fattest one, munching on his third burger—rubbernecked the rumbling Harley, easing his efforts to locate Nova Krenshaw.

Eight faces were glimpsed before he found the FBI agent. She was forcing herself to finish her buffalo chicken wrap and fries, despite not even being hungry when she'd placed her order. Ever since she'd heard about the trouble at the Olivine, she'd lost her appetite. Her boss would fire her if he'd found out she'd passed up the opportunity to bring in Trey Radisson—one of the most wanted men in the country. It would also cripple her chances of finding a new job if, because of her decision to not arrest him, the Chromes had killed or reacquired him. For the past half hour, she'd been worried sick; with the terrorists' ill-timed interference, the odds of her never seeing Trey again were quite high.

But here he was, making an entrance the Fed would never forget.

"Over there," Trey directed, pointing. He was overjoyed to find her since it confirmed she'd had nothing to do with the terrorist activity.

Sonya rolled the bike up to the table of the lone black woman who scarce believed what she saw. Trey dismounted the steaming motorcycle as it backfired, startling every witness. Then he nonchalantly scooted a chair back and took a seat at the shocked agent's table.

Peering over her glasses, Nova gawked at Sonya for a moment, recalling the pale face, curly black hair, and maroon helmet she'd seen in a picture of her. As Sonya reached for the key to kill the overheated engine, it died on its own again. Shaking her head, she set the kickstand and climbed off, not seeing what happened next. As she walked away from her two-wheeler, the kickstand buckled. The heavy bike thudded loudly on the tile floor inches behind the boot heels of the startled owner.

A small fire erupted on the engine, which had been redlining for most of the trip. Sonya's wide eyes gave her surroundings a panicky once-over before finding a fire extinguisher. She hastened for the heavy red bottle, unhung it from the wall, and pulled its pin. With a deafening hiss, she squelched the flames as a few diners moved away from the white cloud of nitrogen. She let the extinguisher fall noisily from her hands. A wave of her arm conveyed how she'd had enough of the ancient Harley.

Nova's attention returned to Trey. His head turned from the ruined motorcycle to check the time on his watch. It was ten minutes after eight. Meeting the agent's gaze, he rested his clasped hands on the table and cleared his throat.

"Sorry I'm late, ma'am," he apologized, as if he'd been delayed by a round of golf.

DALLAS/FORT WORTH INTERNATIONAL AIRPORT

At 2130, a fully fueled Dassault Falcon on the wet runway shrieked up to takeoff speed. The white aircraft's landing gears left the tarmac and retracted seconds after the jet turned airborne. Displaying FBI in bold black letters on the tailfin, the twenty-three-meter plane climbed into darkness northwest of the city.

Inside the deluxe cabin, a well-dressed stewardess served Trey and Sonya the sodas they'd asked for as they sat comfortably in well-cushioned leather seats. Across their small mahogany table, Nova sat and talked to someone on her smartphone. At the galleria, she'd led the odd pair from her table to a parking garage where two of her subordinates had waited in a white van. Then they were driven to the airport to board the aircraft. On the way there, the senior agent had called her other team at the Olivine to fetch the couple's belongings from their room, as they'd requested, and load them on the plane. Aside from the Chromes wrecking half of Dallas, everything had gone according to plan.

"Yes, sir," Nova said to the man on her phone. "I have Mr. Radisson *and* Sonya McCall. No, not Jane Doe, her *real* name is Sonya...McCall. *McCall.* M-c-c-a-l-l." Her eyes rolled. "We're in the air now. We'll be there soon. Okay, bye." The call was disconnected and she faced Sonya and Trey. "Sorry, guys; my boss is a bit slow and needs a new hearing aid. He should have retired years ago."

"No prob," Trey said and sipped his Sprite. "So, where are we going?"

"The NSA. Some of the top officials want to interview you two and learn all you know about the Chromes."

"Sounds like fun," he groaned and looked out the dark window.

Sonya squeezed his hand that gripped the armrest between them, as if telling him to not fret. Then she faced Nova. "Thank you for getting our stuff from the hotel."

"No problem at all. By the way, what's in the locked briefcase?"

You mean the money we stole from Chrome Falcon? she thought, taking a nervous swig from her Dr. Pepper.

"Just my private stuff."

"What kind of private stuff?"

"You don't want to know." She noticed Trey's reflection in the window. Like her, he couldn't suppress a smile.

The agent's eyebrows flew up. "Oh, *that* kind."

Well, that *answer worked. This is kind of embarrassing, but how else will I keep her from looking in the briefcase?*

"Don't worry, Sonya; your secret is safe with me," Nova reassured her.

"How do you know my name?"

"On the night I first met Trey, I had my people watch him from a satellite." The scientist faced her, wanting to hear the story. "They saw him get in a cab and take it to the Olivine. Then I went to the hotel with most of my team to have a private talk with the senior manager. We showed him Trey's picture and had him play back surveillance tapes. Once we saw what room Trey went in, the manager looked it up and—"

"Found the room taken by *me*," Sonya finished, nodding.

"Exactly."

Trey craned his neck to see the lights of Dallas behind the aircraft. The clouds and distance made the city impossible to see. As he recalled all the destruction Captain Ferch and his team had caused from trying to catch him, his heart ached for the victims. With elbows on the table, he let out a deep sigh and cupped his forehead in his hands.

"Are you all right?" Sonya and Nova asked together.

The inventor shook his head, feeling a bit nauseous. "I want to know how many in Dallas died because of me," he said quietly without looking up. Sonya's consoling arm around his back did not help.

Nova took a deep breath, trying to think of the best words. "Mr. Radisson, what happened in Dallas was very tragic, but—"

"Tragic?" he huffed, looking annoyed at her. "That's putting it mildly, Nova. The Chromes turned the city into a warzone!"

"You can't blame yourself for—"

"Please! How many."

She gave him a long, serious look. "They're still counting. And the current count is not a number you want to live with. Trust me."

He felt his nausea worsen. "Excuse me." Sonya leaned back as he stood, dodged her knees, and entered the aisle. With one hand over his mouth, he hurried to the back of the plane for the lavatory. Seconds after the door slammed shut, the two women heard the muffled sound of him retching.

An uncomfortable minute crawled by. The only sound was the soft drone of the jet's engines. Then Sonya's curiosity drew a question for the agent. "How do you think the Chromes found us at the hotel?"

"Well, let me ask you this: what was that helmet doing in your room? My people have seen helmets like that before, so they know it belonged to the Chromes. They found it when they went to get your things."

"Trey and I had to disguise ourselves so we could escape the Chromes' command center."

"There was a bug in the helmet. They bug *all* their helmets. The reason it took the Chromes so long to find your exact location in Dallas is because the bugs can only be detected from eight hundred feet away."

Feeling stupid, Sonya sighed and combed her fingers through

the top of her raven-black cloud of hair. "I can't believe it."

"What?"

"I let Trey wear the *other* helmet all the way from the Olivine to the mall. No wonder the Chromes tailed us so well." She guzzled more soda and checked behind her headrest, verifying the lavatory was still closed. "Let's keep the thing about the helmets between us."

"Agreed. He clearly has enough on his mind right now."

"That's true. So, what else do you know about the Chromes?"

"Chrome Falcon is a terrorist organization with ambitions of becoming an entire empire. The group began nearly three years ago when Dr. Harbison teamed up with Glenn Casprite, a self-proclaimed general."

"I've heard of Casprite, but who is Dr. Harbison?"

"According to my limited sources, Harbison is a scientist who invented the prototype for some sort of teleportation device. Advanced versions may have been made by Harbison's team and then duplicated. If the theories about this revolutionary technology are true, it would explain how the Chromes have been able to elude the authorities and U.S. military so well."

"Teleportation device," Sonya said slowly as if tasting the words. Then she pondered the info. "I've got bad news: the theories *are* true. The Chromes call them Green Gates. So far, Trey and I have passed through two of them."

"I knew it!" the agent exclaimed. "Where were they?"

"One was somewhere in the Rockies. The other was…I don't know where. The plane had no windows."

"Oh. Well, that's not much help. Uh…when you and Trey were at CFCC, did you get to meet General Casprite?"

"No, we just heard him once over their PA system. He was summoning all the colonels to a meeting. Where did he come from?"

"He's a former colonel in the U.S. Army who was dishonorably discharged."

"For what?"

"I don't know. Lots of things, I heard. No matter what the issue was, he believed he was always right. Of course, it doesn't really matter what he believes. He's a complete psychopath who was well known for criticizing the way our country is run."

"Lots of people disagree with that."

"He does more than disagree. He's insane, stupid, and arrogant enough to think he can lead our nation better than any president in U.S. history. And that's just what he intends to do if he ever manages to establish enough hidden bases to set the stage for a hostile takeover."

"Huh. I've got to hand it to him, he sure sounds motivated."

"Motivation is good…until mixed with stupidity; *that* makes it hazardous."

"True. I prefer *lazy* idiots who never leave home; at least they're not out hurting people. But if this general is a stupid man, how has he gotten so far?"

"He's a very skilled leader and speaker. Being skilled is not the same thing as being smart. Also, General Casprite is a walking, talking bottle of pure evil—essentially, a modern-day Hitler. He also has connections worldwide with drug lords, human traffickers, and various other bad apples that help finance his expanding army and arsenal. For two years, he has been recruiting Americans and non-Americans who are down on their luck and just as disgruntled at the U.S. government as he is. To supplement his still-inadequate army, he also employs hundreds of terrorists from every continent but Australia and Antarctica. He thinks of the terrorist recruits as expendable assets and a means to an end."

Sonya nodded. "I met a Chrome Falcon colonel from the UK, which I thought was very odd. Why would a *British* person join them? The UK is one of our best allies, right?"

"Of course they are, but every nation in the world has a few haters of the American way. We can't fault the good U.S. of A for that though; there is no such thing as a country that everyone on the planet agrees with a hundred percent. *Every* nation in the world has its share of lovers and haters. The only reason the focus is on America is because of how long the U.S. has been policing the world."

"I see. And people don't want to be policed; they want the freedom to keep doing what they know is wrong."

"Exactly. As if that isn't bad enough, they try to justify their wrongs with their culture and history."

Sonya puzzled over her discourse with the agent. "How do you know so much about the Chromes?"

"The whole Bureau knows all I've told you. In the past eight months, the FBI has managed to locate and incarcerate a few people who lawfully work and live with the rest of society while secretly supplying the Chromes with money, weapons, info, whatever. Then we sat these covert supporters before professional interrogators. I heard that we got a *huge* break last week. The Chromes had been bribing a corrupt cop to give them sensitive info for over a year. The cop was arrested a month ago. Then, in exchange for leniency, he gave us enough names for us to bring down a whole nationwide *network* of shady police who were secretly serving the Chromes."

"That's awesome. Lawless living just doesn't work, does it? That sort of life is like a house of cards. You take out one, the entire thing falls. I don't know why people even try it."

"Do you know what sets you and Trey apart from everyone the FBI brought in for questioning about the Chromes?"

"What's that? That we're actually innocent?"

"Not only that, but you're the only ones who have actually been to CFCC. You two have lots of valuable knowledge *and* nothing to hide…I assume."

"Of course we have nothing to hide. I think I speak for both me *and* Trey when I say I want to offer so much info, the U.S. military can force General Casper to surrender before Christmas and shove the American flag right up his—"

"General Casp-*rite*," Nova corrected.

"Whatever. I like Casper better."

"And don't you think the American flag deserves far better treatment than what you almost said?"

"Of course it does. I meant figuratively." She nearly fumed with bloodlust for the loathsome terrorist leader as she recollected the cops she'd witnessed his minions slay. "And, if he *won't* surrender, I say we turn Casper into a friendly ghost." Ignoring the agent's mirth, she downed the last of her Dr. Pepper and set it in her cup holder. "I'm serious." She waited for the end of Krenshaw's hilarity before speaking again. "Can you do me a favor and have the stewardess bring me another soda?"

"Absolutely. I owe you more favors than that."

"You owe *me* favors? Why?"

"If not for you, the Chromes would have captured Trey again today. You evaded them while delivering the poor man straight to me, even though your method was very unorthodox."

Sonya smiled again. "Well, what can I say? When I have a tail as relentless as the Chromes, I get unorthodox."

"I'm sure you do. *And* you managed to lose that tail before you found me. Because of that, the Chromes have no idea you two are now under FBI protection. As far as they know, the both of you *still* have no safe haven. You have been very helpful and that's why I should repay you with a better favor than just another beverage. It can be anything you want. Well, *almost* anything. You have to be reasonable."

Squinting at the reading lights in the ceiling, Sonya mulled this over. Then she went saucer-eyed. "I've got it!" Immaculate teeth were exposed as she grinned. "Boy, have I got it."

"Go on."

"Have the FBI in California find and arrest the Screamon Demons. It's a biker ring that mostly resides in Sacramento. They like to rob people, sell drugs, and worse things. Their leader, Levi North, wants me dead. I can give you names and addresses." Her smile vanished from the agonizing memory of her last phone call with Becky Lugo. "They also murdered my friend in Carson City."

For 1700 the following day, Nova made a reminder on her smartphone to question Sonya about the gang. "We'll talk tomorrow about that. I've never heard of the Screamon Demons, but you can most likely consider those thugs history."

"Thank you." *There goes another house of cards.*

Sprawled across a full-sized bed in the back of the plane, Trey continued to grieve for the hapless innocents in Dallas, still feeling responsible for all of them. His face was buried in a lumpy pillow until he raised his head to fix his large welling eyes on a clock built into the wall across the dark room. Displayed in bright blue digits was 10:47. Once the plane landed in Maryland, he would be two hours ahead of Dallas—way past his preferred bedtime.

Who cares? I doubt I'll be sleeping tonight, he thought, returning his face to the pillow.

Gloomy thoughts of a wasted life filled his brain. The VV1 had been his number one goal for years. Hundreds of hours had been misused on its creation—hours he'd never get back. As if this wasn't bad enough, he'd never dreamed the abysmal device would bring him a future like this. And it didn't even exist, except in his memory. The more he reflected on it, the more convinced he was that *he* was America's biggest problem.

How many people would have been saved if I'd not *been saved? Why was I born with the ability to create that horrible machine? In fact, why did I have to be born at all? I am nothing but a curse to this world. I can't think of one worthwhile thing I've ever done in my life. Instead of escaping CFCC, I should have stayed and found a way to make the place self-destruct.* That *would have been a marvelous way to end my hollow existence.*

✞

Slowly and quietly, the door opened. Light from the rest of the plane silhouetted Sonya's form while landing on the bed next to Trey.

"I prefer it dark," he said without looking up.

"Okay," she replied in a near whisper, closing the door soundlessly. She ambled up to the side of the bed and waited for a reaction—which never came. Her clothing rasped softly as she lowered herself gently to sit on the bed's edge without rocking him. Two minutes crawled by with no response from him. She put a consoling hand on his back and scratched gently through the cotton of his plaid shirt.

"What do you want?" he muttered, face still in the pillow.

"I came to see if you were feeling better."

"Nope."

"Sorry. You know, I don't feel good about what happened in Dallas either, but you shouldn't keep beating yourself up over it. We didn't make the Chromes wreck half the city and blow up innocent motorists. *They* chose to do those things."

"Because *I* chose to not cooperate with them."

"Trey, I…" Sighing, she let her head loll forward.

"Do you have a gun?"

Curls flew as she spun to see his scarcely visible head in the dark room. "What?"

"Do you have a gun?"

The question haunted her. There was only one reason a man in his glum disposition would ask such a thing. She pushed the thought from her head, determined to keep him talking.

"No, I do not. They took it from me at the airport. Remember? Why do you ask?"

He switched on a reading light over where the bed and wall met. Then he rolled over to face her, remembering how attractive she was. "You know the Chromes don't care how many people they have to kill just to get to me, right?"

"Right."

"I could save a lot of lives by taking my own. Think about it."

Her disbelieving eyes were fixed on his face with more intensity than he could endure. After ten uncomfortable seconds of it, he rolled his head away to eye the wall.

"I can't let you do that," she said.

"Why not? If it's because I'm your only friend, I'm sure you can find a much better one."

"No. Just listen to me." She reached out to grab his jaw, making him face her again. "Listen. Do you remember when the Chromes picked us up in that jumbo jet near Denver?" He nodded. "Remember what I told you just before that happened?" His guileless gray eyes blinked as he harked back to that day. "I told you that I was helping you because God wants me to. I said that it was a long story and you said that you wanted to hear it some time. I think *this* is the best time. Do you still want to hear it?"

"Go on."

"A few minutes before we first met near Colorado Springs, I asked God what I should do with my life. As soon as I begged for a sign, that gunship flew over me and led me to you. Call it coincidence if you want, but the longer I'm with you, the more convinced I am that *you* are my sole purpose in life. More than once, you've saved my life and I've saved yours. That proves to me that you and I need each other. It hasn't been easy, but we both know my efforts have *repeatedly* kept you breathing. Are you really cold enough to make my hard work a total waste by putting a gun in your mouth?"

He blinked a tear away, then shook his head on the pillow. "No, Sonya. You're right. You're absolutely right." He sucked in a shaky breath. "I don't want to do *anything* unfair to you, even end my trivial existence."

"It's *not* trivial."

"Perhaps." His gaze drifted thoughtfully to the ceiling. "I just don't know why I ever made that vile machine. Or why I had to meet Zuri and be stupid enough to show it to her. Man, I hate that woman. She's a terrible, terrible person."

"Yeah, I know. It sure felt good, shooting her in the butt with that dart gun."

He chuckled with her. "Yeah, and I thought it felt good watching you do it."

"Of course, using her Glock would have felt even better."

"After you sedated her, you made the best use of an antique coffee table that I've ever seen." They shared another laugh. "Until I saw that, I always thought those things were useless."

"Me too." A third spell of mirth.

"Thank you for saving me again," he said warmly.

"From what? Your suicidal thoughts?"

"Exactly."

"Well, that's what I'm here for."

As he continued to beam upward at her, she adored the smile lines that flanked his large nose. Then she brought to mind his other admirable qualities. Though they'd shared a room for weeks, he'd never once tried to take advantage of her. Every night he'd chosen to stay in his own bed—something most men would not have done. There were some nights he'd unknowingly showed signs of longing to close all the space between them. She could tell it was mostly out of respect for her that he restrained himself—not fear of her dislocating his arm, which she could have done with little difficulty.

Why have I only been attracted to men who were tougher than me? she thought. *I don't care if I can kick Trey's butt. So what if he can't protect me as well as I can protect him. Society would tell me that those roles should be reversed. Forget stupid society! Trey is sweet, gentle, humble...and perfect for me.*

She was abruptly overawed by their history together, coupled with how courteous he'd always been to her. A weeks-old impulse in her veins blossomed to proportions she could no longer keep in check.

Seizing a fistful of his plaid shirt, she coaxed him to sit up straight. Then they shared a profusion of zealous kisses. Her warm mouth and embracing arms had more than their intended effect on him. Every agonizing thought in his head melted away, making room for a blissful dream that was transforming into a perfect reality. In seconds, he'd gone from feeling like the world's biggest problem to feeling like the luckiest man on earth.

Giving him time to breathe, she rested her chin on his shoulder and held him tighter. Then she whispered anxiously in his ear. "I know things don't make sense right now, but, please, no more thoughts about ending your life. I *need* you. I haven't lost my faith, so don't lose yours. God will give us answers. He put you on this earth for a reason. I don't know why, but we'll find out soon. You have to be patient, Trey. You *have* to."

"If I can wait for the answers while in the comfort of *your* arms, I'll never run out of patience. Trust me." She squeezed him so hard, he could scarcely take in air. Then her arms loosened, but still encircled him. "Does this mean that you're my girlfriend now?"

"Of course." Her lips neared his ear again. "Pray with me."

FORT MEADE, MARYLAND

The day after, Trey and Sonya spent hours in the imposing, high-tech surroundings of the NSA, being questioned by more faces than they could remember. There were generals, admirals, civilians in suits, all desperate to know everything the couple could tell them about the Chromes and CFCC. At first, the former scientist and former biker were interviewed separately for three exhausting hours so the VIPs could see if their stories matched. Then they were quizzed together for four more hours.

Nearly every bigwig who interrogated them knew Nova well and honored her requests to treat the couple with respect, give them anything they wanted for lunch, and, in exchange for their cooperation, wipe everything negative from their records in addition to a few more favors. It wasn't too much to ask since the odd pair had given the NSA names, explained how the Green Gates worked, and revealed everything they'd seen at CFCC. They were especially praised for crippling the terrorists' ops by destroying their only cargo plane.

At 1600, Trey and Sonya were in an elegant conference room, seated across a polished mahogany table from a trio of suits. Can lights limned paperwork scattered in front of the well-dressed officials to aid them in the tiring half hour of questioning. Then, Trey was given the most awkward inquiry of the day.

"Mr. Radisson, there is one more thing I want to ask," Barry Reynolds, the top executive in the room, said in a deep voice. His baggy blue eyes peered seriously over narrow reading glasses. "The Chromes could have gone after any scientist they wanted, but they singled you out. What do you know that sets you apart?"

Trey swallowed and exchanged glances with his new girlfriend. He gave the man of seventy-one years a grave look and chose his words carefully. "I know how to make something they want, sir."

"Something…like what?"

"Something I invented three years ago and then destroyed shortly after. Something I will never make again, for humanity's sake."

"Interesting." Barry clasped his wrinkled hands on the table. "Tell me about this 'something,' Mr. Radisson."

"I'm terribly sorry, sir, but that secret will die with me."

The three senior citizens exchanged whispered words for a minute. Then the leader spoke again. "As you wish. It is your right to have secrets, as long as they never become a threat to our national security."

"I understand, sir."

"It *is* for the sake of national security that he will never, *ever* reveal his secret," Sonya chimed in, squeezing her beau's shoulder. "He may be cursed with much-wanted knowledge, but you should have heard all the things he said last night. He proved to me that he is more than ready to die for our country."

"What do you mean?" the balding man to Barry's right asked.

"Do you know how devastated he was by what the Chromes did in Dallas? I had to talk a blue streak to convince him he shouldn't—"

"What she's trying to say is quite simple," Trey interrupted, too embarrassed by his past thought of suicide to have it voiced. "There is not a thing on this planet that will change my mind about taking my threatening secret to my grave."

"Well, I'm very delighted to know that," Barry said. He removed his specs and cleared his throat. "I think we can all move on to a more positive topic now. What about Christmas? It's only three weeks away. Have any plans?"

"No, but I would like to call my parents and *make* some plans. I haven't spoken to them for months."

"And you shall have that opportunity. You and Ms. McKill are heroes and we will send you anywh—" The elder to his left tapped his shoulder and whispered in his ear. "Okay, let me try that again. You and Ms. Mc*Call* are heroes and we will send you anywhere you want to go." He smiled after seeing the couple grin over his mispronunciation of Sonya's last name. Covering his mouth, Trey thought about what she'd done with a shotgun the last time they were on the roof of the Olivine Hotel. "And, for your protection, until the Chrome Falcon threat is finally over, we will utilize our satellites and have eyes in the sky on you at all times…unless you don't want that."

"Actually, I *do* want that."

"So be it. By the way, Trey, we are forbidding the media, nationwide, to come near you and your family. They will not speak of you or your girlfriend ever again. Not on the TV, Internet, or papers. Any overzealous news nut who fails to honor our directive will face prison time."

"That's great, but what about the First Amendment?"

"A waiver has already been made and emailed to every top media executive in America. They *will* honor it, and they will verify everyone beneath them honors it as well. The executives know that if they *don't* take the waiver seriously, they will lose millions to our government's steep fines…as a start. We will also provide both of you a copy of the waiver. You can think of it as a restraining order or no-contact order against the press."

"We really appreciate this, sir," Sonya said.

"Well, you two have earned this favor since the media destroyed your reputation. And they did it based on nothing but a theory of one blabber-mouthed cop. Before you leave, we need contact info from you. We will provide you an attorney to assist you with a settlement sometime next month."

"Settlement?" Trey queried.

"That's right, a settlement…with the media executive who allowed his people to think it acceptable to serve you all that injustice without solid evidence. You have a very strong case against that not-so-bright millionaire. He made the entire nation starting with Colorado hate your guts. You do want to sue him, don't you?"

"Absolutely." A chuckle stressed Trey's smile lines. "Ironically, Colorado is where I want to go for Christmas."

WINTER PARK, COLORADO

At 7:40 P.M. the following day, snowflakes peppered the Christmas-colored municipality as a white limo from the Denver airport entered. With her back to the driver, Agent Krenshaw was seated in the stretched sedan across from Trey and Sonya. The couple held hands as they gazed merrily out the windows at everything they passed. Multiple holiday-lit homes were the main thing seizing their attention whenever the snow-caked evergreens didn't block the view.

"Is it good to be back in your hometown, Trey?" Nova asked, gratified she'd had a lot to do with the pair's bliss.

"I can't remember the last time I felt *this* good," he replied, drawing a smile from the black woman. His excitement swelled as the car followed serpentine mountain roads leading to the address he'd given the chauffer earlier.

"You'll probably feel even better next month once the settlement is concluded. The odds are very much in your favor that you will both end up with a few million."

Trey exchanged a look of shock and elation with his girlfriend. They shared another kiss before he faced the agent. "Are you for real?"

"Absolutely. On the very rare occasions that the media links terrorists to an innocent man and woman, completely ruining the couple's lives, the press pays the price…sooner or later."

"But the media never used Sonya's real name. They didn't know it."

"That doesn't matter. They still put her picture on TV and made the entire country hate her as much as you. Her settlement may not be as big as yours, but it will still be pretty high."

"I think I speak for both of us when I say that I could thank you for all your help a hundred times and it still wouldn't feel like enough."

"Well, it's my pleasure." Hearing a chime, Nova looked down at her smartphone. After reading the newest text, she looked up at Sonya. "They've just made three arrests in Sacramento. I'm expecting many more tomorrow."

"Thank God," Sonya replied, and then mentally beat herself up for waiting three years to report all she knew about the Screamon Demons; she'd been too worried the authorities would discover her participation in a few Sacramento robberies. Had she *not* waited, Becky would still be alive.

"Arrests? Is she talking about the biker gang you used to be in?" Trey asked.

"That's right. But let's not bring that up around your family, okay?"

"That's *very* okay."

Sonya faced Nova. "Have any plans with *your* family this Christmas?"

"Don't have one. I was an only child and my parents passed years ago."

"Like me. No husband or kids?"

"Nope. I'm married to my career. But it's always a pleasure when I can reunite *other* families. I've always been hooked on helping people. I just can't get enough of it."

Trey's bulging eyes praised the FBI agent. *Why can't the world have more people like her?* he thought, then faced his sweetheart. "I never thanked you for what you did on your birthday—acted up in that fancy restaurant."

"*Thanked* me? What for? I got drunk and embarrassed you."

"I know. That's why I went off the next day to eat alone. If not for that, I never would have crossed paths with Nova…who gave us our lives back."

Sonya's eyeballs wiggled as her brain digested this fact. "Oh. I, uh…I guess you're right." She turned to the black woman again, honoring her with her own eyes. "I have an idea. Go sit next to her," she said to Trey.

"What for?"

"Picture time." Sonya pulled her smartphone from a pocket in her wool coat and switched on the camera app. Trey got up and crossed the limo to take a seat to Nova's right. Sonya sat on the agent's left and held the phone out for them all to see. Once all their smiling faces were on the screen, she tapped it, drawing a flash from the device. "Good. Now we can remember this moment for the rest of our lives."

"I would like a copy," Nova said. Sonya got the pic ready to send and passed the phone to the agent so she could type in her email address. The image was sent and the phone handed back. "That reminds me, I need to give this to you." Nova took an extra phone from her purse and handed it to Trey.

"What's this for?" he asked.

"So you can call me anytime you want. Until the reincarnated Nazis are history, I need to be able to reach you. You never know when Chrome-related trouble might brew around you again. If that happens, I can warn you about it now. For a few weeks, I'll be staying at the FBI office in Denver."

"Thanks."

He returned to his seat so Nova wouldn't feel crowded. Sonya did the same.

"So, what are your parents' names?" Nova asked.

"Rody and Mitzi Radisson."

"How did they react when you called them up and told them you'd be home for Christmas?"

"They were hysterically happy."

"You told them about *me*, right?" Sonya asked, throwing an arm around his shoulders.

He met her caring eyes with his own. "Of course. They know you're coming." They kissed again. "In fact, my mom told me she would have an extra room ready for you. She and my dad can't wait to meet you and hear about all our experiences together."

"We're almost there," the driver announced and turned right onto White Gales Drive, which had been made an official street less than three years ago. After a quarter mile, the stretched sedan made a left at a mailbox with all but the lid embedded in a decorative plinth. On each side of the granite block was an engraved rosette centered below a recessed copper plate, sporting a raised *47* in Old English digits.

"I guess their wait is over."

The limo slowed to a halt in the driveway of a mountain lodge-style home with fieldstone walls and log accents. Snow coated a slate roof edged with long icicles and sparkling Christmas lights. Studding a wall with three garage doors were four wrought-iron lanterns, bathing the driveway in corn-colored light.

When the chauffer opened the back door, Sonya was the first to step out. Her azure eyes drank in the massive, custom-built house. "What do your parents do for a living?" she asked Trey as he and Nova exited the car.

"My dad's a retired doctor who also invented some kind of medical equipment that's used all over the world," he explained, giving the home a similar look. "My mom just keeps him company. Until a year ago, they lived over on Timber Drive. So, it's my first time here too." He followed the salted steps leading to an arched front entrance. Sonya and Nova followed, donning wool stocking caps for their cold ears.

The trio neared double doors of ironbound oak befitting a castle. Hanging on the left door was a wreath with three cherubs and a red-gold ribbon coiled around the greenery. Trey's gloved hand reached for the doorbell's glowing button, centered in an engraving-smothered escutcheon. Hearing the muffled *ding-dong* inside, he looked back to exchange smiles with Sonya. As the indigo sky sprinkled white flakes across her jade hat and curly black hair, he admired her stylish winter clothing, believing the holly pinned to her wool coat's lapel was a nice touch.

With a *click*, the right door was tugged open, revealing a ruddy round face, framed by chopped graying hair. Smile lines like Trey's formed beneath the plump woman's oversized glasses. Chubby hands went skyward as Mitzi let out a delighted scream at the sight of her son. Then she threw her arms around him, giving him all the bliss he'd been hoping for.

"Welcome home! Welcome home! Welcome home!" she tittered, hopping as she squeezed him.

"I missed you, Mom," he said, patting the back of her red holiday sweater.

"Well, get inside, will you? All three of you. It's freezing out there." Once everyone entered the foyer, Mitzi closed the door and faced Sonya. "Jaaaaaane!" Trey's girlfriend gave him an awkward look as his mother embraced her. "I saw you on the TV." She gripped Sonya's shoulders and held her back to give her a sidelong grin. "Just remember, Jane, if you're dating my son, he shouldn't be on the back of your motorcycle anymore. Those things are dangerous. I once heard about a guy—"

"Mom, Mom, Mom," Trey interrupted.

"What, what, what?"

"Her name is not Jane."

"Sure it is, Trey. That's what the TV said. She's *Jane*. Jane *Doe*."

"The cops called her that because they didn't know her *real* name. Anyway, enough about that. Sonya, I'd like you to meet my mom, Mitzi. Mom, this is Sonya. Sonya McCall."

"Sonyaaaaa!" The bespectacled woman embraced her again, drawing a smile.

This woman cracks me up, Sonya thought, not sure if her voice was amusing or annoying.

"By the way, ma'am, I'm done with motorcycles," she reassured Mitzi. "After an experience I had in Dallas, I'm sticking with cars from now on."

"Well, bless you, Sonya. Bless you." She squeezed Trey's girlfriend tighter for a moment before releasing her.

"And this is Agent Krenshaw with the FBI," Trey introduced Nova.

"Krenshaaaaaw!"

The black woman chuckled as she accepted Mitzi's embrace.

"Is that you, son?" a stocky man with a short red beard intoned as he entered the foyer. He set his coffee mug down on an end table and neared everyone.

"It is, Dad," Trey replied. They hugged and slapped each other on the back. "This is a nice new place you've got here. Definitely bigger than your old house."

"I'm glad you're finally getting to see it, son."

"Hi, I'm Sonya," the tall young woman introduced herself after Trey's father let go of him. "You must be Rody."

"That's me. Nice to meet you, Sonya." He seemed impressed with her grip as they shook hands. Then he shared an eyebrow-raising glance with Trey, as if saying, *How did you win the heart of a beauty like her?*

"I'm Nova with the FBI," the agent told Rody and shook his hand next.

"Nice to meet you…I think. Is anyone I know in some kind of trouble?"

"Not at all. I'm just helping Trey. And I heard you've had cops and news crews at your door, asking crazy questions about your son, right?"

With eyes closed behind narrow glasses, he gave a revolted head shake. "Oh, man, I tell you what, all those nosy nitwits with their mics, lights, cameras, and—"

"Well, sir, I just want you to know that I have friends in high places and all that hogwash is over. No one will come to your door again with those harassing inquiries."

"Well, I sure do appreciate that, ma'am."

"You all take care. I need to go once my driver brings in your luggage."

Trey and Rody followed Nova outside to assist with the bags. Sonya trailed Mitzi further into the house.

"I'm making some hot chocolate. Want some?" the old lady offered.

"That would be great," Sonya replied.

"Okay. Make yourself comfortable. I'll be back."

As Trey's mother headed for the gourmet kitchen, Sonya doffed her snow-covered cap and eyeballed the cozy surroundings of the great room. At a low volume, "Christmas Cannon" played from a costly sound system. Exquisite creations from Rody's favorite hobbies—hunting and taxidermy—graced every wall. He'd hunted deer, elk, moose, mountain goats, bighorn sheep, pheasants, and ducks. Deerskins were draped over railings and rustic furniture. Twinkling lights coiled around greenery that festooned the vaulted ceilings and timber beams.

The next thing to seize her attention was a gorgeous Christmas tree, adorned with shiny ornaments and lights that kept changing colors. Firelight bathed her face as she gravitated toward a warm hearth of fieldstones stacked floor to ceiling. She smiled ear to ear when she saw the Christmas stockings hanging over the flaming logs; the red sock next to Trey's green one had JANE on it. She didn't care if the name was wrong; the fact that Mitzi had thought to make a stocking for *her* made her heart melt with euphoria.

The McCall family had never cherished this time of year as much as she'd wished. The synthetic tree she'd grown up around was small and pitiful. Christmas dinner was—on a good year—a bucket of fried chicken and a few sides. Her grandma and father had told her that Christmas lights were too expensive.

Worst of all, no one ever came to see them, even on holidays. Despite Iza's sincerest efforts to help everyone get along, her siblings had always despised each other. As if that wasn't bad enough, they'd allowed the hatred to be passed on to their children and grandchildren. Sonya never knew how many relatives she had since they all shunned each other. She'd always believed the word "family" was synonymous with "fighting."

The Radissons were nothing like that. They'd welcomed her as if she was already one of them, regardless of the fact that they knew little about her. Moreover, despite how well-off they were, they'd not allowed what they had to turn them into snobs. With the exception of her and her late grandmother, it took very little financial gain to turn anyone in her line of McCalls into a snob. Milly, one of Iza's four sisters, had married a millionaire and, within a year, started telling every sibling who called about coming to visit the most appalling words: "Your shabby cars just wouldn't look right in my classy driveway."

Still beaming, Sonya plopped down on the well-upholstered sofa, deciding there was nothing she would change about the moment.

DENVER

The evening after his ex-girlfriend arrived at Winter Park, Levi North was abed in a ramshackle room at the Lone Drifter—a cheap motel in the roughest slum of Colorado's capital city. For several weeks, he and his followers had been scouring every street for signs of the deserter, never knowing she'd been in Texas for almost the entire time.

The five bikers had grown a bit more demoralized every week. They'd had to buy warmer clothes as winter approached. They were running low on money. Everyone they'd mugged had not carried much cash. They missed their lives in Sacramento. Worst of all, there were not many biker gangs this far north. The ones they'd found in Denver had never seen or heard of Sonya McCall. Every time Levi showed her picture to someone in a bar, all he got was a headshake.

"Now *that* guy can tackle!" he raved, referring to the game on TV. One of Pittsburgh's linebackers had clobbered the player with the ball, keeping the Steelers nine points ahead of the Kansas City Chiefs. "Yes, sir, that's my boy! You disagree?"

He faced left, as if expecting an answer. The dead prostitute lying next to him said nothing. He'd snapped the curvaceous blonde's neck an hour ago when she'd denied him the refund he'd demanded for her "humdrum" service.

"That's what I thought," he snorted, taking a final drag on his stogie. "You better *not* disagree!" The cigar sizzled as he put it out in the body's pierced navel.

A chime on his smartphone drew his attention from the TV. He took up the phone to read four texts from Wade Grimes.

boss, dont com bak 2 Sacramnto evryone I know has been bustd.

no one will answr ther phone. had 2 leav my house n hide

Feds all over drug plant. dont kno wher they got info

Dont bothr replying im ditchn this phone b4 its traced

The burly leader of the Screamon Demons jumped out of the queen-size bed, wearing only skull-studded boxers. His heart sank as he read his phone's screen again and again.

I don't believe it! How did this happen? Who ratted us out? How will we sustain our fortune without our drug profits?

He let the phone fall from his hand, wondering if it, too, was being traced. His Taurus revolver was taken up from his nightstand with clumsy haste that spilled an ashtray across the stain-studded carpet. He aimed the gun at the phone a moment, and then changed his mind; even in this cut-rate motel, someone might call the police after hearing gunshots.

To get closer to the device, he dropped to his knees, feeling the tough carpet fiber bite into his skin. The phone was pistol-whipped to pieces. Recalling the last thing the shattered screen had said, he let his eyes fall closed and inhaled deeply.

Those stupid, party-pooper Feds! They've ruined me! I can't think about this anymore. It's making me sick. I need a drink or two...or ten.

Minutes later, he exited room 17, fully dressed for a cold ride to the nearest bar.

Maybe Melvin and Jed will join me for beer and shoot some pool with me. I think Rex and Ajax are still busy with a trio of call girls. All four of them can wait till tomorrow to hear the bad news. For right now, I just want to go enjoy myself.

Lighting another stogie, the depressed gang leader moseyed over to room 18. A large chip of the door's peeling paint fell off as he pounded a gloved fist on it. He was surprised when the almost-latched door swung open—into a dark room. When he flipped on the light switch, antique lamps limned two full-size beds with cigarette burns in their flannel coverlets.

One bed had a note on it. He stomped forth to snatch the piece of paper.

Boss,

We heard about Sactown. All four of us have left to go find jobs and new homes, as we've been thinking about doing for weeks. This stupid life of crime is just not working out for us. And we have wasted enough time on your ridiculous quest for vengeance on your ex. Good luck to you.

Melvin

The note was crumpled in his large fists as his blood boiled with unfathomable rage. He couldn't recall the last time he'd felt more livid and alone than he did right now. The plan to find a bar was still on; he would just need stronger drinks than what he'd had in mind earlier.

Tomorrow, I will keep hunting for Sonya. I will never stop, no matter how long it takes. Once I'm finished with that slut, I will make a new *hit list. No follower of mine ditches me for a stupid job and gets away with it! Once you're a Screamon Demon, it's supposed to be for life! But first things first.*

He scanned the room for things to break.

RADISSON RESIDENCE

Three weeks in Rody's and Mitzi's comfortable house were filled with events that made Sonya smile so much, her face hurt. There were heartfelt hugs from Trey's mother and two sisters, their sidesplitting stories of his childhood over mugs of eggnog and hot cocoa, and the shenanigans of his niece and two nephews. Sonya was further charmed by Mitzi's snowman-shaped sugar cookies, her friendly Pomeranian in a red and green sweater, two fluffy Persian cats that often chased each other, chimes from an elegant grandfather clock, and holiday comedies on the TV. Never in her life did she feel more at home.

On Christmas Day, when everyone gathered at the table for dinner, Sonya faced the only thing she would have changed about her time with the Radissons. Sitting across the table from her with a nonstop mouth was Jeff Allen—the fiancé of Trey's younger sister, Sherri. After loading up his plate with turkey, stuffing, cranberries, and mashed potatoes, Jeff's first insolent question was for Sonya's boyfriend in the chair next to hers.

"Yo, Trey," the long-haired chatterbox spoke over the platters. Trey tore his attention from stories about the kids to face Jeff. "You ever thought of getting a haircut? Jewfros aren't really in style anymore, dawg. Know what I'm sayin'?"

Who are you to talk about haircuts, Mr. Ponytail? Sonya thought.

Remembering the black dye was fading from his shock of yellow curls, Trey replied, "No, Jeff, I haven't." He cut the turkey slice on his plate. "Do you think if I got a haircut, I might be more socially acceptable?"

"Absolutely, dawg. Know what I'm sayin'?"

"I used to care about that. Later, I realized that people who matter *don't* care."

Jeff's tired-looking brown eyes went from Trey's hair to his attractive girlfriend. She gave Jeff a blank look, unable to remember him saying anything else to her beau. *Of all the words he could have said first, he'd chosen a crack about his hair?* she thought.

"Do you ever smile?" Jeff asked Sonya.

Now I've just heard his first words to me. *What's his problem?*

"Sometimes I do," she answered before spooning some of the green bean casserole into her mouth.

"Prove it. Smile for me."

Instead of obliging Jeff, Sonya chewed her food and recalled what a nuisance he'd been. She could tell she wouldn't like him, even before he'd entered the house the first time that week. Three days ago, she'd heard vulgar rap music booming outside. Then she went to a window in the great room to find the source—Jeff's yellow Dodge Challenger. He'd arrived with Sherri for his first visit that month, which was Sherri's third. Before coming inside, he'd tossed his cigarette on the driveway of his future in-laws. Later, he'd dominated most conversations with boastful, sarcastic remarks and told inappropriate jokes that only *he* laughed at.

The next thing Sonya recalled was from a week ago. On her way to the bathroom, she'd passed a dark room and heard Sherri on the phone. Since the door was not completely shut, Sonya had caught Sherri's alarming words to her future husband: "Jeff, if you're not ready to be a father, why did you keep placing the order? Did you not listen in biology class? I can't believe I accepted your negative feelings about condoms. Or the fact that you thought buying me an engagement ring gave you the right to stop wearing them! Gosh, you're so stupid! I'm so stupid! I should have stayed chaste, like my parents told me to do, but, noooo; I had to care too much about what you want! What? Don't talk stupid! Yes, you are! How dare you tell me our unborn baby is part of God's plan? God never made anyone pregnant since the Virgin Mary! You have some nerve, trying to play that card! We both know you're not even a believer!"

Besides the three of them, no one else in the house knew Sherri was expecting. Sonya was set on keeping her lips sealed about it. She felt bad for Trey's sister and wondered how long Jeff would stay faithful. She'd often caught his half-closed eyes appraising her face and figure with lustful peeps, unbeknownst to his fiancée. To Sonya, Jeff was nothing but a clone of half the lowlife boys she'd met during her teen years.

"Hello?" Jeff called out, snapping his fingers over the table.

After swallowing the tasty bite of Mitzi's casserole, Sonya blinked twice and shook her head from her musings. "I'm sorry, what?"

"Welcome back to Earth. Now, let's see you smile. Go on. Smile for me."

"Why? So I can be a phony, like you?"

Rody chuckled at her remark, letting cranberries spill off his spoon.

Dropping his fork, Jeff raised his hands in surrender as if Sonya were aiming a gun at him. "Whoa, calm down, girl. Damn! I'm just kiddin' around with ya. Just calm down! Know what I'm sayin'?"

Calm down? You're speaking much louder than me, moron!

"Sweetie, please be nice. It's Christmas," Sherri implored, patting Jeff's shoulder.

"*Me* be nice? What the f— What the heck did *I* d—" She tugged at his sleeve, giving him a serious look with one finger over her mouth. "Fine, fine." He slurped the last of his water. "I guess I just need a proper refill." He discreetly pulled a stainless-steel flask from his pocket, unscrewed the cap, and poured the intoxicating contents into his empty glass.

He sniggered when Sherri rolled her eyes and gave him a disapproving slap on the arm. "Jeff," she whined.

"What? This stuff warms me up. Know what I'm sayin'? I still feel the bite from outside a little bit. It's too damn cold out there. I am soooo ready for summer. Then I can do fun stuff again, like skydiving." For five minutes, Jeff gabbed about his past experiences with jumping out of planes. Then he faced the couple across the table. "Ever tried skydiving?"

"High-risk activities aren't really my thing," Trey replied as he cleaned his plate.

"*Whaaat?* What do you mean they aren't your thing? That's no way to live, dawg." He looked at Sonya. "What about *you*?"

"Nope," she said bluntly, spearing a bite of turkey.

"You guys need to get out more. Try new things. Know what I'm sayin'?"

"We don't need to try new things; we've already found the *best* things, starting with God. Besides, life is already too short. Why risk cutting it shorter with adrenaline-junkie jackassery?"

As Trey and his parents commended her last remarks, Sonya thought of the wild motorcycle ride across Dallas and through the shopping mall—an experience that belied her words. Then she reminded herself that she'd had no other choice.

"That's horse sh— Hockey. Horse hockey, dawg!" Jeff protested. Then he voiced more of his daring experiences, mostly around mouthfuls of food. Later, he got carried away with tedious stories of his achievements and good fortunes.

While washing down his dinner with a deep swig of water, Rody decided he'd heard enough from his daughter's betrothed. "Jeff, no good ever came from showing off or boasting, as you are so inclined to do," he huffed, setting his glass down. "News that only benefits you is not news worth sharing. So, why don't you give others a chance to speak for a while? Know what I'm sayin'?"

Scattered fits of laughter at Jeff's expense were heard around the table. Once the dinner concluded, Mitzi counted raised hands for her pumpkin pie, then again for pecan pie. After the scrumptious dessert course, everyone moved to the great room to be entertained by the children. The eight- and ten-year-old, Dustin and Tyler, sang Christmas carols as Mallory, their sister of thirteen, deftly supplemented their off-key voices on the upright piano. Flanking Sonya and Mitzi on the sofa were Sherri and the children's mother, Denise. All four women over-applauded the completion of every tune, drawing hysterical barking from the dog.

Nathan, Denise's husband, shared more amusing stories of the kids with Trey, Rody, and Jeff. The trio sipped mugs of cocoa as they heard Nathan's tales—which included one of Mallory when she was smaller.

"They had her play Mary in a Christmas play at church," the father of three explained. "However, Mallory's heart was clearly not into this, so she made one heck of an entrance. She's carrying a baby doll, which was supposed to be Jesus. She and the little boy playing Joseph walk out onto the stage. As soon as Mallory is near the manger, she just drops the doll in it and sits down. Didn't even hear the gasp from the audience. I couldn't decide if that was a win or a fail."

Nathan's audience laughed and faced the kids as an ovation faded for "Go Tell It on the Mountain." Then the boys and their mother tossed around ideas of what to sing next.

"Hey, kids!" Nathan called from across the room. "Do you remember the one I taught you last week?"

A few voices praised the idea as Denise objected. Tired of the arguing, Mallory, once again, pounded on the piano keys, cueing her brothers. The boys did a jig to the lyrics they sung.

Randolph, the bowlegged cowboy, had a very shiny gun.
And if you ever saw it, you would drop your pants and run.
All of the other cowboys used to laugh and call him names.
They never let poor Randolph play in any poker games.

Then one sunny Christmas Eve, Sherriff came to say,
"Randolph with your gun so bright, won't you shoot my wife tonight."
Then all the cowboys loved him as they shouted out with glee,
"Randolph, the bowlegged cowboy, you'll be hanging from a tree."

As the men chuckled and applauded, the women expressed their annoyance by rolling their eyes or shaking their heads.

"Why did you have to teach them that?" Denise scowled at her husband.

"I don't know," Nathan replied, shrugging. "Because it's... funny?"

"Do you know who wrote that?" Trey asked.

"I heard it was some kid in 1962—a girl in Buffalo, Texas, named Cindy Heil."

"That's nothing, dawg. Ever heard *this*?" Jeff chortled before quoting what he'd heard from an obscene friend. "'Twas the night *after* Christmas in my dad's rundown house. I found some porn when I clicked on the mouse. Dad's out of town and my mom's smoking grass. I'm on her laptop, staring at—"

"Enough, Jeff," Rody protested.

"I'm just kidding around, dawg."

"I don't care. There are children in this house." As Rody turned to go answer his ringing landline, Trey, Nathan, and Jeff exchanged other examples they'd heard of Christmas parodies. The old man returned, holding his portable telephone. "It's for you," he whispered, putting the silver phone in his son's hand. "Probably the FBI."

✞

Trey glanced nervously at the Panasonic portable and his father, who kept everyone talking, not wanting the jovial mood to fade. *Is this Nova?* he thought. *No one else knows I'm here. It must be her. What on earth does she want now?* Clearing his throat, he brought the phone to his ear.

"Hello?"

"Hi, jackass," Zuri Navarro replied hotly.

What? Zuri? Suddenly feeling dizzy, he almost dropped the phone. *Not good! So! Not! Good! Of all the people who could call me right now, why her?*

Chills ran down his spine and his heart hammered in his chest. His worst fear had come to life—the Chromes had discovered where his family lived.

Are they watching me right now?

A splendid wall of windows on the opposite side of the great room was the first place he looked. No one was peeking inside. There were no signs of choppers either; only a majestic view of a meadow and mountains.

Sonya's wandering eyes found him standing frozen and petrified with a fallen jaw and orbs that looked about to fall from their sockets. The sight of her beau impelled her to stand and make a similar face. She didn't know who was on the line, but could guess by Trey's face that the caller was big trouble.

As the kids began another Christmas song, none of their audience took any notice of their Uncle Trey leaving the room with his girlfriend trailing him.

"I guess I have your attention," the Filipino woman continued.

Determined to calm his nerves, he entered the hall bathroom and flipped on the light. Sonya shut and locked the door behind them and did a quick scan of the room for hidden cameras, finding none. Trey faced the bathroom's only window above a corner whirlpool tub. The grid of thick wavy glass was impossible for a potential intruder—or sniper—to see clearly through.

Taking a deep breath, he put his ex on speakerphone. "What do you want?"

"I want you to listen," she hissed. "What I have to say is for you and *only* you. Are you alone?"

"Am I alone?" Trey repeated. "I'm in the bathroom. What do you think?"

"I think it sounds like I'm on speakerphone! Why?"

"I like talking that way."

"I don't care what you like! Take me off the damn speaker!"

"Hang on." After he switched it off, Sonya put her ear close to his to hear the phone. With a finger over his mouth, he glanced at her. Understanding, she nodded. "Is this better? What do you want?"

"What do you *think* I want? I want your cooperation. What about you, Trey? What do *you* want? To die? For your family to die?"

"Of course not."

"Good, because I will let that happen if you don't do exactly what I tell you! You are completely surrounded by snipers with RPGs. They have that fancy house in their crosshairs, understand?"

The threat incited Trey's fury, which briefly chased away his fear and anxiety, emboldening him. "What the hell's wrong with you? It's Christmas!"

Sonya slapped a hand over her mouth, not wanting laughter to escape. As if terrorists would give a rat's behind about that.

"You shut up!" Zuri flared. "Shut up and take this seriously... before I give the snipers the go-ahead!"

Time to cut the stupid jokes, Trey, he scolded himself, getting the same message from his girlfriend's annoyed look. "Okay, okay, I'm listening," he ground out.

"Do you have any idea how hard it was for me to convince the colonel not to kill you? Do you know how much trouble you've been? Because of you, we've lost millions in cash and equipment! This buffoonery stops now! Otherwise, you and everyone you care about will not live to see New Year's Day!"

To no avail, he tried to push a dark future from his mind. It seemed this was the end. He would never again see his parents or sisters...or his beloved Sonya. For the rest of his life, the Chromes would force him to support their mission of tearing the country to pieces.

Maybe I could build a bomb disguised as my invention, he thought spitefully. *I could take out myself and as many terrorists as possible—a much better alternative to aiding them.*

"Well?" Zuri pressed, jarring him from his bleak musings.

"Just give me one thing," he implored in a soft voice. "Please?"

The Filipino woman sighed. "What?"

"Just...one more day...you know...to say good-bye to my family? My parents? My nieces and nephews? Please?"

"That was the colonel's plan anyway. He told me to allow you *half* a day to think about this. You know, to let your situation soak through your thick skull. We need you thinking clearly when we take you back to CFCC. You need time to let go of those ridiculous ideas about resisting us…for the sake of your family. Am I right?"

"Of course."

"Tomorrow morning at 9:30, you will wait outside the house. We expect to find you where your driveway meets the street. Be on time and be alone! Between now and tomorrow morning, if the snipers see anyone else—and I mean *anyone* else—step outside that house, like your trouble-making whore, she is dead! They'll shoot her fifty times and waste your entire worthless family! There will be nothing left of that nice house…but a pile of dust. Do I make myself clear?"

"Crystal." *You go to Hell!*

"Good. Oh, and one more thing: I want my briefcase back!"

When Trey heard the click of Zuri ending the call, he let the phone drop to the carpet. In out-and-out distress, he sat on the floor and combed fingers through his shock of hair. Dark thoughts of the days ahead returned to trouble him further. Sonya's consoling arms around him didn't help much. She thought hard for something to say.

"Dear God," she prayed in a whisper, cupping her man's face in her hands with her forehead against his. "Dear God, please, I beg you, don't let this happen. We need you. Please, God, please. Do som—"

A ringtone like an ancient rotary phone blared from Trey's thigh.

"What the…" he gasped, feeling it vibrate too.

Sonya's hand went in his pocket to fish for the source of the ringing. Her fingers came out gripping a smartphone—the same one Agent Krenshaw had given him. "Look!" she said, excited by the screen that blinked NOVA CALLING.

Feeling hope return, Trey took the phone and swiped the screen to answer. Then, for Sonya's benefit, he touched the corner for the speakerphone.

"Nova?"

"Yes, Trey," she replied coolly.

"The timing of your call suggests you've just heard my last conversation."

"Every word. We had your father's phone tapped in case this happened."

"Is there any chance the Chromes can hear us?"

"Not at all. This line is completely secure."

"I hope you have good news for us," Sonya chimed in.

"Good and bad. First the good. Ever since I brought you to that address, we've had the entire area under surveillance. Not just from orbit, but also from concealed ground units. I'm talking about a circle fifty miles across with that house in the center. We've been watching the area like a hawk and are ninety-five percent sure of what the Chromes will do tomorrow and where they are going. We have a surefire plan ready to acquire the coordinates of CFCC and end Chrome Falcon for good."

"Great," Trey replied. "What's the bad news?"

"Unfortunately, the plan will not work unless you do exactly what the psycho lady you were just talking to told you to do."

"What? You mean I have to let them take me to CFCC, right?"

"Wrong. They won't make it that far. You just have to get in their vehicle and let the FBI do the rest. And don't look out the window of the car, as if you're expecting help."

He exchanged dubious looks with Sonya. "I have to get in their vehicle? There's got to be another way."

"Of course. You and Sonya can spend the rest of your lives looking over your shoulder for armed Chromes disguised as innocent civilians. The Bureau can spend months tailing you and trying to protect you until they decide it's no longer worth it. Meanwhile, the threat of Chrome Falcon will continue to grow."

"Or I can be the bait that lures them into your trap, right?"

"Exactly. Believe me, I don't like the idea at all of putting you in that hazardous situation. But consider this: once this is all over, you will become the main American to thank for ending our nation's greatest threat."

For nearly a minute, Trey chewed this over. Spending a few minutes under the Chromes' control didn't sound as bad as the alternative. His eyes met Sonya's, asking what she thought. She slowly nodded her head—as he was hoping deep down she would do.

"Okay, I'm in."

"Good. Now, go pack a suitcase."

"Pack a suitcase?"

"The Chromes have ordered you to live with them at CFCC. If they come to pick you up and you're not carrying a suitcase filled with clothes, it will look suspicious."

"Oh. Good point."

"And, like 'Miss Miser' told you, don't forget the briefcase full of dough."

"What?" He recalled Zuri demanding the briefcase. She'd said nothing about the contents of it. "You knew about that?"

"I've known ever since we left Dallas. Before it was put on the plane, security checked it. You may recall the time I asked Sonya about its contents. She called it her private stuff."

Sonya blushed. "I'm sorry I wasn't completely honest about that."

"Don't worry about it. Trey, I need you to leave that smartphone with Sonya before the Chromes come to get you. I'm pretty sure they will thoroughly search you, so don't have anything on your person…except your wallet. In the next hour or so, you should warn your loved ones that they can't call anyone and they can't leave the house until you tell them otherwise. Don't say a word about what's going on. If they ask, just tell them the FBI said so because of suspected terrorist activity in the area—activity that may or may not be related to you."

"Uh…okay. And how do I explain my leaving, especially with two carrycases?"

"Tell them the Bureau is coming to pick you up and you can't say why. You also can't say what's in the cases. Just tell them you plan to be back in a few hours."

That's going to be awkward, he thought. "Fine."

"Trust me, Trey, my whole team and I are here for you. Call me anytime if you have any questions."

"Okay. Uh…bye, for now."

"Good luck."

The call ended.

"Can I go prep your suitcase while you warn everyone?" Sonya asked.

"Yes, please," Trey replied.

The couple came out of the bathroom, finding Jeff waiting to use it. "Oooh, what were *you* two doing in there?" he intoned with a sassy grin.

"You'll never know," Trey answered nonchalantly as his girlfriend gave the randy man a hard look. The lewd inquiry was the last thing they needed right now.

"I'm just kidding. Geez. Lighten up."

Sonya couldn't take any more of the rowdy, degenerate slob. She'd seen enough and heard enough out of him. Now, *he* would hear *her*!

"I barely know you, but I can already tell you talk too much," she told him tartly. "Not only that, but I think your favorite words are 'I'm just kidding.' Am I right?"

"I've noticed that too," Trey put in, also recalling Jeff's unlikable behavior. "If that's your best punchline, stop trying to be funny. You never will be."

"Come on, guys." Jeff's arms made a gesture of mock regret. "Don't be a pair of Scrooges. Where's your Christmas spirit?"

Sonya brought her face inches from his, boring into his shameless soul with her icy blue orbs. "We left it in the great room where it belongs, smarty-pants!" she countered, striving to keep her voice down. "If you want to sit in the can and sing 'Silver Bell,' be our guest! Better yet, go in there and think about what you did to bring out this side of us. Trey and I are good people who cherish Christmas. You might have realized that, but you were too busy yapping about yourself like a spoiled nine-year-old. Don't lecture us about Christmas spirit, jackass! The only thing crushing *anyone's* spirit is your intolerable lack of manners. So, grow the hell up!"

With a fading smile, Jeff cowered from her piercing gaze and nervously eyed the floor. He finally grasped that he'd gone too far as her decisive words replayed themselves in his infantile brain. Moreover, not only was she three inches taller than he was, but the sleeveless shirt she'd worn a day ago revealed sinewy muscles he'd not soon forget. Her arms were clearly stronger than his, but not enough to understate her feminine shape. He no longer doubted Sonya could put him in the ER if he pushed her buttons enough times.

"We don't have time for all this!" Trey scowled. "Our lives are in danger!"

"Yeah, you're right," Sonya agreed and checked down the hall for curious faces. To her relief, no one had heard her tirade over the piano or children's voices.

"Danger?" Jeff asked fretfully.

"I'll explain later," Trey promised. "Just come back to the great room when you're done in the can. I need to talk to everyone. I know you're not much of a listener, but trust me, you want to hear what I have to say today."

✝

Before closing the bathroom door, Jeff watched the toughest woman he'd ever met devotedly follow her beau down the hall. Sonya's raven-black hair was a gorgeous curtain of ringlets swaying behind her hourglass waist. Further down, flaring hips and muscular legs filled her black denims quite well.

Nerdy or not, Trey is the man! Jeff silently praised. *How did he ever steal the heart of that feisty beauty? And, geez, if only* Sherri *looked that good in tight jeans.*

Trey steeled himself for his departure at 9:25 A.M. the next day. He slowly exited the front door, baggage in hands. Keeping him warm was a black winter cap and a blue-and-yellow parka his father had given him. With a pair of aviator shades on his hawk-like nose, he nervously descended the salted steps. His anxious breaths steamed in the chill air as he gave the darkness beyond the surrounding evergreens a few once-overs. If the snipers were out there, they were hidden well.

Strolling past a parked pair of Dodges—Nathan's green Durango and Jeff's yellow Challenger—Trey took one last look at the largest windows of the house. With hopeful eyes, Sonya, Rody, Mitzi, Sherri, Jeff, Denise, Nathan, and the three children watched him from the great room with their hands on the glass. It had not been easy warning them to stay in the house without understanding anything beyond the "suspected-terrorist-activity" explanation. Calming them down had also been difficult, albeit Sonya had been helpful. It was also useful to have Nova's permission to blame the Bureau for the odd warning and for his unexplained departure.

The words "I love you" could scarcely be read from his girlfriend's lips as the windowpanes reflected the cloudless sky. Recalling what occurred ten minutes ago—their possibly-good-bye-forever kiss—he put down the carrycases to say "I love you" the way a deaf person would. Nearly everyone inside made the same words for him in sign language, not realizing he was only talking to Sonya. The mixup made him smile. His message might as well have been for the entire family since he deeply cherished all of them. If there were any exceptions, it would be Jeff.

He recalled how upset his sweetheart had been that she could not accompany him this time. If she put even a toe outside, the snipers would shoot her and fry the house with everyone inside. Trey wanted to mouth more words, like "I'll be right back," but chose not to. What if the snipers could read lips? What if the FBI failed him and he did *not* make it back?

Hearing only snow crunching underfoot, he headed further down the driveway. The house vanished behind a stand of cedars as he neared White Gales Drive.

✝

At 9:45 A.M., Trey was still puttering around his parents' mailbox, wondering what was taking the Chromes so long. A fleeting look at his watch showed him the extremists were fifteen minutes late. He kept his hands warm in his pockets as the nippy morning air continued to make his fretful breathing visible. Mostly out of boredom, he meticulously scanned every direction for any sign of a man holding an RPG or a rifle with a scope. He still felt utterly alone and wasn't at all surprised; the forest offered plenty of places for the radicals to stay invisible.

"What's keeping you psychos?" he groused, verifying the mailbox's address number had not been concealed by the last snowfall.

Then the first vehicles he'd seen all morning on the quiet street came into view. Two Toyota 4Runners made the final turn before the Radissons' driveway. His heart raced as the SUVs approached. When the silver one in the lead passed him, he saw three occupants wearing shades and civilian clothing. The two people in the front looked unfamiliar. The woman in the back looked like Zuri.

The silver 4Runner parallel parked on the wrong side of the

road, three yards left of the driveway. Four men occupied the black 4Runner as it parked near the mailbox. Both SUVs flanked Trey, as if prepared to counter any resistance. He shot worried glances right and left.

A bearded terrorist, seated behind the black vehicle's driver, got out to level an HK433 at Trey. Scowling, the stocky gunman scanned the trees, verifying the man in his sights was alone. With his heart hammering at the sight of the assault rifle, Trey allowed a dozen terrible thoughts to worry him.

Will he really let me live? Or is he verifying there will be no witnesses as he murders me? I have been Chrome Falcon's biggest problem. Maybe they've decided I'm no longer worth keeping alive. Maybe Zuri's words were meant to cow me out of the house and make myself an easy target. Please, God, don't let this be the case. Am I going to survive this day? Of course I am! Don't be ridiculous, Trey! The snipers hidden around the house could have ended you at any time.

All but the driver exited the black SUV. The terrorists' winter clothing gave no hints of who they served; they thought it best to leave their uniforms at CFCC and come dressed as residents of Colorado. With stylish specs on his nose, the black man from the front seat beckoned Trey over. He complied, bringing both carry-cases with him.

"Martinez, check the bags," Specs ordered in a deep voice. The other man from the backseat, a short Puerto Rican, strode up to take Trey's cases away. "Lose the coat, Mr. Radisson!" Sighing, Trey unzipped and doffed the parka, letting it fall on the snow-caked road. Already, he felt the bite of the chill air. "Hands on the hood! Spread 'em!"

Specs shoved Trey in the back and kicked his inner ankles. As the former inventor was frisked head to toe, he watched Martinez unzip his soft blue suitcase and empty its contents. The clothing was kicked around in the snow as he searched for anything suspicious.

"*This* bag is good, Captain," Martinez humbly assured the black man.

"Throw it all in the trees and search his coat."

He complied. "Coat's good."

"Now, the briefcase."

The leather container was set on the black 4Runner's hood. After Martinez found the latches to be uncooperative, he faced the captive.

"Three-one-two, nine-seven-eight," Trey sighed the combination. The briefcase was opened. Most of the money packets were still in it. Not knowing how much it contained before, Martinez closed it.

"Well, Mr. Radisson, I see you brought no weapons *or* a phone," the captain voiced his observation. "I guess this means you've finally learned your place and you're ready to start taking us seriously now, aren't you?"

Trey nodded, thinking it best to feign further hopelessness. "Why can't I bring my luggage?"

"Don't worry. We'll give you *new* clothes…starting with one of our uniforms."

"Uh…okay." *I'd rather wear a muumuu.*

The Puerto Rican tossed Trey his parka. After he caught it, he didn't hesitate to put it back on as the freezing temperatures made his jaws clatter together. Once he zipped up the coat, Martinez tightly secured his hands behind him with a cold pair of handcuffs. Trey could already feel the metal restraints draining body heat from his wrists.

He didn't see Zuri coming from the other vehicle until she was three strides away. The sloe-eyed Filipino brought her livid face near his. Then her gloved hand flashed out, slapping his cheekbone and tossing his shades in the snow. Nearly losing his balance, he thought of nothing for five seconds but the sting in his chilled face and the ring in his ears.

"That's for what you did to Dillon!" she flared, shaking a wisp of her lank black hair from her face. With a muffled *crunch*, she spitefully stomped on his sunglasses.

"Come on, Zuri," Trey whined, staying in character. "I didn't make your crazy boyfriend fly his helicopter inside a shopping mall."

"I don't care what you say he did! There's two sides to every story!" She opened the briefcase, noting crossly that some of the cash was gone. Then she checked the empty side pocket. "Where's the diamonds?"

"I sold them. Sorry." He hung his head, praying his ex-fiancée didn't shoot him in the foot or something similar.

She slammed the lid closed, secured the latches, and scrambled the dials to ensure the briefcase didn't fall open. "You dumb bastard! You're gonna pay for that!"

"Lieutenant, we need to leave now," the captain cautioned. "We don't have time for this."

"Fine." The petite woman took the briefcase off the SUV's hood. Then she pulled a .45 from her wool coat and pressed the cold muzzle under Trey's chin.

Stay calm, he told himself, feeling a bead of sweat crawl down his temple, despite the icy air. *She won't kill you; she needs what's in your brain too much.*

"You're riding with me," she hissed.

"How nice."

"Do anything stupid and I'll aim this at your knees…or maybe someplace you'll never need." The firearm was held against his groin. "Got it?"

"Got it." Once she backed the gun away, he headed for the silver 4Runner.

"Slow!" She followed him, keeping the pistol trained on his back with her right hand as her left carried the briefcase. "Passenger side. You're riding shotgun." When she opened the specified door for him, a weather-beaten face turned to scowl at them. "Get out, Wilcox. You're riding in the back with me." Groaning, the man threw down his cigarette and gave up his seat to the captive.

Without the aid of his cuffed hands, Trey awkwardly climbed into the leather seat. Then Zuri shut the door. Trey found only one thing to like about sharing a vehicle with the enemies—the heater worked well, instantly relieving the chill in his bones. Next to him was the driver, a doe-eyed beauty with an unruly mass of auburn curls. Taking a drag on her own cancer stick, she regarded him derisively. Then she put her shades back on, blowing a noxious cloud at him. Showing no contempt, he turned his straight face down for a coughing fit. Wilcox and Navarro got in and pulled the rear doors shut.

"Let's go, Blake," Wilcox told the haughty redhead. She cracked open her window long enough to toss out her Newport, put the vehicle in drive, and eased off the brake. The silver Toyota made a U-turn and headed down the road with its black twin tailing it.

After half a mile, Trey slowly twisted his neck to study the duo seated behind him. Zuri still gripped her .45 and was in the perfect spot to shoot him if he did anything reckless.

"What are you looking at?" Wilcox bristled. He looked ready to punch the scientist's beaklike nose.

"Turn around!" the Filipino spat.

Wearing a despondent face, he obeyed and regarded the windshield as the 4Runner made multiple turns, climbs, and descents on the serpentine mountain roads. Next, he thought about the discomfort of the handcuffs and wished they were not behind his back. After that, he thought of the unbearable wait he'd endured on his parents' driveway.

"You guys showed up a little later than 9:30," he said casually, trying to slow his pulse.

"What about it?" Blake huffed, unsure if he was slighting her driving competence.

"Did you have trouble finding the place?"

"Not that it's any of your business, but, yes, we did," Zuri replied after exchanging looks with Wilcox. She decided to elaborate after an awkward silence. "Three years ago, you told me your parents lived in Colorado. I just couldn't remember which town or their first names. So, after we lost you in Dallas, I searched the Internet for every Radisson in Colorado. For days, I called multiple numbers, asking if Trey was there."

"Then she realized she was misspelling your name," Wilcox interjected, snickering.

"Do you mind?" she snapped, causing his smile to fade.

"I can't wait for this drive to be over!" the redhead added. "Both of you men are complete windbags!"

"So, I corrected the spelling," Zuri continued after more silence. "Then I tried more numbers. It wasn't until yesterday that I tried the number that happened to belong to your father. Twenty minutes ago, we went to the address that was listed with that number and all we found was a house for sale. So, I did a more meticulous search and discovered your parents had recently moved to White Gales Drive, but kept their old phone number."

"I see," Trey said, trying not to laugh. *If only I could have seen your face when you found my dad's* old *house.*

✠

As the pair of 4Runners moved deeper into the Arapaho National Forest, thoughts on the mission were exchanged in the black SUV.

"This is ridiculous," the bearded man carped. "This is a very important op and I feel like we're far too vulnerable right now. Why couldn't Colonel Epperson get more men and equipment for this task?"

"I heard that General Casprite won't let him have any more," the nearsighted captain said. "After the failed op in Dallas, the general lost too much faith in the colonel to entrust him with more gear and personnel."

"The Dallas op cost us a lot while gaining us nothing," the driver added. "Colonel Epperson made a big mistake by putting that idiot Captain Ferch in charge."

Near Winter Park Resort, the two SUVs climbed numerous twisting roads rarely used by the locals. Not once did Trey see any signs of FBI among the trees. Despite Nova's warning, he wasn't worried about raising suspicion with his bulging eyes fixed on his window; it only made him look curious about where they were going.

Come on, Nova! Where are you? Where are your people? You've got to get me out of this! he thought fretfully.

✞

Satisfied with the distance from the Radisson home, Zuri subtly pulled out her smartphone and selected a name on her contact list. A message was typed up and sent. Her lips barely rose at the corners as her eyes shot daggers at the back of Trey's head.

And this *is because I don't like your girlfriend*, she thought.

The recipient of Zuri's message was Sergeant Felton. He was staying warm inside his olive dome tent, smoking and playing videogames on his smartphone. Then the text from Lieutenant Navarro interrupted his game.

Destroy the Radisson home now.

"Well, it's about time," he grumbled, unzipping the tent's entrance. What his commanding officer had told Trey yesterday was not entirely accurate—Felton was the *only* sniper. Warm camouflage clothing hid him well in the evergreens as he finished his Camel cigarette and stood to regard the isolated target one last time. The lodge-style home was across a ravine about a quarter mile from his vantage point.

Felton readied his RPG and eyed the back of the house through his optical sight. He'd been warned to not approach the target from the road; the Radissons could have seen him and called police.

With the largest window in his crosshairs, he fired.

Leaving a cloud of sour smoke, the rocket hissed away. Felton watched as the deadly projectile soared over the ravine and closed in on the point of entry. Windowpanes crumbled from the rocket's swift passage before it exploded. Debris and fire thundered from every window. The blast made enough holes and cracks in the roof to collapse it. Then, things quieted as smoldering ruins settled under a rising black cloud.

"Got rid of *you* rich fatheads, didn't I?" the sniper whooped and cackled, not knowing what stood in the home's front yard—

—a Realtor's sign.

After going to the wrong house, Navarro had searched the Internet again. When she'd found the *correct* address, she'd forgotten to inform Felton.

✞

"I don't know about the rest of you, but I'm making a beeline for the dining hall when we get back," Wilcox said. "I'm starving. Any idea what they're serving for lunch today?"

"It doesn't matter," Navarro told him. "As soon as we're back at CFCC, I'm getting out with Trey. You and Blake will drive back through the gate after the guys behind us reactivate it."

"Huh? What for?"

"I need you two to help them pack up all the gate's equipment. After that, follow them to the *permanent* gate near Kremmling."

"Oh, come on, Lieutenant. Don't do this to us."

The driver sighed, sharing Wilcox's discontent.

"Stop bellyaching! You guys can go eat somewhere in Granby. It's on the way to Kremmling."

Ignoring everyone, Trey continued to watch the evergreens go by. He still hated how his cuffed hands felt between the seat and his lower back.

The silver Toyota slowed to a halt, reminding him he'd not observed the windshield for over a minute. The road ended at a large clearing in the cedar forest. A portable Green Gate had been set up a few yards ahead. Two hexagonal posts jutted vertically from a pair of chocked carts. The only thing left to do was activate the field and drive through it, sending the SUV and its occupants to CFCC.

"Wilcox, go punch in the code," Navarro ordered as Blake put the vehicle in park. The weather-beaten man got out and made tracks across the snow to the left pole.

Come on, Nova, help me out here! Trey thought nervously.

A twelve-button keypad was exposed after Wilcox raised a panel installed where the shaft was connected to its four-wheeled cart. With a series of bleeps, he entered an eight-digit code and hit the pound sign.

Red lights atop the black posts flashed once. Emitters extended up and down the poles with a chain of clicks. Green, translucent energy formed a buzzing rectangle between the columns, distorting the view of pines behind it. Two seconds later, the glow faded and the view sharpened as the power field's transparency nearly matched the 4Runner's windshield.

Displayed over the buttons were bright red numbers of a digital timer. After the time limit of half a minute was up, the gate would shut down. The seconds began ticking away: 0:30…0:29…0:28…

Nova, now would be a good time.

Wilcox took three hurried strides back to the SUV—

—then collapsed in the snow after a spray of blood escaped his skull. No one had time to determine the source of the bullet that had gone through the man's head.

Navarro's gun, visible to anyone outside her window, fell from her hand as another shot punched a hole through her window and wrist. Crying out in agony, she yanked off her scarf to use as a bandage.

Turning the windshield white with a thousand cracks, a third round entered the vehicle. The slug drilled deep into Blake's forehead. With a crimson leak, her face thumped down on the steering wheel, sounding the horn. Her shades fell off, revealing unblinking green eyes fixed on the dashboard.

Trey huddled behind the console as Zuri continued to fumble with her scarf to stop the bleeding. Both were startled by an RPG that met the other 4Runner behind theirs. All four men inside died instantly in a blast that tossed the vehicle high in the air. In a bundle of fiery ruins, it boomed back down to Earth with its collapsed roof resting where the tires had been.

The silver Toyota's only two living occupants gaped out the rear window, scarce believing what had just happened to the escort vehicle. Everything had transpired so fast; Wilcox had collapsed only ten seconds ago.

Then Trey's attention returned to the front and he wondered how many snipers were outside. The windshield disintegrated on its own, showering the dashboard with tiny pebbles of glass as it revealed the view. Two men in black FBI jackets had come out of hiding and were standing near the Green Gate, observing the timer's remaining seconds: 0:15…0:14…0:13…

One Fed was holding a grooved, light-studded device the size of a three-liter soda bottle. The second after Trey noticed it, the sophisticated-looking gadget was tossed into the energy field. With a static sound, it was sent instantly to the enemy's command center.

The other agent busted one side of the gate with a vicious swing of an axe, cutting off possible reinforcements or any chance of the device being thrown back. Sparks burst as the energy field winked out. Both hexagonal poles groaned, powering down.

Euphoria washed over Trey when he spied what emerged from the trees—ten more Feds armed with automatic weapons. Most of them formed a ring around one man staring intently through his glasses at the flat device in his hands—an electronic tablet half the size of an average computer monitor.

This team must be under Nova's command, Trey deduced since he was now the only one unscathed by the ambush.

The SUV's bothersome horn was still blaring stridently. More blood escaped from the bullet hole in Blake's forehead and ran down her pretty face. *What a shame*, Trey mused, noting the ringless fingers of her dangling arms. *With a better attitude, respect for the law, and no nicotine addiction, she could have made someone a lucky husband.* With one foot, he shoved the redhead's corpse against her door so her bleeding head would slide off the steering wheel, ending the irritating noise.

"It's about time you Feds showed up," he voiced his next

thought, mainly to infuriate Zuri, who'd already noticed the FBI group outside.

"What?" She glowered, then her eyes enlarged to such an extent, she no longer looked Asian. "You knew this would happen? What's going on? I thought the FBI believed you were with *us!* How did you—"

She shrieked again as glass pebbles showered her from a shotgun's stock busting through her cracked window. The brawny man holding the gun—an agent whose approach she'd not noticed—spun the weapon with both hands to train the barrel on her face.

KA-CHAK!

"Don't move!" he warned, letting her cradle her injury; she clearly wasn't interested in picking up her .45 from the floor mat.

"You wouldn't dare shoot a pregnant woman...would you?" Zuri asked him with a phony smile.

"You let Dillon the Degenerate knock you up?" Trey scoffed without looking at her. "You're a special kind of stupid, aren't you?"

"Shut up!"

Looking cross at him, she didn't see the female agent approach the 4Runner. The woman aimed a pistol through the shattered window and squeezed the trigger.

SNAP!

Zuri gritted her teeth from the sleeping agent fired into her neck.

"*You* shut up," the Jewfroed man shot back.

Seeing the Filipino's injured hand, the agent called for a medic and rounded the back of the SUV. After turning woozy and getting blurred vision, the petite lieutenant plopped across the backseat for a sixty-minute count. Trey gave her a pleased glance.

A lanky guy with a mustache opened Trey's door so he could get out. "Are you okay, Mr. Radisson?" he asked, picking at the locks on his cuffs. His female comrade put a comforting hand on Trey's back.

"Yeah, I'm fine," he assured them. "Couldn't be better, in fact. You must be Agent Krenshaw's team."

"That's us," the woman replied. Then she turned to check the medic's progress on Zuri, wanting her alive for questioning.

The male agent finished his work on the handcuffs, letting them drop in the snow. Trey immediately rubbed his sore wrists, delighting in the freedom to use his hands again.

"I'm Agent Cline," the man introduced himself with an offered hand.

"Very nice to meet you, sir," Trey replied with a huge grin and shook Cline's hand. "Thanks for coming to rescue me from these psychos." Then he remembered what he'd left in the silver 4Runner. "Well, let's go see how Agent Riley's doing."

After pocketing Zuri's pistol and taking the briefcase from the SUV's backseat, Trey shut the rear door and joined the ring of FBI formed around Riley—the man with the tablet.

"Wait, here it comes!" he announced, quite agog as he watched the activity on the touchscreen. A forty-eight percent became fifty-three and the number continued to rise. A green status bar bleeped and stretched across the screen. Filling the background was an aerial view of wilderness—zooming in. "The signal is strong. Here it comes! Here it comes! And…" When the status bar reached its full length, the zooming stopped. The bar and 100 percent were replaced by lines of info. "*…bingo!* We have Groovy's coordinates!"

"Groovy?" Trey queried.

"Right, Groovy—the transmitter/robot we tossed through the Green Gate a minute ago."

"Oh, okay." *So,* that's *what that gadget was. I would have picked a better name for it though.* "Why didn't the Chromes destroy it?"

"Groovy is doing more than sending us a signal," Cline explained. "Groovy is also releasing a giant cloud of sedative gas. So, no one at CFCC can see Groovy right now, much less go near him… unless they want to pass out."

"Really? That is pure genius!"

"Groovy also has a block of C4 inside him, which I'm about to spark off," Riley informed everyone as he selected a different app and tapped the screen here and there. "That way, the terrorists will never know what kind of device he *really* was." In another series of bleeps, DETONATING flashed in yellow. "Okay, that's done. I bet

Groovy took out over a dozen of those modern-day Nazis."

"Send the coordinates to Krenshaw," the man who'd pitched the transmitter through the Green Gate said.

"Already done." The mobile device chimed as Nova's reply came in. "Excellent! She just confirmed she has their location. In seconds, the military will know where to strike and blow that peak back to the Dark Ages."

"What peak?" Trey asked.

"*This* one." The agent selected his first app and showed him the tablet's screen. The background had become a colorful elevation map with the terrain's significant features labeled. In the foreground, four lines of text spelled out details of CFCC's precise location.

> **COORDINATES:** 45.4407708°N, -110.139632°W
> **APPROX. ELEVATION:** 10,138 FEET (3,090 METERS)
> **USGS TOPO MAP QUAD:** CHROME MOUNTAIN
> **FEATURE TYPE:** SUMMIT

"You've got to be kidding me!" Trey exclaimed. "Chrome Mountain? Chrome Falcon's headquarters is inside a place called... *Chrome* Mountain? I didn't know such a place was even real." Next, he recalled the dream Sonya had told him about when they'd stayed at the Olivine. She'd mentioned someone controlling a trio of CF Gunships...within a mountain. *Now,* that's *scary!* he thought.

"Where in the world is Chrome Mountain?" Cline asked—a question no one but Riley knew the answer to.

"Montana," Riley said, eyeballing the touchscreen again. "It's between Livingston and Custer Gallatin National Forest."

"I still don't know."

"Oh, well, if the military sends in any ground forces, they will probably use Main Boulder Road to get there."

Trey had seen and heard enough. His part in this was finished. Now, he wanted to return to his concerned family. "Sorry to interrupt," he apologized. "But can I go back home now?"

"Soon, Mr. Radisson," Cline vowed.

The scientist regarded what was left of the silver 4Runner. "How will I get there? The same way you guys got *here*?"

"No, the same way that Asian with the hole in her wrist is leaving." At an upward angle, he pointed to a distant 520N NOTAR helicopter thrumming toward the clearing. "The pilot will drop you off right before rushing her to the nearest hospital."

"That will be interesting." He couldn't wait to see the looks on his family's faces when the chopper landed near their house and he got out of it.

"What have you got there?" a different agent asked Trey, eyeing the briefcase in his hand. "Is that your luggage or something?"

"Uh…that's right," he answered tensely.

"Cline, come in!" Nova's voice demanded between two bursts of static.

The lead agent reached inside his jacket for the two-way radio clipped to his tactical vest. He held in the *PTT* button. "Go, boss."

"Take cover, now! More Chromes are coming! We have help on the way!"

Confused, Cline and his charge gave their environs an uneasy once-over, finding nothing to be alarmed about. Trey looked again at the black NOTAR, growing louder with nearness. Backgrounded mostly by the clear azure sky, the copter was dwarfed by something further away—a hot air balloon floating beyond a pine-cloaked ridge. In Wide Latin text, WINTER PARK RESORT ran across the colossal envelope, patterned with zigzagging bands of maroon and navy. Even if he'd brought binoculars, he wouldn't have been able to see who was riding in the delicate aircraft's gondola; it was hidden behind the treetops.

Again, he studied the small chopper, hovering without the need of a tail rotor. The bold white FBI was very apparent on the shiny fuselage. Not so apparent was the pilot. After hearing the concern in Nova's voice, he wanted to know if he should be worried about who was in either one of the aircraft.

Cline raised the radio to his face again. "Are they on the ground or—"

RAT-TAT-TAT-TAT-TAT-TAT-TAT-TAT-TAT-TAT!

A fusillade of tracer rounds exited the immense heated envelope, perforating the NOTAR's fuselage.

"Never mind," the agent told the radio. All eyes were on the Swiss-cheesed rotorcraft as its engine stalled. Leaving a smoke trail, the aircraft nosedived behind the nearest ridge. Seconds later, the echoing rumble of the unseen crash came, followed by a rising black cloud.

"Impossible," Trey gasped, staring upward at what seemed to be the source of the twenty-millimeter shots. "How can a hot air balloon fire from *there*?"

It made no sense for a terrorist to choose such a helpless aircraft. He or she would be a sitting duck. As far as Trey knew, a heavy machine gun could not be installed inside the balloon itself. Even if it could be done, why bother? Fixing the gun to the gondola would have made more sense. By shooting down the chopper the way they did, the villains had only deprived themselves of their ability to stay airborne. What Trey didn't know was why.

Then the illusion dissolved.

The slowly deflating balloon sank low enough to reveal what was behind it—the *true* source of the bullets.

A CF Gunship had fired through the fragile obstacle to reach its intended target. The Chromes had locked weapons on the FBI rotorcraft just before it flew behind the mammoth inflatable.

Though he was close to all-out panic, Trey found time for two unhelpful thoughts: *What a way to make an entrance! Those gunships look a lot bigger in daylight.*

"Take cover!" Cline echoed his superior on the radio.

In the gunner's seat of the massive battle chopper, Colonel Epperson scanned the uneven green-and-white terrain below. Minutes ago, while landed near Kremmling, he'd been on his smartphone with a subordinate at CFCC to verify the scientist had been returned. Instead, he'd heard something different.

"Something is wrong," the lieutenant at the command center had said. "The first car should have come through the gate by now. Wait, here it comes. I— No, that's not— What the hell...what is that? Colonel, something just came through the field. What is that thing? Someone go check that— Wait! Get back! Everyone, get back! Colonel, I don't know what this thing is, but it's releasing a lot of smoke. I think you'd better go see what's going on in Winter Park."

The officer had rambled more before losing his life to Groovy's C4 explosion. Epperson couldn't determine why the call had ended or why the lieutenant didn't answer when he'd tried to call back. Then General Casprite had texted him about a bomb going off at CFCC.

What is that bloody scientist up to? the colonel had thought. *Someone must have helped him escape from my team in Winter Park. But who?* Then his question was answered once he'd spied the FBI chopper.

A major piloted the gunship and flew it over the sinking balloon. He was somewhat disappointed the colonel had not fired more holes through the maroon-and-navy inflatable; he'd wanted to watch the elderly couple in the wicker basket plummet too fast to survive.

Epperson found the place that interested him—a large white clearing atop the next mountain ahead. This was no doubt the destination of the FBI chopper he'd targeted seconds before it flew behind the balloon. He adjusted an eyepiece on his helmet, getting a zoomed-in view. The remains of his team's two SUVs were there. So was the portable Green Gate, which was no longer activated and appeared to be damaged. Then he saw the last two Feds in the clearing dash for the evergreens to hide.

How many FBI chaps are up there? the colonel questioned himself. *Is Trey Radisson with them? What have they done? Have they killed my entire recovery team? Do they intend to acquire the Green Gate technology?*

Then he decided his thoughts were no longer relevant. Whatever these Feds were up to could only mean trouble for the Chromes. Moreover, they had seen too much and, as far as he could tell, the plan to recover the scientist was now hopeless.

"No witnesses," he thought aloud, arming rockets.

The big black rotorcraft contrasted vividly with the clear blue sky as it neared the mountain. With immense fright in his gray bug-eyed gaze, Trey stood next to Agent Cline and watched the approaching chopper from their evergreen seclusion. With his assault rifle's scope against his eye, he put the aircraft in his crosshairs and clicked off the safety. The scientist dropped the briefcase and plugged his ears as nine-millimeter slugs were sprayed from their position. Hearing their leader's stuttering gun, nine other scattered agents also opened fire on the copter.

The shower of bullets startled the pair in the gunship. Sparks flew by the hundreds as most of the rounds barely dented the fuselage and scratched the canopy while a few slugs found places to burrow themselves.

"They're everywhere! Kill them, Colonel!" the pilot bellowed.

Gnashing his teeth, Epperson eyed his targeting screen while adjusting a multi-buttoned joystick. He zoomed in on the first target—one of the repeating gun flashes. The monitor showed a red triangle forming around the tree-shaded sniper—

—then blackened behind the words VIEW LOST.

Shrieking with rage, the gunner pounded a gloved fist on his console, knowing he could no longer preset the trajectory of his rockets.

"Colonel, what's going on?"

"They just took out my damn targeting system! What a bloody lucky shot! I need you to aim for me!"

"You need *me* to aim? Far easier said than done, sir."

"Just do it, chap!"

Everyone on the ground watched as the first three rockets were fired. The trio of projectiles missed everything, whistling over the peak to eventually meet the side of the next mountain.

The chopper's nose tilted further down than the pilot intended, letting the gunner's next four rockets blow up trees and boulders well away from the snipers. Automatic rifles kept firing upward. There were more misses than hits as the airborne target made evasive maneuvers. The armed Feds found the pines to be a mixed blessing; though the agents were secluded from view, the greenery made it difficult to anticipate the gunship's next move.

More explosive projectiles hailed down and missed. Evergreens toppled, smoking craters formed in the clearing, the silver 4Runner exploded, the black SUV was hit a second time, and Navarro's unconscious body was blown to pieces seconds after the medic deserted her.

"What the bloody hell is wrong with you, Major?" the gunner barked after another slug bounced off the canopy. "Aim like you aim between a whore's thighs!"

"I'm trying, sir!" the pilot swore. "I just wish I knew what to aim *for!* These Feds are too well hidden!"

"Good point. I've a better idea." Epperson regarded the diagram of the aircraft on his touchscreen. The rocket count in the nose was zero. Instead of swapping the empty launcher for a full one, he selected a different weapon. "Let's do some vegetation control and give these wankers nowhere to hide!"

Like a ferocious dragon, the rotorcraft scorched the wooded terrain with its flamethrower. Agents raced to avoid the fire as the chopper completed its first strafe. Trey stood near Agent Cline and watched the aircraft pause its burning discharge and move in a U, preparing for another flyby charring.

"Come with me, Mr. Radisson!" the Fed told Trey. "I have orders to get you out of harm's way!"

"But your men—"

"They can take care of themselves! Come on!"

Threading through the pines, Cline and his charge darted from the area.

Behind them, the gunship's flamethrower roared again, torching another strip of trees. Agent Mosley, who'd earlier taken out the black 4Runner with an RPG, returned with haste to his launcher to reload it. Once this was accomplished, he stood and aimed the launcher upward, one eye against the optical sight. Through a gap in the treetops, he could see the chopper turning again for a third pass. As soon as the airborne foe was in Mosley's crosshairs, he squeezed the trigger. The projectile hissed off through the pines, closing the gap between itself and the target.

The gunship's incendiary weapon reactivated. Behind another blazing emission, the fuselage disappeared from Mosley's view. When the RPG met the shield-like stream of fire, it exploded too early. If not for the chopper's flamethrower, the grenade would have flown further and likely downed the aircraft. Instead, the blast only forced the helicopter a few yards back the way it had come.

Scattering ignited propane, the fuselage spun once. The pilot regained control of the rotorcraft, completing his strafe as if nothing had happened. The gunner did not release the trigger as the aircraft neared Mosley, who was trying to reload the launcher with his shaky hands. There was no time. He fled from the gunship's path as the inferno consumed the evergreens surrounding his launcher. For protection, he crouched behind a boulder an instant before his stash of reserve grenades exploded.

✞

For nearly a quarter mile, Trey stayed in Cline's wake, huffing downhill while staying in the shade of the boughs. The winding course of their full-out sprint had them rounding boulders, hurdling logs, ducking low branches, and skirting a deadfall. An occasional slip on ice or trip on roots scarcely hindered their progress as they rolled back to their feet every time.

At another clearing in the woods was Cline's goal—a row of six parked snowmobiles, all with FBI across the black side panels.

"So, *that's* how you Feds got up here," Trey panted. Doing a face palm, he remembered the briefcase he'd left behind.

Grow up, Trey! he advised himself. *This is no time to think about the money. Survive today, look for the briefcase tomorrow.*

"Get on!" the agent ordered as he straddled the nearest vehicle. With a forceful tug on the pull cord, he brought the machine to life. The duo boarded their ride, propping their feet up on foot pegs. Then they put on goggles dangling from the handlebars. Trey held on tight as Cline gunned the throttled. With an earsplitting roar, caterpillar tracks spun through idler wheels, dusting the nearest tree with snow.

The snowmobile followed the same winding path that had led the Feds up the mountain. After cresting the trail's first ridge, Cline applied the brakes till the sled halted.

"What are you doing?" Trey asked in a fretful tone.

"Looking for our next ride," the agent hollered over the idling engine while his shielded eyes searched the clear sapphire skies. The lack of trees on the hilltop offered a nearly panoramic view of the stunning white-and-emerald landscape.

A dark speck in the northern sky caught Cline's attention. Even from the great distance, he could tell it was a chopper. Since it was coming toward them from a different direction than the one they'd traveled, he knew it couldn't be the enemy rotorcraft.

"Here comes the 'help on the way' that Krenshaw told me about," he cheered, pulling a flare gun from his jacket. Sparks showered around them as he fired skyward to signal the distant helicopter.

✞

The flamethrower paused as the massive chopper hovered over the blazing half of the forest. "This idiocy is not working!" the gunner groused, hearing two more slugs glance off the canopy. "Wherever the Feds are, they keep escaping the fire and finding other places to snipe us from. Maybe I should try gas canist—"

"Colonel, look!" the pilot bellowed, pointing. "What is that at our two o'clock?"

Two pairs of eyes were on the bright object floating beyond the treetops a mile away. It was the gleaming shot from Cline's flare gun, hanging in the air like a smaller version of the sun.

"I don't know," Epperson replied as the flare burned out. "Let's investigate."

"But the Feds."

"We'll deal with them later. That flare could mean a bigger problem."

✞

After sliding his goggles up to his forehead, Cline held binoculars to his eyes, scarcely able to determine the shape of the approaching copter did not resemble a CF Gunship.

"Are you sure it's not another one of them?" Trey asked fretfully as he got off the snowmobile, trying to get a better look.

"I'm sure," the agent guaranteed his charge, passing him the optical instrument. He raised his goggles and focused in the same direction.

The thump of rotor blades reached their ears. It sounded too close to be the aircraft Trey was fixated on. Then the sound boomed thrice as loud as its source appeared over the treetops like a titanic wasp.

The gunship from CFCC had come for them.

It was worse than last time; not only were they out in the open, but they were without the protection of Cline's gunmen.

Albeit he was not far from losing bladder control, Trey somehow found the valor to keep standing where he was and move the lenses to the closer chopper. Then he focused on the canopy—

—and recognized the British man.

He was inside in the front seat, staring right back at him. Memories of their chats at CFCC returned to his mind.

In utter shock, he dropped the binoculars, giving Colonel Epperson a clear view of his face. The gunner repositioned his helmet's magnifying eyepiece, confirming he'd found Trey Radisson.

"I don't believe it!" he exclaimed as the scientist returned to his seat on the sled.

"Who is that, sir?" the major asked, watching the snowmobile bolt away.

"I'll tell you who that is. He is the source of all our problems—the lab geek who can build us cloaking devices. We're not returning to base until he's..."

"Until he's what? Captured?"

The colonel considered his next words. Trey had somehow managed to acquire FBI protection, despite his damaged reputation. None of the minions on the ground had survived the Fed attack. Even if there *were* survivors, they still had no way to reacquire the scientist. The Green Gate had been damaged, none of Epperson's team was qualified to repair it, and the only vehicles they had to drive to another gate were destroyed. The nearest functioning gate was several miles away. If the colonel and his pilot managed to stop the sled without killing Trey, they couldn't return him to CFCC after capturing him; there was no room in the chopper.

"No, *not* captured; that cause is lost!" Epperson groaned, recalling the time he'd had Trey and his girlfriend bagged near Denver. The couple had escaped CFCC the following day in a way that had cost the terrorist organization a fortune. Their actions had also given General Casprite a very negative perception of the colonel—he was even considering demoting him.

"Then, what, sir?" the pilot asked, impatient.

"I want that lab geek dead! Dead, dead, *dead*!" the gunner boomed.

The accelerating snowmobile entered Winter Park Resort, jumping a netlike fence of orange nylon that marked the ski area boundary. Trey hung on to Agent Cline for dear life as the runners and tracks made a bumpy landing. Skiers and snowboarders scarcely avoided the speeding vehicle's path in time and shouted curses after it, not understanding the driver's haste till the great black rotorcraft soared over the tree-lined ridge with a *WHUMP-WHUMP-WHUMP!*

Oh, man, this has to be the worst wrong turn I ever made, the Fed thought. *Because of my screw-up, that CF Gunship might kill innocent skiers while trying to hit me and Trey.*

The sled's speed climbed from sixty to seventy miles an hour. It turned airborne as it shot over a hill in the broad ski trail and cleared a large yellow sign that read SLOW. Shortly after landing, the vehicle jumped a second slope, landed again, and nearly grazed one end of a man's snowboard as he stood with his smartphone in both hands, preparing to take a picture. If not for the loud techno music blaring in his earphones, he might have heard the activity behind him.

"We're ready, Chad," the snowboarder's wife called out to him as she stood with their two teenage sons ten yards downhill.

"Say cheese," Chad intoned. Instead of smiling for the picture, the man's family shrieked and dispersed. "Wait, guys!" He watched the trio vamoose further down the trail on snowboards. Confused, Chad held his arms out sideways, unaware of the massive gunship sixty yards behind him and closing fast.

Desperate to outdistance the petrifying rotorcraft, a veteran skier in maroon spandex moved at breakneck speed toward Chad. Not wanting to collide with him, the skier made a sharp turn, spraying the confused father with icy powder.

"Hey, you jerk!" Chad spat, frowning at the dark red skier gliding away. He was certain the slope pro had to be the rudest person around—a theory that changed when the helicopter thundered over him. The rotor wash dusted Chad tenfold.

✞

The FBI had sent in an armed reconnaissance and attack compound helicopter to counter the threat to Agent Cline's ground team. The flare he'd fired had not been necessary; the pilot flying the advanced co-axial copter had already seen the CF Gunship. Where it flew, he would follow. Over the sleek canopy, two main rotors—one stacked atop the other—spun in opposite directions from the same mast. The tri-bladed rotors kept the aircraft balanced without the need of a tail rotor. However, one still spun between two tail fins, blowing aft for speed instead of sideways for stabilization. With the aid of the pusher propeller, the high-tech FBI chopper exceeded two hundred knots—a speed never matched by a CF Gunship.

"We'll be within firing range in forty-five seconds," the pilot assured his gunner.

✞

After two sprays of fire missed the snowmobile target, the touchscreen on Epperson's console showed his propane depleted. He'd used too much from trying to incinerate the rest of the FBI team. Cursing, he pushed the button to spin the chopper's enclosed turntable, swapping the spent flamethrower with a full rocket launcher.

Once it was armed, he hit the firing button.

The first rocket came down and exploded, missing the speeding sled by several feet. The second flew upward.

"What do you think you're doing, Major?" the colonel barked, not knowing why the rotorcraft was suddenly climbing.

"Avoiding the ski lift, sir," he replied.

As one cable carried empty seats down the mountain, another conveyed occupied chairs uphill. Awestruck skiers riding in the ascending seats rubbernecked the gunship as it cleared the cables by a few feet. The noisy aircraft soared by, tossing freezing wind in curious faces. Losing ski poles and winter caps, the skiers' awe turned to ire.

After dodging a dozen more skiers and snowboarders, Cline steered the snowmobile toward a stand of pines—where no innocent civilians would be. Clenching his teeth, he meticulously zigzagged through the trunks. Trey craned his neck to look at the sky behind them, happy to see a web of greenery instead of the relentless chopper.

A trio of rockets whistled down and turned into bright orange blasts at their four, six, and nine o'clock positions. The gunship's target exited the conifer stand seconds after another projectile detonated against a dead tree, severing it at the base. The timber column toppled, crashing down three feet left of the snowmobile.

Cline drove the vehicle into more wooded terrain, nearly losing control as the ground steepened.

Wait a minute, Trey thought, remembering Zuri's .45 in his coat pocket. *I could at least* try *to shoot that crazy colonel...before one of his misses hits an innocent civilian. It would be a very lucky shot if I did, but what good is the gun if I don't use it?*

As the forest floor leveled out, Cline slowed the snowmobile; the rockets were hitting further and further away. Then they stopped completely, but the roaring rotor blades were still loud with nearness. The aircraft was hovering somewhere, waiting for the agent and scientist to come out of hiding.

The pair glanced upward in twenty different places. Through a gap in the cedars, Trey spied the front end of the helicopter. It had gone still, encouraging his idea. He got off the snowmobile, pulled Zuri's pistol from his coat, and trained it on the rotorcraft. Beyond the sights, he saw two helmeted heads swivel back and forth inside the bulletproof canopy. Epperson and his pilot watched every edge of the forest, waiting for their target to emerge.

"Mr. Radisson, where did you get that piece?" Cline demanded, still straddling the idling sled. "Put it down! You might give away our position!"

Didn't think of that, did you, moron? he chided himself, lowering the firearm. Through the break in the greenery, he beheld the chopper as it still hung in the same place. Under the six whirling airfoils, the fuselage slowly turned counterclockwise.

With a sound like a gun firing through a silencer, the nose ejected a gas canister. It dropped in an arc through the trees and landed several yards away—too far to become a concern. More steaming cans followed as the aircraft kept swiveling with the intent to gas the entire area. A sedative cloud from the nearest canister was slowly drifting toward the snowmobile. In under a minute, Cline and his charge would have no choice but to evacuate the woods.

"*Now* can I shoot them?" Trey groaned when they noticed the tail about to point in their direction. There was enough time to empty the entire magazine before the duo in the gunship had any chance of seeing the source of the bullets.

"Fire away and then get back on the sled," Cline told him. "Hurry! We need to leave while there's still time."

Trey raised the .45 upward. In his sights was a small hatch in the fuselage directly under the tail boom. He guessed the panel was covering a fuel cap. If this was the case, it would likely take a miracle to ignite the fuel with a shot from the small pistol. If not, perhaps he would get lucky and hit a hydraulic line. Trying not to think of how ineffective Cline's team had been with their assault rifles, Trey squeezed the trigger.

✞

With weapons locked onto the unaware CF Gunship, the FBI's co-axial helicopter stayed scarcely visible behind treetops less than half a mile away.

"Fire!" the pilot bellowed as he steadied the rotorcraft.

Thrice, the gunner squeezed the trigger. A trio of rockets launched from the left pod and crossed the distance to the target. The two-man crew of the FBI chopper grinned when their projectiles were three seconds from the weapon pod's right half.

✝

In three seconds, Trey fired off eight rounds at the airborne foe. When the ninth shot came, fire blasted from the side that was concealed from his vantage point by the treetops.

"I got them! I got them!" he exclaimed gloriously, not knowing rockets from another copter were the true cause of the damage.

"Good, now get back on!" Cline ordered, more concerned about the nearing cloud of soporific gas. Trey complied and the vehicle weaved through a dozen trees before returning to the exposure of the broad ski trail.

As the driver steered the sled further downhill, the passenger glimpsed behind them. The gunship was spinning out of control while leaving a trail of black smoke.

✝

"We're hit! We're hit!" the pilot shrieked over a warning buzzer, fighting to regain control of the sinking chopper. The fuselage's gyrations slowed to a halt as the aircraft stabilized.

"Damage report!" Epperson bellowed, facing right. It looked as if Godzilla had taken a huge bite out of the helicopter. A third of the munitions pod was missing. "Never mind. That side only had bullets and expended weapons. Otherwise, we'd be dead." Like the pilot, he shot glances in every possible direction. "Did someone fire an RPG at us?"

"I don't know." The pilot noticed something contrasting with the white ground—the dark dot of the sled moving away. The passenger's blue and yellow parka confirmed it was the same one they were hunting. He pointed. "There they are!"

The gunner futilely pressed the trigger to fire, getting no results. The damage had made the entire weapon system unserviceable.

"I can't fire! Use the rotor! Cut that wanker's head off!"

Swallowing fear of his possible death, the major shared the bloodlust. He steered the crippled copter the best he could toward the man responsible for so much damage to his beloved organization. From the unbalanced weight, the rotorcraft fishtailed as it closed in on the speeding snowmobile. Onlookers on skis and snowboards kept their distance from the vehicle's path and its airborne pursuer.

Trey glanced anxiously behind them. "Faster!" he shouted. His voice was no match for the sled's earsplitting motor, coupled with the deafening rotor behind them. The bright orange needle encased in the snow vehicle's speedometer reached the ninety. Albeit the snowmobile could go faster, the uneven terrain made further acceleration too risky. Even ninety miles an hour was not safe.

The wobbly gunship drew closer, regardless of the quivering flames and comet-tail of black smoke escaping its damaged side. Then it tipped forward so the radiating airfoils twisted ten feet over the snow…and less than thirty from the zooming sled.

When the trail narrowed for fifty yards, a metallic ring was heard as trees on both sides were sliced up. Without slowing, the unrelenting rotor came further down like an oversized saw blade. Trey checked the chopper's progress with more fretful glimpses to his six. The sight in the sled's wake made him recall the most petrifying dream he'd had in his youth. A swarm of flying foxes followed him as he sprinted down a treeless hill that offered no places to hide. But none of that was real. The massive rotorcraft, hell-bent on chopping him into tiny pieces, was very real and made the giant bat nightmare trivial.

He tried to not think of what would happen when the shrieking ring of death came much closer. The gruesome likelihoods refused to leave his brain. Through the blurring rotor, he briefly made eye contact again with the beet-red face of the incensed colonel. The sextet of airfoils spun like colossal machetes fifteen feet away.

Then ten feet.

Eight feet.

While the lethal speed circle blared closer, Trey remembered an event from Dallas. On the roof of the Olivine, Sonya had fired a shotgun at one of the Chromes. The twelve-gauge round had tossed the sergeant off the roof. Then he plummeted to his gruesome demise—on a gunship's rotor. Trey had been certain he'd never die in such a horrific manner. Now, he was *not* so certain.

WHOOSH-WHOOSH-WHOOSH-WHOOSH-WHOOSH-WHOOSH!

He begged for God's forgiveness for every sin he'd ever committed. Other thoughts followed.

Please, God, don't let this be it for me.

Five feet.

Please! I don't want to die. Have mercy on me.

Two feet.

One.

Sparks erupted inches below the passenger's behind as the snowmobile's taillight was chopped off with a steel clang.

I swear I will turn my back entirely on science and dedicate the rest of my life to serving You, praising Y—

Three more rockets breached the bottom of the slanted gunship. Their source was the unnoticed FBI copter that had joined in the chase.

Terrified shrieks from Epperson and his pilot filled the cockpit when the enormous rotor kissed the ground. An immense explosion of snow formed behind the fast-moving sled, swallowing most of the enemy aircraft and, momentarily, its fleeing prey. The copter was finally finished, no longer capable of staying airborne. Inside the mammoth white cloud, gyrating rotor blades chimed as they kicked up more powder. Then they bent and broke against the slope. Once the nose was grounded, the entire fuselage flipped forward. The tailfin came down two feet from the snowmobile's right ski. Before they sped away, Trey and Cline endured a brief, chill dusting from the still-spinning tail rotor.

Seconds later, the downed rotorcraft exploded.

In over ninety directions, smoldering debris flew from a fiery orange blast that swelled to the size of a house. The sled jumped another ridge that shielded it just in time from the rim of the explosion. With more distance, the snowmobile barely escaped the hailstorm of smoking helicopter fragments.

"Okay," Trey panted, tremendously fright-winded by the last twenty minutes. "Okay, let's not ever do that again." *Thank you, God.*

"*Ever!*" Cline agreed, braking to safer speeds.

"*Now* can I go back home?"

The agent chuckled. "Show me the way."

Sergeant Felton was in his dome olive tent, feeding his face till there was nothing left of his MRE. For the past hour, his fingers had stayed busy on his phone's touchscreen. He kept switching between a video game and sending texts.

litenant Navarro, where r u

why wont u answer my calls or my texts

why wont ANYONE anser my calls

whats goin onn

???

is anyone comin 2 pick me up

where r u guys

what kind of sik joke is tthis

its nott aprl fools day

what did I do to deserve this ☹☹☹

✞

The snowmobile was stopped at the turn to White Gales Drive. Agent Cline got off and put distance between himself and the idling motor so he could hear his handheld radio. Trey followed him, wanting to listen to the conversation.

"Krenshaw, come in," Cline said, pressing the radio's *PTT* button.

"I'm here," the radio's speaker replied in Nova's voice. "Report."

"I have Mr. Radisson with me. We're about half a mile from his family's home. He just remembered to inform me there may be snipers in the area. Is it safe to proceed?"

"Rog. Our satellite shows no heat signatures near that property. However, there *is* one in the trees near the Radissons' *previous* home. Well…what's left of it."

"Are you saying there is only one sniper and he blew up the wrong address?"

"Exactly."

"Stand by." Cline and Trey laughed so hard, their eyes watered. Once the Fed finally had the mirth out of his system, he spoke again. "What's your plan as far as dealing with the sniper?"

"We think he's waiting on a ride back—a ride that won't be coming. As soon as he gets tired of waiting and heads for the nearest road, we have a unit nearby that's ready to arrest him."

"Copy. I'm proceeding to the Radisson address."

"Rog. I'll meet you there. I need to speak with the Radissons."

"What's your ETA?"

"Two hours."

"Copy."

The snowmobile was boarded and cruised down White Gales Drive. After making the turn that Trey pointed out, the sled was parked by Nathan's Durango. The Fed's charge climbed off and jogged up to the front door. The moment Trey let himself in, he found a group hug awaiting him.

✞

Over two hours later, Nova and Agent Cline were in the great room of the Radisson home, sipping on steaming mugs of cocoa Mitzi had offered everyone. At the Feds' request, Trey's sisters and their families played outside so they could be alone with Sonya, Trey, and his parents. The two agents were slouched on a well-upholstered loveseat that faced a matching couch where Trey sat with Rody and Mitzi flanking him. Rubbing her beau's shoulders, Sonya stood behind the sofa, heeding every word of the updates the Feds had for the family.

"The U.S. military has already breached Chrome Mountain," Nova explained elatedly. "By the hundreds, terrorists are eating bullets or surrendering. And I was informed five minutes ago that General Casprite has taken his own life. Dr. Harbison and his entire science team are now in our custody. They also discovered the Chromes were developing their second base underground in Mississippi. The day you arrived in Dallas, the second base was expecting a shipment to be dropped from the air to land near the base's hidden entrance."

"So *that's* where the plane was headed," Trey realized aloud. While going through the jumbo jet's payload, he'd noticed equipment for another Green Gate—which would have become the second base's primary entrance and exit had he not destroyed the aircraft. "And there are no other bases?"

"None. The Chromes haven't been allowed enough time to start others. Thanks to you, my team located CFCC and forwarded their coordinates to the U.S. military so they could end the free world's greatest threat. You were the bait that lured the Chromes straight into our trap."

"Now you know why God gave you that gift," Sonya whispered in his ear. He nodded, knowing the word "gift" meant his ability to build cloaking devices.

"Because of you," Agent Krenshaw continued, "everyone in my division of the Bureau will be lauded and probably promoted.

There's no other way to say this, Trey: you're a hero to the entire nation!"

Applause filled the room as Trey was filled to the core with euphoria. He watched the agents clap their hands, eyeing him with keen gratitude. He looked both ways to see his beloved parents do the same. He faced behind him, seeing the love of his life applaud him. After she stopped clapping, she seized his face in both hands to give him a deep kiss.

"So, what happens now?" Trey said eagerly after Sonya released him.

"Anything you want," Agent Cline replied. "How about a party in your honor at our Denver office…as a start? You can have televised praise and a trip to D.C. so the president can thank you in his own way. He will want to do exactly that when we reveal the fact that you were the key to our mission's success. And I do mean the most significant mission of our careers."

As the trio surrounding Trey grew excited by the possibilities, he raised two hands in objection. "Please, sir, none of that. I've been on TV enough. And I don't need thanks and praises from people who know next to nothing about me. What's going on right now inside these walls is more than enough for me. Believe me, I will cherish this moment for the rest of my life."

"As you wish, Trey." Nova chuckled. "You don't strike me anyhow as someone who desires celebrity status."

"You hit the nail on the head."

The black woman faced Rody and peered over her glasses. "What about you, sir? Is there anything I can do for *you*? Contact your homeowner's insurance perhaps?"

"For what?" Trey's father replied.

"You didn't hear?" Cline said. "The terrorists wasted your other house."

"What? You mean the one I'm trying to sell?" He looked at everyone in disbelief.

"That's right, sir," Nova said. "The terrorists looked up the wrong address and thought every member of your family, except

Trey, was inside your *previous* house." Rody, Mitzi, and Sonya felt chills run down their spines. "By the time I'm done speaking with my superiors and your insurance company, you will own *two* more large homes here in this county…if you're interested."

Speechless from the generous offer, Mitzi beamed back and forth between her husband and the agent.

"Well, I— I mean— I…" Rody spluttered then cleared his throat. "How on earth can I say 'no' to that?"

Cline's smartphone chimed. He read the new text and met eyes with Trey. "One of my men found your luggage. He's bringing it over now."

Sonya looked down at her boyfriend, noting his smile as he remembered the briefcase full of cash. "Luggage?" she queried in his ear.

"Your 'private' stuff," he whispered back. The couple beamed, not sure how the day could get any better.

✞

Under a wool blanket, Sergeant Felton was still in his tent, curled up in the fetal position for warmth. From late afternoon to sundown, unnoticed texts from his smartphone kept coming.

im freezin my butt off up heere ☹

out of food

wil someone pleas answer me

PLEASE

??????????????????

Answer mee

why do u all keep iggnorin me ☹☹☹

ANSWER ME!!!!!!!!!!!!!!!!!!!!!!!!!

is this the thanks I get for blowin up tha Radison hoouse like u told me 2 do

som reeeal gratitud

☹☹☹☹☹☹☹☹☹☹☹☹

youknow what YOU SUCK!!!! ALL OF YOU SSUCK!!!!!!!!!!!!!!!!!!!!!!!!!

tomorow Im moving 2 Mexico or somthin

DENVER

Small, decrepit houses, built more than eighty years ago, lined the streets of a destitute neighborhood. One of the least visited homes was the residence of Matilda Stanton, a lone widow who'd seen seventy-six winters, including the current one. Daily, she pined for the company of her estranged son and his three children who rarely returned her phone calls. For months, no one had come to her door—till five days ago. Since that day, she'd been lying deceased in her hall bathroom. A beastly intruder, looking for somewhere to stay rent-free, had strangled her to death after she'd made the mistake of answering the doorbell. Now, the trespasser was resting comfortably in her living room.

Levi North sat on a legless couch that he guessed was older than he was. For five days, he'd been staying warm in the old widow's house, eating her food, pocketing all her cash and jewelry, watching her satellite TV, and enjoying hot showers in her master bathroom. He didn't know who she was and didn't care. To him, killing her and tossing her frail body in the bathtub made more sense than tying her up. As long as he kept the hall bathroom closed, the stench of her decomposing wouldn't assault his nostrils.

Though his last bundle of stolen hundreds could have extended his stay at the Lone Drifter Motel, he wanted to reserve the money strictly for unforeseen survival expenses. For several weeks, he'd been far too careless on his quest for vengeance against Sonya McCall. His negligence had cost him the loyalty of his four cronies. Moreover, if it weren't for his addiction to booze, cigars, and hookers, he wouldn't be down to his final wad of cash—the main reason he'd felt compelled to invade the elder's diminutive dwelling.

He didn't know what he would do once the fridge, freezer, and pantry were empty. He could go look for another house that gave no hint of someone who'd be missed soon. *How long can I keep living that way?* he'd often asked himself.

He'd wanted to return home to Sacramento. This desire changed when he'd heard the most demoralizing news of his life—the Screamon Demons were no more.

How did that happen? Who told the FBI all my gang's secrets and ruined everything? Whoever opened their big mouth, I don't want that rat dead; I want that rat alive and chained to a bed for years to experience every method of torture I can think of.

That would never happen. The turncoat had gotten away scot-free, leaving no clues of his or her identity. Levi was certain he'd never find out who blabbed in Sacramento. Moreover, he didn't care anymore; knowing would not put things back the way they were. He'd lost everything...except his thirst for revenge. His double-crossing ex had broken his heart, robbed him of 70,000 dollars, and taken his license plate, which led to his incarceration of twenty-eight months—time he'd never get back.

From a certain perspective, what Sonya had done to his life paled in comparison to what the "traitor in Sacramento" had done. But it didn't matter; he would never find the rat if he didn't even know the rat's name. Therefore, he would have to settle for finding his ex. Killing her with his own two hands was the only thing left on his bucket list. He'd sacrificed far too much to give up now.

Levi shoved a handful of animal crackers in his mouth and crunched noisily. Then he raised the TV remote to change the channel. The reports of auto mishaps on icy roads were getting old. *Click.* The next channel showed a weight-loss commercial. *Click.*

A divorce lawyer advertisement. *Click.* An infomercial on cardio equipment. *Click.* A tampon ad. *Click.* A laxatives ad. *Click.* Yeast infection.

"Oh, come on!" he thundered at the screen, wanting to hurl the coffee table at it. Instead, he settled for the display cabinet left of the entertainment center. The small table was chucked and went deafeningly through the glass doors. Inside the cabinet, glass shelves split and toppled, spilling an assortment of figurines.

Spanky, the dead widow's white cat, had been hiding behind the cabinet from the intruder. Deciding it was no longer safe, the feline entered the back of the partition under the TV with the intent of escaping through the front. Levi watched with amusement as Spanky's face appeared, bumping against the compartment's glass doors. The terrified cat wasn't strong enough to shove them loose from the magnets keeping them closed. For a moment, he thought he was trapped. Then he found another way out and scrammed from the living room.

Chuckling, the brutal biker plopped back down on the sofa. He'd tried to catch Matilda's pet a few times to give him the same lethal treatment he'd given her. The always frightened feline had been too quick every time. Levi didn't look forward to the day Spanky starved to death and fouled the air.

He pointed the remote at the TV again. *Click.* News regarding bedlam in Winter Park was on. The report snared his attention the second he heard about Chrome Falcon's involvement.

RADISSON RESIDENCE

After dark, only four individuals remained at the Radisson domicile; the daughters and their loved ones had returned to their own homes in Denver. On an upper-level patio, Trey conversed with his mother and father in the relaxing warmth of their spa while enjoying a panoramic view of the surrounding peaks. While sipping tall glasses of cold lemonade mixed with grenadine, the trio's eyes drank in the majestic wilderness beyond greenery and Christmas lights coiled around the railing of the spacious balcony.

Sonya came outside, flip-flops crunching across the snow-caked planks of the cypress deck. The steaming water looked very inviting as she neared the hot tub. Every hydro jet was open. A dozen soft blue lights studded the spa shell. Native American meditation music played from the tub's sound system.

Perfection, she thought, doffing her warm fleece robe from her curvy physique in a black two-piece.

Rody had been babbling on for over ten minutes about places in Colorado he'd considered living and why he'd chosen not to. Then he paused in midsentence at the alluring sight of Sonya's shapely muscles. Two flawless globes of flesh swayed a little beneath her swimsuit top as she climbed into the spa.

After catching the direction of Rody's eyes, his wife slapped the back of his head. He instantly continued rambling about housing and found it easier to not stare once the woman's athletic body was neck-deep in the bubbling water.

"Well, enough about all that," Rody sighed.

"Thank you," Mitzi said.

"Trey, do you ever miss your life in San Antonio?"

"Not so much," he answered.

"What about you, Sonya?"

"I'm done with New Mexico and *definitely* California," she replied.

"What? I didn't know you lived in California," Mitzi exclaimed with interest, recalling distant friends who'd lived in various parts of the Golden State. "What town?"

"Sacramento, Stockton, and Modesto. All three places were mistakes…at least for me. Not necessarily for others."

"Maybe you would have liked San Francisco more."

"Nah."

"Oakland?"

"Nope."

"San Diego?"

"No way."

"LA?"

"LA?" Making a gagging noise, Sonya pointed down her open mouth, imitating a woman trying to make herself vomit.

"What about Hollywood?"

"I never have and never will want to live near Holly-weird."

"Holly-*weird*?" Rody repeated and chortled. "Good one! So true too. It *is* weird. So, where *do* you two want to live?"

"I don't know yet," Trey admitted.

"I like it here," Sonya said. "But I don't know if I could afford a home in *this* county." Her thoughts turned to the briefcase filled with cash. Then she recalled her bank account's balance, still swollen from selling Zuri's diamonds. She wanted her half of the wealth to last for decades—a dubious hope if she chose to live in a pricey area. "Well, maybe a much smaller home than this one."

"Really?" Mitzi asked with a puzzled look as she poured a bath salt into the soothing water. Everyone's nostrils were pleasantly filled with a vanilla-jasmine scent. "You like it here in Winter Park? You may not like it here for very long. Won't riding a motorcycle through the snow get old after a while?"

"It *would* get old. That's why I'm buying a car soon."

The elderly lady set down the salt jar and took Sonya's hand to pat the top of it. "God bless you. Those motorcycles are dangerous."

"I thought I told you my first night here that I'm finished with Harleys."

"Sorry. My memory is not what it used to be."

"You got that right," Rody said, earning another thump on the head. He faced Sonya. "So, I guess you don't have that Harley anymore that I saw on TV?"

"No, it died on me."

"In a shopping mall in Dallas," Trey added.

"In a what?" his father gasped. "Okay, I don't want to hear about this. I've *got* to hear this! Tell me everything."

Sonya filled in every unintended gap Trey left in the story about the trip from the Olivine to the mall. The agog elders listened raptly to every word. Then Trey got to the meeting with Agent Krenshaw where his girlfriend badly wanted to finish the story.

"And that's when Trey said, 'Sorry I'm late,' like we'd been Christmas shopping or something," Sonya said. The senior couple were misty-eyed with laughter.

"Well, I'll tell you what I want to do," Rody began. "Once this deal happens between me, the FBI, and State Farm, I want to buy two more homes the size of this one—right here in Winter Park." He pointed at his son. "One for you." His finger moved to Trey's girlfriend. "And one for *you*."

The young couple stared in disbelief at Rody. Then Trey began to stammer.

"Dad, that's uh…that very, *very* generous, but I— Uh, I don't think I really deserve—"

"Don't be ridiculous, son."

"Yeah, Trey," Sonya added, lightly slapping him atop the head through his shock of curly hair. "Don't be ridiculous."

"Listen, son. Do you know the only thing that gives me more pride than being an American?" Trey shook his head. "It's knowing my boy *saved* America. I heard that FBI agent loud and clear. Now, don't hurt your poor old man's feelings. Take my offer."

Trey shot glances and smiles at the three pairs of eyes praising him. He cleared his throat. "Well…how can I say 'no' to *that*?" Sonya grabbed his face and put her mouth all over it. "Hey, come on, not in front of the family."

Chuckling, Rody and Mitzi clinked their glasses together.

FRASER, COLORADO: FOUR MONTHS LATER

With a sparkly engagement ring on her finger, Sonya pushed her shopping cart down the cereal aisle of a grocery store. Her fiancé reached for a box of Frosted Flakes to put in his own cart.

"No," she said. Sighing, Trey swapped it for Lucky Charms. "Seriously?" He reluctantly put it back and took a box of Wheaties. "*Now* you're thinking healthy. Trust me, you'll thank me for this later."

He dropped the Wheaties in his cart. "I'll miss that stuff," he groaned, giving the sugary cereal one last look.

"Yeah, but your *health* won't miss it; too many carbs and sugars. I've told you that."

"Yeah, I know." He gave a glum stare at his cart's contents, scarce believing he'd chosen lean turkey meat for his sandwich instead of tasty bologna. However, what he wanted more than junk food was a long, healthy life with his remarkable fiancée. She'd taught him much about health and fitness...and was far from finished.

They approached the main aisle in the back of the store and paused to avoid the path of the nearest shopper—a fiftyish woman weighing at least four hundred pounds. Honey buns, oatmeal crème pies, soda, ice cream, corn dogs, pizza, and a box of Lucky Charms filled the wire basket of her motorized cart. As she coasted by, the first thing that seized the couple's attention was the shopper's eyes—they were closed.

Highly amused, the duo stood quietly and watched the handicap cart drift another nine yards down the quiet aisle. The snoozing customer awoke with a start when her overloaded ride collided with the end of the soup aisle. A set of shelves toppled, spilling large juice bottles that were on sale. Four of the plastic containers landed hard enough to leak. A purple puddle quickly spread across the linoleum floor. The obese culprit reversed three feet and steered down the soup aisle as if nothing had happened. Heads of other shoppers turned as her wheels made yards of violet tracks on the white tiles.

"And *that's* why you shouldn't eat Lucky Charms," Sonya jested as they moved to the next aisle. "Let's get water." From a low shelf, they took two jugs at a time and put them in their carts till they each carried eight.

"Is some kid getting his arm amputated?" Trey asked, hearing a high-pitched scream.

Sonya went to peek down the next aisle. "No," she said indifferently after returning to the baskets. "It's just his mom denying him candy."

"What a brat!"

"No kidding. Let's go to the cold aisles."

Trey shadowed Sonya as they pushed their shopping baskets toward the edge of the store. "*Which* cold aisle?"

"The last one." They strode down a broad passageway lined with glass doors that kept shelves of frozen food cold. She stopped in front of the wide selection of fruit and veggies. "I need time to decide what I want to put in my smoothies next week. Can you go get two cartons of almond milk? They're in the last aisle we passed. Sorry."

"No problem." He strolled off, leaving his cart.

"No sugar, please," she called after him.

"Got it. Low sugar." He didn't pause.

"*No* sugar!"

"*Mo* sugar!"

"Shut up, sugar!"

Grinning, he disappeared around the corner. He could hardly wait for the next two weeks to pass. They would be married in a small ceremony, Sonya would move into his new home, and they would rent out her house to a responsible tenant. He'd proposed to her on Valentine's Day and she'd accepted the ring with no trace of reluctance. They didn't know what they would do with the rest of their lives. As far as they were concerned, the future at this point didn't really matter, as long as they were allowed to face it together and pray together. Their keen love and respect for God and each other was all they would ever need.

As icing on the cake, the settlement they'd received was more than enough for them to live on. The meeting with their lawyer, the press official, and *his* lawyer had gone very well. And, thanks to Zuri's briefcase, the engaged couple would never need to make cash withdrawals at an ATM again. Life was good.

Trey stood before the choices of milk and found the kind Sonya had requested. Two cartons were taken up and he headed for the back end of the aisle, walked in a U, and paused at the entrance of the last aisle.

When he'd been searching for the milk, he'd not noticed the bearlike policeman who'd passed his aisle before entering the one Sonya was in. The hulking cop, unaware of the man behind him, stepped purposefully toward the tall woman.

In his gloved hand was a black semi-automatic pistol.

Trey went saucer-eyed as he realized the cop's intent. No one was in the aisle except the three of them. He'd not brought a weapon and was certain his fiancée was also unarmed.

He silently set down the milk and studied the menacing lawman. Ironed slacks grazed the top of his polished patrol boots as he walked. The shiny belt bore all the tool of the trade: cuffs, Taser, police-walkie, magazine pouches, and his firearm's holster. In bold yellow letters, POLICE ran across the back of his jacket as dark blue as his trousers. A coiling cable linked his walkie-talkie to the mic clipped to his shoulder. His sleeves bore the chevrons of a sergeant and patches reading DENVER POLICE DEPT. Trey couldn't fathom why the cop would be over an hour away from his area of jurisdiction. From behind, he could see no features of the sergeant's head except the nest of curly gray hair.

He tiptoed forward, staying three yards behind the lawman. It was imperative he be close to the cop, giving him no time to aim his gun at him when he seized his right wrist. He doubted he could disarm the hefty man by himself; he needed Sonya's aid.

All these thoughts made sweat bead on his brow as his heart hammered fiercely in his ribcage. His need for air swelled from the adrenaline, making it far more challenging to keep his breathing silent.

Beyond the policeman, he saw his girlfriend comparing calories on various bags of frozen food. If not for the pop music emanating from the supermarket's speaker system, she might have heard the sergeant's footfalls at her eight o'clock position. Trey couldn't warn her too early; they both had to be near the errant cop to have any chance of disarming him before he could level the pistol at one of their heads. This wouldn't be easy; the sergeant was twice Trey's size. Fortunately, Trey and Sonya were equal on height and weight, which might even the odds.

The badge had only ten strides remaining. But his weapon was still at his side with a finger on the trigger. He intended to shoot Sonya at pointblank, regardless of the surveillance camera capturing his face from the front of the aisle. With the pistol still clearly visible, he seemed unconcerned with what would happen to him or his career in law enforcement if he carried through with the murder.

With no pause to his stealthy strides, Trey stayed in the sergeant's wake. Numerous thoughts raced through his head.

Who is this cop? Why does he want to execute my beautiful fiancée? She's a wonderful woman. What could she have possibly done to him?

Trey wanted to marry Sonya. They had been planning on getting married since February and their wedding was only two weeks away. He wanted to live a long life with her, to see her smile when he gave her gifts on birthdays, anniversaries, and Christmas. He wanted to grow old with her. She was his soul mate. She kept him happy with her witty remarks, her indomitable spirit, her enthusiasm about his company, her devotion to God.

But this madman in uniform was about to take all that away. He was about to destroy Trey's future.

Please, no! God, don't let it end this way! I need Sonya. I love her. Please take complete control of our imminent actions. Help us defend ourselves. We need you, Lord.

The cop was five strides away.

Wait for it.

Four strides.

Wait for it.

Three.

Now!

"Sonya!" he shrieked, lunging for the lawman's gun. By the time the distracted cop had turned in search of the one who'd yelled her name, his wrist had been seized tightly in both of Trey's hands.

With her sable mane fanning out, Sonya swiftly spun her head to her beau's voice, already knowing by his tone that something was wrong. Her azure eyes went straight to the firearm in the sergeant's hand. The love of her life was trying to disarm a larger man before he could overpower him and shoot him. He needed help and he needed it now. Dropping a bag of frozen broccoli, she pushed her cart aside and dove into the fray.

Trey kept the pistol pointed skyward where it couldn't hurt anyone, and his only free finger found the magazine-release button. With thirteen rounds still in it, the clip slipped out and clattered to the floor, leaving the gun's grip hollow. But there was still one round in the chamber. He wouldn't stop struggling till he pulled the semi-auto from the brute's grasp.

Screaming with rage, Sonya jumped up and shot her right arm around the cop's thick neck like a python seizing its prey. Gnashing her teeth, she squeezed like her life depended on it. With help from gravity, her efforts collapsed the man's windpipe. As her feet dangled over the floor, her free hand took a fistful of the lawman's hair to inflict more pain.

The nest of gray curls slipped off the sergeant's shaved head.

Shocked, Sonya gaped at the wig in her hand for a second. Then she chucked it away and used both her arms in the chokehold.

Deciding he could breathe later, the cop flung Trey's body across the aisle where he shattered through a freezer door. The firearm was held even with his head, but with the woman strangling him, the lawman couldn't aim well.

BANG!

The shot was too high. The bullet grazed Trey's shock of hair as he tumbled out of the freezer to sprawl across the floor.

The sergeant reached back to club the woman atop the head with the spent pistol. Her feet were back on the floor as she released her hold on him and covered the sore on her scalp. Then, for the first time, she got a look at the face of the "cop."

Levi North.

He'd been wearing the wig to hide the front of his tattooed scalp. To further help with the police disguise, he'd shaved the long hair from the back of his head, going completely bald. He'd also removed the beard and mustache from his ruddy weathered face. Despite all the changes, Sonya easily recognized the naturally livid eyes of obsidian.

Winded from the struggle, they regarded each other for a few heartbeats.

"You big dumb bastard!" Sonya spat, wondering how her ex had found her. "So…we meet again. You sure look ridiculous in that uniform! Why don't you be a good boy and go back to Sacramento, huh?"

"For what, slut?" he shot back. "Everything there is ruined!"

"Surely it's not *that* bad."

"Stupid female! You've been gone too long! A rat leaked all my secrets to the Feds. The entire Screamon Demons gang is gone! *Gone!*"

Grinning, she took her hand off her throbbing scalp. "Oh, yeah,

I almost forgot about that."

The smoldering coals of his eyes burned hotter. "What? It was you? *You* are the rat?"

"Guilty as charged."

His nostrils flared as fury quickened his breath and deepened the red in his face. "I'll kill you, slut! I'll rip your little double-crossing head off and go bowling with it!"

He looked down, searching for the magazine. After glancing three more places, he found it in Trey's hand. Then it was tossed atop the row of freezers behind him. Trey gave the phony cop an "oops" gesture, earning himself a backhand across the face. He spun away and dropped to his hands and knees.

Sonya charged at Levi, only to earn a sidekick in the midriff. Her hair closed around her face as she flew backward, shattering a second freezer. Once her feet returned to the floor, she assumed a fighting stance and shook her black curls away from her eyes. While shuffling sideways out of the pile of glass, she fought to catch her breath after having the wind knocked out of her from the fierce kick. Her waist ached, but it was nothing compared to how it would have felt without the years she'd spent exercising her abs to be rock-hard. Three years ago, the kick would have ended her will to stand, much less fight.

Woozy from the blow to his cheekbone, Trey stood a few strides away, waiting to catch the fake cop unaware.

Levi shot him a glance. Then he pointed at him while giving his ex-girlfriend an incredulous frown. "You left me for *that* wuss? Are you stupid?" he scoffed.

"I would have left you for a tomato!" she countered. "For your information, I ditched you over three years ago, and I've only known the wuss for a few months!"

"Wuss?" Trey objected.

"Nothing personal, babe. As for *you*, you oversized moron, disappear from my sight before I put you in the ICU!"

The empty gun was thrown at her. She ducked, letting it crack a third glass door. From her crouched position, she jumped three feet in the air. Her long hair and open jacket flew as her body twirled once. Before gravity returned her to the tile floor, she extended one leg, walloping Levi's mouth with her hiking boot. The spin-kick did more than interrupt the massive foe's effort to free the Taser from his belt; it also dislodged a tooth from his upper jaw and tossed him through a fourth freezer. Shallow cuts formed on his weathered face from the hail of glass.

Lying on a pile of frozen goods and fallen shelves, Levi eyeballed his ex-girlfriend with disbelief. If not for their last conversation, he would have wondered if she was the wrong woman. The Sonya he remembered wasn't half this tough and needed acidic words and a firearm to make up for it. While her fighting prowess had improved, his had declined. He was pushing sixty and decades of smoking and drinking had finally caught up with him. Moreover, during the months he'd spent searching for the disloyal woman, he'd neglected to keep up on his martial arts training, which had also helped even the odds. The more his hopes of finding her had decreased, the more his waist had *increased.*

Sonya looked both ways, wondering how much store-wide attention she'd drawn so far. Small knots of spectators had formed at both ends of the aisle. Some customers had evacuated the supermarket after hearing the gunshot. Others continued shopping after mistaking the report for a balloon popping.

Both combatants drew more blood and smashed more freezers in another exchange of punches, kicks, and headlocks. When she was not busy ducking or blocking, Sonya delivered speedy combo attacks that never allowed her archenemy enough time to unfasten the Taser from its holster. Before long, he forgot he even had it and grew more interested in trying to defeat her without weapons.

Believing he'd encountered a foiled arrest, one Good Samaritan hurried over to aid the man in uniform. "She's *mine*!" Levi thundered, knocking the shopper down with an uppercut. As the hero-wannabe crawled away, all other onlookers disregarded any thoughts of assisting the "lawman."

Groceries the couple had intended to buy went everywhere as

the struggle knocked over their shopping carts. Trey offered sporadic intervention, kicking the back of the bully's knees or chucking the most solid merchandise he could find. A minute later, his interference paid off.

While a bag of frozen chicken distracted Levi by bouncing off his face, Sonya jump-kicked him in the jaw. Barely conscious, he toppled noisily to the floor, smacking his shaven head on the linoleum. Knowing his stupor wouldn't last, his ex-girlfriend noticed the Taser on his belt. She wasted no time unsnapping the holster strap and ripping the nonlethal weapon free.

The electrodes were fired into the brute's thigh. For over fifteen seconds, she squeezed the trigger, letting the current flow through the coiling wires and into her floored enemy. Trey watched elatedly as the "cop" convulsed and groaned in agony. Levi was very disappointed with himself for not having the electroshock weapon in his free hand when he'd first entered the aisle. He could have been using it after the sidearm was rendered useless. Instead, he'd underestimated the couple and had assumed the pistol would be enough to complete his vengeance.

After pushing another button to retract the tiny conductors, Sonya aimed the nonlethal weapon at Levi's face. She stepped over his arm and squatted next to his head, putting the Taser inches from one of his terror-enlarged eyes. Until now, she'd never seen such an expression on the face of Levi North—a man feared by many in Sacramento.

"If you don't want to be blinded for life, don't move!" she warned, using her free hand to crank the voltage up to its highest setting. "Trey, search him."

Trey kneeled and did a quick frisk of Levi's person, finding no other weapons but the one under his slacks—a hunting knife sheathed at his ankle. He was grateful Levi had lacked the time and interest to arm himself with the Taser or eight-inch blade. The former gang leader's blurry vision was filled with the light-studded ceiling that backgrounded the hovering faces of the two people he hated most in the world.

"So, *this* is your ex, huh?" Trey asked Sonya, not sure why any woman would choose a boyfriend old enough to be their father. Trey faced his sweetheart and noticed her bleeding nose and the handful of minor glass cuts across her face.

She nodded regretfully in response to his question. "What can I say? The old me was a godless idiot who thought she had a lot to prove."

Furious about the attempt made to end her life, Trey shook the saw-toothed blade in front of Levi's face. His free hand gripped the black tie on the collar of the brute's dress shirt. "Okay, you've h—" The clip-on tie came off. He tossed it away and took a handful of the royal blue shirt instead, not seeing Sonya's smile. "Okay, you've had your fun! Are you ready to stop acting like a homicidal lunatic? Just le—"

"Police?" a panicky store manager said on a smartphone. "I have a pair of Bonnie and Clyde wannabes in my store, resisting arrest! Get here quick! Want the address?"

The couple turned in unison to the woman who'd called nine-one-one. Fifteen paces away, she stood with the onlookers at the end of the aisle. Trey and Sonya had almost forgotten they and Levi had an audience. Some of the bystanders were even recording them with their smartphones.

Scowling at the manager—the store's newest employee who'd not seen the couple shop there before—Trey dropped the knife and stood with his arms out. "Are you stupid or what? Would a legit cop have a tattoo on his—"

"Trey!" Sonya cut him off. He looked down at her, heeding her words. "We need to get out of here, now. When the cops get here, they will probably support Levi instead of us. Before they have all the facts, Levi will take one of their guns. Come on." She glimpsed both ends of the aisle. "We'll go out the back." One last time, she met eyes with her supine ex. "Don't follow us."

Trey stayed close behind his girlfriend as she fled the scene. She raised the Taser so the small cluster of ogling shoppers would clear a path. Albeit going through the back meant it would take them longer to reach Sonya's car, the front of the store had too many spectators blocking the way out. Plus, the odds were higher that a bystander would try to stop them.

The couple vanished through double doors that read EMPLOYEES ONLY. They weaved through pallets of consumable goods awaiting shelf space and hit the push-bar of the exit door. Outside, rain fell profusely from the steel gray sky. Annoyed by the sudden turn of the weather, the duo rounded a parked tractor-trailer and huffed on in search of the customer parking lot.

Levi sat up in the frozen food aisle, trying to shake the dizziness and pain from his head. Blood dribbled down his chin from where his last upper incisor had been.

Get to the parking lot, he ordered himself. *Don't let that slut and her geek boyfriend get away! You've worked far too long and hard to find them! Get to their car before* they *do. Once they see what you did to it, they'll run off and hide!*

Shoppers offered to assist him as he stood. He shrugged off the helping hands, returned his knife to the sheath under his slacks, and bustled for the front of the store.

"They went *that* way, stupid!" a senior shouted after him, pointing to the back. Levi ignored the elderly lady and neared the main aisle, where onlookers stepped aside for him.

The grossly overweight woman on the handicap cart had fallen asleep again. She rolled directly into Levi's path when he exited the frozen aisle. A dozen bystanders gasped as the pair fell down in a heap and the cart toppled over, scattering the basket's junk food.

"Rape!" the floored shopper yelped, wide-awake with terrified eyes on the man who'd fallen atop her. "Rape! Raaaaa—"

BAM!

With a right cross, Levi silenced the chunky woman and glanced at her groceries. "Who the hell would rape *you*, Not-So-Little Debbie!" he snarled, getting back on his feet. Knocking down two more customers, he dashed out the automatic door and searched for where he'd parked his stolen police motorcycle. His next thought was on the misery-inducing rain. Levi hated rain. But he hated Sonya McCall a lot more.

✞

Soaked by the weather, Trey and Sonya barreled across the parking lot toward the latter's Toyota Sequoia. As they slowed, the four flattened tires of the midnight blue SUV captured their attention.

"Nooooo!" Sonya cried out, feeling utterly defeated. "That unthinkable bastard!" The slashed tires were the vehicle's first set with under five thousand miles on them. *What a waste*, she thought.

"How long has Levi been stalking us?" Trey pondered aloud. "He must have found out where you live, tailed you to my place when you picked me up today, and then followed us here. Now he knows where *both* of us live!"

"I thought I made my new address unlisted."

"Do you think he bribed some cop to look up your info?"

"Maybe. He's purchased favors from cops before. At least that's what one of my former friends in Sacramento had told me."

Their heads spun to an engine revving from a different side of the half-filled lot. It was coming from a black-and-white BMW motorcycle over ninety yards away. Straddling the bike was the same menacing monster they'd fought inside the store. With no helmet on, he was looking directly at them, making the two-wheeled property of the Denver Police roar a second time. He'd clearly decided the battle was not over yet.

"We've gotta get out of here, Sonya," Trey cautioned. "That guy must have bones of titanium or something. Let's go find somewhere he can't follow us. Come on."

She eyed her beloved, considering his words. The bruise on his cheek had turned purple. Then she faced the last of the Screamon Demons and considered the damage to her own body. Her stomach and scalp still smarted from the fight. She wasn't sure if makeup could hide the mild cuts on her face before she was married and wondered if two weeks was enough time for the sores to heal. She wiped her upper lip and stared at her finger—bathed in blood from her nose. Her eyes returned to the one responsible for her injuries.

"Sonya, let's go!" Trey urged.

She didn't seem to hear him as she daringly moseyed into the center of the paved passage with two rows of parking spaces flanking it. Her eyes were still on the only other person in the lane—the beastly villain from her past. He was waiting at the opposite end of the lot, wondering what she would do next. From a distance, azure eyes clashed with obsidian eyes.

Levi cranked the heavy BMW's handle again. The engine rumbled louder.

"What are you waiting for?" Trey demanded. "We need to go, now!"

Sonya was not cognizant of his voice any more than the rain that pelted her face and dripped from her drenched locks of hair. Her only thought was on the many months of her life she'd wasted dating the atrocious lawbreaker, sleeping with him and using her locksmith skills to help him steal whatever he wanted. She'd never get that time back.

She recalled the innocent victims who had been robbed and tortured by Levi and his cronies after they'd grown bored with quick, direct thievery. Then there was the time she'd last seen the ringleader before today—the night he'd blackened her eye and raped her. Three years later, one of his followers had murdered her friend in Carson City.

How many others died last year...or this *year? In fact, what happened to the cop who used to ride the black-and-white motorcycle?* she thought.

Then she shrugged out of her leather jacket, bearing muscular arms and a sleeveless T-shirt. Across the dark green top was PHILIPPIANS 4:13. As she eyed the white Algerian text printed across her shirt, a memory from her childhood suddenly surfaced. She was in Sunday School, hearing about the Bible verse.

What about me? Can I also do anything through Christ? Of course I can! I can even execute my daring plan to end the threat ninety-plus yards in front of me. Through God, I will succeed...or die trying. Either one is better than fleeing from the problem. I've been trying that for three years and it has accomplished nothing... but getting others killed.

"Sonya, please!" Trey bellowed. "Forget about him! We have too much to live for! Just run away!"

"I don't think so," she said, mostly to herself. "I'm sick of running away. I'm not running again. Not anymore."

Hearing only the murmuring rain, she looked daggers at the single headlight of Levi's ride while steeling herself for her hazardous plan's execution. Dropping the jacket on the wet blacktop, she allowed lines of wrath and resolve to crease her damp face, quivering from all her ex's dark deeds that replayed in her head. Then she thought of the slashed tires of her new SUV and everything the vile creature had done in the store. He'd tried to take her life—the only one she would ever have. He'd tried to take her *soulmate's* life.

Enough is enough!

"Not! Any! *More!*" she repeated.

Puddles of rainwater splashed underfoot as she charged forth, her saturated mane flying in her wake. From the distance, her target watched her as disbelief and rage competed for dominance of his face.

Levi gunned the throttle. The rear tire briefly squealed and steamed on the wet pavement. Then the police cycle rocketed forward with a quickly climbing speedometer.

Sonya's full-out sprint carried her past numerous parked cars that varied in make, model, and color. None of the scattered vehicles had occupants to witness her mad dash; they were all in the supermarket, waiting for a letup in the unexpected rain. With fifty yards to go, she'd moved out of earshot of Trey's pleas for her to stop playing chicken with a felon on a motorcycle. He hastened in the same direction, knowing she might need medical attention if she came out of this alive. As he watched her zip away like an adept track athlete, he prayed for God's aid while admiring her unparalleled valor.

Gnashing her teeth, Sonya thought of nothing but her fervent wish to overcome the revolting brigand who accelerated toward her. *You assaulted me in every way possible*, she thought as the gap between her and Levi shrunk to forty yards. *You murdered my friend.* Thirty yards. *You tried to kill my fiancé and me.*

Twenty yards.

Now, I will take...

Ten yards.

...you...

Five.

...down!

Instead of letting a head-on collision with the steel two-wheeler destroy her flesh and bones, she did what the rider never saw coming—she leaped.

Turning airborne, she let out a livid scream. One of her legs folded beneath her as the other extended ahead of her. The speeding bike's handlebars passed under her body, and her flying kick took down the windshield. Screws that secured the Plexiglas's base dislodged themselves as her foot kept going.

The rubber treads of her hiking boot found their mark—Levi's face.

POW!

The in-flight kick tossed the criminal's skull back far enough to break two neck vertebrae. The bones formed sharp edges as they fractured, severing the spinal cord they were meant to safeguard. Losing consciousness, Levi rolled backward off the seat of his stolen ride.

PLOP!

He kissed asphalt, prone and spread-eagled.

Sonya landed on her feet next to him and windmilled her arms to avoid falling. She didn't bother watching the activity behind her—the BMW bike popping a wheelie and clattering stridently to the soaked blacktop. Despite the rain's loud whisper, she heard the nearing footfalls of her man scurrying up to her. He watched her shove Levi over with her foot so he would lie supine. Then she held the Taser ready. The couple's feet stood still as they flanked the disguised bandit's chubby face.

"Is he dead?" Trey queried. The answer came when the crook's eyes slowly fluttered open. He gazed up through the falling rain at the man and woman looking triumphantly down at him. The pair looked menacing from this point of view. Lightning flickered across the gray sky behind their looming figures.

Sonya waited for the rumble of thunder to fade before she spoke. "Some people never learn! They don't know when to quit! What did I tell you in the store, dumbbell? 'Don't follow us!' Remember those words? Do you have a hearing problem?"

Levi said nothing.

"I wonder where he got the uniform and bike from." Trey glanced at the fallen motorcycle. "You think he murdered a cop to get that stuff?"

"Probably. It must have been hard to find a cop with a uniform big enough for him." She read VELOZESPINAL on the nametag of Levi's police jacket. "He picked a victim with a very rare name, didn't he? This…Veloz-Whatever must have been one huge guy."

Beyond the applause of the rain, she could hear police sirens from afar. The cops had responded to the store manager's nine-one-one call.

"Now he's going to answer for the lawman's death," Sonya went on. "He'll answer for a *lot* of things. Are you ready for that, Levi? Ready to face justice, stupid?"

"I'll see you in Hell, Sonya," Levi muttered.

"That's not where *I'm* going, jackass. If you ever want to meet again, get saved. Find God. He still loves you, despite all you've done."

They waited for him to say something.

"He's awfully still, isn't he?" Trey mused aloud. He stomped on Levi's hand, shocked by the complete lack of response. "I think you paralyzed him."

Sonya considered this, letting the Taser fall from her hand and clatter. "I'm only four years late, aren't I? Let's get out of here." For the final time, she met eyes with her ex. "Levi, I'll be praying for you."

Trey took two strides to follow her, giving the heavy villain nothing to gaze at but the rain-filled sky. Then he came back and crouched, putting his grinning face back in Levi's view. Looking down at the fallen brute one last time, Trey spoke his final words.

"Remember, don't follow us," he jested.

Levi's voice was barely audible as he cursed the couple who left him behind and headed for the distant Toyota. Despite the flat tires, they got in the front seats for shelter from the rain. Sonya turned over the engine and cranked up the heat so they wouldn't freeze in their saturated clothes. She left the lights off, not wanting it to be obvious her blue Sequoia had occupants.

Trey wiped his fogged window so they could watch Levi's motionless form, still lying supine and alone in the drenched parking lot. Further away, blue-and-red lights flickered atop three police cruisers. Two parked next to the store, and one explored the parking lot till its headlights were shining on the downed "sergeant." When the black-and-white stopped, two cops in rain ponchos got out to check Levi's vital signs. Minutes later, he was on a gurney with a neck brace as a hospital crew loaded him into an ambulance. Another three-man team removed the police motorcycle from the area after securing it to a flatbed truck. After most of the emergency responders left, only a few cops were inside the supermarket to take statements from witnesses.

"We should call a cab and go home before anyone finds us," Trey suggested. "I don't know about you, but I'm in no mood to explain all this to four or five cops. I still have plans for today. Tomorrow, we can come back and have new tires put on this car."

Sonya said nothing as she stared out the window at where they'd last seen Levi.

"Are you okay?" Trey asked.

"I can't convince myself that my scumbag ex is no longer a

problem," she said. "I know he's helpless now and none of his minions came with him to the store."

"Maybe they're all in jail. Do you think the FBI missed a few?"

"No. If the Feds *did* miss any of Levi's cronies, they would have definitely come here with him. Levi never works alone. Plus, he never once struck me as someone who would put on a police uniform, as much as he hates cops. He must have been extremely desperate to do that."

"Well, then what are you worried about?"

"If Levi followed us to this store, then I'm positive he knows where we live. Some corrupt cop must have given Levi our addresses for a bribe. There's no doubt in my mind."

"If such a cop exists, why wouldn't he have come here to help Levi execute you?"

"Maybe Levi didn't pay him enough to put his career in that much risk. Since Levi can still talk, he could call the shady cop and offer him more money to go to our homes—where there are no witnesses—and shoot us in the head."

"Good point." He puzzled over her last words. "Wait a minute. Why didn't *Levi* just try to kill us at our homes? Wouldn't that have been easier?"

"He must have found my house today—right when I was leaving to come pick you up. And he didn't want to wait on me to return home. I know how he thinks. He's rash and his patience is very limited. Plus, he didn't mind shooting me in public because, after everything I've put him through, his vengeance against me was probably the only thing he had to live for."

"And, now, he's not even going to have *that*."

She grinned. "Nope. And there is no doubt in my mind that he wishes he didn't survive my last attack."

"Well, a lot of people would rather be dead than paralyzed."

"Levi would rather be dead than *impotent*. That vile pig thought he and his manhood were God's gift to women. There is a dark side of me that hopes the bastard will have to wait ten years to die—because I know he would much rather wait ten *seconds*."

"That's perfectly understandable." Trey thought of Sonya's theory about the crooked police officer. "Well, let's see what we can do about keeping the unethical cop away from us."

He pulled his smartphone from a jacket pocket. From his list of contacts, he selected NOVA KRENSHAW and hit CALL. After two rings, she picked up. Trey put her on speakerphone so Sonya could hear.

"Hi, Trey," she answered cheerfully after seeing his name on her screen. "It's been awhile."

"Hi, Nova. Are you busy?"

"Always, but I will put all that on hold for you any day. What's going on?"

Trey and Sonya reminded her of Levi North, explained the relevant events of the past hour, and gave her the store's address. Then they told her what the former gang leader was wearing and voiced their worries about him knowing where they lived.

"You two just go on home and don't worry about a thing," the agent consoled them. "Right now, I'm looking up the nearest police department and the nearest emergency center to the address you gave me. I'll make sure all the right people know who the 'cop' with the broken neck *really* is. Mr. North will be very heavily guarded by security for his entire stay at the hospital. He won't receive any visitors, nor will he make or receive any phone calls. By the time I'm done, once he's released from the hospital, they'll lock him up and throw away the key."

"Best news we've had all year. You can really make all that happen?"

"Absolutely. You might be surprised how much dirt the Feds in Sacramento have gathered on Mr. North. They coaxed lots of incriminating info from his partners in crime. A few weeks after those rebel bikers got busted, they were ready to say anything in exchange for a little leniency. If Levi North doesn't receive a death penalty, he will get at least three life sentences."

"Thank you so much, Ms. Krenshaw," Sonya said with wholehearted gratitude. "I don't know what we would do without you."

"Well, you're quite welcome. Oh, I will also make sure the

police in your area don't concern themselves with who you two are or your involvement. And, if you send me pictures of your tires, I'll square everything away with your auto insurance."

"You're the best, Nova."

"Well, I try. I need to hang up now. I have a lot of work to do."

"I understand," Trey reassured the agent. "I'm sure our crazy situation has made your hands quite full."

"Exactly. You two take care. I'll be in touch. Bye." She hung up.

"Man, I love having her for a friend!" Sonya said chirpily.

"Me too, honey. Crossing paths with her is probably one of the best t—"

The smartphone rang while blinking MOM CALLING. He swiped the screen to answer, forgetting to put Mitzi on speakerphone.

"What's going on, Mom? Nothing. Just doing a little shopping. Hey, Mom, you won't believe who Sonya and I saw today."

His girlfriend turned saucer-eyed. "Shut up," she warned voicelessly, gesturing for him to end the call.

"Some overweight lady who fell asleep on her motorized cart. It was hilarious. She was so enormous, she probably exceeded the cart's weight limit. Anyhow, she just drove by with her eyes closed and knocked down a bunch of juice bottles."

We were almost killed in that store and you're thinking about her? You are so nuts, Sonya thought, slipping into an uncontrolled bout of hilarity. *That has to be the funniest thing you've ever done. I guess that's one of the hundred reasons I want to marry you.*

"That's just Sonya, Mom," Trey continued. "Yeah, she's still laughing at the fat lady." Sonya's spell of mirth increased. "I don't know if the lady was diabetic. Narcoleptic? Maybe. What? Low blood sugar? Uh, Mom, never mind. Just never mind. I— Mom. Mom! I'm sorry I brought it up. Sorry. Because, you missed the whole point of the story, Mom. I wasn't doing medical research; I was just trying to tell you something funny that happened. Never mind. Let's talk about something else."

"Oh, my Lord," Sonya panted, wiping away humor tears.

"What, Mom? Uh…good question. I honestly don't know. Hang

on a sec." He lowered the phone to talk to his fiancée. "She would like to know where we plan to go for our honeymoon."

"Our honeymoon? Oh, I never thought of that. Let me see." She watched the rain drum on the windshield while considering the question.

MONTANA: EIGHTEEN DAYS LATER

From afar, it looked like any other peak. Evergreens, grass, dirt, and snow cloaked Chrome Mountain in blotches of brown, white, and two hues of green. From a nearby hiking trail, two pairs of eyes drank in the view, made all the more vibrant by the high noon sun. Trey was not impressed; for days, he and his new wife had encountered far more majestic scenery. They'd savored horseback rides and other hikes across the varied landscape of Custer Gallatin National Forest—their chosen place for their three-week honeymoon. Every daytime event was nearly as blissful as the "events" at night in their rented cabin.

"That isn't quite how the mountain looked in my dream," Sonya thought aloud, her voice laced with mild disappointment.

"I'm not impressed either," Trey replied. From behind a cedar stand, he saw an older couple appear on the serpentine trail after descending a mile of switchbacks. They were hiking from the same peak Trey and Sonya were headed toward. "Hello," he greeted them as they passed. "Sorry to bother you. I just had a question."

Both pairs of hikers stopped to regard each other.

"Fire away," the old man said pleasantly.

"That *is* Chrome Mountain, right?"

The eyes of the seniors followed his pointing hand across myriad treetops to the summit beyond. "It is. Thinking of going there?" The younger duo nodded. "Don't bother. A few miles ago, we encountered some U.S. Army guys who made us turn around."

"They wouldn't say why," the man's silver-haired wife added. "But there's a rumor going around that a whole army of very bad people hollowed out much of that mountain a year or two ago to make a base for themselves."

"Yeah. Now everyone thinks the military has been up there to salvage their equipment. No one will ever know the whole story. Pretty soon, there will be barricades instead of troops to keep everyone away from that peak."

"If mountains are what you guys are interested in, do yourselves a favor. Go visit Mount Hague, Mount Wood East, or Saddleback. They are more photogenic."

"Yeah, and don't forget to check out Mystic Lake and Stillwater Plateau."

"Okay, thanks," Trey replied and, like Sonya, waved good-bye to the elderly pair.

"Too bad," Mrs. Radisson sighed.

"Sorry," Mr. Radisson said, putting a consoling arm around her.

After watching the seniors disappear over a rise in the path, they faced Chrome Mountain together. They enjoyed a minute of quiet, broken by birds trilling in the trees that swayed faintly from pine-scented wind. The mild breeze fluttered a wisp of black hair across Sonya's blue eyes. With one hand, she combed the curl away to bask in the view awhile longer.

"I was hoping we could go carve our initials on the peak," she said. "I think we've earned the right to do that at least a hundred times. Don't you?"

"Oh, well, I don't think I would have made it to the top anyhow." Trey dubiously eyed the steep slopes. "That mountain looks—"

"Oh, please, you would have been fine." She returned the half-embrace and kissed his temple. "May I remind you that we are devout followers of God? That means there is *no* mountain we can't overcome."

About the Author: Ben Schneider was born in Oklahoma. In 2003, he earned a B.A. in Graphic Design at Oklahoma University, married his fiancée, and joined the Air Force. Ben and his wife, Suzy, have been stationed in Italy, Okinawa, and Alaska. Aside from writing fiction, Ben's other interests include drawing cartoons—primarily his *Airman Artless* comic strips. *Chrome Mountain* is his debut novel.

CPSIA information can be obtained
at www.ICGtesting.com
Printed in the USA
FSHW011718090921
84596FS